THERE IS

A DOOR

IN THIS

DARKNESS

THERE IS
A DOOR
IN THIS
DARKNESS

by Kristin Cashore

DUTTON BOOKS

DUTTON BOOKS

An imprint of Penguin Random House LLC, New York

First published in the United States of America by Dutton Books,
an imprint of Penguin Random House LLC, 24

Copyright © 2024 by Kristin Cashore

Visit us online at PenguinRandomHouse.com.

Library of Congress Cataloging-in-Publication Data is available.

ISBN 9780803739994

1st Printing

Printed in the United States of America

LSCH

Design by Anna Booth
Text set in Adobe Garamond Pro

for Faye Bender,
sine qua non

THERE IS

A DOOR

IN THIS

DARKNESS

2020

Frankie used to make the world shine, or at least that's how Wilhelmina Hart remembered it.

Frankie, Esther, and Aunt Margaret—the aunts, as Wilhelmina's father called them—lived together in the country. Aunt Margaret was her father's actual aunt and Frankie and Esther were Margaret's companions. Wilhelmina used to spend her summers with them. Wilhelmina would wake in her attic room, patter down the stairs to the smell of coffee or French toast. Step out into the yard with the grass cool on her feet, join Frankie in her garden. Wilhelmina's memories of those summers were golden; the sun always infused them with a wash of warm light.

Most days, Aunt Margaret and Esther went to work and Wilhelmina stayed home with Frankie. Frankie grew things, digging into the cold earth with strong hands, humming and praying, guiding the magic that brought forth flowers, vegetables, and herbs. "Every year is full of endings and beginnings," she told Wilhelmina. In the giant, wild yard of that castle of a house, she taught Wilhelmina the difference between a maple and an oak tree; a sycamore and a beech; a blue spruce and a hemlock; an acorn that grew into a red oak versus one that grew into a white oak. At the end of every summer, when Wilhelmina returned to her life in the city, she forgot the lessons, but she never forgot the feeling of Frankie teaching her. Frankie would come back to her in dreams, small, tanned, and sunlit, kneeling in the dirt with her silver hair tangled and stuck against her damp neck. Teaching Wilhelmina the names of herbs in English, then sometimes in Italian; telling her which ones would soothe Wilhelmina's nerves, ease her joints, wake her up when she was sleepy.

Frankie had ovarian cancer. She had always had ovarian cancer, or anyway, "always" from the perspective of Wilhelmina, who was five, then seven, eleven, thirteen, fifteen. Frankie was one of those people who lived with cancer longer than her doctors could account for.

The aunts wanted Wilhelmina to come stay with them for more than a summer—for a whole year—when she was older, take a year to live with them, so that they could teach her all their best lessons and she could teach them her own. The aunts were like that, especially Frankie. They didn't think that just because Wilhelmina was young, she had nothing to teach. Wilhelmina looked ahead to that long, golden year. She liked that her life was a string of lights, one for every summer she'd spent with them, leading to a warm, kind sun she hadn't lived yet.

And so, when Frankie died, Wilhelmina wasn't expecting it. Why would she? For Wilhelmina, Frankie's cancer was something Frankie lived with. Like Esther's arthritis. Like her own mother's seasonal allergies. Not some bad magic that could actually suck away her life.

The dreams ended when Frankie died, and the lights went out. For one brief, horrible stretch, the sun itself seemed to have fallen into a void, Wilhelmina dragged in with it. It was cold in there, and Wilhelmina was alone. There was an inertia too: once in there, staying alone hurt less than reaching for her friends; keeping still hurt less than moving. It took Wilhelmina a long time to realize she would rather try to claw her way out.

It was around then, while Wilhelmina was just beginning to reach her hands up, that lights began to turn off all around the world.

FRIDAY, OCTOBER 30, 2020

On the Friday eight days before Wilhelmina stepped into her own, she drove Aunt Margaret into Cambridge, to an eye appointment in Harvard Square.

This was more difficult than usual, because it was snowing. In October! Big, wet, clumpy snow. And it had been so many months since Wilhelmina had driven in snow, and so much had happened since then, that she forgot all the things you needed to do. She didn't clean the snow off the side mirrors. She didn't clean the hood or the back. She didn't clean the windshield wipers adequately, so they flung chunks of snow all around while she drove.

"So beautiful," Aunt Margaret kept saying. "So beautiful!" As she peeked through the foggy windows with her foggy vision, she said, "Wilhelmina, dear, isn't it beautiful?"

Wilhelmina was listening for the ding that would herald an important text from Julie while also looking for parking where Aunt Margaret could step into the narrow streets without landing in a snowbank. She did not find it beautiful. "Okay," she said, taking her best guess at where the white lines were and bringing the car to a halt. "What do you need to do to check in?"

"Oh, I'll just give them a call," said Aunt Margaret. "You go ahead and start your errands."

"I don't want to leave you here alone," said Wilhelmina. "What if they're not ready for you?"

"I would rather wait here in this beautiful storm than in their waiting room anyway. Go, Wilhelmina," said Aunt Margaret. "Give an old lady a few minutes to herself. Do you know how rarely I get a minute to myself?"

Aunt Margaret was having retinal surgery. No unnecessary humans were allowed to accompany her into the building due to Covid pandemic protocols. It was enough of an impertinence sending her out into Harvard Square to have surgery all alone without first abandoning her in the car, but on the other hand, Wilhelmina didn't begrudge her a moment to herself. Aunt Margaret and Esther had moved from their house in rural Pennsylvania to stay with Wilhelmina's family during the pandemic. Wilhelmina; her parents; her ten-year-old sister, Delia; her four-year-old brother, Philip; and the aunts were all living together these days, in an apartment too small for seven people.

She groped around inside her coat until her fingers touched the duplicate car key beside her phone.

"Okay," she said. "Keep the heat on, and take this when you go. I have another key."

"All right."

"Do you need anything?"

"I have everything I need, dear. Remember to enjoy being out in that storm."

"When they tell you how long it'll be, will you call me? I don't want to keep you waiting."

"You have grown into such a responsible young woman, Wilhelmina," said Aunt Margaret, gazing at Wilhelmina with an expression of unruffled benevolence.

"Thanks," said Wilhelmina. Then she pushed herself out into the snow, obscurely guilty about what a relief it was to escape.

WILHELMINA PRESSED HER WAY THROUGH a sloppy, wet world, unable to see where she was going, because her mask fogged her glasses. She wondered if her phone was too deeply buried inside her layers to be heard or felt. Julie was supposed to be in Harvard Square today, and Wilhelmina would not be okay with missing her. She unearthed the phone, held it in her hand, and tried to see through the mostly transparent top edge of her glasses.

Glasses were, in fact, the nature of Wilhelmina's first errand: she was picking up a new prescription for herself. She hadn't expected it to feel like Shackleton forging a path to the South Pole. When the glasses-store person finally let her in and locked the door behind her, she was a cold, wet, dripping, foggy, despairing grouch with a tickling nose.

And then, of course, she wasn't allowed to touch anything in the store except for her new glasses. And when she put them on, they distorted her depth perception and made her dizzy, as new glasses always do. Not to mention that she couldn't tell how they looked on her face, because she wasn't allowed to take off her mask.

The glasses-store person tucked the glasses into a cute black bag with red ribbon handles and released Wilhelmina again into the storm. The path to her next errand took her past the car. The engine was still running.

With a sigh, Wilhelmina climbed back in, pulling her mask down. Aunt Margaret watched her with a sweet, expectant smile.

"Still waiting?" said Wilhelmina.

"I just now got permission to go up," said Aunt Margaret. "But can I see your glasses first?"

Obediently, Wilhelmina unearthed her new case from the bag and handed it over.

"Oh, Wilhelmina!" said Aunt Margaret, opening the case to reveal chunky red frames. "These are you exactly." She removed the glasses and slid them onto her nose. "What do you think?"

Now that Wilhelmina could see the glasses on Aunt Margaret's face, she realized she'd made a mistake. Aunt Margaret was pinkish-pale, small, and plump, with hardly any wrinkles. Her hair, wavy and pure white, hung loosely down her back. Her winter coat was pale green. She had a Mrs. Claus look, and Wilhelmina's red glasses were gigantic on her face.

They're Christmas glasses, Wilhelmina thought, despising them. *I got myself Christmas glasses.* "You look great," she said, her voice all wrong.

But Aunt Margaret only smiled serenely. "They'll suit you as they could never suit me," she said, handing them back. "All right, wish me luck, dear. They said it should be two hours."

Two hours! The most recent estimate Wilhelmina had heard had been thirty minutes. More time with Julie, then? Maybe they could have a snowy walk in the cemetery? She was so focused on wiping away the moisture she'd just discovered on her phone that, as Aunt Margaret swung the door open and climbed out into the storm, she forgot all the things she'd meant to say. *Are you nervous? It'll be fine. I've heard only good things about this doctor. Call if you need me. I'm here.* As the car door slammed and Aunt Margaret shuffled away, Wilhelmina tried to reach after her with those kinder thoughts.

ALONE IN THE CAR with her phone in her lap, Wilhelmina turned off the engine. For a while, she just sat. The snow blanketing the windshield transformed the car's interior into a white cave. She liked it, despite herself. A part of her wished she could stay just like this, alone in a bright white car, for the rest of time.

Eventually, she pulled her mask, scarf, and hat away. Then she tried the new glasses on in the rearview mirror.

The burst of pleasure surprised her. The chunky red frames looked just right on her big, pretty, pale face, her gray eyes standing out against the red rectangles, her dark hair clipped close. They weren't Christmas glasses at all.

You'll be okay, Aunt Margaret, she thought again, knowing that her aunt was heading into surgery, and was not, in fact, particularly nervous. Aunt Margaret wasn't the type to get ruffled.

Wilhelmina had more errands she could do. Less despondent now, she wound herself up into her winter things again, opened the door, and pushed herself out into the snow.

WILHELMINA WASN'T TALL, but she was always steady. She had strong, steady legs and big, steady Hart feet. She always pictured her steady great-great-grandmothers climbing rocky crags in Ireland, looking out over the sea, in search of their husbands and brothers coming in with the catch. She had no idea if her ancestors had fished, or even lived near the sea, but she liked the image. She thought she might like to climb some rocky crags someday. Her boots made big, slushy footprints on the sidewalk as she advanced toward the clock shop.

When she got there, the clock man let her in, took the clock she handed him, then disappeared with it into the back. It was a small enamel clock in the shape of a barn owl, belonging to Aunt Margaret and Esther, who'd lost the key needed to wind it up. Wilhelmina had heard their sad voices behind the door of her young siblings' bedroom, which had become the aunts' bedroom when they'd moved in. She'd heard them groaning as they knelt to look under the bed, sighing when the key wasn't found. With a familiar sinking feeling, she'd knocked on their door. Wilhelmina had no school, no job, no plans, and no purpose. "There's a clock shop in Harvard Square," she'd said. "Want me to get you a new key?"

"Oh, Wilhelmina," Aunt Margaret had said. "You're an angel."

In the foyer of the clock shop, her phone finally dinged.

We're here, wrote Julie. *You here?*

We? responded Wilhelmina.

Yeah, we've even got the kids, texted Julie. *And we can't stay long. Sorry. We're in the alley near the post office*

"We" meant four people: Julie, Bee, and both of their little sisters. Wilhelmina had thought she was getting Julie to herself. *Five minutes,* she responded, just as the clock man emerged from the back and said gruffly, "Three hours."

Wilhelmina was dismayed. "Three?"

"Three," the man said firmly, peering down at her through tortoise-shell glasses. "I have several jobs ahead of yours, and I'm all alone." He wore a pin-striped mask that matched his bow tie, a dark gray vest with silver buttons, and a crisp white shirt. She respected his style, but he'd just complicated her afternoon further. Now she would have to wait for Aunt Margaret, drive her aunt home to Watertown, then drive back for the clock.

"All right. Thank you," said Wilhelmina dismally.

His eyebrows forming a V, the man strode around the counter and pushed the door open. She would've liked a minute to organize her snotty, dripping self before she set out again, but she guessed he was eager to be the only human breathing air in the shop during a pandemic.

Wilhelmina made her way to the alley near the post office, struggling to see where she was going. She heard the kids first—Julie's seven-year-old sister, Tina, and Bee's seven-year-old sister, Kimmy, chasing each other, throwing snow and screeching. Then she saw Julie and Bee, the two loves of her life, huddled together in winter coats and gloves over steaming cups of coffee, and needed a minute to battle her jealousy back. Her two best friends were in a quarantine bubble together so that their little sisters could attend second grade jointly. It was the new, pandemical shape of her life: a tight-knit group of four that included Julie, Bee, and two seven-year-olds, then Wilhelmina off to the side. It was like when you poured M&M's into your hand and one of them bounced away and rolled under the couch, where it moldered eternally, living a pointless existence. Bee was Wilhelmina's oldest friend. She'd known him since preschool. Julie had graduated high school virtually with Wilhelmina last year and lived in the apartment above hers. Once, Julie and Wilhelmina would've been the pair texting Bee to tell him where they were going. Not anymore.

They look like a couple, Wilhelmina thought as she approached them. It was true, they had a couple vibe, practically leaning against each other, their faces—their beautiful, uncovered faces—flashing grins at each other whenever they pulled their masks down to sip their coffees. She could tell they'd done their makeup together. Above Julie's dark eyes, a green sparkle of eyeshadow blended into gold, and Bee had mascara-thick lashes and beautifully smudged silver eyeshadow. He also sported a wedge of pale pink near the front of his otherwise dark head of hair, which meant that someone had bleached the hell out of it for him. And given him a haircut. Wilhelmina wasn't even allowed to touch them, or even stand beside them, but apparently Julie was up to her elbows in Bee's hair.

Not their fault, she told herself. *Let it go, Wilhelmina. Channel your inner Elsa.*

"Hey, elephant," said Julie as she arrived.

"Hey, elephants," said Wilhelmina. It had long been their traditional greeting when they were alone.

"Great glasses," said Julie.

"Yeah, the red is you, Wil," said Bee.

"Thanks," said Wilhelmina. "You guys look amazing. What's up?"

"Fortune teller's having a snowstorm sale," said Bee, nodding at a person sitting at a folding table nearby. "I'm trying to decide if I have a question."

Wilhelmina studied the alleged fortune teller, whose folding table was situated against a brick wall spotted with snow. The sign hanging from her table said ASK MADAME VOLARA, but she was bundled in so much winter gear that she could've been anyone. Instead of a mask, she wore purple scarves wrapped around her face, and aviator goggles. A year ago, Wilhelmina would've thought this strange. Now she just figured the woman didn't want anyone breathing germs into her eyeballs.

A smaller sign on Madame Volara's table said FORTUNES $20. TODAY ONLY: $5, SNOWSTORM SALE!

"Steep discount," said Wilhelmina.

"Exactly," said Bee. "I feel like it's too risky to pass it up."

"Are you kidding me right now?" said Julie. "Are you, like, completely unaware of manipulative advertising techniques?"

"Seriously, Bee," said Wilhelmina. "It could be Mr. Rochester in there, for all we know."

Julie hooted, which made Wilhelmina warm up inside.

"That was a book reference," said Bee intelligently.

"Aw, elephant," said Julie, reaching up to pat his shoulder. Bee was tall. He was also a year younger than Wilhelmina and Julie, and thus accustomed to their literary condescension.

"Okay, I have my question," he said, taking a step toward Madame Volara, who sat before a lavender crystal ball into which she might have been gazing, though it was hard to tell under all her wrappings. At any rate, she straightened as Bee approached, and raised her hands in a welcoming manner.

"Greetings," she intoned. "Ask me what you will."

"Okay," said Bee. "Will I get a soccer scholarship?" Bee was a senior, currently in virtual school, working on his college applications.

Madame Volara gazed into her milky crystal ball, then began to undulate her arms like a cartoon octopus.

"Wow," said Julie, taken aback.

"Wow!" screeched Julie's seven-year-old sister, Tina, who came running past with Kimmy in close pursuit. Kimmy threw a snowball. Tina swung at it with the thing Tina was always holding, her favorite pandemic tool: a long stick with a grabby claw at the end. Her grabby stick decimated the snowball, and her momentum spun her in a circle, her stick drawing a hard, sharp circumference in the air.

"Oh my god, Tina," said Julie. "If you hit someone with that thing, I'm never taking you anywhere again."

"There's no one around!" shouted Tina.

"Kimmy!" said Bee to his sibling. "No more snowball baseball."

"You're not *Mom*," said Kimmy.

"I'm Mom's deputy," said Bee.

Madame Volara made a dramatic arms-above-her-head gesture that drew everyone's attention. Then she spoke.

"I see a spotted sphere," she said. "I see a tall, white boy with pink hair and fabulous makeup running across a grassy field, pursued by rivals who fall away in the wake of his impressive speed."

"He's the *goalie*," Tina shouted.

"Teeny!" said Julie. "No being mean."

"Don't call me that!" said Tina. "Anyway, it's *mean* to lie to your *customers* about the *future*."

"Teeny!" cried Julie, grabbing Tina's arm and trying to drag her away.

"Okay, I have a question," said Wilhelmina, who didn't really, nor did she want to lose five dollars. But she needed to help Julie, whose anguish felt spiky and panicked, and awfully sudden. "Um," she said, grasping for a question.

"Ask her when we'll go back to *school*," shouted Bee's little sister, Kimmy.

"Ask her who's going to win the *election*," shouted Tina. "An old white man? Or an old orange man?"

"Ask her, will Santa be able to come for Christmas?" shouted Kimmy.

"Um," said Wilhelmina, "okay. What's going to happen tomorrow?"

"Tomorrow!" Madame Volara intoned, beginning her arm-waving routine again. "Tomorrow, superheroes will roam the streets of your town."

"They will?" said Wilhelmina, surprised.

"Tomorrow's *Halloween*," shouted Tina.

"Oh, right," said Wilhelmina, disappointed. She'd liked the notion of wandering superheroes. The world needed them right now.

"Also," said Madame Volara, then stopped, making a small, choked noise.

"Yes?" said Wilhelmina, taking a step forward. "Are you okay?"

The fortune teller sat up, ramrod straight. She threw her shoulders back and lifted her chin, and suddenly she seemed bigger. In fact, she seemed to be expanding, which was really weird, and she was also getting brighter at the edges. She looked like the sun in eclipse, and then, even though she was wearing scarves and goggles, Wilhelmina could see her face. It took form through the fabric and leather: flat cheeks and beaky nose, tufted ears and round eyes, made of flowers and leaves and shining light. Her raised arms took the shape of gigantic, feathery wings. Wings!

"AAAK!" cried Wilhelmina, a garbled, inarticulate shriek, as she backed across the alley as far as she could go. She pressed her body against the opposite building's cold, wet stone, watching the woman grow.

"YOUR DOUGHNUT WILL BE STALE!" cried Madame Volara, in a voice like wings beating against the wind. "YOUR . . . DOUGH-NUT . . . *WILL BE STALE!*" She was standing now, towering, enormous, and above her, lights were glittering. Flashes of white and gold. The lights were forming letters. *W . . . I . . . L . . .* Then a dash. *H . . . E . . . L . . . M . . .* Then another dash. *I . . . N . . . A . . .* Wilhelmina watched her own name, oddly divided, glitter in the air above the enormous fortuneteller. *WIL—HELM—INA!!*

Then the lights subsided. Madame Volara sat down. She was small again, masked, goggled, and ever-so-slightly shivering. All the noises in the alley were normal. In fact, everything in the alley was normal, except for Wilhelmina, who was pressed against the far wall, gasping and shaking.

"Wil?" said Bee, who stood closer to Wilhelmina than he should, really—both Bee and Julie were huddling around her closer than they should, their eyes wide, their hands reaching toward her uselessly. Tina and Kimmy stood behind their older siblings, looking a bit frightened.

"Wil!" said Julie. "Are you okay? Are you having a panic attack?"

"I . . ." said Wilhelmina. "I . . . no! What do you mean? Didn't you see that?"

"See what?" said Bee.

"The fortune teller!" said Wilhelmina. "Turn into a big bird and start glowing! The lights with my name! The prophecy!"

"Huh?" said Julie.

"Prophecy?" said Bee on a sharp note.

"Wil," said Julie. "What the actual fuck are you talking about?" Julie's incredulous voice brought her into focus for Wilhelmina. Julie's hair was wrapped in a black-and-white zigzag scarf to protect it from the snow, and her coat was brilliant green, like her eyeshadow. Her eyes flashed dark in her brown face. A necklace spilled out of her collar on a gold chain, a small gray elephant with crimson-and-orange butterfly wings. Wilhelmina had given Julie that necklace, the same day she'd given Bee an elephant-unicorn necklace, and shown them the elephant necklace with lilies sprouting from its trunk that she'd gotten for herself.

Julie's necklace dragged Wilhelmina back to reality, where she began to understand that her friends had not seen what she'd just seen. This worked for Wilhelmina. She hadn't seen it either. She put a steadying hand to the wall, then peeked over the little girls' heads at Madame Volara. The fortune teller sat quietly at her table, her head propped on her fist, idly watching the foot traffic at the end of the alley near the post office. Wilhelmina's glasses fogged and cleared with her breaths, fogged and cleared, but the fortune teller didn't change.

"I must be really stressed," she said.

"Yeah, you think so?" said Bee, acid in his tone, but it was an acid Wilhelmina recognized. All of them were worried, and tired, and similarly stressed. "It's not cool to see weird shit that's not there."

"Yeah, you scared us, Wil," said Julie. "Are you really okay?"

"Yeah," said Wilhelmina, who was thinking about the glowing letters that had spelled her name. Because they *hadn't* spelled her name, not really; they'd spelled *WIL—HELM—INA*. She didn't spell her name like that, with dashes, or pronounce it that way either. Which meant that none of this had been for her benefit. Right? It wasn't just that it hadn't happened. It hadn't happened to *her*.

"What was the prophecy?" asked Tina.

Wilhelmina focused on Tina's small, familiar face. Her mask was bright yellow, with a print of black cats wearing top hats. She wore her hair in two high Afro puffs, dampened by a scattering of snowflakes, and her dark eyes were narrowed, skeptical. Tina didn't believe Wilhelmina was okay.

" 'Your doughnut will be stale,' " said Wilhelmina.

"What?" cried Tina, delighted.

"Wilhelmina!" said Kimmy, giggling. "You got us."

Wilhelmina decided to go along with that explanation, even though she hated practical jokes and never would've staged one so random and weird. Bee was looking at her funny. So was Julie. They knew better. She avoided their eyes.

"Here," said Tina, who'd stepped back and was attaching a piece of paper awkwardly to the grabby claw at the end of her stick, using the squeeze grip at the top. "Maybe you need this."

She pointed the end at Wilhelmina, who took the paper, realizing then that it was a sheet of rectangular stickers.

Spell for Goblin Banishment, said one. *Wise Woman Potion,* said another. *Good Luck Spell.* Each sticker contained a heading, followed by instructions, illustrated with witches on broomsticks, cauldrons, black cats.

"Wow," said Wilhelmina. "Thanks, Tina."

"I can't believe tomorrow's Halloween," said Julie. "It doesn't feel like Halloween."

"Yeah," said Wilhelmina, matching Julie's doubtful tone, but wondering if Julie and Bee were planning to have Halloween without her this year. Private Halloween, without her. Would they do that? "You guys doing anything?"

"What would we do?" said Julie, shrugging, which was vaguely reassuring. But Wilhelmina wished, when they all left the alley and Julie and Bee set off together with the girls, that she could hug her friends, hold them against her trembling body for a moment. That she could see the bottom two-thirds of their *faces*, for crying out loud. But that wasn't an option.

So she gripped Tina's stickers tight in her hand and pushed through the snow, steady-footed. When she remembered Madame Volara's prophecy, she told herself that her vision was unreliable today, and anyway, the message hadn't been for her.

BACK IN HER CAR, Wilhelmina decided to go for a snowy walk by herself, less because she wanted to and more because there weren't a lot of other options. She could go home while she waited for Aunt Margaret—her town was only a couple of miles away—but Wilhelmina was not in need of family time.

She knew where to go: Mount Auburn Cemetery, which would be empty in this weather, and pretty, and would soothe her jangled spirits, and maybe even amuse her too. Wilhelmina liked the headstones. Early Bostonians had funny names.

She cleaned the snow off the car again, this time remembering the side mirrors, the windshield wipers, et cetera. Inside, with the defrost roaring, she inched her car back onto the road and drove through the storm to the massive cemetery's tall iron gates.

She was right. Inside, she found hardly any cars on the cemetery's winding roads. Wilhelmina crested small hills, turning randomly onto narrow drives that were sheltered by trees reaching down to her with beautiful snow-covered limbs. It was peaceful.

She kept poking at thoughts, then pushing them away. Like the makeup. Wilhelmina hardly ever bothered with makeup anymore, but she could've done hers too, if she'd known it was a thing. She liked to blend colors just as much as they did. She liked experimental eyes. But they hadn't told her, so she'd shown up makeupless, which had felt naked and boring alongside their own looks, which had probably evolved organically while they were hanging out together, laughing, touching each other, breathing the air of the same room. Why would it even occur to them to text her? Why would they think of her face?

As she drove, she realized she was clutching her scarf, her hand in a fist at her throat, because it was the closest she could get to her own necklace. Wilhelmina had acquired the trio of elephant necklaces last Christmas, Christmas of 2019, just months before Covid happened. It'd been her and Julie's senior year, Bee's junior year. Wilhelmina had been starting to feel some stirrings of excitement about the future, which had been an unexpected sensation, and a nice one. She'd thought she might like to go to UMass, in Western Massachusetts, and study something. She wasn't sure what yet. Botany? Philosophy? Fashion? Julie had applied to faraway places only: Atlanta, Philadelphia, Chicago, California. Julie didn't know what she wanted to study either, but she wanted a new corner of the world; Julie wanted to live in all the corners of the world. Bee still had one more year, but he was thinking about colleges too, which had been interesting, because of the unexpected revelation that Bee *did* know what he wanted to study. "Psychology and medicine," he'd said, "and French and Spanish."

Julie's eyebrows had shot up. "Monsieur Docteur Bee?"

"Señor Doctor Bee?" Wilhelmina had added.

Bee had grinned bright, then shrugged. "Not sure yet."

"Well, I can see it," Julie had said. Wilhelmina had seen something too: that everything was changing. It had made her want to bestow a symbolic treasure upon her friends, a small, portable container of love. Elephants had been the obvious choice, because of the Elephant Incident of 2016, which had involved a hypothetical question that had gone awry.

"If I were an elephant in an elephant sanctuary," Julie had asked one day, "would you guys be able to tell which one was me?"

"Oh, no problem," Bee had said. "You'd be the one reading a fantasy novel to the other elephants."

"Yeah," said Wilhelmina fondly, "flopped down in the middle of the floor."

Julie was, in fact, flopped on Wilhelmina's rug during this conversation, sprawled on her back with one knee bent and her arms stretched out. Julie had a way of always looking comfortable, as if surfaces molded themselves to her body. She was catlike that way. Wilhelmina and Bee lay on the bed. It was November, almost Thanksgiving. They were fourteen.

Julie spoke to Bee. "You'd be the elephant trying to help the other boy elephants connect to their feelings."

Wilhelmina grinned. "Yeah. You'd start a feelings circle."

"You'd start a space program for the elephants," Bee told Julie. "Elephant astronauts. Astrophants?"

They were feeding off of each other, the way they did sometimes. Wilhelmina always felt cozy while she listened. "You'd invent bath therapy," Julie said to Bee.

"What's that?" said Bee, wrinkling his nose.

"Like, elephants swimming in warm water to soothe their anxiety," said Julie.

A tiny needle of unfairness stung Wilhelmina at this. Of the three of them, she was the swimmer. She swam miles when she was in Pennsylvania with the aunts. "Would you guys be able to recognize me?" she asked.

"Of course," said Bee. "You'd be separate."

The word didn't surprise Wilhelmina, exactly, but it hurt a little. She thought she knew what Bee meant by it. Bee and Julie both played soccer. Julie was in chess club. They had other groups, other people outside their official best-friendship with Wilhelmina, whereas Wilhelmina had Julie and Bee and mostly kept it at that. She was perfectly friendly to other people, it wasn't that; she just didn't *need* more friends. She spent her entire summers in Pennsylvania, with three old ladies.

"Separate," she said carefully.

"Yeah, you'd be the queen elephant," said Julie. "With three aunt elephants around you, and people would have to take a number."

"Wait, what?" said Wilhelmina, floundering up to a sitting position. This was unexpected. "Take a number? Like, to approach me?"

"I mean," said Julie, propping herself on one elbow. "I didn't mean it in a bad way, Wil."

"Am I unapproachable?" said Wilhelmina.

"No!" said Bee, also sitting up. "That's the opposite of what we mean."

"But you think I'm, like, unapproachably separate from the other elephants?" said Wilhelmina. "And, like, a queen? Like, am I *bossy?*"

"No!" said Julie. "Oh my god, Wil. Could we maybe start over with this?"

Wilhelmina was stumbling around inside herself in confusion. It wasn't like her to get so upset all at once, or feel this injured at something Julie or Bee said—or maybe it *was* like her? Maybe she was a spoiled, melodramatic queen, and she'd just never realized it before?

"I have to pee," she said, blundering for the door, but not stopping at the bathroom, continuing on through the kitchen and out into the yard. The backyard of Wilhelmina's and Julie's duplex was a tiny space, full of dirt and patchy grass, dropping steeply to trees and a retaining wall where some crows were cawing. Wilhelmina stood there in her socks, watching the crows with her arms wrapped around her middle and her feet growing cold, her neck beginning to ache. She could feel every discordant squawk inside her own body, like she was the one crying out in pain.

Behind her, the door opened. "Wil?" came Julie's voice.

"I'm sorry," Wilhelmina said, not turning yet, because she was crying, which was embarrassing. "I overreacted."

"I shouldn't have said 'separate,'" said Bee. "I didn't mean separate from *us*, Wil."

"Okay," said Wilhelmina, not believing him.

"No, really, Wil!" he cried. "I only meant that you—you're different. You have something the other elephants don't have! It's, like, hard to describe. It's your aura."

"A snobby aura?" asked Wilhelmina.

"No," said Julie firmly. "It's, like, a comforting aura."

"Yes!" said Bee. "Thank you."

"It's like safety," said Julie.

"Yes!" said Bee again.

"That's why the other elephants are taking numbers to be near you, Wil," said Julie. "They want to feel how it feels to be your friend."

Wilhelmina was confused again, because all of this sounded a bit unlikely. She turned to study her friends. Julie looked dead certain about what she was saying, and Bee was nodding with his entire face scrunched up in thoughtfulness.

Wilhelmina knew their ways, their expressions. They weren't making shit up just to placate her. Okay, then. She was the comforting, safe elephant?

"Do you guys feel like you need to take a number to be with me?" she asked, because she didn't want that.

"Nooooooo!" said Bee, going high-pitched with it, like a siren of protest.

"You're *our* elephant, Wil," said Julie. "The other elephants better take a number."

"Yeah, they can't have you," said Bee.

"Okay," said Wilhelmina. "Can I be part of your space program and your feelings circle?"

"Of course!" said Julie. "But do you really want to be part of Bee's feelings circle?"

Wilhelmina didn't actually want to be part of either group. She just wanted to know she was welcome. But she recognized the invitation to tease Bee, and return things to normal. "Maybe not," she said, snorting.

"Hey," Bee said, in pretend indignation. "I'm doing good work."

Wilhelmina stepped toward her friends. A bit shyly, she held out her arms. "Could I have an elephant hug?"

"Of course," said Bee, practically leaping across the yard to her. Julie followed.

"I'm a little sensitive, maybe," Wilhelmina admitted while they hugged. "I'm sorry I made it a thing."

"We're all a little sensitive," Julie said, which was true. It was November 2016, and a pretty obviously awful person had just been elected president. People loved him. It was bewildering. And it was hard to know what was coming.

As Wilhelmina drove through the cemetery, she remembered how it had felt four years ago to believe, if only for a few confused minutes, that her friends considered her the separate elephant. The one who didn't belong. She'd felt herself falling into a funnel of loneliness. But Wilhelmina had been fourteen then. She hadn't known who she was yet; of course she'd misunderstood. Wasn't it different now?

Didn't they look like a couple today? she asked herself again, directing her car up a small rise and around a corner. *They did, right?*

On the road ahead, beside a massive willow that hung with snow, Wilhelmina saw a woman walking around a parked car. Wilhelmina didn't want an interaction with a stranger. She would drive past the woman, find another road to turn onto, and park where she could continue to be sad and alone.

She neared the woman, driving in that slow-motion manner unique to snowstorms, when the world is silent except for your own blasting heat and the squeaky crunch of your tires on snow. Then Wilhelmina realized that the woman wasn't a stranger. White and white-haired, wearing a black peacoat and a flowered scarf, this was Mrs. Mardrosian, who lived around the corner from Wilhelmina and Julie in a giant house. Giant in the sense that it was probably twice as big as the building Wilhelmina and Julie lived in, plus their building was a duplex, Julie's apartment above and Wilhelmina's below. Mrs. Mardrosian owned her house and lived in the whole thing.

Wilhelmina still had hopes of sneaking by unrecognized. There was nothing wrong with Mrs. Mardrosian, precisely. But she'd been Wilhelmina's dad's boss years ago when he'd worked at the public library, which meant she would ask Wilhelmina questions. She would want to know how the Harts were doing in the pandemic. She would ask how Wilhelmina's father Theo liked his new library job in Cambridge. She would talk about the election, which Wilhelmina definitely didn't want to talk about while not knowing for whom Mrs. Mardrosian was voting. Also, there was without a doubt something wrong with Wilhelmina's eyesight today, because Mrs. Mardrosian was ever-so-slightly glowing at the edges. *Agh.* Wilhelmina tried to hide behind the most fogged-up part of her windows.

But then she looked closer at Mrs. Mardrosian's car, a big, old, taupe Mercedes sedan, and saw that it had a flat tire.

With a sigh, Wilhelmina pulled over.

"Mrs. Mardrosian?" she called, climbing out, pulling up her mask. "Do you need help?"

Mrs. Mardrosian hardly seemed to notice her. She was digging around in the snow beside the road with her ice scraper and talking to herself. Wailing to herself, really; she almost sounded like she was weeping. At least she was no longer glowing.

"Mrs. Mardrosian?" Wilhelmina called, stepping closer. "Did you lose something?"

"My keys," Mrs. Mardrosian wailed. "Oh, it's hopeless!"

"Your keys?" said Wilhelmina. "To your car?"

"What? Oh, hello, is that you, Wilhelmina?" said Mrs. Mardrosian, straightening, turning to her. "Oh, thank heavens. I may need to ask you for a ride."

Wilhelmina didn't love the idea of giving an elderly woman a ride during a pandemic while she lived with two other elderly women and an asthmatic father she was meant to be protecting, but of course she was going to have to do *something*. "Help me understand," she said. "You have a flat tire *and* you lost your keys?"

"I never used to get into these situations," said Mrs. Mardrosian. "Oh, what would Levon think?"

Wilhelmina remembered a conversation then, a recent one between her parents. Mrs. Mardrosian had lost her husband. "All alone in that big place," Theo had said. "I feel for her. She was a rotten boss, but I feel for her."

Now Wilhelmina was feeling for her too, imagining what it would be like to lose one's husband *and* one's keys, then get a flat tire, in a cemetery, in a snowstorm, in a pandemic. And she remembered a tall, spare man walking a small dog around the neighborhood. Somehow she knew, though she'd never met him, that that had been Levon Mardrosian. He hadn't been friendly. He hadn't smiled at the dog, and he'd never even looked Wilhelmina's way. But he'd bent down with a groan and scooped the dog's poop into a bag with meticulous attention, and then he'd carried it off, instead of dumping it into a neighbor's garbage can.

Wilhelmina walked toward Mrs. Mardrosian's car, stopping as she neared the woman. "Would you mind stepping back?"

"What? Oh, yes," the woman said distractedly, moving away, then digging in the snow near a headstone topped with a mournful angel.

Wilhelmina didn't know why she was compelled to do what she did next. She walked all around Mrs. Mardrosian's big Mercedes, sticking her hand into the tire wells, under the bumpers, and behind the license plate. She knew what she was looking for, but she didn't know why she expected to find it.

Her fingers touched a small, metallic box stuck to a metal ledge in one of the tire wells.

"Mrs. Mardrosian?" she called, yanking the magnetic box away from the car, then sliding it open to confirm that there was a key inside. "It looks like I found your extra key."

"My what?" cried Mrs. Mardrosian, staring at Wilhelmina with her ice scraper held before her vertically, like she was illuminating the scene with a candle.

Wilhelmina displayed the box in her hand.

"What—how—oh, Levon must've done it. Levon must have known I would lose my head," said Mrs. Mardrosian.

"I guess so," said Wilhelmina. "Now, can I change your tire?"

Mrs. Mardrosian lowered her ice scraper and goggled at Wilhelmina. "*You* know how to change a tire?"

Wilhelmina knew how to do a lot of things. It was part of the competence required when one was the eldest Hart child in a pandemic, with two small siblings aged ten and four to care for, two distracted parents, and more recently, two great-aunts at home. She could cook and shop and research health insurance and supervise virtual school and drive everyone everywhere and unclog the drains and fix the Wi-Fi and bring in the mail and budget and cut hair, and yes, she could change a tire.

"Of course," she said, hearing that her own voice had dropped to a lower register, the way it did sometimes when she was annoyed. It was a new development, Wilhelmina's "serious" voice, one that kept taking her by surprise and one of which she despaired, because her mother's voice did the very same thing, and Wilhelmina had always found it intensely irritating. Cleo was a therapist. Whenever Cleo was moved to say something profound and corny, it always came out in that resonant, cello-like timbre. Wilhelmina felt betrayed by her own vocal cords.

"Would you like to wait inside the car?" she asked Mrs. Mardrosian, trying to raise her pitch, but possibly warbling like an intoxicated songbird. "Or outside the car, at least six feet away from me?" She added that last part because Mrs. Mardrosian, who wore no mask, kept trying to edge too close.

"Oh," said Mrs. Mardrosian, backing away. "Of course. Perhaps I'll keep looking for my keys. After all, once I drive home, I'll need a way into the house."

Wilhelmina used the hidden key to open the trunk of Mrs. Mardrosian's car. There she found a jack, a spare tire, a lug wrench, and some beautiful leather work gloves that looked like they'd never been used, all of which she guessed Mrs. Mardrosian was unaware she owned.

"Maybe your husband hid an extra key outside your home too," she said, hauling on the tire, then beginning to feel a painful tightness in her neck and pectorals. "In the mailbox? Or in one of those fake rocks?"

"What? Oh. Yes. That does sound familiar. Levon died. Did you know? He died, and he didn't tell me all these things first. I just can't get over someone like you changing a tire," said Mrs. Mardrosian, who was scratching in the snow by the road again.

Wilhelmina said nothing to this, because she wasn't sure what Mrs.

Mardrosian meant, and there was a good chance she was better off not knowing. Someone like her, meaning a girl? A nice white girl, specifically? Someone short and fat? Someone in black ankle boots, red leggings, a knit turquoise dress, red glasses, and a red coat with a wide belt snug around her middle? Wilhelmina didn't want to know which part of her person disqualified her from the useful skill of tire-changing in the mind of Mrs. Mardrosian, so she stretched her hurting neck once, then got started removing the hubcap.

Mrs. Mardrosian came too close again. "Regardless, you're an angel," she said, pointing her ice scraper vaguely at the angel on the headstone nearby. "You saved me, Wilhelmina. I may even have time to early vote when you're done."

Wilhelmina really, really did not have the wherewithal to talk about the election. She didn't want to know which side Mrs. Mardrosian was on. She worked with the lug wrench, trying to seem like she was far too busy for conversation.

Then she saw Mrs. Mardrosian with her shoulders slumped, poking at the ground. Dabbing her eyes with her sleeve, and sniffling. Muttering to herself, "Oh, Levon."

Wilhelmina decided she wanted to be changing Mrs. Mardrosian's tire, no matter what they talked about.

AT LEAST THE CAR INCIDENT killed some time. Afterward, Wilhelmina went walking.

She could remember other solitary walks in this cemetery. It was a place she'd once liked to visit alone, because it was beautiful, and quiet enough that she could hear her own feelings. Then, at the beginning of the pandemic, the cemetery had closed to walkers, and in the disruption of everything changing, she'd forgotten how much she liked the hills and trees and the old gray headstones. She liked the geese, the wild turkeys; the hawks that dropped down suddenly from the sky. She'd seen a snow goose here once with Frankie, its huge, white wings tipped with black. The sight of it had made her perfectly happy. That was a thing Wilhelmina had been capable of once: pure, plain happiness.

She'd never seen the cemetery looking like this, though. In late October, the trees were always vibrant with fall foliage, but today they were heavy with snow too. Red, orange, and gold burst through blankets of white. And some of the trees hadn't even started to turn yet. Thick with green leaves, their snow cover was an anomaly, two seasons manifested at once.

Wilhelmina almost forgot to look at the gravestones. She wandered among them with her eyes raised to the trees, occasionally remembering to glance down. She stumbled upon a family named Crowninshield, then one named Worsnop. *Wilhelmina Crowninshield,* she thought. *Wilhelmina Worsnop.* She stopped at a stone with a single word: SPARROW. *Wilhelmina Sparrow. Pretty good.*

She noticed the carved dogs, the angels—Wilhelmina had always been drawn to the angels—but mostly watched the snow collect in the branches above. No one was around, so she lowered her mask. This improved her vision vastly; she had to keep wiping her glasses dry, but the inner fog problem went away. The new-glasses distortion remained, but Wilhelmina had steady feet.

She rolled her shoulders. Wilhelmina had chronic pain that always started in her neck and shoulders, then grew achier the more she used her hands. Cold made it worse, as did stress. Stretching helped.

So when Wilhelmina came upon a giant maple, brilliant crimson leaves clogged with snow, she propped one forearm against its trunk, then the other, bracing her Hart feet on its roots and stretching her pectoral muscles until they cried out from the relief of it.

Then she saw something through the branches above. Something dropping from the flat, sunless sky, like the falling snow . . . except that it was big, winged, and white. No, not winged. It was—a parachute? A great white parachute, floating down from low, thick clouds. With no airplane above it. In a cemetery, in a snowstorm.

Wilhelmina burst out from underneath her maple, following the path of the parachute, trying to keep sight of it through glasses that beaded with falling snow. She half ran, almost tripping over a low gravestone. The parachute sank evenly, aiming for a cluster of trees in a low basin nearby.

Squinting, Wilhelmina could see no person suspended below its canopy. It was dropping not a human, but a package: something small and rectangular. The package glinted yellow and gold, painful to look at, difficult for her eyes to define. And then, when she entered the cluster of trees, she *did* see a person. Someone like her, on the ground, pursuing the parachute with eyes to the sky just like she was, but from the opposite direction.

Aggravated, Wilhelmina pulled her mask up, continuing to bolt along, feeling like it was a competition now. That was *her* parachute, dammit, and that person—that guy—

Wilhelmina faltered, realizing then that the person was James Fang, a boy she half knew from school. He was new-ish, or anyway, he'd moved to Watertown from somewhere nearby at the beginning of junior year. He was one of those sporty, athletic types, and he'd graduated last year, like her. She didn't falter because he was sporty and athletic. Nor did she falter because she'd lost her competitive spirit. No, Wilhelmina faltered because James Fang's Italian-Chinese-American family owned a doughnut shop, Alfie Fang's, which her family had patronized for many years. Wilhelmina had had enough of inexplicable events involving doughnuts for one day.

Except that now, James was bounding gracefully into the space between the trees like an antelope, clearly on an interception path with the parachute, and that was too much for Wilhelmina. She put on another burst of speed.

He got there first, dropping to his knees just as the sparkly, gold thing bumped gently to the ground. He put his hands on it, and he was inspecting it—he seemed to be untying a glittering bow and pulling a ribbon away from it—when Wilhelmina arrived.

"Wait!" she cried.

Starting in surprise, James looked up, then raised his hand as if blocking a great light. Wilhelmina saw a glow reflected in his dark eyes; he almost seemed to wince at the sight of her. Wilhelmina had just enough time to find this insulting before James dug into the collar of his puffy sky-colored coat and pulled up a mask.

"I'm sorry," he said. "The sun is behind you. The—this thing—"

"I saw it falling," said Wilhelmina.

"It's a present," he said, pulling the ribbon away, then folding back a kind of wrapping paper made of—leaves? And flowers? Fuchsia, scarlet, and green leaves and flowers seemed to fall away, until James was holding a small, glittering object, rectangular and flat, with brilliant light across it that spelled out a message. Wilhelmina saw the words on the object clearly. They said, TRUST WIL-HELM-INA.

James looked up at her again, still blocking his own view with his hand, as if dazzled. "You're Wil-helm-ina, right?" he said, pronouncing the word "helm" in the middle, just like it was written.

"No," said Wilhelmina firmly. "That's not me."

"You're not Wilhelmina Hart?" he said, pronouncing it correctly this time. "I saw you at school every day. You're memorable!"

Wilhelmina didn't know what that was supposed to mean. "Yeah, but my name doesn't have dashes, and it's not pronounced like that. The second *L* is silent. Look, see? It's not me."

Creasing his brow, James studied the small, glittering object in his hands. TRUST WIL-HELM-INA, it blared.

"Is this the time to get picky about punctuation?" he said.

"Definitely," said Wilhelmina, with feeling.

"Okay, but," said James, then squeaked in astonishment—and then Wilhelmina was squeaking too—because the little sparkly sign in James's hands broke apart, then vanished. It vanished! Wilhelmina came closer, too close, trying to see if he'd dropped it into the snow. But he was turning his hands over and scrabbling around looking for it. It was gone.

"What?" he cried.

"Where did it—"

"It was here, wasn't it?" he cried. "We didn't imagine it?"

"I saw it," said Wilhelmina, then immediately changed her mind. "But you're right. We imagined it."

"Joint hallucination?" he said, glancing at her skeptically. "At least you're not glowing anymore."

"I wasn't glowing."

"You were most definitely glowing. But what happened to the flowers?" said James, looking around again. "The ribbon?"

"What happened to the *parachute*?" said Wilhelmina, pushing her mind back in an attempt to remember. When had she last noticed the parachute? She had the eerie sense that it had disappeared from her sight the very moment the package had hit the ground.

"What parachute?" said James.

"It dropped from a parachute."

"What? No! Didn't it drop from an owl?"

"An *owl*?"

"A gigantic snowy owl?" said James. "Flew out of the tree and dropped it?"

"What are you even talking about?" cried Wilhelmina, then added in growing aggravation, "This is Massachusetts! Snowy owls live in the Arctic!"

"Maybe it did look like a parachute," said James doubtfully, "now that you mention it."

"Well, which one was it?" said Wilhelmina. "An Arctic bird, or a parachute? They're not the same!"

"I . . . don't know," said James, who was rubbing snow out of his wavy dark hair and craning his face up into the trees. "Flimflammery," he muttered under his breath. "This is flimflammery."

"'Flimflammery'?" said Wilhelmina. "What the fuck does that even *mean*?" She knew she was speaking in her cello voice again, indignant and profound. She knew that she sounded like she was accusing him of something. She couldn't help it. Wilhelmina was frightened.

But James didn't even seem to notice. "Why are we even *here*?" he cried to the trees.

It was a good question. Why were they here, James kneeling in the snow with the knees of his jeans soaked through, Wilhelmina standing above him?

She backed away a few feet. They were solitary, alone. No parachutes, owls, flowers, or sparkly packages present to help them make sense of this interaction. Just tree branches clumped with snow, stretching across the sky. James was staring up at the branches, as if waiting for another owl to arrive with a placard bearing an explanation.

"Well, anyway," said Wilhelmina. "I should go."

James turned his dark, inscrutable eyes to her face. "I'm supposed to trust you," he said.

"Or some other person," she said. "Wil-*helm*-ina."

"You're the only Wilhelmina here."

"Okay, then," said Wilhelmina, doggedly backing farther away. "Trust me when I say we hallucinated this."

As she increased the distance between them, James pushed his mask down from his face, watching her. His expression was incredulous, dazed with wonder, but he was also smiling. And kind of adorable. James Fang had a smile that was made of pure joy.

"Shouldn't we at least exchange numbers?" he called out.

"I have to get to Harvard Square," she said. "I need to pick up my aunt and a clock." *Shaped like an owl,* she didn't add, because she didn't want to make any more connections.

"You can find me at the doughnut shop!" he called after her, but Wilhelmina was already speeding away.

Frankie hadn't had family of her own, at least not any she ever talked about. She always lit a candle on the same day every June. Wilhelmina knew it was for Frankie's father, but whenever Wilhelmina asked questions about him, Esther and Aunt Margaret would . . . not shush her exactly, because they weren't the types of aunts who shushed children. But they would form a sort of soft but protective barrier between Frankie and all questions. Wilhelmina could feel it thickening the air as the aunts murmured and ho-hummed. They would tell Wilhelmina, "Frankie may not want to talk about it. Let's wait for her to volunteer." Which Frankie never did.

Frankie seemed to have no pictures either. Wilhelmina imagined a picture of a shortish, sturdy-ish man in old-fashioned clothing, with tanned skin and thick silver hair like Frankie's, maybe with Frankie's generous nose and warm smile. When Frankie lit the candle, she always set a little battered metal crucifix beside it that hung from a short chain of black beads, like it was part of a broken rosary. She'd grown up in a town not far from the aunts' Pennsylvania house, on a small farm that was no longer a farm but a housing development, plus a shopping complex at which she never shopped. Aunt Margaret and Esther shopped there sometimes. Frankie didn't mind. "It's a long way to the next Target," she would say, watching from the vegetable garden while Margaret or Esther emerged from the car with the telltale shopping bag. Then, with her usual familiar creaks and groans, she would stand, wipe the dirt from her knees, and extend her hand, which was always warm and rough when Wilhelmina took it. "Shall we go see if they've brought us any treasures, Wilhelmina?"

Aunt Margaret had also grown up nearby, in the same town as Frankie. Aunt Margaret and Frankie had gone to school together, then met Esther in college. Aunt Margaret's childhood house was still standing; Aunt Margaret always said it did and didn't look the same. She could recognize its shape, but the color had changed, and the shed was gone, and the lawn was perfectly landscaped now, the neighborhood around it gentrified. It made her feel a bit unsettled to drive by it, she said. Wilhelmina's family was her only remaining kin. Her brother, Wilhelmina's paternal grandfather, had died a long time ago.

Esther, in contrast, had a very large family seeming to hail from everywhere, with hubs in Miami and New York. Most everyone was Cuban or Jewish or both; Esther had had a white Jewish mother and an Afro-Cuban dad, and had grown up in Washington Heights. The refrigerator door was crammed with pictures of this grandniece's bat mitzvah, that cousin-three-times-removed's quinceañera, and dozens of babies. Her phone conversations were sprinkled with Spanish or Yiddish or both, depending on who was on the other end of the line. Her sister and many of her cousins still lived in New York. At least once every summer, one of them would pass through on their way to somewhere else and stay for a couple days. Once, two of her ancient tías came, not because they were passing through, but just to visit; Tía Maria and Tía Rosa, two tiny wrinkled women who spoke little English but kept up a constant joyful conversation with each other and Esther in Spanish, and Frankie a little too, because Frankie knew some Spanish. They liked to sit in the sun, stretching their feet out and drinking Frankie's iced tea. One of them, Tía Rosa, drew sometimes, in a sketchbook. Wilhelmina peeked once and saw a butterfly, a toad, a ladybug, a dandelion in a patch of grass, the sycamore tree that stood outside her own bedroom window.

One summer, when Wilhelmina was seven—it was 2009—Esther's cousin Ruben visited. He stayed a few days because he was handy and the aunts had a list of tasks he declared he was happy to perform. He set up a TV he'd brought with him, a hand-me-down from one of Esther's cousins. He fixed the gutters. He replaced some missing shingles on the side of the house, then painted them. He even built Frankie a low kneeling bench, which wasn't on the list. He constructed it to be sturdy but light, so that Frankie could move it around easily in her garden. After he'd nailed the last nail and sanded the last edge, he came to the border of the vegetable patch, where a tangle of big leaves hid the baby pumpkins. Then he held it out with his chin to his chest, almost bashful, as if he thought his help might be rejected. When Frankie saw him standing there, she cried out, "Ruben, you dear!" and smiled a smile so radiant that Ruben's face burst into happiness.

Bee was there with Wilhelmina that summer. Bee was invited to stay with Wilhelmina and the aunts every summer, but this was the one summer his parents actually let him come. He was almost, but not quite, seven, and he was called Tobey then. While he and Wilhelmina played in the yard or worked with Frankie in the garden, Ruben carried the ladder from one part of the house to another, climbing it with a hammer in his belt and nails in his mouth, passing from shade into sun. Sometimes he climbed so high, right up to the roof tiles, that Wilhelmina, watching, felt the emptiness beneath his feet and had to look away, whirling with a dizziness that Ruben himself did not seem troubled by. She would push her hands into the dirt beside Frankie and the earth would stop spinning.

Every morning, the aunts and Ruben had breakfast before Esther and Aunt Margaret left for work. One day, very early, while Wilhelmina was pattering down the stairs with sleep still sweet and heavy in her limbs, she heard them talking in the kitchen.

"You know what I've always wondered?" said Ruben. "Do you three ladies sleep together in one big bed?"

"Ruben, dear," said Aunt Margaret, with flint in her voice. None of the aunts had a habit of sharpness, but the kitchen suddenly felt full of sharp aunts. "Is that your business?"

"Uh," said Ruben. "No."

"Is it a respectful question, furthermore?" Esther put in.

Ruben's apologies were immediate, profuse, and heartfelt. "Honestly, Ruben," Esther said a few times to her cousin, but every time she said it, she sounded a little less exasperated, because it was clear that Ruben understood the rebuke. All three of the aunts returned to sounding like themselves, their voices a melodious counterpoint as they talked with Ruben of other things.

After Esther and Aunt Margaret drove off, Ruben began his chores. Wilhelmina and Bee went out to play near Frankie, who was picking beans in the garden.

Curious, Wilhelmina sat in the yard, watching Ruben carry his ladder around. Ruben didn't look like Esther. Esther was tall and slender with pale brown skin and dark hair streaked with silver that she wore in braids, and a soft smile that appeared often, sometimes teasing, sometimes ironic, other times a bit secretive. Also, she was stylish. "A sharp dresser," Frankie always said approvingly, "whereas I am a sparkly dresser," which was true. Frankie always had a sparkling pendant, or something shining in her ears.

Ruben, in contrast, had a rare but bright smile and a big voice, he wore a Mets cap over curly pale hair, and he had short, powerful limbs and pale skin, more like Aunt Margaret than like Esther. He wore baggy shorts and T-shirts. His face was different from Esther's; she looked Black, and he looked white. Their laughs were different. He sang while he worked, in a rough, scratchy timbre; Esther didn't sing much, but when she did, her voice was smooth and clear. When Ruben talked, though, a New York accent like Esther's came pouring out of his mouth.

Wilhelmina watched him carry the ladder past the rosebushes that grew wild against the old, sagging carriage house, then around the corner of the big house and out of sight. A moment later he came back, collected a can of paint from the shed, and disappeared again. Her thoughts followed him. Wilhelmina was thinking about Ruben's question.

Nearby, Bee—called Tobey—lay on his back in a patch of tall grass, watching lilies bob and sway above his head. A bee was bumbling from lily to lily. It brought to mind the low drone of a tiny announcer's voice, starting and stopping, starting and stopping, like the man who introduced the players coming to bat at a baseball game.

"Do you remember that boy at the baseball game?" said Bee.

Frankie, who loved baseball, had taken them to a minor-league game weeks ago. It was funny that they were both thinking about it now. "What boy?" said Wilhelmina. "Tobey?" she added, when he didn't answer. "What boy?"

"The boy sitting right behind us. His grandfather kept calling him Raimondo."

That sounded familiar. "Sort of."

"And he kept saying, 'Stop calling me Raimondo.' "

Wilhelmina hadn't been paying much attention, but she could hear that boy's voice in her memory. "Yeah, I think so."

"The grandfather finally said, 'All right, what should I call you then? Can I call you Ray? Will you be my Ray of light?' "

"I missed that part," said Wilhelmina, who liked the idea of being someone's ray of light. "You were really listening in, weren't you?"

Bee didn't speak for a while. Wilhelmina watched Frankie push up onto her feet and carry her new bench and her basket to the cucumbers. Frankie wore her long, silver hair in a twisted braid that wound around her head like a crown. Wilhelmina thought it made her look like a queen, even if her jeans were muddy and her fingernails caked with dirt.

"My dad's name is Tobey," said Bee.

Wilhelmina hugged herself. Bee's dad was a doctor, and Wilhelmina had noticed that everyone was always super nice to him. Actually, he wasn't just a doctor; he was an emergency room doctor, which meant he saved people's lives all the time. People turned away from other people when he entered a room and held their hands out for him to shake, looking into his face admiringly. They watched him when he moved off to talk to someone else. He was tall, dark-haired like Bee, and supposedly very handsome. People certainly acted like he was handsome. But to Wilhelmina, he'd always had the feeling of a false smile and hard eyes pasted to the outside wall of a cold, empty cave. When he'd just woken up or when he hadn't slept for days—two states in which Wilhelmina encountered him fairly often because of his strange work hours—the impression was heightened. When his eyes touched hers, Wilhelmina shivered. And she knew that Bee was afraid of him.

"I feel like my name is something else," said Bee.

"Something else?"

"I mean, not Tobey."

"Oh," said Wilhelmina, surprised. "What do you think your name is?"

Bee sat up. "I think it's Bee," he said, looking into Wilhelmina's face with his own face scrunched up in perplexity. "Like a bumblebee." Then, just as abruptly, he lay down again.

Wilhelmina looked from Bee to the bumblebee bumbling around the lilies, then she lay down too. It was a lot to take in. He didn't much resemble a bumblebee. His hair was thick and wavy, his eyes were greenish-brown, and his skin was flushed with summer freckles; he was skinny and long, not squat and round. He didn't bumble or buzz. He was quiet, and thoughtful, and serious. He didn't sting. "I think it's cool to choose your own name," she said.

"I don't think my dad will let me," he said.

Frankie's voice rose from the garden. "Your father has no power over your name, Bee," she said. "Should I call you Bee?"

"Yes," said Bee, who sounded pretty sure about it.

"Lovely," said Frankie. "It is a pleasure to make your acquaintance, Bee. Your father can refuse to call you by your name, and he can refuse to let you change it officially until you're an adult. But that has nothing whatsoever to do with what your name actually *is*. It's *your* name. *You* know what it is. Names are powerful. They're more powerful than one opinionated man."

Wilhelmina closed her eyes, thinking about names. Imagining them as powerful. The grass tickled her neck. She could tell that Frankie was in the tomato patch now, because the earthy, unmistakable smell of tomato vines was filling her throat. *Wilhelmina,* she thought. *Bee. Wilhelmina. Frankie. Ruben. Wilhelmina. Bee. Tobey.* She shivered again. Already, "Tobey" felt wrong. Tobey was her friend's father.

"I like Bee as a name," she said, which was true, even if she didn't understand it as a name for her friend.

"Thanks," said Bee.

"I'm worried I'll forget and call you the wrong name."

"It's okay," he said. "I'll remind you."

Wilhelmina remained on her back with her eyes closed, idly musing. Her mind returned to Ruben's question this morning. When Frankie moved away from the tomatoes to examine the garden's single promising eggplant, Wilhelmina knew she'd moved, even though she couldn't see Frankie. She searched her senses for signs of Ruben, and knew he was still on the far side of the house, climbing the ladder again.

"Bee?" she said.

"Yes?"

She could hear something new in his voice, because she'd called him *Bee*. It was a kind of confused happiness. "Bee," she said, wanting to cause him more happiness. "Can you always tell where people are?"

Bee thought for a moment. "What do you mean?"

"Like, when you wake up in the middle of the night," said Wilhelmina. "Can you tell where everyone is in the house? Or, say you closed your eyes now and Frankie went to the shed, and I went inside. Would you know where we were?"

"I mean, I could guess where you were," he said. "But how would I *know* where you were?"

"Just by," said Wilhelmina, "I don't know. By how it *feels*."

"I mean," he said again, "I think I could, maybe a little. But I think that's just because I would probably hear shed noises or something."

"Yeah," said Wilhelmina, understanding, and wondering if that was what she meant too. If when she came awake during that early part of the morning when it felt like an extra door had opened in the world, when the other humans in the house were asleep and the house was still and waiting, when the owls were coming home and the robins were just starting to stir, if the reason she knew where Bee and Ruben were, and whether the aunts were sleeping all together that night, or all apart, or in some other configuration, was because of the noises she almost didn't realize she was hearing.

Frankie's voice, warm and scratchy, broke into her thoughts again. "Some people have more of a sense of those things than others," she said.

Wilhelmina sat up, blinking. Looking for her aunt. Finding her in the eggplant patch, exactly where Wilhelmina had known her to be.

As Frankie wiped the sheen of sweat from her brow, her skin glowed with the sun. She gave Wilhelmina her megawatt smile. "Maybe it's part of your magic, Wilhelmina dear."

On the Saturday one week before she stepped into her own, Wilhelmina woke early, to silence, cold, and a stiff neck.

She also woke to a noise, but as she came more awake, she realized the noise must've been a dream. It had been the distinctive, birdlike squeak of the pulley-and-rope system she and Julie had used when they were little, to connect their bedroom windows. The rope was gone now, and the pulleys had rusted into place long ago. Gone also was the little locked box they'd tugged back and forth from window to window, with their secret messages inside. It had been a wonderful innovation, one that had become instantly obsolete once they'd both possessed phones.

Wilhelmina slipped on her new glasses. Then she grabbed her phone, but no one had texted. Creeping out of bed, she groped around on the floor in the dark for her fluffy, deep purple bathrobe. Wilhelmina wasn't normally the type to throw a precious possession like her purple bathrobe onto the floor. The bathrobe was full-length and had thumbholes and a hood that made her look like Emperor Palpatine. It was perfect. But things had changed since she'd started sharing her room with her ten-year-old sister, Delia, who was a pig. No, not a pig: Frankie had told Wilhelmina once that pigs were, in fact, quite tidy. Delia was a junk bug. She carried the carcasses of her victims around on her back after sucking them dry, so that predators would think she was gross and avoid her.

Wilhelmina found her robe, and beside it, one fuzzy sock. She couldn't find the other sock. She snuck past Delia's bed and into the hall, tiptoeing, barely breathing, trying hard not to make a sound. Once, before the pandemic, Wilhelmina had always been the first person awake. For half an hour or so, even longer on weekends, she'd had the apartment to herself. But Esther and Aunt Margaret lived here now, and they were early risers too. Something told Wilhelmina—the scent of a beeswax candle, or the quality of the silence—that they were awake this morning, in the living room at the apartment's other end. And if anyone descended upon Wilhelmina with *good morning* or *how did you sleep, dear*, she was going to implode. Or maybe explode; neither would be good.

In the bathroom, Wilhelmina tried to move around without touching her right foot to the frigid tile floor. It required a sort of improvised ballet. She removed her nightguard from her mouth and cleaned it. *Yuck.* While she was sitting on the toilet with one leg awkwardly extended, Julie's furnace turned on. The Dunstable family's furnace, ancient and angry, lived downstairs, right under the Hart bathroom. It sounded like a propeller plane and made the floor shake. If you happened to be sitting on the toilet, as Wilhelmina was, you had the sense that a commanding voice should start the countdown to lift off.

Wilhelmina was remembering the rope-and-pulley system again. She and Julie had built it together, or anyway, they'd tried to. They'd both been ten when Julie's family had moved from Boston to Watertown, into the apartment above Wilhelmina's. It had been late August, right before the start of school. Almost in the same moment that the girls had understood the relative positions of their bedrooms, a little bell had chimed in both of their minds together, the first of many synchronous thoughts.

"Wait," Wilhelmina had said, leaning out of Julie's bedroom window, the one with the window seat that was the reason Julie had chosen this room for herself. Underneath the seat was a shelf that she'd already crammed with her favorite books. If Wilhelmina knelt on the seat and leaned out far enough, she could see her own bedroom window: one floor down, two rooms over. "Julie, come here, look!"

When Julie had joined her in the window, looked where she was looking, Julie had said, "Oh! We could—from there—"

And Wilhelmina had said, "Maybe with a bucket?"

And Julie had said, "My dad has pulleys, because of Math in the World!"

Wilhelmina had understood this. Julie's dad—Mr. Dunstable— had been Wilhelmina's own math teacher in third and fourth grade. Possibly nothing had ever astonished Wilhelmina more than her own math teacher appearing outside her house one day with a moving van, then moving in. With an amazing daughter! Anyway, every Friday at the end of class, Mr. Dunstable did a thing he called Math in the World, where he taught his students some mathy thing that was the basis of some part of life everyone took for granted. Like, for example, the way a massive weight could be lifted by a relatively small force, with the help of a simple shape, like the circular head of a pulley.

The division of labor had been clear. This was because (1) the notion of pawing through her math teacher's belongings looking for pulleys was inconceivable to Wilhelmina, and (2) Julie happened to have a broken arm, from a soccer accident. So Julie would collect the supplies, and Wilhelmina would drill screws into the outside windowsills to attach the pulleys. Bee hadn't been there that day. Wilhelmina couldn't remember why, but he'd had a broken arm at the time too. Both Bee and Julie had started school that year with purple casts on their arms.

Being ten, Wilhelmina had never drilled anything before. She was pretty sure she probably shouldn't have been drilling anything now, but it was different when it was Julie's family drill, and when Julie kept telling her it was totally fine. Julie kept saying that it would be super speedy, just two quick screws. How bad could something be,

Wilhelmina thought, if it only lasted a total of, say, ten seconds? An interesting question for an episode of Math in the World, perhaps, but Wilhelmina's capacity for philosophical speculation soon faltered, because the drilling wasn't going well. She'd seen people drilling screws before. It was easy: you slotted the drill bit into the screw, you pointed the screw at the spot, you pressed the button, and the thing happened. But it was different kneeling in Julie's window seat, leaning out Julie's window, and holding a pulley, a screw, and a drill all sideways and weird, then pressing the drill toward the windowsill in a direction that was aimed toward yourself. Her first attempt made a lopsided nick.

"The windowsill is really *hard*," she said to Julie. "It's, like, *bizarrely* hard."

"You did a really good job, though," said Julie, who was leaning out of the window with her purple cast cradled against her chest, watching closely. Julie seemed as comfortable hanging out a window as when she was flopped on a bed. Her contentment was encouraging. "It just needs to be deeper. Want to try again?"

Wilhelmina's second attempt turned the nick into more of a conical gouge.

"Girls?" came Mr. Dunstable's voice from Julie's bedroom doorway. "That's not the drill I'm hearing, is it?"

Wilhelmina was so startled by the hearty, booming voice of Mr. Dunstable that she let out a tiny screech and dropped the drill, the pulley, and the screw. All of them landed in the yard below.

Julie, who'd watched the hasty descent of the items with her mouth forming a small O, spun around and said honestly, "We don't have the drill, Dad."

Wilhelmina spun around too, trying to look innocent for Julie's sake. But there stood Mr. Dunstable, one of her foremost authority figures, his face friendly and trusting, his close-cropped twists showing new glints of silver probably because of the headaches caused by disobedient children. However she might have been able to prevaricate to her own parents, Wilhelmina couldn't do it to her math teacher. Her eyes went wide, and she kept opening and closing her mouth like a fish. As Mr. Dunstable, with a changing expression, stepped into the room, she screamed, like a subject under torture, "It was me! It was all me!"

"What?" cried Julie, staring at Wilhelmina with utter incredulity. "Don't you do that, Wil! It was *me*! Dad, I'm the one who told her to do it!"

"No, it was me!" said Wilhelmina. "Julie has a broken arm!"

"But it was all my idea!"

By this point, Mr. Dunstable had crossed the room and joined them at the window, where he looked down and spotted the drill and other detritus lying in the yard. Then he found the mangled hole in the exterior windowsill.

"Juliana," he said. "Did you take my drill without asking?"

"Well, um," said Julie. "Um, yes, kind of, yes."

"Do you have any idea how dangerous a drill is?" he said, his voice escalating in pitch, while also, Wilhelmina noticed, decreasing in volume. Apparently, when Mr. Dunstable got upset, he sounded like a distant canary.

"We were only going to use it for a few seconds," said Julie, whose voice was growing wet with tears.

"A few seconds!" squeaked Mr. Dunstable. "Julie! A few seconds is all it takes for a child to fall out the window!"

"We were only doing Math in the World," wailed Julie, bursting into tears.

"It was my idea, Mr. Dunstable," wailed Wilhelmina, who was also crying, because Julie was crying, and Wilhelmina couldn't bear Julie being so sad.

"Oh," Mr. Dunstable moaned, clasping his forehead with one hand. "Oh, oh, oh." Then he sat on Julie's bed and pulled his sobbing daughter into his lap. "Wilhelmina," he said, patting the spot beside him and Julie, "sit down."

Wilhelmina sat down. At a tragic glance from Julie, she took Julie's hand. Julie grasped her hand tightly and wailed, "Just go ahead and yell at me!"

"Honey, I'm not going to yell at you," said Mr. Dunstable. "It's probably time I taught you how to use the drill. But we're going to have a conversation about not taking my power tools without permission, *or* leaning out a second-story window, *or* making holes in the property we are renting."

"I made the holes," said Wilhelmina. "I know the landlord. I'll tell him I made the holes."

"No, stop it, Wil!" cried Julie. "Daddy, we did it together."

"Yes," said Mr. Dunstable. "I've surmised that you did it together. You girls need to make better safety decisions, but it's good to see you trying to protect each other." Then he pulled Julie closer, tucking her head under his chin. "Moving has been hard," he said. "Your arm's been hurting. I'm not angry, Julie. But we're going to talk about this until I'm convinced I'm never going to find you or Wilhelmina teaching yourselves how to use power tools ever again. Got it?"

That weekend, Mr. Dunstable built them a rope-and-pulley system. Every time he so much as picked up the drill, he wore goggles and a dead serious expression.

"I'm surprised he's not wearing a helmet," Julie muttered, rolling her eyes at Wilhelmina.

"I'm surprised he's not wearing armor," said Wilhelmina.

"I'm surprised he didn't set up caution tape and make us wear hard hats."

"And put a trampoline under the window, in case he falls out."

"I can hear you, girls," said Mr. Dunstable. "The more suggestions you make, the more I think I might take you up on your bright ideas, especially the one where you both wear hard hats until you're eighteen. Now come here, and I'll show you how to get a good angle on this thing."

Wilhelmina's father, who was a librarian, came home that day with a small, red, metal lockbox that had a handle and two keys.

"This is from the library," he said. "It's been in my desk as long as I can remember. No idea where it came from."

"Oh my gosh," said Julie.

"It's where they kept the library fines!" said Wilhelmina.

"A hundred years ago!" said Julie.

It had become the box in which, on a rope between two squeaky pulleys, they'd passed each other what they called Introductions. It was a concept they came up with together.

"We've been apart for, like, *years*," Wilhelmina had said, thinking of her friendship with Bee, whom she'd met in preschool.

"Oh my gosh, I know," said Julie. "Like, you probably don't know what it's like to live in Roxbury with, like, five restaurants around the corner."

"You had restaurants right on your corner?" said Wilhelmina, to whom this sounded extremely sophisticated. "I have to walk like ten minutes to a restaurant!"

"We can catch each other up on everything we've missed!"

I spend my summers with my 3 aunts in PA and you need to come visit. SHRED THIS NOTE! wrote Wilhelmina.

We drive to NC every summer to visit my grandparents and it's so hot there I carry around a teeny fan. SHRED THIS NOTE! wrote Julie.

I don't like the Red Sox, wrote Wilhelmina, *I like the Phillies. SHRED THIS NOTE!*

I'm really good at chess, wrote Julie, *but I kind of hate it. The tournaments stress me out. SHRED THIS NOTE!*

Tournaments? wrote Wilhelmina. *Are there audiences? Would it help if I came?*

Oh my gosh, it would bore you to death.

I bet it wouldn't!

I think it might be weird if you came. But could we always hang out when I get home?

Yes!

Bee's dad scares me, wrote Wilhelmina, one afternoon after both girls had swung by Bee's house to pick him up on the way to the park, and Bee's father had unexpectedly answered the door. *Sometimes, when I know he's nearby, I get an instant stomachache. I feel awful about it, because I don't want to be anywhere near him, but Bee has to be with him all the time. I wish he didn't. I wish I could do something. Don't tell anyone, okay?*

I don't like him either, wrote Julie, *obviously. Want to try to always both be there if he's around?*

Yes!

I know it's not like I'm the only Black kid at school, wrote Julie one day in October, *but it was so different at my old school. Like, half the school was Black kids. I wish I didn't stick out so much. Please don't tell anyone, okay?*

When Wilhelmina got that note, she asked her librarian dad to help her look up some statistics, because she was curious. She didn't tell him why, of course; Julie had asked her not to. It was the fall of 2012. In the Watertown schools, about 4 percent of students were Black, 9 percent were Asian, 11 percent were Hispanic, 4 percent were mixed race or other, and 72 percent were white. It matched what Wilhelmina already knew, but seeing the numbers next to each other was a helpful kind of Math in the World.

I'm so sorry, Julie, she wrote. *4% is small. (I looked it up.)*

You did? Can you show me where?

Of course! You can see all the school districts in Massachusetts. Will you show me your old school in Roxbury?

Of course!

There was a way in which writing things down, folding them up, and locking them in a box for which only one other person had the key made it easier to share complicated things. The next time you saw your friend, the conversation had already begun, and you already knew a little bit about where your friend was coming from. Wilhelmina thought about this when Julie told her that her mother was pregnant, and Julie was trying to act happy about it. *Really, I'm just so mad at them*, wrote Julie. *Why does everything have to keep changing?* She thought about it when she told Julie that Frankie was having another surgery for ovarian cancer, and everyone kept asking her if she wanted to talk about it, and of course she didn't want to talk about it, but was it okay if sometimes she sent Julie notes about it, notes that Julie would promise to shred? And actually, could Julie maybe never bring it up in conversation later?

Here, today, Wilhelmina was still in the bathroom, still sitting on the toilet. The floor under her was still shaking.

Wilhelmina sighed. She'd thought that she and Julie had done a good job of catching up to each other, across the years. Hadn't they?

Her phone buzzed.

It was Bee. *Miss your face, elephant. Happy Halloween.* He'd sent a photo from the Halloween when they were really little, seven or eight, the time Wilhelmina had dressed as a zebra wearing polka-dot pajamas and Bee as a giraffe in striped pajamas.

Wilhelmina smiled. *No one recognized our genius that year*, she dictated back.

Showed it to Julie yesterday, he said. *She laughed so hard she fell off the bed*

Wilhelmina didn't want to hear about Bee and Julie together on a bed. She flushed the toilet, washed her hands, and went to make some coffee.

WILHELMINA LIKED THE ROUTINE of making coffee. She liked the whickering sound of the water filtering through the grounds, she liked the smell, and she liked choosing a mug. Her favorite was the ceramic one with brown-and-gray glaze, shaped like a cauldron and big as a soup bowl. Technically, it belonged to the aunts; they'd let her bring it back to Massachusetts one summer.

While she was adding a solid foundation of sugar to its bottom, Aunt Margaret wandered in from the living room. She wore her long, pale green winter coat, a fuchsia knit cap, and a patch over one eye, and she smelled of the cold.

"Good morning, Wilhelmina dear," she said crisply.

"Good morning," said Wilhelmina. "Were you outside?"

"I was just checking the mail."

"At six in the morning?"

"You know we're waiting for our ballots, right?"

Right. Esther and Aunt Margaret had applied for their Pennsylvania mail-in ballots ages ago, but the ballots hadn't arrived yet. With the election in three days, they were running out of time. Wilhelmina had voted by mail too. She'd done it at the very earliest opportunity, and now she didn't want to think about it anymore. Thinking about it made her feel panicky.

"How's your eye?" said Wilhelmina.

"It aches a bit," said Aunt Margaret, "but my doctor says that's normal."

"You have a follow-up soon, right? On Monday?"

"No, it's today."

"Saturday?" said Wilhelmina, surprised.

"They're doing weekend appointments to make up for having fewer people in the office at once."

"Ah. What time?"

"Two."

"Okay." The coffee machine beeped. "Would you like to choose a mug?" said Wilhelmina, pouring her own cup. "I'd give you this one, but I've already added the sugar." As she did every morning, on purpose, so that one little thing in the free-for-all of the Hart kitchen could feel like hers.

"I'll get my coffee, dear," said Aunt Margaret. "You enjoy yours. Are you missing a sock? Here, could this be a match?"

Aunt Margaret produced a sock from her coat pocket, which was a weird thing to do. "Thank you," said Wilhelmina, taking the sock, but not asking why it was in her aunt's coat pocket, because she didn't want to talk anymore. The sock was cold to the touch. Maybe Aunt Margaret had found it in the mailbox. Why not? Once she'd pulled it on, it warmed up quickly against the skin of her foot, and it was, in fact, a match. Wilhelmina badly wanted to carry her beautiful, warm coffee into some room where she could be alone, but the only option was the bathroom, where Julie's furnace was roaring like a dozen jackhammers and where it was only a matter of time before someone knocked.

Esther glided into the kitchen from the living room, tall, and with silver hair peeking out from under a silver scarf. She wore a robe that was purple, but with more of a rose tone than Wilhelmina's. In one hand she balanced an extinguished candle, golden and fat, that smelled like beeswax and warmth. She smiled softly at Wilhelmina. "Good morning, bubeleh."

"Good morning."

"How did you sleep?"

"Fine."

"I had a dream my mother was in the circus," said Esther. "The flying trapeze. Papi was with me in the audience. She wore a leotard made of purple asters, the ones that grow along our fence. She had butterflies!" Esther said, standing still with glowing eyes, as if she were seeing the dream inside herself. "All around her!"

"How lovely!" said Aunt Margaret. "Did you know that the flying trapeze was invented by a Frenchman named Jules Léotard?"

"I confess, I did not."

"He used a swimming pool as his net."

"Very resourceful."

"But tell us about your dream, dear," said Aunt Margaret. "Did you get to talk with either of your parents?"

"They had no messages for me," said Esther. "But oh! She was exquisite."

Wilhelmina decided to carry her coffee back to her bedroom and sit with it in the dark while hoping Delia wouldn't wake up. She remembered now that she'd also had a dream. It was a recurring dream of hers, one that had visited her often in the two years or so since Frankie's death, and one that she hated. Really, it was more of a sense than a dream. It was a kind of dream flavor. She'd be dreaming about something—school, or her family, or anything—and she would know that if she could just keep dreaming, Frankie was about to appear. She would try to hold on to the dream, waiting for Frankie. But Frankie never arrived in time. Just at the moment when her arrival was imminent, Wilhelmina would wake up.

"Doughnut Saturday, Wilhelmina?" said Aunt Margaret to her retreating back.

Doughnut Saturday was a long-standing Hart tradition, one to which the aunts had taken with enthusiasm. Wilhelmina had a new plan never to eat another doughnut ever. But she could see no way to avoid procuring doughnuts for the rest of the family.

She stretched her aching neck, dropping her head down and raising her mug so she could inhale the scent of coffee at the same time. "Yes," she said. "I'll go soon." At least if she was running an errand, she could escape her family for a bit. She just hoped James Fang wasn't working today.

NOT ONLY WAS JAMES WORKING, but he was working the register.

This was unusual. In all Wilhelmina's years of doughnut pickup, while she could remember seeing glimpses of James in the kitchen doing things like sliding doughnuts in and out of the fryer and covering doughnuts with clouds of powdered sugar, she couldn't remember him ever working the register before.

Maybe this was because he was bad at it. Standing on her marker six feet removed from the next in line, Wilhelmina heard the customer at the counter say, "Wait. You gave me way too much change."

She couldn't hear James's response because of his mask and the plexiglass barrier. But she could see his high eyebrows and his confused expression. She could also see that he had a bat on his head. It was quite realistic, its segmented wings spread wide and its beady eyes glinting down at the customers. Of course, it was attached with a piece of red yarn tied in a bow under his chin, which somewhat ruined the terrifying effect, and also made him adorable, which was annoying.

Wilhelmina focused on the doughnut shop instead, Alfie Fang's. The Alfie part of the name was for James's mom, Alfie, and the Fang part was James's dad, whose first name Wilhelmina didn't know. She supposed she didn't know Alfie's last name either, now that she was thinking about it. The shop, which served a range of treats from classic glazed doughnuts to Chinese doughnuts to doughnuts with impressive portraiture in icing, occupied a glass-walled corner at the base of a tallish office block called the Lupa Building. The original structure was an old Art Deco beauty from the 1930s, made of white reinforced concrete, with sharp, stylized wolves carved above every entrance. The Museum of Armenia was in this building, as was Wilhelmina's dentist.

The doughnut shop was small and filled with light. The customer area was a triangular wedge, a counter in black and pink marble making up one side, glass walls making up the other two. Big black and white squares tiled the floor. Behind the counter was a mural, constructed in miniature tiles, showing a forestscape with bears and wolves, foxes and owls, and the Boston skyline beyond the trees. Skyscrapers peeked out, and bridges, and far to the left, the obelisk that was the Bunker Hill Monument.

It was Wilhelmina's turn. She stepped up to the plexiglass.

"Wilhelmina Hart!" said James. "Good morning."

"Good morning," she said, feeling awkward. What did one say to a person with a bat on his head with whom (the person, not the bat) one had recently experienced a joint hallucination? "I placed an online order," she said.

"Right," he said, reading something on his screen. "One RBG, one Kamala Harris. Two honey crullers. One youtiao. Two plain cake doughnuts covered with every pumpkin, bat, witch, black cat, broomstick, and orange sprinkle we have in the shop."

"Those two are for my little brother and sister," Wilhelmina said apologetically. The doughnuts her siblings chose always made her feel like her family didn't adequately respect doughnut artistry. She was trying to think of a way to ask for reassurance that the doughnuts weren't stale today, without insulting him further. "Which of the doughnuts are freshest, do you think?"

"Freshest?" he said, peering at her doubtfully.

"Yes."

"Well, the honey crullers just came out of the fryer," he said. "Have you been having freshness issues with our doughnuts?"

"No!" she said. "Never! I just really . . ." She jabbed the air for emphasis, which immediately made her feel like an idiot. ". . . wanted an extra-fresh doughnut."

"Hm," he said. "Okay. How will you be paying?"

"Credit card."

"Good. I can hide from you how hopeless I am at making change. Any strange messages drop down on you from the sky since yesterday?"

"No."

"Me neither," he said. "Do you think maybe we should talk about that?"

"Um," said Wilhelmina, pretending to be occupied with the card reader. While it beeped and buzzed, James's mother, Alfie, came forward from the kitchen, her hair honey brown, gathered in a knot on top of her head. She glanced at her son, then turned with interest to see to whom he was speaking.

"Wilhelmina, right?" said Alfie, who was tall and hazel-eyed, graceful, and always, for some reason, made Wilhelmina think of Frankie when she spoke. Sort of as if they had a similar accent, except that neither Frankie nor Alfie had an accent she'd ever detected.

"Yes, ma'am," said Wilhelmina.

"You look beautiful every time I see you, Wilhelmina," she said, "and I like those glasses. Enjoy your doughnuts."

While Wilhelmina was still stammering a startled thanks, Alfie spun back to the kitchen. It wasn't every day that people out in the world gave unsolicited compliments to short, fat, masked individuals like Wilhelmina, even when their hair was cutely tousled and their glasses were new and red and, okay, maybe they'd chosen a close-fitting black knit dress and swirly leggings to wear under their close-fitting red coat, just in case James Fang was at the doughnut shop.

James slid Wilhelmina's doughnuts through the opening in the plexiglass, saying nothing, just looking at her very hard. She couldn't tell what kind of look it was. She wished she could see his face.

She transferred the doughnut box into the handled bag she'd brought for the purpose. Handles always meant less pain. Then she gave him, and his bat, an exasperated glance before turning away.

OUTSIDE, Wilhelmina squelched through mucky patches of snow and slush. It was warmer today, barely, but still wintry, white in places. A small group of children in costumes passed by. She saw a princess, a honeybee, a ladybug, but no superheroes. Poor kids. Trick-or-treating was so weird this year, with face masks, and no knocking on doors. Candy left on stoops. Hand sanitizer beside the treats.

Wilhelmina's neighborhood was situated on a long, steep hill that she was used to climbing. A block from home, she changed her route, so that she could walk by Mrs. Mardrosian's giant house and look for signs that Mrs. Mardrosian had made it home safely. That meant walking by Bee's place too, because the Sloanes—Bee, Kimmy, and their mom—lived in an apartment in a converted Victorian a few doors down from Mrs. Mardrosian.

She found Bee on his stoop, looking sleepy, wearing ripped jeans and a pale pink hoodie that matched his hair. He was maskless, and Wilhelmina's heart filled to see his face. He'd grown so gigantically tall, and he had a shadow of stubble on his jaw, but he still had the same big, greenish-brown eyes, and he still smiled the same sweet smile when he saw her.

"Hey, Wil," he said. "Love your face. Those glasses suit you."

"Thanks."

"Did you get me a doughnut?"

"No, but you can have mine."

"Nah," he said, "I wouldn't do that to you. Hey, what happened yesterday? That was some weird shit, with the fortune teller."

"Oh," said Wilhelmina. "Yeah. I think I'm just tired, you know?"

Bee gave her the same pursed-lip, skeptical look he'd been giving her since he was three and they were in day care together. "Sure, okay," he said. "But what actually happened?"

"Nothing," she said. "I'm sure it was nothing. Do you know James Fang?"

"Varsity track," he said. "Moved from Waltham like two years back. He's good. One of those steal-the-competition situations. Don't his parents have the doughnut shop?"

"Yeah."

"Why are you asking about him?" said Bee, then shivered. "Brr!" As he pulled his hood up, she caught sight of his elephant-unicorn necklace, glinting in the sunlight. Then it disappeared inside his clothes. "And come on, Wil," he said in a sharper tone, "what happened yesterday? I'm worried about you."

"Why are you sitting out in the cold?"

"I'm contemplating a walk. Maybe I'll go ask James what's going on, since you won't tell me."

"You wouldn't dare," said Wilhelmina, grinning.

"Oh!" Bee said, his smile growing bigger, and sweeter. "Is that how it is now? Something *is* going on with James?"

"There's nothing going on with James," said Wilhelmina, "and don't you embarrass me."

"When Julie gets here," he said, "maybe we'll walk to the doughnut shop."

Wilhelmina turned away. "Great," she said. "Enjoy your walk."

"I'm worried about you, Wil," he called after her. "Don't you disappear on me." But she held up a hand in salute and didn't look back.

A moment later, she came abreast of Mrs. Mardrosian's house. It was one of those giant Victorians with a tower room, gingerbread decoration, four chimneys, and gorgeous tall maples dropping leaves poetically across the lawn. Mrs. Mardrosian's old Mercedes was parked in the driveway, which meant she'd gotten home. Great. Wilhelmina walked on, stomped around the corner, and immediately saw Julie walking toward her.

Wilhelmina almost began to cry. It was a sudden and unexpected reaction. Bewildered by her own body, she stomped harder, then took a few big, gusty breaths, trying to get her feelings in order.

"Wil!" said Julie, rushing toward her with a mix of happiness and concern on her face. "Are you okay?" She stopped some distance away. "I've been worried about you."

"I'm fine," Wilhelmina said weakly.

"Hey, don't brush me off," said Julie. "Are you really okay? You look upset."

It was breaking her heart to see Julie's face, her mouth, the soft dimples that hid in her cheeks. Her big hair was braided across the front, and she'd wrapped a long, pale pink scarf around her neck about a hundred times. The scarf was breaking Wilhelmina's heart too, because it matched Bee's hoodie, and it matched his hair. They were matching on purpose.

"That was really weird yesterday," said Julie. "You seemed scared. Want to come walk with me and Bee?"

Wilhelmina didn't want to walk with Julie and Bee. She wanted to walk with Julie. Or with Bee. Or with both of them, fine, but not like this, as an afterthought! How had she become an afterthought, when she used to be integral? Would Julie have built a messaging system with any old person? Could Bee have attached himself to any old kid in preschool? Was it just about who was there? Because it wasn't just about that for Wilhelmina.

"Thanks, but I have to deliver the doughnuts," she said, indicating her bag.

"Okay," said Julie. "You're being kind of mysterious, though, you know?"

That wasn't what she wanted either. "Do you know James Fang?" she said.

"Doughnut hottie," said Julie.

"Yeah. Well," said Wilhelmina. "I went to the cemetery yesterday after I saw you guys. For a walk."

"Okay," said Julie. "Did something happen?"

"Aren't you going to be late?" said Wilhelmina. "Bee's waiting."

"He'll survive," said Julie. "What's going on here, Wil? You keep deflecting. Do you want me to drag it out of you or do you want me to leave you alone? Give me a clue about what you need here, okay?"

Wilhelmina wished she knew what that was. "James Fang was in the cemetery," she said. "And, well. A shiny thing fell from the sky."

"A shiny thing?" said Julie. "What do you mean?"

"Just, this *thing*," said Wilhelmina. "But when we ran to catch it, it sort of . . . disappeared."

Julie raised her eyebrows. Then she tucked her chin to her chest and looked worried, a posture so characteristically Julie that Wilhelmina's heart ached. "Disappeared," she said carefully, "like you couldn't find where it landed?"

Wilhelmina swallowed, then sighed, overcome by a kind of surrender. "No," she said. "We found it. It was, like, a sparkly rectangle. It said 'Trust Wilhelmina' on it, like, in little lights, but with weird dashes in my name. I mean, it *wasn't* my name. Then while we were examining it, it vanished. Like, it was just *gone*."

Julie's mouth twisted. She reached into her back pocket and grabbed her phone.

"What are you doing?" Wilhelmina cried.

"I'm finding someone who can send me James's number," Julie said, scrolling fast. "So I can give him shit for playing pranks on you."

"No," said Wilhelmina. "Don't do that, Julie. I don't think he's playing pranks. I think he's as confused as I am."

"Then how do you explain it?" cried Julie, not looking up from her phone. Then her fingers stilled. She exhaled. She raised her face to Wilhelmina. "How do you explain this, Wil?"

"I've been carefully avoiding trying to explain it," said Wilhelmina.

"Okay," said Julie. "Then let me explain it: As of yesterday, you're seeing things. Things that aren't there."

"Okay," said Wilhelmina, "yes. But James is also seeing things."

"Joint hallucinations are a known phenomenon. It happens, like in cults. Or like in the Salem witch trials. You know the theory about the rye?"

"What? Rye?"

"There's this theory their rye flour got moldy that winter and they all ate a hallucinatory fungus," said Julie. "So when they started acting crazy, everyone decided they must be witches, because that's how people thought in the seventeenth century. Did you and James eat anything?"

"No!"

"How well do you know him anyway? I think he's friends with Eloisa Cruz. You know her? She's in Bee's year. I think Bee likes her. She's Dominican, always stars in the musicals?"

"Yeah," said Wilhelmina.

"Want me to pick her brain?"

"No!" said Wilhelmina. "Could you maybe just . . ."

"Yes?" said Julie.

"Stop, for now? Like, maybe just give me a minute?"

"Give you a minute," said Julie, who didn't look happy. She was doing her worried chin tuck again. "I mean, of course, Wil. I can give you like a minute and a half. But did you tell Bee?"

"Not yet."

"Can *I* tell Bee?"

Wilhelmina was beginning to wish she'd kept the whole weird, fucked-up thing to herself. "Sure," she said tiredly.

"Okay," said Julie, who seemed relieved by this. "Bee and I will get back to you. One last thing: Did you dress sexy to go to the doughnut shop?"

Now Wilhelmina was smiling a little. "Bye, Julie."

"You tell me when you want some recon on that boy, okay?"

"No recon, Julie."

"Okay, but tell me!"

"I'll tell you. Bye."

"Bye, elephant!"

WILHELMINA FOUND ESTHER just inside the front door. She was perched on one of the steps that led up to Julie's apartment, her shoulders straight and her posture graceful, still wearing her rose-purple robe, but somehow making it look like a careful fashion choice. Wilhelmina couldn't see Julie's cat, who was also named Esther, but she knew the feline must be present. Human Esther visited cat Esther on the stairs often, sitting with her silently.

"Hi," said Wilhelmina.

"Hola, bubeleh," said Esther. "Doughnuts achieved?"

"Yes."

The cat emerged from behind the human then, arching her back against Human Esther's outstretched hand. Esther the cat was a pale gray that complemented human Esther's silver locs rather nicely, actually, now that Wilhelmina was noticing.

"You two would make a nice painting," she said.

"Would we?" said Esther, with a soft smile. "Thank you kindly."

"Would you like your doughnut?"

"Do birds fly?" said Esther. "I'll come inside soon. I'm telling Esther about my mother."

"Okay," said Wilhelmina, who didn't have the wherewithal just then to indulge Esther's oddness. The aunts in the apartment up close for months on end during a pandemic was a different phenomenon entirely from the aunts for a summer in their spacious Pennsylvania home. Especially without Frankie. Wilhelmina went inside.

IN THE ENTRANCEWAY, Wilhelmina spent some time shaking one foot, then the other, trying to get her slushy boots off.

Her father's voice rang out from the kitchen. "They won't take the precautions because they think the precautions are a hoax," Theo said. "Then, when they get sick, they expect the medical care that's based on the same science as the precautions."

"That sounds like an eminently human thing to do," said Aunt Margaret mildly.

"In the sense that humans are ignoble animals, sure."

"Ignoble *and* noble, Theo dear."

Finally freed from her boots, Wilhelmina stomped into the kitchen with her doughnut bag. She plunked it onto the table around which Aunt Margaret; her father, Theo; and her mother, Cleo, were sitting. Then she kept on walking, disappearing into her bedroom before anyone could try to engage her in a debate about humans.

In the bedroom, Delia lay on her back in bed, blinking at the ceiling.

"Your disgusting doughnut is here," Wilhelmina said.

Delia emitted a tiny squeal. Then she sat up, scrabbled around in one of the mountains of clothing on the floor, extracted a sweatshirt that said UNICORN! CAKE!, slid it on over her pajamas, and bolted out of the room.

Alone at last, Wilhelmina went to her bed and climbed under the covers. She lay on her back, resting her neck, touching the little enamel elephant at her throat.

After a moment, she unearthed her laptop from her blankets. All computer work—and phone time too, really—came with some pain for Wilhelmina, who couldn't type in the normal way and needed to be militantly careful never to hunch over her devices. But when she was lying on her back, she could open the laptop as flat as possible and perch its bottom edge on her stomach, then look at things. Sometimes Bee and Julie lay to either side of her and watched stuff with her. In fact, Julie had some games she loved so much that after she'd played them once herself, she would play them again with Wilhelmina on her own laptop, the two girls tucked together, Julie doing all the mousing and keying, being Wilhelmina's hands while Wilhelmina made the decisions.

Bee was usually nearby, providing commentary or futzing on his phone, or distracting them with rhetorical questions. "Do you guys think numbers are real? Or, like, just a human construct?" (Wilhelmina: real. Julie: real. Bee: construct, though Wilhelmina thought he might be playing devil's advocate.) "Would you rather have an extra arm or an extra leg?" (Wilhelmina: leg, because her arms often hurt, and imagine how surefooted it would make her while climbing rocky crags in Ireland. Imagine the power of her kick while swimming. Julie: arm, in case she ever lived on a spaceship, in free fall. Also so she could eat/do her hair/carry things/hold an umbrella while reading a book. Bee: arm, because he was a soccer goalie, and also for self-defense.) "Would you rather eat a brownie the size of a couch, or a tiny turd?" (Wilhelmina and Julie: refusal to engage with this question.)

The three of them had tried to keep playing games together in recent months, Julie streaming over Twitch for Wilhelmina, all three of them video-chatting on their phones. Julie had seemed to enjoy it. Wilhelmina hated it. It made her feel like Julie, Bee, and the game were across the universe from her, or unreachable at the bottom of the sea. When Bee and Julie were in the same room while it was happening, Wilhelmina hated herself for how jealous it made her. It was better to watch things alone.

With a minimum of mousing, Wilhelmina pulled up one of her favorite makeup video playlists. She thought about the conversation she'd overheard. Were humans noble or ignoble? Her friends were noble. There was never any question about that. It was why she yearned for them. But Wilhelmina was feeling a bit ignoble herself today: disgruntled, resentful, selfish. Humans, it turned out, could be the worst. Wilhelmina hadn't always thought so; it hadn't occurred to her to have such ambivalence on the topic, until the day a giant minority of them had chosen someone for president who mocked disabled people, laughed about assaulting women, and wanted to keep Mexican people behind a wall. Then loved all of his choices. Believed all of his lies. It was very confusing. Sometimes Wilhelmina felt cut off from her entire species. Other times, she felt like humans got just what they deserved.

Wilhelmina pressed play on a cat-eyes video she'd watched before. The video helped: watching gentle humans transform other humans soothed her. Some humans, at least, were kind magicians, with hairbrushes and creams, heat and water, eyeliner and eyeshadow.

SOMETIME LATER, when she sensed that Cleo was working behind a closed door and her siblings had gone out with Esther, Wilhelmina emerged.

She found Theo and Aunt Margaret in the kitchen. Theo was tapping on his laptop at the kitchen table. The doughnut box sat behind it.

"Hi, honey," he said, his square, pink face brightening at the sight of her. Theo looked like Wilhelmina and Aunt Margaret, stout, pleasant, not particularly tall. "Did I tell you I like your new glasses?"

"Thank you for getting the doughnuts, Wilhelmina," said Aunt Margaret. She stood at the counter, packing chicken pieces into the slow cooker.

"Should you be cooking a day after eye surgery?" said Wilhelmina.

"Oh, I'm allowed to use my hands," she said. "Your father got the slow cooker out of the cabinet for me. We left you a honey cruller, dear."

"Hm," said Wilhelmina, eyeing the doughnut box suspiciously. "Who ate the other honey cruller?"

"I did," said Aunt Margaret.

"How was it?"

"Even more delicious than usual."

"Fresh?"

"Divinely fresh."

"Okay," said Wilhelmina, not moving toward the doughnuts.

Peering around his screen, Theo pushed the box toward Wilhelmina. Inside it, she could see the golden ridges of the honey cruller, shining with glaze. "Go for it, hon," he said.

"I don't know," said Wilhelmina. "I might be off doughnuts."

"Off doughnuts?" said Theo, his forehead crinkling in concern. He was going to need another haircut soon; his arrangement of uneven, graying brown wisps was getting long around the ears. Every haircut Wilhelmina gave Theo was uneven, because it didn't matter how many YouTube videos you watched if your subject kept bending his face to his phone to read the news.

"Don't you feel well, Wilhelmina?" said Theo. "Any nausea?"

"No," said Wilhelmina, who was used to her father turning everything into Covid. "I meant I might be off doughnuts forever."

"Forever!" said Theo, changing tack. "You mean like a diet?"

"No!" said Wilhelmina. "I just don't want the doughnut! Why are you freaking out?"

"I'm not freaking out," said Theo. "It's only that I can't bear the notion that any of my beautiful children might think they need to go on a diet."

"It's not a diet, Dad!" said Wilhelmina. "Geez!"

"Okay," said Theo. "I apologize. You don't have to eat the doughnut."

"Well, now I feel like you'll be watching everything I eat," said Wilhelmina. "Examining me to make sure I'm not on a diet."

"I wouldn't do that."

"I sure hope not."

"If it's an unwanted doughnut, may I have it?"

Theo's hand reached toward the box, and it was in that moment, as matters approached the point of no return, that Wilhelmina understood that she *had* to eat the doughnut. Because it was only by eating the doughnut and finding it as fresh and delicious as Aunt Margaret's that Wilhelmina would be able to dismiss every strange thing that had happened since yesterday.

"I changed my mind," she said, marching toward the doughnut and snatching it out from under her bewildered father's hand. She raised it to her mouth. Then she bit into a cruller as dry and scratchy as the bristles of a broom.

"What the fuck!" she shouted, pitching the doughnut across the room.

Theo jumped up, rigid with alarm. "What is it?" he shouted. "Have you lost your sense of taste?"

"It was stale!" Wilhelmina shouted.

"Oh, that's too bad," said Aunt Margaret serenely, peering one-eyed at the doughnut, which had landed at her feet. "You should go back to that nice shop and get another."

"Stale?" said Theo. "Are you sure? Can you smell things?"

"Dad!" said Wilhelmina. "I don't have Covid!"

"Okay, okay," said Theo. "You threw your food!"

"I'm very—upset," said Wilhelmina, who was shaking, but also understood how this looked.

"Wilhelmina, honey," said Theo. "You scared me. Do you think maybe you overreacted?"

"Yes," said Wilhelmina. "Could I take the car?"

"To do what? Go get a new doughnut?"

"I just need the car, Dad," she said sharply.

"Indeed," said Aunt Margaret, "maybe Wilhelmina would benefit from some time to herself." She started to bend down toward the doughnut, then stopped. "I think bending is on the list of things I'm not supposed to do."

Wilhelmina rushed forward to collect the doughnut from around Aunt Margaret's feet. As she pressed it into Aunt Margaret's hand, her phone buzzed. A message from Julie. *Hey. I can't find my necklace. I had it this morning. Let me know if you see it?*

"The car?" said Wilhelmina in her involuntary cello voice. "Dad?"

"You may have the car when you ask me for it politely," said Theo, a bit flushed.

Once again, Wilhelmina was fighting back sudden, unexpected tears. "I'm not a child," she said. "I run all the errands. I do Delia and Philip's school. I get the food. I drive the aunts to their appointments. I'm not even supposed to *be* here. I'm supposed to have gone away. Is there something you need the car for, Dad? Why do I even need to ask for permission?"

Theo looked pink and puffed up and confused, and a little bit foolish. That was how he looked when he was sad. Wilhelmina hated when she made Theo sad.

She took the cruller back from Aunt Margaret, who was presenting it to her benevolently, like a white-haired, patch-eyed angel. She found the car key—it was in her own pocket—and left.

IN THE CAR, Wilhelmina kept replaying her words, and her father's face. Theo had asthma. It was unsafe for him to venture out into the world during the pandemic, which wasn't his fault. Cleo had no risk factors, but she was a therapist who specialized in conspiracy theories, which meant she was overbooked with clients right now. Not clients who believed conspiracy theories; conspiracy theorists, by definition, were unlikely to reach out to therapists, since they had all the answers already. Cleo's clients were the people those people had left behind, like the husband who'd lost his spouse to QAnon and couldn't figure out what to do.

Anyway. In addition to being overwhelmed professionally, Cleo was in the midst of the worst attack of seasonal allergies Wilhelmina could remember, which included the constant fun of wondering if it was Covid. The drugs Cleo was on made her too spacey to drive. Esther's driver's license had expired early on in the pandemic. Aunt Margaret was recovering from eye surgery. It was lucky for the family that Wilhelmina could drive.

Everyone was doing all they could. The aunts and Theo took turns cooking. Everyone—not just Wilhelmina—took turns supervising Delia's and Philip's school. Wilhelmina was fortunate she could jump in the car and get away. Theo was a librarian with no library to go to and no patrons, working on his laptop in whatever room was available, stir-crazy and worried, and hardly ever complaining.

Wilhelmina pulled over and reached for her phone.

Theo had texted approximately thirty-seven times. *I'm sorry hon.*

You're right, you shouldn't need to ask permission for the car.

If you'll just confirm that no one else needs it, you can always take it.

You are our rock, Wilhelmina.

Furthermore, you are my protector. I appreciate that more than I can say. It shouldn't be like this. I'm the parent. I should be protecting you.

I'm sorry I treated you like a child.

Sniffling, Wilhelmina texted back. *It's okay Dad. I'm sorry too. I was rude*

He responded immediately. *I love you.*

I love you too

As cars swarmed by, Wilhelmina sat for a while, staring at the steering wheel with her phone in her lap. She wasn't sure what she was waiting for. To stop feeling like everything was wrong? She expected she'd be waiting a long time.

Julie's message about the lost elephant necklace rose through the muck of Wilhelmina's mind. She dictated a text to Julie. *Hey, sorry about the necklace. I'll keep an eye out.*

Her palms were beginning to burn, which meant she needed to stretch her neck and shoulders soon. So she eased into traffic and continued toward her destination. She passed a skinny white man who stood in the middle of a five-way intersection where it was hard to parse what lane you were supposed to choose in order to get where you wanted to go, unless you'd driven it dozens of times, as Wilhelmina had. At peril to his life, the man waved a gigantic flag bearing the name of the president. This man was often there with that flag. Wilhelmina had turned her feelings off to him long ago. She drove past him without looking.

When she reached her destination, she got out of the car, found a spectacular, yellow-leaved maple, and stretched her neck and chest with her arm braced back against its trunk. Wilhelmina was in the cemetery again. She'd decided to feed her stale doughnut to the birds.

Wilhelmina walked. There were more people in the cemetery today, masked friends traversing the roads six feet apart from each other, yelling conversation across the chasms between them. Wilhelmina kept to the footpaths. A thin sun peeked through the clouds, unhurriedly melting the snow. When she saw a flock of turkeys in a clearing, she tromped toward them down a grassy hill that ran with streams of meltwater.

It wasn't until she entered the clearing that she realized this was the same spot as yesterday, the little basin where all the weird things had happened.

No thank you, thought Wilhelmina. She turned around and was about to hightail it away when she heard a great cracking noise above, as if a tree was falling. Next, James Fang fell from the sky. He fell from the sky! He swooped down on a parachute and crashed beside her!

"What are you *doing*?" Wilhelmina cried.

"Falling," said James mournfully, collapsed in a heap on the ground, his limbs entangled with—something gray and brown? The parachute? A cloak? She surged toward him, obeying her human instinct to assist another human who was down, then remembered the pandemic. Stopping herself, she watched him push to a seated position and begin rolling his shoulders, bending and testing his arms. His expression was dazed.

"I'm sorry to just stand here," she said, fishing her mask out and pulling it up. "Do you need help? Are you okay?"

"I seem to be," he said, bending and straightening one leg experimentally, "though I don't think I should be."

"But where did you *come* from?" said Wilhelmina. "I mean, seriously. Were you *skydiving*?"

"No!" he said, staring up at her incredulously. "Wilhelmina Hart, are you seeing parachutes again?"

Wilhelmina realized then that the parachute, or cloak, or whatever flappy thing she'd thought she'd seen above and around James was gone. Of course it was gone. Why would she expect anything else? James sat in the clearing, the butt of his jeans soaking up a small pool of melt-water, wearing his puffy sky-blue coat. No cloak, no parachute.

Also, he was faintly glowing around the edges.

"Are you playing a prank on me?" demanded Wilhelmina.

"No!"

"Then why did you just fall out of the sky?"

"I was in the tree," he said, pointing up.

When Wilhelmina craned her neck, she saw a thick web of branches, impossibly far above. Twenty feet? Twenty-five? An icy drop of something plopped onto her forehead. Ugh!

"You were up there?" she said. "And you *fell*? How are you not hurt?"

"I don't know!" he said. "My legs should be broken. But doesn't it seem like a lot of things aren't happening the way they should?"

Suddenly, Wilhelmina remembered the doughnut she was still clutching. Almost in a passion, she began shaking it at him. "My doughnut was stale!" she cried.

"Okay," he said, startled. "I'm really sorry about that. We can get you a replacement."

"But your doughnuts are never stale!"

"Yeah, the shop's a mess at the moment," said James. "My dad's sick—not the virus," he added. "Probably it's affected our quality control."

"You don't understand," said Wilhelmina, who was now holding the cruller in both hands, extending it toward James, like an offering. "Yesterday, a fortune teller in Harvard Square prophesied my future. She told me my doughnut would be stale."

James clearly needed a minute to process that one. He cocked his head sideways and blinked a few times. Then, slowly, he stood, testing each limb before applying pressure to it. He wiped his wet hands together, then rubbed his head. His dark hair was sticking up funny on one side, which was cute. Everything about James was cute. Nearby, the turkeys wandered in circles, pausing occasionally to dart suspicious glances at the humans.

"Flimflammery?" James finally suggested.

"You said that yesterday," said Wilhelmina. Another drip plopped onto her head. "I think we need a more advanced theory."

"Well, it *is* Halloween."

"What does that matter? Do you think *ghosts* lowered you gently to the ground?"

"Both my grandmas would say it matters," said James. He took a breath, then raised his eyes to the branches far above. He gazed at the web they made for a moment, then added thoughtfully, "I guess one of my grandmas works with a different calendar, but I still think she'd take this in stride. Okay, here's the deal. I was climbing that tree. I slipped and fell out. It was terrifying. I knew I was going to break my neck. Then something that felt like a giant flapping bird surrounded me, and the next thing I knew, I was on the ground, all in one piece, and *you* were there. I mean, of course you were. That part shouldn't surprise me. But—what *happened*?"

Wilhelmina had no answer to that. "You're really okay?" she said shakily.

"I think so."

"Why were you climbing the tree?"

"I was looking for an explanation for that thing that fell from it yesterday."

"Did you find anything?"

James's lips puckered up. He shrugged. "Seems like your basic tree." Then, belatedly, he noticed Wilhelmina's mask, and started digging into his collar for his own. "Sorry! I forgot. I don't know what's going on. It's been a deeply weird couple of days. Why are *you* here?"

Wilhelmina sighed, then held up her doughnut again. "I wanted to feed my stale doughnut to the turkeys."

"Ah," said James. "Technically I think that's, like, a crime against nature. And it's definitely against the cemetery rules, but I feel like we're beyond that now, don't you? It'd make the turkeys happy."

The two of them considered the turkeys quietly for a moment. Bulbous and ungraceful, with startlingly beautiful feathers shining on their throats and arrayed along their wings, they stalked and clucked among themselves, poking their beaks at the wet ground—except for a single outlier, who was climbing onto tombstones. She jumped from one to the next, flapping herself up onto a high plinth topped by a marble fruit basket. Then she seemed to pose there, considering her surroundings like a queen.

James chuckled. "Rafter?"

"Huh?" said Wilhelmina, who was pretty sure James had just asked her the question, "Rafter?"

"Is that what a group of turkeys is called?" he said. "A rafter? I think that's right. You know how groups of animals have funny names?"

"I know about a murder of crows."

"I wonder what a group of owls is called," mused James.

"You'll have to find out," said Wilhelmina, "and tell me the next time you see me."

For a moment, James peered at Wilhelmina and Wilhelmina peered at James, carefully, each studying the other, but coming to no conclusions. Or, anyway, Wilhelmina came to no conclusions. James Fang was surprising. He had an earnest energy that she couldn't help liking. She also liked the way he talked. And the way he looked, though that wasn't a new revelation. James had always been one of those noticeable people at school. She liked the way he looked *at* her. It was strange to think of the dozens, maybe hundreds of times she'd passed him in the halls of the high school, catching and holding his eye, knowing who he was, noticing that he was attractive, but never realizing what he was *like*.

He was still faintly glowing at the edges. *Sigh*. And Wilhelmina's cruller was turning her hand into a sticky mess.

"Is it really a crime against nature to feed doughnuts to the turkeys?" she said.

James scrunched up his eyes, considering. "Nah. It can be our Halloween offering."

Wilhelmina didn't know what that was supposed to mean. But she tore the cruller in two pieces, then gave half to James, so that he could make the turkeys happy too.

DINNER, which was chicken, dumplings, and caramelized brussels sprouts, was delicious.

"Your eye trouble has not impeded your cooking, Margeleh," said Esther.

"Thank you," said Aunt Margaret. "The doctor says everything looks just fine."

"When's your next appointment?"

"Saturday."

"Did your ballots come?" asked Theo.

"They did not," said Aunt Margaret grimly.

Wilhelmina sat at the table, quiet as usual, pressed up against her father on one side and Delia on the other, ignoring Theo's concerned, sidelong glances. Ignoring the intrusive eyes of her mother too, who sat across from her. The constant, aggressive banter of Delia and Philip, plus the patient intercessions of Theo, annoyed her, but Cleo's silence annoyed her more. Wilhelmina was sure that Theo had told Cleo about her earlier outburst, and she didn't like when the eyes of her therapist mother studied her from across the dinner table. There was always something so compassionately diagnostic in Cleo's face, even today, when Cleo's eyes were puffy and bloodshot. Her nose was chapped almost scarlet, her reddish-brown hair gathered in a messy ponytail. Cleo's hair was exactly the color of a chipmunk.

"Margie and I will be roasting hazelnuts after dinner," said Esther. "It was a favorite Halloween tradition of Frankie's."

"You mean in the fireplace?" said Delia.

"Yes, and any of you children may join us," said Aunt Margaret. "Though of course we understand if you have more exciting plans than roasting hazelnuts with your old aunties."

"I want to roast hazelnuts," said Delia, rather combatively. Delia was dressed as a banana. Theo had taken Delia and Philip on some abbreviated pandemic trick-or-treating before dinner, and it hadn't met Delia's expectations. Delia had wanted to trick-or-treat with her friends Eleanor and Madison as in years before, not to mention that it was weird and uncomfortable to take candy from people who wouldn't let you anywhere near them. She refused to remove her banana costume, she slumped from room to room shooting people martyred expressions, and she spoke only in aggrieved tones.

"Me too, me too, me too," said Philip, whose passions in life alternated between idolizing Delia and avoiding baths. He was dressed like a slice of watermelon, and he smelled. Wilhelmina's number one goal for the evening was to avoid being the person responsible for getting Philip into the bathtub. As the dinner ended, she volunteered for dish duty.

Then Theo led Philip away with a successful bribe: a bath, in exchange for being allowed to roast hazelnuts with Delia and the aunts. Cleo disappeared to bed in an antihistamine haze, as she'd done every night for the past two weeks. Delia went off to choose the best pajamas for fireside activities, and the aunts receded down the hall to the living room to get the fire started.

For twenty-odd minutes, Wilhelmina was alone in the kitchen

with leftovers, pots and spatulas, and warm, sudsy water. It was nice to put things in order by herself.

When she entered the living room afterward, Delia was wearing star pajamas and her temper seemed to have sweetened. So had Philip's aroma. When Wilhelmina sat on the rug by the crackling fire and her little brother climbed into her arms, she was able to give him hugs that were nothing but genuine.

"You smell like soap," he told her.

"That's you, silly," she said, kissing his damp, wispy hair, hugging his wriggling body, surprised to find herself choking up again. Wilhelmina had become one of Philip's default caretakers at the start of the pandemic. Philip was thrust upon her often, especially when Cleo had allergies. She took him outside to play in the wet and cold, made him lunches he complained about, cut his hair while he bounced and squirmed, wiped sticky things like peanut butter and jelly from his face and hands. She went on walks with him around the neighborhood, making him promise first that he would keep his mask on. When he tore it off, threw it, laughed in her face, Wilhelmina was shocked sometimes by her own anger. She read him stories at night willing him to fall asleep. She was always counting down the minutes until he became someone else's responsibility. Somewhere along the line, she'd forgotten that not too long ago, she'd adored him.

Aunt Margaret, sitting on a pillow before the hearth, held a funny little pan with a long handle, for roasting things in fireplaces. The part that went into the fire was coppery, round like a cookie tin. Wilhelmina recognized it; it had used to hang beside the fireplace in the aunts' Pennsylvania home.

While Aunt Margaret dealt with the roasting pan, Esther moved around the room's perimeter placing candles in the windows. Esther was a big one for candles. She lit Shabbat candles on Friday night and meditated to a candle most mornings. But tonight she was outdoing herself: She carried an unlit green candle to one window, a yellow to another. A blue to the old rolltop desk in the corner and a red to the wide boot bench that sat beside the front door. Then she placed smaller white candles onto every remaining surface at the room's edges that she could find, on top of bookcases and side tables, in more windowsills and on the mantle, so that the candles made a sort of circle containing the room's activities. Esther wore a shirt, actually, that contained blocks of bright colors just like the candles, crisp twill over dark jeans.

Next Esther swept around the circle with a lighter, lighting the candles one by one. Philip shouted her name once—"Esther!"—and she shot him a smile. But when Philip tried to climb out of Wilhelmina's lap to run to his aunt, Wilhelmina held him tight and whispered, "Wait. Let her finish." Something about Esther's passage around the room creating a trail of winking flames was mesmerizingly elegant. Wilhelmina wanted to watch the circle's completion.

When Esther lit the last candle, Wilhelmina let Philip go. He shot up and ran to Esther, who bent down to him, took his hand, and brought him to the hearth, where Aunt Margaret was teaching Delia how to hold the roasting pan. The room was beginning to smell wonderful, like woodsmoke and warm Nutella. For some time, Wilhelmina enjoyed the sensation of being enclosed in a wide circle of candlelight in a warm, good-smelling room. Then she pushed herself up and went to the windowsill beside the desk. One of the aunts had arranged a few small treasures there in a line, and Wilhelmina was curious.

It was cold by the window, the outside air creeping in. Esther's candles danced, their light licking at the odd little assortment of decorations she or Aunt Margaret had placed there. One was the owl clock Wilhelmina had carried through the snowstorm just yesterday. It was small and enamel with a flat, heart-shaped face, brown glass eyes, brown painted feathers, and a clock in its round belly. Two other items were carved wooden owls as well, with big eyes and knowing expressions.

Wilhelmina thought one of them might be a great horned owl, because it had little tufts positioned like ears. She didn't know what kind of owl the other one was. Two more items were small ceramic figurines of other kinds of birds—a robin and a female cardinal—and one was a miniature plastic model of a snow goose.

Wilhelmina took to the snow goose immediately. It had a head on a long neck that was weighted at the end where it attached to the goose's body, so that the head gently swiveled and bobbed, as if the goose were observing the entire room. It had a painted pink bill, intelligent dark eyes, and white feathers with black plumage peeking out underneath. It reminded Wilhelmina of the snow goose she'd seen with Frankie in the cemetery once a long time ago, startling her at the edge of a pond.

Next to the goose was a small ceramic statue of a pink-skinned man, wearing a brown robe with a rope around his middle. Birds sat on his hands, arms, and shoulders. He had a halo around his head.

"That's Saint Francis of Assisi, dear," said Aunt Margaret, coming to stand beside her. "Frankie's namesake. He was a companion to the animals. Made friends with a wolf, and talked to the birds as if they were his sisters."

"I didn't know Frankie was named after a saint," said Wilhelmina.

"Her parents were very religious," said Aunt Margaret. "Frankie's life took a different path, but she always liked her namesake. Now, I'm afraid I must ask you not to eat these particular hazelnuts," she said, placing a tiny bowl on the windowsill beside the other items. The bowl contained three hazelnuts. "But you can come to the fire and eat the others."

"These are all Frankie's things, aren't they?" said Wilhelmina, who knew it somehow. She could feel it, just as she would've known Frankie's voice.

"Yes," said Aunt Margaret. "These are her treasures."

"Including the clock?"

"Yes. That's why we cherish that clock."

Wilhelmina had a moment of regret for the resentment she'd felt toward the clock. "Are those hazelnuts—for her too?"

"Exactly," said Aunt Margaret. "They're our offering."

Aunt Margaret went back to the hearth, where she knelt beside Esther and helped her add more hazelnuts to the roasting pan. Wilhelmina watched them together, more conscious than usual of Frankie's absence. If Aunt Margaret and Esther were doing some project together in the living room, wasn't it natural to assume that Frankie was somewhere else in the apartment? That she would come in suddenly from the kitchen, then cross the room to Wilhelmina with the sun in her smile? The aunts had used to be like the points of a triangle. As they'd moved around, the shape of their triangle had stretched and changed, but there had always been a way to feel surrounded, enclosed by their happiness and warmth. Now they'd lost one of their points. Aunt Margaret and Esther were a closed segment, passing ideas back and forth to each other. The warm space was gone; Wilhelmina couldn't find a way back in.

She whispered a text to Julie. *Any sign of your necklace yet?*

Nope, said Julie. *Happy Halloween though, elephant*

Happy Halloween, elephant

She texted Bee next. *Miss you, elephant*

Miss u, he texted back, adding an elephant emoji.

Then he texted again. It was a selfie of him and Julie in his bedroom, huddled together against pillows on his bed. Bee was smiling big and Julie was holding her fingers up in the shape of a heart. He was still in his pink hoodie, and she was still wearing her pink scarf.

Wilhelmina waited for another text. "Bee and I will get back to you," Julie had said. She tried inhaling the scent of hazelnuts. She tried to enjoy the snow goose with the bobbing head. Her phone didn't buzz.

Wilhelmina left the room, crossing out of the circle of candles.

Theo was tapping on his laptop at the kitchen table again. She practically ran past him.

In her cold bedroom, she crawled under the covers with her laptop and found a YouTube video of a hairstylist, a man with dark hair and beautiful dark eyes who looked just a little bit like James Fang. She watched him give a woman with long, wavy red hair a thick crown of braids.

One of the reasons Wilhelmina loved visiting the aunts was the conversations they had that she wasn't supposed to hear.

At night, Wilhelmina had a routine. When it was her bedtime, she climbed into bed in her own little bedroom that the aunts kept for her at the top of the house. They kept it for her year-round. No one else slept there. It was one of those cozy rooms, small, with slanted walls and dormer windows that were always left open in hot weather. Wilhelmina's bed was pressed against one of those windows, and a sycamore rustled outside. At bedtime, someone, usually Frankie, would visit her or read to her, then tuck her in. To the sound of the wind in the leaves and the distant voices of her aunts rising from the open kitchen window two floors below, Wilhelmina would fall asleep.

Sometimes she slept through the night; and sometimes, after an hour or two, she woke up, knowing that the aunts were talking about something that mattered. She couldn't make out their words through the window. But maybe she could recognize something significant in their tone? Or maybe it was part of whatever inner sensitivity always told Wilhelmina where people were. Once she heard salsa music, and knew somehow, maybe from the breathless feeling of the laughter she could just barely catch, that they were dancing.

An old Victorian house nearing its century and a half birthday is not a quiet space for sneaking. When Wilhelmina slipped out of her bed onto the rag rug Frankie had made, then crept down the first staircase and along the second-floor corridor, then onto the next staircase, the floorboards creaked. One of the steps on the upper staircase practically screamed, and Wilhelmina's legs weren't long enough to skip over it. But the aunts never came looking to see what all the noise was. It never occurred to Wilhelmina that they knew what the noise was, and didn't mind.

It was during the summer after the summer when Bee had been allowed to visit, when Wilhelmina was eight—the summer of 2010—that she heard the aunts talking about Frankie and the owls. It was a cool night. As Wilhelmina settled into her usual spot halfway down the stairs, she almost wished she'd pulled a hoodie on over her pajamas, but it was too much work to go back. She hugged her legs with her arms and half closed her eyes, focusing sleepily on the rectangle of yellow light at the bottom of the stairs that was the doorway to the kitchen. She could hear the water turning on and off, and the clatter of dishes being washed. Esther and Frankie had made dinner together, fish and chips and a giant salad, the fish flaky and tender and the breading perfectly crunchy and light, and Wilhelmina had noticed a lot of bowls and pans. She could also hear a pen scratching on a page, and someone shaking the newspaper open.

"Oh, Frankie!" said Aunt Margaret. "Some sad news here. Mrs. Mancusi died."

The pen stopped. "What!" said Frankie. "Are you sure?"

"Concetta Mancusi," said Aunt Margaret. "That's her, right?"

"Yes. Oh!" said Frankie. Then she was quiet for a while. The water stopped running and all the aunts were quiet, except for footsteps and the sliding of chairs, then some low sniffling.

"There, mi cielo," said Esther softly. When the aunts were alone, Frankie was Esther's sky, and Aunt Margaret, "mi corazón," was her heart. Esther had a name for Wilhelmina too, but it was Yiddish, not Spanish: Wilhelmineleh.

"There, there," said Esther. "Oh, my hands are wet."

"It's okay," said Frankie, her voice full of tears, and muffled against someone else's body. "I suppose she wasn't young exactly. But she can't have been old either, right?"

"I'll check in a minute," said Aunt Margaret, whose voice was also muffled.

"Now, help me remember," said Esther. "Was this the woman who showed you how to turn back the odometer?"

"That was Mrs. Ferrari," said Frankie. Then she let out a teary, wet snort. "Why haven't I ever noticed it's funny that Mrs. Ferrari helped me with the car?"

Another moment passed, and more scraping of chairs. Wilhelmina heard footsteps and a thump, and thought Esther might be back at the sink again. Frankie's pen resumed scritching.

"Our car was the furthest thing from a Ferrari, of course," Frankie said, after a while. "An ancient Ford that only went into reverse if you threw your whole body into it."

"I remember that car," said Aunt Margaret. "Mrs. Mancusi was our senior-year math teacher, Esther, the one who came by every day after school and brought Frankie her lessons."

"The *only* one who did that," said Frankie. "Some of the other teachers sent lessons with her, but Mrs. Mancusi was the only one who came herself. She didn't care what I'd done. She taught school, then she came to the Harts' house and taught me."

"And dutifully ate my mother's burnt cookies," said Aunt Margaret, who was crinkling the newspaper again.

"Your mother's cookies weren't that bad," said Frankie. A chair moved. Frankie's footsteps. "Here, Esther, let me get that out of your way."

"Well, Mrs. Mancusi wasn't coming for the cookies," said Aunt Margaret.

"She was coming because she was an angel," said Frankie firmly.

"Ah, here it is," said Aunt Margaret. "She was seventy-five. Survived by three children, seven grandchildren, and eighteen great-grandchildren!"

"Good heavens," said Frankie. "All that at seventy-five. Do you remember how young and pretty she was?"

"I remember the day you got out of bed and actually did your hair," said Aunt Margaret, "because you wanted to try the crown braid she wore in *her* hair. I went out into the yard so I could cry without you knowing. I was so relieved. You were so depressed, Frankie. I kept expecting to find you hanging from the ceiling."

"It was a dark time," said Frankie. "I remember I missed my mother's cooking, but I didn't miss my mother. I felt guilty about that for a long, long time."

"That which you water, grows," said Esther. "That which you don't water, dies. Your mother starved that garden."

"You missed the barn owls," said Aunt Margaret.

"Oh, I did miss those barn owls!" said Frankie. "They were such beauties. They knew all my secrets too. All the animals did. They even watched Mrs. Ferrari take apart the odometer!"

"She did that in your own barn?"

"Yep. At night while my parents slept. She sat in the front seat with a flashlight and a couple of screwdrivers and her Sunday hat on her head. Here, Esther, I can dry that. Told me her unscrupulous brother had a used car dealership and at least she'd learned something from it."

"Here," said Esther. "That one's soaked."

"I remember when she finally turned off the flashlight," said Frankie. "It was so dark in there, so suddenly, that we both squealed. And then, one after another, the owls hooted, and I thought to myself, *They're thanking her for helping me.*"

"I suppose Mrs. Ferrari is long gone," said Aunt Margaret. "She wasn't young then."

"And now Mrs. Mancusi has joined her," said Frankie. "Bless her heart. She's the only reason I ever finished high school."

"And now I learn that your hairstyle comes from her too," said Esther.

Frankie gave a gentle laugh. "I suppose so, yes."

"En paz descansa," said Esther. "May her memory be for a blessing. Should I light candles for them both?"

"Yes," said Frankie. "And for Margie's parents too. They took me in. I wasn't alone."

There were a few things Wilhelmina didn't understand about this conversation. She didn't know what an odometer was, or why Mrs. Ferrari's name was funny. She wasn't sure just how literal Frankie was being when she talked about the animals knowing her secrets. It seemed possible to Wilhelmina that Frankie was being quite literal indeed. She certainly didn't know what thing Frankie had done to make her have to leave home, and it was a revelation to learn that Frankie had lived with Aunt Margaret's family instead of her own. Wilhelmina thought back to every time Aunt Margaret had ever driven past her childhood home and said, "I grew up in that house right there, dear. Can you believe it?" Wilhelmina had imagined a young Aunt Margaret in that house, maybe Wilhelmina's age, maybe looking a lot like Wilhelmina herself, in old-timey clothes. Now she retroactively changed all her imaginings so that a teenaged Frankie, dark-eyed and lonesome, with long, dark hair and at least one unhappy secret, lived there too.

There was one part of the conversation Wilhelmina did understand: she knew what it was like to miss owls. The woods around the aunts' house were thick with owls in summer. Wilhelmina heard their low call in her dreams sometimes and knew she wasn't actually dreaming. At the end of every August, when she returned to Massachusetts, her sleep felt empty for a week or two, until she got used to nights without owls. When Wilhelmina returned to her warm bed that night after listening to her aunts' conversation, she thought she heard the hoot of a distant owl as she drifted back into her dreams.

In the morning, after Aunt Margaret and Esther drove off to work—Aunt Margaret had some job with math, and Esther did some kind of consulting—Frankie sat quiet and still at the kitchen table, nursing her coffee longer than usual. Her recipe box was nearby and she had a pen in her hair, but she didn't seem conscious of either. Wilhelmina was allowed to look inside Frankie's recipe box whenever she wanted. It contained cards with lists of ingredients, notes, and questions. "Turmeric for E's joints?" "M's eyes: avoid St. John's wort." "Breathe a blessing in through the feet." Frankie's handwriting was a bit wild: spiky in some places, bulbous in others.

Like the plants in her garden, Wilhelmina thought. Wilhelmina was quiet too this morning. She was wondering what an odometer was.

"May I call Bee?" she finally asked. The aunts let Wilhelmina call Bee whenever she wanted to, as long as she didn't talk too long.

"Yes, dear," said Frankie absently. So Wilhelmina ran upstairs to use the phone in the second-floor sitting room, because that room had a door that closed. She could ask Bee to find out what an odometer was without Frankie hearing. Of course, the aunts had a computer; they had dictionaries, and even an ancient encyclopedia. But she wanted to know from Bee. She wanted to tell him what she'd heard, and get his thoughts.

Bee's father answered the phone. As an emergency room doctor, he worked long, unpredictable shifts. Wilhelmina always knew, even before he spoke, that he was the one on the other end. She could hear something hollow in the air.

"Tobey isn't home," he said. "Which of his girlfriends is this?" He always asked that, which of Bee's girlfriends she was, even though she wasn't Bee's girlfriend and Bee didn't have any girlfriends and she was probably the only girl who ever called him anyway. Bee's father thought it was hilarious. It made Wilhelmina extremely uncomfortable, because saying, "This is Wilhelmina," as if it were an answer to the question he'd asked, always felt like a betrayal of Bee. Yet there was no other way to get past Bee's father to Bee.

For some reason, that morning, the situation made her hang up the phone, very hard and loud, without responding.

When she returned to the kitchen, Frankie had removed the pen from her hair and was flipping through her tarot cards. Wilhelmina knew Frankie's cards. They were soft with use, and colorful, and Frankie tended to pull them out when she was in a quiet and thoughtful mood. Wilhelmina didn't understand most of the cards. This was partly because there were so many of them: seventy-eight. Most of the deck was made up of suit cards, like the four suits of playing cards, except that these suits were called cups, wands, pentacles, and swords. But twenty-two of the cards in the deck were separate. When you laid them out side to side, they told the story of a person traveling through life. Some of them showed the trials the person would face; some of them showed the helpers they would meet. Some of them, like card zero, the Fool, and card nine, the Hermit, showed the person themselves. Wilhelmina liked these twenty-two cards best, because whenever Frankie worked with them, she told Wilhelmina a story.

Frankie kept her cards wrapped in a piece of dark fabric scattered with tiny golden bumblebees. Wilhelmina always noticed it because it made her think of Bee. Today Frankie spread the cloth onto the table before her, then slipped a few cards out of the deck, choosing them deliberately, placing them onto the cloth. They were all cards from the part of the deck Wilhelmina liked best. One showed a turning wheel and was called the Wheel of Fortune. One showed a woman in a garden wearing a dress with a print of pomegranates and a crown of stars on her head, and was called the Empress. And one showed an angel pouring water from one cup into another, and was called Temperance.

Frankie peered keenly at Wilhelmina. "That was quick. Are you all right, dear?"

"Bee wasn't home," said Wilhelmina. "What are you going to do with those cards?"

"I'm thinking about the story they tell," said Frankie, then patted the seat beside her. Wilhelmina sat down, hoping Frankie was about to answer her questions about the things she'd overheard.

"Chance brought me a person once, Wilhelmina," Frankie said, tapping the Wheel of Fortune. "This is the wheel that turns through our lives, bringing us surprises, then surprising us again by taking things away. Bringing us endings, and new beginnings. As we grow, Wilhelmina, we begin our lives again over and over. A long time ago, at a time in my life when I was making a new beginning, fortune brought me a person.

"That person was a woman who was like a mother to me," said Frankie, touching the Empress card. "She nurtured my mind, and my heart too, and helped me to heal when I was hurting. She's also the person who taught me about tarot cards. And she taught me the importance of temperance."

Frankie lifted the Temperance card and handed it to Wilhelmina. The angel on the card had massive red-and-gray wings.

"Have I ever talked to you about Temperance, Wilhelmina?" asked Frankie.

"No," said Wilhelmina.

"It's about time I did, then. I think it's my favorite card."

"Because an angel is like an owl?"

Frankie flashed a smile Wilhelmina recognized: it was her surprised smile. "I hadn't thought of that," she said. "Does that angel make you think of an owl?"

The angel on the card didn't really look like an owl. He looked very much like a person, in a white dress, with blond hair, golden cups held in human-shaped hands, and truly mammoth wings. He had a funny gold triangle on his chest too. It made Wilhelmina think of the giant Citgo sign above Fenway Park. Maybe this was Frankie's favorite card because Frankie loved baseball.

Anyway, he was definitely an angel. But for a moment, she imagined an owl in his place.

"I like owls more than angels," she said.

"It's interesting," said Frankie, "because both have reputations as peaceful, wise creatures, but in fact, both can be quite ruthless."

"Owls are ruthless?"

"Owls are nocturnal raptors. They're designed to blend into the night and keep perfectly still, so still that it seems impossible. It's the stillness of a predator, Wilhelmina. Then they swoop down on little animals who don't even know they're someone's prey until they're airborne. You must never corner an owl. Their claws can hurt you badly."

"I wouldn't corner an owl."

"I know you wouldn't," said Frankie simply. "You're not a person who tries to control the creatures around you. In fact, I believe you're a person who would excel at temperance."

Wilhelmina studied the way the angel on the card was pouring water from one cup to another. "Is it something about drinking?" she said.

"I suppose that for some people, temperance means to abstain from alcohol. Generally, temperance means a kind of moderation, in drinking but also in attitude. In the tarot specifically, temperance is the most beautiful—and practical—quality imaginable. It's a kind of balance. It's when you take all your dreams and imaginings, all the things you most want and all the magic you believe in. And then, next to that, you take all the harsh realities of the way things actually are in the world. And you find the way to balance both sides inside you. So that when you're planning and dreaming, you're also being realistic, and if you find yourself caught in one of the traps of reality, you remember your own magic.

Temperance is the place where magic meets the mundane, Wilhelmina. Remembering the mundane makes us smart; remembering the magic makes us brave."

When Frankie got abstract like this, Wilhelmina didn't always understand. She thought that every time Frankie ever did anything, that was probably magic meeting the mundane, because Frankie was magic. What else could magic be, if not the sense of comfort and rightness that radiated from Frankie?

"Tomorrow I'm going to a funeral, dear," said Frankie. "Esther will work from home so you won't be alone."

Wilhelmina thought about that for a moment. "Did your empress die?" she said.

Frankie gave Wilhelmina another keen look. Sadness was plain on her face. "Yes."

Wilhelmina thought a little more. "Can I come?"

The funeral took place in a church Wilhelmina had noticed before from the car, because it was made of a kind of pale brick that was the same color as her own skin. She liked her skin well enough, but she didn't like the building. It looked like a giant thumb.

She was surprised by how different it was on the inside. From the outside, the windows looked muddy and opaque, but inside the church, the light streamed through them, dazzling her with brilliantly colored designs. Wilhelmina had meant to be a detective. She'd wanted to solve the mystery of Frankie leaving home, and the odometer, and what Frankie had done. Instead, she spent the funeral entranced by the way the light streaming through the windows stained the floor—and sometimes even the people—blue, red, purple, orange, and gold. There was a little boy sitting some distance from Wilhelmina, near one of the windows. He had some scraps of tissue paper cut into shapes Wilhelmina couldn't decipher. He kept hurling them into the air, which upset his parents. It seemed to be the thing to be quiet and still during funerals in churches, not throw stuff straight up into the air. But whenever he threw the papers, the light would catch them, so that they floated down again gently, spangled with changing color. It was so pretty that at one point, Wilhelmina made a noise of appreciation deep in her throat.

Then she glanced at Frankie beside her, worried that she'd been too loud. But Frankie, who had tears running down her face, was smiling. She was watching the spangling colors too.

SUNDAY, NOVEMBER 1, 2020

On the Sunday six days before she stepped into her own, Wilhelmina woke from a dream that was unmemorable, except that Frankie was about to arrive, and never did.

She felt under the covers for her phone. No new messages. It was cloudy, one of those days with clouds so thick and low that the sky was formless and it was hard to believe the sun was out there somewhere. It was also the first day of Standard Time. That meant Wilhelmina got an extra hour today, but she didn't want an extra hour. Not if it meant the sun setting at four in the afternoon all winter long.

Wait, no—as Wilhelmina sat up in bed, she remembered that there had been more to her dream. Frankie had never arrived, true. But James Fang had arrived, walking toward her with a living owl sitting on his head. The dream had taken place in the cemetery. He and the owl had been soaked through, because it had just stopped pouring rain, though Wilhelmina was dry, and warm, and could only remember blue, sunny skies.

"Excuse me," said James, "but I'm freezing in these wet clothes." Then he'd removed the owl as if it were a top hat, and placed it on a nearby gravestone, where it sat looking soggy but inscrutable, water dripping from its eyebrow feathers. He'd removed his coat. Then he'd hooked his fingers around the hem of his T-shirt and pulled it over his head so that he was standing there shirtless, and suddenly, the feeling of the dream had changed.

"Oh my god!" said Wilhelmina to the air of her room. Blundering out from under her blankets, she pulled the cord on her lamp and groped for her glasses. When the room sprang into view, she saw that Delia was up. That was good. She wouldn't have to explain her exclamation, or answer Julie's questions about why she was having a hot flash.

Deliberately, she focused on her room: her boring, unsexy room. This room had been Wilhelmina's once, all Wilhelmina's. She'd used it for homework, reading, planning, daydreaming. For Julie and Bee. When Delia wasn't in here, she could almost imagine it hers again, if she did a little selective observing. Her room was under there, if you took away Delia's bed and Delia's piles. But her old life wasn't under there anymore.

On her dresser, Wilhelmina's big tin of makeup supplies collected dust. Wilhelmina liked trying unexpected things, like a smudge of yellow right in the middle of her eyelids or a silver eyeliner, and she also liked the challenge of understated makeup that looked like you weren't wearing any makeup at all. But the effort felt pointless if most of her face was always covered, and if Julie and Bee weren't there to appreciate it. Lipstick. Wilhelmina missed lipstick!

She supposed that at least she could dust her supplies. That would calm her down. Pushing out of bed, she found her fluffy purple bathrobe and pulled it on, fastening it around her middle. Then, from a nearby hill of clothes, she selected a nice soft T-shirt of Delia's. If Delia was going to ruin Wilhelmina's life, Wilhelmina was going to use her shirt as a dustcloth.

Wilhelmina's dresser was one of those squat, wide affairs with a broad mirror on top framed in wooden curlicues. Long ago, she'd placed a single tarot card into the top edge of the mirror. It was Temperance, and Wilhelmina couldn't remember why she'd put it there. Frankie had told her once, eons ago, that Temperance was her favorite card in the deck; soon after, she'd given Wilhelmina her deck. Given Wilhelmina her own beloved tarot deck! Which Wilhelmina had stored in the desk that was tucked under rows of hanging bookshelves in her Pennsylvania bedroom, leaving it safely with Frankie and the aunts whenever she returned home at the start of every school year—except for this one card, Temperance, which she'd slipped into her suitcase, then stuck in her mirror, where she could always see it. The big blond angel with his cups of pouring water had meant something to her once, something she'd wanted to remember year-round. About the magic all around her? Which had been fine, she supposed, until Frankie had died. The election had happened, then, less than two years later, Frankie had died. Where was the magic now? This angel had abandoned them.

"Frankie loved you," she said to him. Then, grudgingly, she dusted him with Delia's shirt. "That's the only reason I'm leaving you there."

Before her eyes, the angel in the card changed. That was the only way to describe it: He changed. His angel shape morphed into a sort of beak-mouthed bird-woman like the fortune teller in Harvard Square, and below his feet, the word TEMPERANCE changed too. TRUST RAY it said instead, in tiny sparkles, like fireflies.

Wilhelmina cried out, then fell back onto Delia's bed. Then, angry, she surged up again, ready to confront the bird figure in the card; but the card was normal. The angel stared down at the cups in his hands serenely, that silly triangle on his chest. TEMPERANCE, said the letters under his feet. When she blinked, she could see the words TRUST RAY burnt into her retinas. She closed her eyes, trying to hold on to it, but as she grasped at it, TRUST RAY dissolved into blackness.

Suddenly, Wilhelmina was furious, so furious that she was shaking. "Enough," she said. "No more bullshit! Enough!" She found a giant, ratty, button-down shirt she wore when she was cleaning, and flung it over the mirror. She barged out of the room and marched toward the bathroom. As she neared it, Aunt Margaret emerged in a cloud of steam wearing goggles.

"Good morning, dear!" said Aunt Margaret.

"Good morning," said Wilhelmina, pressing past her into the bathroom and slamming the door. Every surface was dripping with condensation and Julie's furnace was shaking the floor. Wilhelmina needed to leave. If she didn't leave, she was going to start screaming. It was Sunday, her least favorite day for running this particular errand, but Wilhelmina was desperate. She would do the groceries.

IT WAS A SHORT DRIVE to the grocery store, but it involved one snaggly traffic circle and at least one intersection where no one followed the rules. Not that this was a problem; Wilhelmina knew how to deal with it.

She and Julie had learned to drive together, in the spring of 2018, as soon as they'd both turned sixteen. Wilhelmina's dad and Julie's mom had taken turns as instructors. It seemed like a decade ago now, because of the way the pandemic stretched time out. *Or maybe it's because those earliest lessons were just before Frankie died,* thought Wilhelmina as she drove.

Julie's mom, Maya, a science teacher who taught kids the properties of physics, had given them straightforward advice. "Line the left edge of the car up with the center line in your own line of sight, Wilhelmina. That centers you in the lane. Yes, that's it, good! Now, when you're in a two-lane traffic circle, girls, it's just like any other two-lane road. You don't change lanes until you've checked you're clear. Right? Excellent!"

Theo, on the other hand, had always reached for metaphors. "Think of yourself as a hawk riding a current of air," he said once while Julie was driving. Wilhelmina, in the back seat, shot her eyes to Julie's in the rearview mirror, then covered her mouth with a hand to discourage her own snort. "Peaceful and serene, in control of your movement, but ready to make a quick adjustment if the air changes, or if you spot a mouse."

"Super-helpful advice, Mr. Hart," said Julie.

"Think of yourself as Schrödinger's cat," he said another time. "You might hit the correct exit lane or you might miss it, but it's no big deal. Don't try to make dramatic corrections in real time. Just keep going, and options will arise to get yourself back on track."

There was a brief silence. Then, from the back seat, because Wilhelmina was driving this time, Julie said, "That seems like a tenuous analogy, Mr. Hart."

"Yeah," said Wilhelmina. "And don't you think it *is* a big deal for the *dead* cat?"

"It worked better in my head," said Theo. "Listen, if you find yourself taking the wrong exit, just go with it, okay? It's dangerous to make last-minute decisions!"

After their lessons with Theo, Wilhelmina and Julie would climb the steps to Julie's room together, clasping each other and laughing. "Think of yourself as El Niño," Julie would say. "Think of yourself as the national anthem."

It helped to laugh, because Wilhelmina was honestly kind of scared of driving, and Julie was too. It was fine when they managed a stretch alone on an empty road somewhere. But Boston traffic was so unpredictable, other drivers made unbelievably terrible decisions, and the intersections through which Wilhelmina's parents had been driving her for her whole life suddenly made no sense. When two different sets of lights were aimed basically at *you*, and you weren't sure which was meant for you and one was red and one was green, at an intersection where five roads came together at bizarre angles and the lanes were unmarked and everyone laid on their horns if you hesitated, what were you supposed to do? Just close your eyes and go?

And yet they wanted to learn, so badly. They wanted to be free.

Then their phones would buzz, both at the same time, because Bee would be texting to ask how the lesson had gone. Bee had been fifteen that spring; he hadn't turned sixteen until September. Wilhelmina couldn't even remember Bee turning sixteen, actually, now that she was thinking about it, though they must've made some sort of fuss. Some party Wilhelmina had sleepwalked her way through? Frankie had died at the end of June.

Wilhelmina had almost reached the grocery store. While she was braking for a red light, a pickup truck roared past her, making her jump. It was flying a Blue Lives Matter flag. A sign on its tailgate said THIS IS MY AMERICA.

Inside the store, indecisive people clogged the one-way aisles, and the checkout lines were long. She waited in line forever, then paid, then drove home feeling irritable and unappreciated. When her father came running out to help her haul the bags in, she bristled, because she wanted to be alone.

"Is Esther on the stairs with Esther?" she asked him.

"She is," he said. "Should I tell her you're looking for her?"

"No," said Wilhelmina, who was not looking for Esther. She was looking for a path through her day that would allow her to avoid having to pretend to be friendly to any more humans than necessary, because Wilhelmina knew she was poisonous today. Esther never visited Esther for long. She would wait outside.

The small yard sloped steeply downhill. Wilhelmina walked its perimeter, trying to appreciate the desultory, mostly dead flowers. The landlord hired landscapers to come by now and then and blast everything with leaf blowers. Every time, Wilhelmina felt like someone was screaming at her soul. She also worried about the ears of the men doing the blasting. And she thought of all the trees at the aunts' Pennsylvania house, and the rakes and wheelbarrow that had always lived in their shed. "Do you push that wheelbarrow around?" she'd asked Frankie once, imagining her small aunt trundling along behind a massive pile of autumn leaves.

Frankie had laughed. "I used to," she said. "Now we hire a pair of young women who live in town. We pay them double so they won't use leaf blowers."

Wilhelmina's neck and shoulders were hurting. As she returned to the front of the house, she propped one forearm upright against a pilaster on the porch and pressed that arm back like an angel's wing, reveling in the deep sensation of relief that stretching brought to her chest and neck sometimes. After thirty seconds, she switched to the other side. A crow had perched itself high in one of the tall hedges that grew against the house, shifting its head back and forth, looking down at her. It was enormous. Wilhelmina forgot sometimes how big crows could get.

A glitter caught her eye. This crow held something sparkly in its beak. The moment Wilhelmina saw it, she recognized it: a gray enamel elephant with red and orange wings, on a shiny gold chain. It was Julie's necklace.

With a cry, Wilhelmina stepped toward the bird. As she did so, the crow dropped the necklace. The chain snagged on a lower part of the hedge very near Wilhelmina, and the crow cawed, jumping and flapping, then landing again in the same high spot. Wilhelmina wasn't afraid of the crow. Maybe she should've been, but she wasn't. She knew this moment was her chance to reach out a hand and retrieve Julie's necklace.

It must've been some instinct besides fear, then, that held her body still, waiting for the very thing that happened: the crow dove to the lower branch, snatched the necklace firmly in its beak, and flew off.

INSIDE, Theo was putting the groceries away. "I got it, hon," he said, when she tried to help. "You relax."

The aunts were at the kitchen table, drinking tea. Philip sat in Esther's lap happily shoving into his mouth one of the bananas Wilhelmina had just brought home. His hair, chipmunk-colored like Cleo's, stood up around his head as if he'd just pulled on a staticky shirt. "Want some tea, W'mina?" he said.

Wilhelmina's phone dinged, then dinged some more. "No thank you," she said, pulling it out of her pocket. Julie. *We're in the square again. You anywhere nearby?*

"Sit down if you like, Wilhelmina," said Aunt Margaret, who'd changed out of her goggles and into her eye patch.

Wilhelmina's phone was still dinging. "No thanks," she said, checking her messages again. *We're kid-free. We might get hot chocolate*

"We're discussing what to do if our ballots don't arrive tomorrow, Wilhelmina," said Esther. "Any thoughts?"

Wilhelmina was feeling pulled in too many directions. "Don't your votes count even if you postmark them Tuesday?"

"Yes, as long as they reach Pennsylvania by Friday," said Esther. "But what if we don't get them by Tuesday?"

"Yeah, I don't know," said Wilhelmina, just as her phone dinged three times. Her father dropped a can of kidney beans that rolled against her foot; Philip squirmed out of Esther's lap and dove for it. In her peripheral vision, she saw her mother entering the room, wearing a blanket cape. Wilhelmina was going to start screaming again. "Does anyone need the car?"

Theo shot her a curious look. "I don't think so, hon," he said. "You can take it."

Wilhelmina blazed a path to Harvard Square.

A LINE OUTSIDE THE CHOCOLATE SHOP stretched down the block. Wilhelmina saw Bee first, probably because he was tall, though he had a feeling to him too that Wilhelmina could always find in a crowd. It was a kind of rooted solidness, like a tree you could lean against. A sweet, sad tree.

When Wilhelmina and Julie were about to start high school and Bee eighth grade—the summer of 2016—Bee's dad died. Tobey Sloane had taken stimulants during his ER shifts sometimes, to keep awake.

He'd taken opioids for pain. Then, when his shifts had ended in the middle of the night, sometimes he'd gone out partying with colleagues. One night, it had killed him: polydrug intoxication. Bee knew that was what he'd died of, partly because he knew some of the things his dad did, but also because Tobey had been brought to his own hospital in cardiogenic shock and Bee had overheard the attending doctor, a bald man Bee had seen at parties at his own house, tell his mother so.

"You mean he had a heart attack?" Bee's mother had said.

"Well, Cindy," said the man, whose face was wet with tears, "multiple drugs were found in his system. Alcohol. Opiates. Cocaine."

"But he had a heart attack?" said Bee's mother.

"Well," the doctor said again, "ultimately, he did experience cardiac arrest."

After that, Bee's mother had started telling people about her late husband's surprise heart attack. She even talked about how worried she was that Bee might've inherited Tobey's bad heart. "Make sure you're getting tested for heart disease," she told people.

If Bee ever alluded to what had really killed Tobey, she became shrill with indignation. "She's so focused on defending him about that, like that's what's shameful," Bee had told Wilhelmina. "Who the hell cares if he had drug problems? He broke my arm once, Wil. He did that while he was sober. You know how many times she's gotten mad at me for bringing that up? Zero. Because she turns off if I mention it. She goes instantly deaf and walks out of the room. I don't even exist, if it means she has to acknowledge that that ever happened."

"Remind me of the spot," said Wilhelmina. It was a few weeks after Tobey's death. They were sitting in Wilhelmina and Julie's steep backyard, in a couple of tottery lawn chairs Theo had put out there because Cleo was pregnant and kept needing fresh air.

When Bee held up his left forearm and pointed to a place near his elbow, Wilhelmina remembered the purple cast he'd worn there some four years ago. She also remembered an overheard conversation: Cleo had reported the incident to the Department of Children and Families. Cleo had also tried to talk to Bee's mom about it. But nothing had changed.

Reaching out to Bee's arm, Wilhelmina touched the place too. "I acknowledge that your dad broke your arm," she said. "While sober."

Bee spoke with tears in his voice. "Thank you."

Then Julie appeared around the corner, and Wilhelmina's heart reached out to pull her in too. "Hey," said Julie. "Saw you from my window seat. You doing okay, Bee?"

"Yeah," he said, wiping his face with his wrist. "My mom won't talk about my dad. Not in an honest way."

"You can tell us anything," said Julie, coming and touching her hand gently to the top of Wilhelmina's head. It made Wilhelmina feel like they were a net for Bee to fall into. "We believe you."

Now here they were, Bee towering beside Julie in the hot chocolate line. The two of them wore their matching pale pink again. Julie's hair was in a twist-out. Bee's was wispy in a calculatedly careless manner that felt very Bee to her, but she wished—almost desperately—that she could see their faces.

Then she noticed a couple of familiar people ahead of them in line and realized she wasn't the only person Julie and Bee had invited. One was a guy named Zach who'd graduated with Julie and Wilhelmina and had played soccer on the school team with Bee. The other was Eloisa Cruz, James Fang's friend, the one who starred in all the school musicals, or used to, when the school had done things like musicals—the one Wilhelmina had specifically asked Julie not to pump for information.

Wilhelmina almost couldn't believe it. Her disbelief—and something else too, something more painful—almost turned her right around. But then Bee saw her and waved.

He was in the middle of a conversation. "I mean, there's value in understanding people," she heard him say. "Hey, Wil!"

"Limited value, in some cases," said Julie. "Hey, Wil! Bee's trying to *understand people* again. Look, we ran into Zach and Eloisa."

It was like an infusion of sweet air: Julie and Bee hadn't invited Zach and Eloisa. And of course they hadn't. Bee didn't even like Zach all that much, and Julie would never have intentionally invited the one person Wilhelmina had asked her not to talk to. As sense returned to Wilhelmina, she was ashamed of herself.

"I mean, take the people who believe his lies," said Bee. "I feel like it's worth knowing whether they *really* believe him, or if they're only pretending to believe him because it suits them. Like, if you hate liberals enough, then any weird lie is justified. Is that it? Or do they really not see the holes in his logic? I get uncomfortable every time I come to the conclusion they're stupid."

"I'm comfortable with that," said Zach, who stood in line six feet ahead of Julie and Bee, his longish hair pulled into a blond ponytail that bounced on top of his head. Eloisa stood six feet ahead of Zach, which put her quite some distance from Wilhelmina. Nonetheless, Wilhelmina thought Eloisa might be touching her with curious dark eyes.

"It's reductive," said Bee.

"Whatever the reason, it makes them rally around a white supremacist," said Julie. "I mean, I don't think the explanation is going to make us comfortable. How you doing, Wil?"

"Fine, I guess," said Wilhelmina, who didn't want to be having this conversation with people she didn't know. "How are you?"

"Excuse me," called Zach. "Would you mind putting on your masks?"

It took a moment to figure out that he was speaking to the man and woman ahead of Eloisa in line. The man glanced back.

"We'll wear them when we get to the door," he said. "We're outside now."

"You're supposed to be wearing them now," said Zach, speaking across Eloisa, who was staring back at Zach with big, frozen eyes that made Wilhelmina wonder if they were friends, or just acquaintances. Eloisa looked trapped. "It's the law in Cambridge."

"My wife is uncomfortable when she wears a mask," said the man. "We're just trying to get some hot chocolate."

"And I'm just trying to protect my sick dad!" said Zach, who was suddenly shouting. "All I'm asking you to do is put a piece of cloth in front of the holes on your face. You selfish prick!"

"Okay, whoa!" said Bee, stepping toward Zach. "Zach! Lower your voice."

"It's a fucking pandemic!" Zach shouted. "The rules exist for a reason!"

"I know," said Bee. "You're right. But you can't be yelling at people on the street."

"Not even to protect my dad from selfish pricks?" yelled Zach.

Julie and Eloisa had pulled together into a unit, stepping out of line and off to the side. "*I'm* the one who was near them," she heard Eloisa say to Julie.

"Yeah," said Julie. "That was awkward for you."

Wilhelmina knew she could join Julie and Eloisa. She wanted to. But Zach was still shouting, still spewing all his anxiety into the atmosphere. Wilhelmina was dizzy with it. She turned around, walked back to her car, and shut herself inside.

AS SHE ENTERED THE CEMETERY, the texts started coming in.

Wilhelmina drove the winding roads, trying to ignore the phone, trying to bury her own thoughts. Looking for some place deep inside this labyrinth of paths where nothing could touch her. But every ding was a sharp little strike against the bell of her conscience.

She pulled over.

Hey, Julie wrote. *What happened? You left us alone with that*

I'm really sorry, Wilhelmina responded. *I shouldn't have bailed like that. But I was going to lose my shit*

It's okay, texted Julie immediately. *But what happened?*

It's like he was dumping his stress on everyone else, said Wilhelmina. *You know? We're all stressed out, but with him, he was hurling it around at everyone else. I just needed to go*

It was a minute before Julie responded. Wilhelmina peered out of the car, craning her neck to see the trees and graves all around, pretending to herself that she wasn't looking for James Fang. A raindrop plopped onto the windshield.

Her phone dinged.

Wil? What's going on with you? asked Julie.

Wilhelmina didn't know why her eyes were suddenly filling with tears. *Nothing*

Is it the weird shit you and James are seeing? Julie asked.

She knew it wasn't that, not really, or anyway, not entirely. *Yeah,* she said.

Her phone rang. Julie. "Hey," said Wilhelmina.

"Hey, elephant," said Julie. "Listen, you're not going to like this. But maybe it's time for you to talk to someone."

Who? thought Wilhelmina. *You? There's no one.* "What do you mean?" she said. "Like my therapist mother?"

"You're seeing weird shit that isn't there, Wil."

That's not the problem. "James Fang is seeing the weird shit too," she said.

"Okay, how about I text James and ask him what he's seen?"

Wilhelmina understood Julie's logic. Julie was worried about Wilhelmina's grasp on reality. As such, Julie knew that if Wilhelmina was seeing things that weren't there, then she could also be seeing James seeing things that weren't there. If James could verify the sightings independently, it would prove that the problem wasn't inside Wilhelmina.

But of course the problem was inside Wilhelmina. All the problems were. "Let me think about it," she said. "Okay? Let me think about it and text you."

"When?" said Julie.

"What do you mean, when?"

"I want a deadline. Please, Wil? Give me a deadline."

"After which, what?"

"I don't know what. I'm worried about you. You seem like you're shutting down."

"What does that mean?" said Wilhelmina. "Are you going to tell my parents or something?"

"Elephant!" said Julie. "Of course not! I don't go behind your back."

"Okay," said Wilhelmina, ashamed again. "Sorry. I knew that."

"How about six?"

"Six?"

"O'clock," said Julie. "Decide by six o'clock if I can text James. Okay?"

"Okay," said Wilhelmina miserably. "Julie? Are you okay?"

Julie let out a short sigh. "I'm fine. I'm hanging out with Eloisa while Bee has a heart-to-heart with Zach about how to get his head out of his butt. We're walking along the river. Don't worry, Eloisa can't hear me right now, and I haven't said anything about James. Honestly, it's great out here. It's amazing not to have Teeny's voice in my ear every second."

Both of Julie's parents were teachers, and both were pushing through the most overwhelming school year of their lives. Like Wilhelmina, Julie had delayed college, mostly to help take care of Tina during the pandemic.

Wilhelmina's eyes were filling with tears again. "I miss you, elephant."

"I miss you too. Listen, it's starting to rain. I should go."

"Okay."

"Six o'clock!"

"Six o'clock."

Outside the car, the drizzle was thickening. Wilhelmina stared at her phone for a minute. When no more calls or texts came in, she pulled onto the road and wound her way deeper into the cemetery, peering carefully through the falling rain, not finding what she was looking for. Raindrops made a nice thrumming sound on the roof. It was comforting to be inside a watery cave. She had a vision of driving alone across America, watching the world happen from the safety of her car. For some reason, another vision kept breaking through: her own self, standing still, waiting for that crow to take Julie's necklace away.

WHEN WILHELMINA GOT HOME, there was a stillness to the apartment, so unusual that she stepped inside almost with a sense of disorientation.

She found Theo in the kitchen with a cutting board, a bowl of potatoes, a knife, and the food processor. The slow cooker bubbled. Wilhelmina smelled onions, tomatoes, peppers.

"Are you making ropa vieja and latkes?" she demanded. These were Esther specialties, and Wilhelmina was surprised to see Theo attempting them.

"Oh, hi, honey!" he said, his flushed face lighting up as he turned to her. "Yes, I am. The aunts'll move back home someday, you know, and I'll wish I learned it while I could."

"Fun to have latkes outside of Hanukkah," said Wilhelmina approvingly.

"Mm-hm. How was your outing?"

He asked that question a little too casually, with a sidelong glance that was a little too curious. "Rainy," Wilhelmina said.

"Well," said Theo, "you should enjoy the quiet house while you can. Your mother's asleep and the aunts somehow convinced both Delia and Philip to take a walk. They even brought umbrellas. But you never know how long they'll hold out."

"Right," said Wilhelmina. "Thanks."

She went to her bedroom. There, she tried watching a hair video on her laptop, but the covered mirror kept distracting her. Wilhelmina couldn't subdue the part of her that wanted to check on the Temperance card to see what it looked like.

Pulling her purple bathrobe on over her clothes, she moved to the empty living room and chose a chair by one of the windows, where she could watch the rain. Frankie's treasures still sat on the windowsill. Wilhelmina bobbed the head of the plastic snow goose gently, looking into its dark, clever eyes. *Frankie?* she thought, then didn't know what to say next.

Her hand touched the elephant necklace at her throat. For her own necklace, she'd chosen an elephant with lilies sprouting from the end of its trunk, because Frankie had grown tall lilies along the edges of the yard, white, gold, and pink. She couldn't imagine a world without Frankie's lilies.

Frankie? she thought, almost with a strange, exhausted surrender. *What should I do?* Then she asked another question. *Frankie? Why did you leave me?*

She thought of the time Frankie's teacher Mrs. Mancusi had died. She remembered that Frankie had pulled out the Empress tarot card, because the Empress was a nurturer like Mrs. Mancusi, glowing with magic. The woman in that card was powerful, peaceful, and surrounded by life, wearing a gown with a print of pomegranates, with a crown of stars on her head. And what other cards had Frankie pulled? The Wheel of Fortune? When Frankie had died, Wilhelmina had lost her own empress. The Wheel had taken *her* empress away. Why? Cancer? What a stupid, arbitrary waste of a person who was made of goodness.

At Frankie's memorial service, Wilhelmina had finally learned—after years of not knowing—why Frankie had left home as a teenager. It was because the priest in her parish had gotten one of her friends pregnant, so Frankie had driven her to nearby New York City to get an abortion. Then, after that, she'd started helping other women get to New York for abortions. It had been the early 1960s, the decade before abortion was legalized; there were women and girls all over Pennsylvania who needed help. Frankie met women at the bus stop and told them the passwords and addresses they would need once they got to the city. Sometimes she even drove them to the city herself, in her father's car. She was a young, slight, plain, Italian-American girl. Though she was eighteen, she looked about fifteen. No one who saw her thought twice about her. She lied to her parents about going to study with friends; she lied about going to the library. She learned how to set the odometer back on the car so her father wouldn't guess how far she'd been driving.

One day, Frankie's parents got a call from the local police because Frankie had been arrested.

"Arrested for what?" her father shouted into the phone.

"For assisting with an illegal abortion racket," said the police.

"Ridiculous!" shouted Frankie's father.

But when the police finally released her for lack of evidence, and when she came home and stood before her horrified, mortified parents, Frankie made herself as tall as she could, threw her shoulders back, and refused to deny it. She believed in what she was doing. "I'm helping oppressed people," she told them, over and over, "just as you've taught me to do."

After that, Frankie's family bore down hard with rules and restrictions, threats and imprecations, and especially guilt. Her father was a shouter, which was hard to bear, but then his anger would fizzle, and he would become sad and bewildered. Frankie's mother was neither sad nor bewildered, and she knew how to shore her husband's anger up again. She was immovable, and knew exactly how things should be. No car, no outings, no unsupervised visits with friends, no unsupervised phone calls. When Frankie told her parents about the priest, they wouldn't believe her. Together, they made her go to his Masses on Sundays. They made her tell him her confession. When she began to lose weight, becoming so depressed that sometimes she skipped school, they told her that if she wasn't going to keep up her good grades, they wouldn't allow her to go to college. College was Frankie's plan of escape. In fact, it had begun to be the only thing she was living for. Was she to have nothing to live for? Some tiny, irrepressible spark inside her refused this. She would survive, and she would thrive. So she left. When she left, her family washed their hands of her. Aunt Margaret's family and one of her teachers, Mrs. Mancusi, helped her build a new life.

At Frankie's memorial service, Aunt Margaret had told this story to everyone present. "She asked me to tell this story," Aunt Margaret said, "because she wanted everyone here to know how deeply she believed that the world is full of people who will help each other survive heartbreak. You just need to find out who those people are for you. It's no small task, is it? She knew it wasn't always easy to see who those people are. But she believed, fervently, that they're all around us. Maybe if you're here today, it's because you're one of the lucky people Frankie touched with that same kindness in which she had so much faith."

Hearing the story at the memorial service, Wilhelmina couldn't remember ever having felt so alone. Which was confusing, because she wasn't alone. Julie sat on her left, Bee on her right. They'd come to Pennsylvania for this, for her, which meant a lot, and yet she felt almost as if they were the ones here and she'd gone off somewhere else by herself, wandering in a cold and airless place. She was angry at Frankie's parents, for preferring to lose their own daughter rather than know her for who she actually was. Thinking about that made her angry at Bee's mom too, for loving stupid ideas about how things should be more than she loved her son. And she was angry on Julie's behalf, because everyone at this memorial service full of white people assumed, when they saw Julie, that she must be Esther's family or Esther's friend. Wilhelmina could feel Julie growing harder and more distant, to protect herself. "Where's your New York accent?" one man asked her, smiling like he was being charming. Wilhelmina rose to that, shot back with, "Why would my friend from Boston have a New York accent?" Then she sank into numbness again.

She was still sitting in the window, still staring at the rain. She kept touching her necklace. Was it hypocritical to wear it, when she'd all but handed Julie's to a crow?

Wilhelmina reached for her phone. She didn't want to think about the weird stuff any more than she wanted to think about anything else, but it was a way to stay attached to Julie.

Okay, she texted Julie. *You can ask James what he's seen*

Julie responded with a thumbs up and a smiley. *I'll text you soon about your fate,* she said.

Gee thanks. Can't wait

Wilhelmina bobbed the head of the snow goose again, watching it swivel. Then she realized something.

If you text me back that James says he saw those things too, she texted Julie, *that could just be my mind fabricating your text*

Yeah, wrote Julie. *I thought of that. You should let me ask him anyway*

Why?

Because I'LL still know, she said. *We look after each other, right?*

Okay, said Wilhelmina. *But for all I know, this conversation isn't even happening*

Okay, breathe, elephant, said Julie. *We have to decide to believe SOMETHING, right?*

Yeah, said Wilhelmina. *That's true.*

But she didn't tell Julie that she hadn't decided yet what it would hurt least to believe.

THE AUNTS CAME HOME with Delia and Philip, all of them crowding through the door and then standing in the entrance, dripping like a forest of firs in a rainstorm.

"I'll hang up your wet things," said Wilhelmina.

"You're a dear," said Aunt Margaret, shouldering her way out of a long trench coat.

"Thank you, Wilhelmina," said Esther, handing her an umbrella. "You know, I remember a time not too long ago when it was not considered normal for a man to fly giant racist flags on his vehicle while driving around town."

"I saw one this morning," said Wilhelmina.

"He sprayed us with water," said Esther.

A knot of furious sadness tightened inside Wilhelmina's throat. "I'm sorry, Esther," she said. "Are you okay?"

"Don't you worry about me, bubeleh," said Esther, touching her shoulder.

Wilhelmina helped Philip out of his soggy clothes, pretending to attend to his cheerful description of every puddle he'd encountered and what had happened when he'd jumped into each one. She had an ulterior motive for taking charge of all the wet things. She'd learned from experience that she could make a barrier in the living room with everyone's umbrellas, then situate the coatrack and the tall drying rack in front of the corner chair, the one in the window that currently contained Frankie's treasures. She could create a small fortress for herself, and no one would look askance. The only person who ever bothered to push his way through was Philip, and for some reason, Philip was always lovely inside the fortress. He seemed calmed by it. Today, when he found Wilhelmina, he crawled into her lap, his skin pink and cold and his hair damp, and fell asleep. Wilhelmina sat there, matching her breaths to his and trying not to think, until it was time to help with dinner.

AT DINNER, Theo asked for Esther's honest assessment of his ropa vieja.

"It's lovely, Theo," Esther said.

"I know it's cheating to throw everything into the slow cooker all at once," said Theo.

Esther's mouth twitched into a smile of assent. "It's true the flavors are finer if you attend to each part," she said, "but you're a man with limited time. I think this is an excellent alternative. Just don't be afraid of garlic!"

"Thank you," said Theo, pinkening. "And the latkes? Be honest. I can take it, Esther."

"The latkes are delicious."

"But are they perfect?"

"I think I could drive us to Pennsylvania," said Aunt Margaret, which brought the conversation to a halt. For a moment, everyone stared at her.

"What?" cried Theo. "Not with that eye!"

"Oh, don't be silly," said Aunt Margaret. "I can see well enough through my other eye."

"I can just imagine what your doctor would say to that, Margeleh," said Esther, who was sitting up straight and looking rather fierce. "Not to mention me, your passenger."

"Oh, come now," said Aunt Margaret. "I would drive very slowly."

"On 84 through Connecticut, you would drive slowly?" said Esther. "Pardon me while I get my will in order."

"Then what are we to do, Esther?" said Aunt Margaret, with a touch of sharpness. "Not vote? This election could be decided in Pennsylvania. What if it's decided by a handful of votes?"

Esther put her fork down, then stared at her plate. "You're right," she said. "I'll drive us."

"You can't, love," said Aunt Margaret, almost on a sob. "Your license is expired."

"That only matters if we get pulled over," said Esther. "We won't."

"*What?*" cried Theo. "Esther! You get pulled over all the time!"

"Yes, Theo," said Esther. "Because my skin is brown."

"Which is reason enough not to risk it!"

"Is it?" said Esther. "Then what do you suggest? Margie and I need to vote."

"I'll drive you," said Wilhelmina.

Now everyone turned their wide eyes to Wilhelmina. She pushed her glasses up and looked back at the aunts. "I'll drive you," she said.

IN THE KITCHEN, Wilhelmina did the dishes under the approving eyes of Esther and the brimming eye of Aunt Margaret. She wished they would stop crowding her with their gratitude and admiration, because it pushed her up against her own guilt. Wilhelmina wasn't doing this for them, or for her nation. She was doing it because she wanted to go to the Pennsylvania house. She wanted to go there and not come back.

They were hanging herbs to dry from the potted plants they grew in their bedroom: coriander, mint, sage, thyme. Delia, who was helping, knelt on the counter so that she could reach the drying line they'd strung high along the windows. It put her butt at Wilhelmina's face level, which was annoying.

"Why is our mirror covered?" she asked Wilhelmina.

Wilhelmina stopped herself from saying, *My mirror. It's MY mirror.* "I didn't want to look at it," she said snippily.

Delia turned to glare at her. "Right," she said, in a voice that dripped with sarcasm. "I'm sure it's terrible to be so pretty."

Startled, Wilhelmina needed a minute; she needed to absorb the sudden relief she felt. Delia was ten. She wasn't particularly fat, but she wasn't thin either, just as Wilhelmina had been at that age. If Delia thought Wilhelmina was pretty, then maybe, if Delia's body grew plump and round at puberty as Wilhelmina's had done, then Delia would have some armor against all the voices in the world that would tell her to be thinner. It was an armor, battered but serviceable, that Wilhelmina had developed for herself somehow, fortified from necessity with stubbornness and rage, family and friends. Wilhelmina's people always told her she was beautiful. Somewhere along the line, she'd decided to believe them.

"I meant because it's dusty," she said to Delia in a milder tone. "Not because I don't like my reflection."

"*What's* dusty?"

"The mirror."

"Even though it looks like you used my favorite shirt as a dust-cloth?" said Delia.

"You're pretty too, Delia," said Wilhelmina. "Didn't you know that?"

"What?" Delia squealed, disbelieving, then studied Wilhelmina with suspicion.

"You are," said Wilhelmina. "Do you think I'd say it if it wasn't true?"

Delia's face transformed into a sort of wondering, yearning hope. It broke Wilhelmina's heart. She wanted Delia to be too young to know what the world was like, but maybe no one was ever too young.

After Wilhelmina finished the dishes, she returned to her fortress in the living room. She sat in the chair in the window, reaching a finger out to each of Frankie's treasures in turn. *I'm going to your home tomorrow,* she told the goose, because that was the plan. Tomorrow was Monday. If the aunts' ballots didn't arrive in the mail, Wilhelmina would drive them home to Pennsylvania. On Tuesday, after they voted in their own local fire hall, she would drive them back again.

Everyone was acting so proud of her. Wilhelmina tried not to think about it.

She checked her phone often and stayed up too late, but Julie didn't text.

The summer Wilhelmina was ten and Bee was nine—the summer of 2012—it almost seemed as if Bee was going to be able to come to Pennsylvania with Wilhelmina again. But on the morning they were supposed to leave, Bee's father changed his mind.

Wilhelmina overheard Cleo on the phone to the aunts, calling ahead to report the change of plans. "I couldn't get an explanation out of Cindy," she said in a low, rapid voice Wilhelmina wasn't used to. "I'm sure she doesn't want to admit that his moods rule that house. A summer away would be good for Bee, and now of course, with Wilhelmina gone, we won't be able to check in on him as much. She's so disappointed, Frankie. If you could've seen her face fall, you would've cried. I'd like to break his nose."

It was at that point that Wilhelmina realized why she didn't recognize her mother's voice: Cleo was furious. She'd never heard her mother talking about one of her friends' parents like that before. It made her feel less lonely in her dislike of Bee's dad. She hadn't thought any grown-ups shared it. And Cleo was almost right: Wilhelmina was disappointed. But mostly she was heartbroken for Bee, who'd wanted to go to Pennsylvania badly. Sometimes Wilhelmina wished that Bee were her brother so that her parents could be his parents. Maybe her parents didn't always understand her perfectly, but even that was consistent. They were reliably who they were. She never had to tiptoe around them, not knowing who they were going to be that day.

It was Theo who drove Wilhelmina to Pennsylvania, and for Wilhelmina, it was a confusing drive. She was always so happy to be setting out for the aunts, and she couldn't help feeling that same joy, but she was crying a little bit too. Her father kept pointing out license plates from "interesting" states like Wyoming and Alaska, or trying to get her opinion about the music on the radio, and she wished he would just let her sort out her thoughts. *Bee, Bee,* she kept thinking. "If Dr. Sloane changes his mind again," she asked her father, "how will Bee get to Pennsylvania?"

"If that happens, honey," said Theo, "your mother and I will bring him to you personally."

"With Delia?" asked Wilhelmina doubtfully. Delia, who was two, always threw up on long car rides.

"Well, yes," said Theo. "We're not quite ready to let Delia fend for herself at home."

"Okay, well, make sure you remind him she's going to puke."

"I promise to remind him," said Theo. "But honey, I don't think Dr. Sloane is going to change his mind again."

When they pulled into the aunts' driveway, Frankie came out of the garden to greet them, wiping her dirt-covered hands on the tails of a long purple shirt. When Wilhelmina heard her happy voice and saw her silver crown of braids and her radiant face, she began to cry in earnest. Frankie took one look at her and held out her arms. Wilhelmina, who had been too old for her mother's attempts at comfort a few hours ago and who'd tried to hide her tears from her father in the car, walked into Frankie's arms and sobbed against her chest.

"I've been thinking it might be nice to send Bee some care packages this summer," said Frankie quietly to Theo over Wilhelmina's head. "We'll send them to you so that you can deliver them to him personally. You can bring the first one back with you tomorrow. Would you like that, Wilhelmina?" she asked, speaking into Wilhelmina's hair while she hugged her. "Maybe we can find ways to share our summer with Bee."

It became the summer of searching for treasures small enough to send through the mail. Some were obvious: a perfect leaf from one of the aunts' many maples. Flowers from Frankie's flower beds or from the wild rose bramble in front of the carriage house, which Wilhelmina lined with wax paper and pressed between the volumes of the ancient encyclopedia that lived in a glass-fronted bookcase in the second-floor sitting room. Facts Wilhelmina found in the encyclopedia, which was from 1924, and had belonged to Aunt Margaret's great-aunt Eileen. "Even when I was little," Aunt Margaret had told her, "that encyclopedia was funny and old!"

"I've been looking up birds," Wilhelmina wrote to Bee. "Listen to this. 'Hummingbird. The nest of a humming-bird is a tiny cup-shaped affair, such as a fairy might build, and it is made of quite fairy-like material, plant-down, stuccoed with moss and spider-web.' 'Robin. The robin's friendly trustfulness has won for him the love of all classes of people.' Do you think they made a point of polling all classes of people? 'Pelican. Mr. and Mrs. Pelican feed their babies from a cupboard which they carry about with them. This cupboard is a sack of elastic skin grown from the underside of the beak.' 'Penguin. Seen from a distance, a colony of these strange sea-birds of the Southern Hemisphere might easily be taken for an assemblage of little men.' 'Pigeons and doves. There is not a single living specimen of the passenger pigeon anywhere in the world. The last of the captive passenger pigeons died—an old, old bird—in the zoological garden of Cincinnati in 1914.' I googled that passenger pigeon. Her name was Martha and she was twenty-nine years old. This encyclopedia has like ten volumes. Can you believe people used to buy that many books, just to know things? Then a few years later, they'd be out of date! It smells like . . ."

Wilhelmina paused in her missive, trying to decide what the

encyclopedia smelled like. "It smells a little sweet and a little stale," she wrote. "Like a doughnut you left out too long in the sun." Of course, that wasn't completely accurate, nor did it make much sense. If you left a doughnut out in the sun here at the aunts' house, it would last about three minutes before a squirrel or a chipmunk, or one of Esther's beloved stray cats, or any of about a dozen species of birds picked it apart or carried it away. But Wilhelmina liked how it sounded. Her letters to Bee gave her an opportunity to practice being poetic.

She called him on the phone sometimes too, although she didn't always get to talk to him. "Tobey's at soccer practice," his father would say, or "Tobey's out playing catch." Tobey was playing football. Tobey was chopping wood. Chopping wood? What wood? Wilhelmina wasn't sure whether to believe these reports, partly because Dr. Sloane always sounded too pleased with himself, like he was making a hilarious joke, and partly because it didn't sound like Bee. Bee enjoyed soccer, but he hated football. It was as if his father were reading from a list of "Things Boys Do" or something (chopping wood?), and in the meantime, Bee was probably upstairs in his room watching *Princess Mononoke*.

"Is this Wilhelmina Hart?" Bee's father asked her once, even though he knew perfectly well it had to be her. "Did you and your aunties make these brownies you sent? Thank you. They're delicious."

Wilhelmina imagined Bee's father eating all the brownies she and Frankie had made for Bee, and began to hate him. She called her parents. "Did you give the last care package to Bee directly?" she shrieked at her mother. "You have to give them to him directly!"

"All right, Wilhelmina," said Cleo, who sounded startled, and also frazzled. Delia was screaming in the background. "We will," she said, "I promise. Honey? I promise. Will you tell me what happened?"

Wilhelmina told Cleo about the brownies, feeling less panicked. She was ten years old and it didn't occur to her that her parents couldn't easily knock on the Sloanes' door with a package, then refuse to relinquish the package to anyone but their nine-year-old son. Nor did it occur to her that her parents were, in fact, already worried about Bee, as much as their busy lives would permit. But she knew that voice of Cleo's. Cleo meant her promise.

After that, almost unconsciously, Wilhelmina switched her focus to treasures that Dr. Sloane wouldn't recognize as treasures. On weekends, the aunts often took her to a small lake nearby. Aunt Margaret loved to swim, and maybe it ran in the family, because Wilhelmina did too. Sometimes Frankie came along, although often she stayed home "for a little time to myself." Esther often came. She was highly suspicious of lake water, but she loved to people-watch while pretending to read. "Plus, who doesn't want the company of two happy fish," she would say, watching in delighted amazement as Wilhelmina set out to swim clear across to the other side of the lake. "Wilhelmineleh! You're a wonder."

Pressed against a thicket of brush and trees on the other side of the lake was a tiny, pebbly beach. On the beach was a scattering of distinctive blue stones. Sometimes you had to search a long time before you found a blue stone. Wilhelmina always did, or at any rate, Aunt Margaret always did—Aunt Margaret had an affinity for finding things—and she always gave what she found to Wilhelmina. She also let Wilhelmina swim with a special little swimming bag she owned that strapped around the waist, so that Wilhelmina could bring the stones back with her. The bag made her feel like an adventurer. The final section of the swim involved swimming through tall grass that felt slick and grabby against her skin, which heightened the feeling. And on the pebbly beach, she and Aunt Margaret were usually alone. Most people didn't bother to swim that far, or turned away when they got to the grass. Wilhelmina liked to believe that no one else knew that the beach, if you achieved it, yielded tiny blue treasures.

She also believed that a soulless person like Bee's father, upon opening a box, wouldn't realize or care that blue stones were treasures, but

Bee would recognize them instantly. The summer he'd come to stay, Wilhelmina hadn't been big or strong enough yet to swim all the way across the lake, but Aunt Margaret had brought some back to them.

The weekend after the brownies incident, Wilhelmina swam across to the beach. It was a hot day, and the lake was full of children. Some of them were playing in the water farther out from shore than the rest. When Wilhelmina reached them, then passed them, then continued moving steadily beyond them, one of them, a boy about her age, shouted with obvious admiration, "Are you migrating to Baja California?"

Wilhelmina didn't understand what this meant, but she liked it anyway. Probably it was a reference to some other animal that swam very well, like her.

She stayed on the beach for a long time, because she wanted to send Bee as many stones as possible. At one point, Aunt Margaret swam ashore. "Wilhelmina, dear?" she said, pushing herself up out of the water into the sun, then standing there dripping happily. "Please do remember that a bag of stones will weigh you down as you swim back."

"Oh," said Wilhelmina, startled, because she hadn't thought of that. "How many stones do you think I can swim with?"

"How many have you collected so far?" asked Aunt Margaret.

"Three," she said, holding her palm out to show Aunt Margaret the luminous stones. A lot of stones glimmered when they were underwater, but the blue stones glimmered all the time. Wilhelmina knew, from the three she kept on her bedside windowsill in the aunts' house, that they even caught the moonlight.

"Lovely," said Aunt Margaret serenely. "Let's say five total, assuming the next two are of a similar size. Are you cold or hungry?"

"No, I'm fine."

"All right, I'll leave you to it. You know," she said, pointing to the far edge of the little beach, "I think I see a blue sparkle over there, beside that big, black rock. You see the rock shaped like a bird's nest?"

Wilhelmina couldn't see a blue sparkle, but she did see the bird's-nest rock. "Thanks," she said, moving toward it carefully. Part of the slowness of the blue-stone search was due to the discomfort of traversing a pebble beach with bare feet.

She found two more blue stones near the bird's-nest rock and tucked them into her bag with satisfaction. She wanted to bring one to Frankie, which left four for Bee. Then, slow and steady, she swam back to shore. When she got there, she discovered that she was, in fact, a bit cold and hungry. She ran across the sand to the aunts, who were sunning themselves in beach chairs, and wrapped herself in a towel, shivering. "Hot soup, dear?" said Aunt Margaret, handing her a thermos. Aunt Margaret was the only person who ever seemed to understand that sometimes on a warm summer day at the beach, a swimmer might appreciate a thermos of hot soup. It was her favorite too, ham and bean, made by Frankie. Wilhelmina sipped it, perfectly happy.

The boy who'd shouted the thing about Baja California was sitting on a beach blanket nearby, also eating something. Whatever it was, he kept breaking off pieces and handing them to a man lying in the sun beside him, a thin man with a graying ring of hair who accepted them cheerfully. The man had a rumbly voice and a sweet smile.

"You're a really good swimmer," the boy called out to her.

"Thanks," she said. Sometimes, when Wilhelmina was chilled through but also wrapped in a towel and sitting in the sun, she felt like nothing was wrong in the world. "What did you mean about Baja California?"

"Oh!" he said. "I meant you were like a gray whale. They migrate farther than any other whale. They swim from the Arctic all the way to Baja California! Anyway, that's what I meant." He looked a little sheepish. "Sorry. My sister tells me I boysplain things."

"I asked," said Wilhelmina.

"I guess you did!" he said. "Gray whales are completely marvelous. Oh! But maybe you don't like being compared to a whale."

"I like it," said Wilhelmina, who was ten, and too sturdily built to be called skinny, but had never doubted what he meant. Whales *were* marvelous. She liked how considerate this boy was. In a fit of generosity, she reached into her bag and pulled out the blue stones. Choosing a nice one, she held it out to him. "Want one?" she said. "I found it across the lake."

"Oh!" he said, clambering to his feet and coming to crouch in front of her. He took the stone and turned it around in his hands. One of his front teeth was crooked, crossing in front of the other, in a way that made his grin kind of cute. He had very dark eyes.

"Blue!" he said. "That's really pretty. Thanks! Do you like doughnuts?"

"Of course."

The boy went back to the graying man on the blanket, then returned, carrying something. "Want one?" he said. "I know it's shaped funny, but it tastes normal. The skinny part might be overcooked."

He handed her a—glazed doughnut? It was stretched into a lopsided oval, way too skinny on one end and too fat on the other. It looked like it had once been an even ring of dough, then someone had hung it on a hook and left it there. "Thanks," she said, taking a bite of the fat end. It was delicious. When she alternated bites of the sweet doughnut with sips of Frankie's savory soup, it was basically the best meal ever. *Some days are perfect,* thought Wilhelmina.

That evening after dinner, while the aunts cleaned up, Wilhelmina sat at the kitchen table composing a letter to Bee. She felt strange about letters to Bee now, almost as if she should be writing them in code just in case Bee's father was reading them. "I met a boy at the lake today who told me I swim like a gray whale, which was a compliment," she wrote. "I looked gray whale up in the encyclopedia afterward but there wasn't an entry! But listen to this about gravitation. 'Gravitation. From the beginning of time a very remarkable thing has been happening, and few except very little children and very great philosophers have thought to ask why. That is, things have invariably been falling to the ground, and never in any other direction.' Don't you wish people still talked like that? Anyway, I wished you were there at the lake," she added, because she didn't want Bee to think she'd found a replacement boy.

"Are you sending these stones to Bee, dear?" asked Frankie, stopping by her chair. The three stones she'd chosen for Bee sat on the table above the letter she was writing.

"Yes," said Wilhelmina.

"Good," said Frankie. Then she rested one hand atop the stones, closed her eyes, and took a breath.

"What are you doing?" asked Wilhelmina.

Frankie opened her eyes. "I suppose you could say I'm praying," she said.

"For what?" said Wilhelmina.

"Oh," said Frankie casually, "I suppose for Bee to be well."

A few minutes later, Esther stopped by Wilhelmina's chair and did the same thing.

"Are you praying for Bee too?" said Wilhelmina.

"In a manner of speaking," said Esther, "yes."

When Aunt Margaret came by sometime later and put her hand on the stones, Wilhelmina didn't ask her what she was doing. She just watched. She was having a memory of every time one of the aunts had ever put a hand on her own shoulder and stood there quietly, just like that. After Aunt Margaret left, she put her own hand on the stones and felt Aunt Margaret's warmth.

At the end of the summer, the aunts and Wilhelmina received some good news: when Theo and Cleo came to stay for a few days, then bring Wilhelmina home, Bee was coming too.

But when the car pulled into the drive and her parents climbed out, Bee wasn't there. The only person in the back seat was Delia, who smelled faintly of vomit.

"I'm sorry, honey!" said Theo, leaning into the car, struggling with Delia's buckles. "We meant to warn you. Cleo, did you text Aunt Margaret?"

"I thought you said you were doing it!" said Cleo.

"Oops."

"I'm really sorry, sweetie," said Cleo, coming to hug Wilhelmina, kissing the top of her head. "We saw him last week down at the field. Soccer game. Did he tell you he's been playing goalie? He's good!"

"Tall for his age," said Theo, his head still inside the car. "Good at covering the angles."

"Listen to you, Theo," said Aunt Margaret fondly. "Sounding like you know what you're talking about."

"Hey, I'm a librarian," said Theo. "I either know or have access to all information."

"Hand me that pukey baby," said Aunt Margaret. "I want to give her hugs."

"You're a saint, Aunt Margaret," said Theo, finally extracting a sleepy Delia from the car. "We did change her clothes."

"I don't care."

"Hello!" called Frankie from the porch. "Welcome! Come have iced tea!"

"Can I call Bee?" said Wilhelmina.

But Bee wasn't home.

Then, when Wilhelmina herself got home, Bee and his mom were away. She could tell because when she went to his house, which was a giant one set into a hilly yard a short walk downhill from her apartment, his mom's Lexus was gone; the light his mom turned on in the front room when she wanted to trick robbers was shining through the window; and Wilhelmina found a few days' mail crammed into the mailbox. She had a feeling Bee's father was home. He lived like a vampire when he wasn't at the hospital, so the signs of an abandoned house never meant anything, and he didn't usually go on family trips. So Wilhelmina didn't knock on the door. But she was beginning to feel panicked again.

It wasn't until a few days before the first day of school that she finally clapped eyes on Bee. She was dutifully "playing" outside with Delia, who would yell something garbled, then throw a ball badly while screaming. The problem with throwing a ball outside their apartment was that if it hit the sidewalk or the road, the steepness of the hill was so extreme that only the most headlong rush would prevent it rolling about three blocks.

Unless a soccer goalie was walking up the hill, which one was. As Wilhelmina began to race after Delia's stupid ball, Bee, dark-haired and quiet, familiar and dear, rounded the corner, assessed the situation, and put out one neat foot. Then he bent and picked up the ball one-handed, and Wilhelmina's initial rush of relief, which had changed almost instantly to an irrational rage at Bee for being so calm when she'd been so worried, transformed next into a sick sorrow. He had a purple cast on his left arm.

Wilhelmina began to cry. "What happened to you?" she said. "Does it hurt?"

She knew his answer before he said it. "My dad pushed me down the steps," he said, speaking as matter-of-factly as ever. He looked into her eyes and held them, his chin raised as if he was daring her not to believe him, but of course she believed him. He wasn't crying, but there was something upsetting in the way he was standing there, like he was ready to flinch at any sudden movement. Wilhelmina wondered if he'd done a lot of crying on his own. The thought made her feel a little frantic.

"The stones didn't work," she said.

"The stones?" he said. "The blue stones from the beach?"

"They were supposed to keep you safe," she said. "The aunts prayed over them."

Bee's eyes widened. "They did?"

"Yes."

"For me?"

"Yes!"

"Huh," he said. "No one's ever done anything like that for me before."

Delia was standing in the yard looking down at them, yelling, "Bee! Bee!" delightedly. It was one of the few words she could say well. As Bee carried the ball to her, Wilhelmina followed. She didn't know what to do with herself. She was furious again, but she couldn't figure out why. She was thinking of the gentle hands of the aunts on her shoulder, and hating Bee's father, and wanting to hurl the blue stones off a cliff if there was nothing she could do to make Bee's life less unfair.

"I'm sorry they didn't work," she said.

"It's okay," he said. "It'd take a lot with my dad. Anyway, I love them. They're like family talismans now, right?"

A moving truck was lumbering up the hill. Wilhelmina positioned herself between Delia and the road and Bee shifted too, ready to intercept the ball, should Delia choose that moment to fling it. "Family talismans?" said Wilhelmina.

"You went on a quest to find them, and then your aunts made them powerful," said Bee. "And then you gave them to me."

"Oh," said Wilhelmina. "I guess so." Then, to her surprise, the truck pulled up to their curb and her math teacher climbed out.

"Mr. Dunstable?" said Wilhelmina in amazement.

"Hello, Wilhelmina," said Mr. Dunstable cheerfully, pocketing a giant key and wiping his hands together. "Hello, Bee. Now, don't tell me one of you lives here?"

It was so strange to see her math teacher standing there outside her home, wearing shorts and a Red Sox T-shirt. Mr. Dunstable wore slacks and sweaters normally, and, to her knowledge before this, did not have hairy legs or muscular arms. Math in the World was Wilhelmina's number one favorite part of school. Mr. Dunstable had taught them how a musical piece reached its climax because of the particular mathematical relationship between its notes. He'd taught them the way electoral votes during presidential elections were counted in strange, uneven, state-sized clumps until one of the candidates reached two hundred seventy. He'd taught them that every attempt by humanity to communicate with aliens involved speaking in math, because mathematical concepts were believed to be universal in a way that other concepts, like God or democracy or literacy, were not. Why was this marvelous grown-up standing on her curb?

"*I* live here," said Wilhelmina. "Why are you here?"

"Because I'm your new neighbor," said Mr. Dunstable, "apparently."

Before Wilhelmina could absorb the revelation that one's math teacher could live in one's own building, a car pulled up behind the truck. A woman Wilhelmina had never seen before got out. Mr. Dunstable was a Black man with dark, golden-brown skin, and the woman looked like she might be Black too. Her skin was pale brown, like Esther's. Then a girl who looked more like Mr. Dunstable came around from the passenger seat, wearing shorts and a giant white hoodie so oversized that maybe she'd borrowed it from one of her parents. Her hair was gathered in a high puff on top of her head.

"I'm Julie," she said, coming up to Wilhelmina and Bee.

"I'm Wilhelmina," said Wilhelmina.

"I'm Bee," said Bee.

"Are you going to be my upstairs neighbor?" said Wilhelmina, her voice ending on a squeak she hadn't planned for. Wilhelmina, who'd been away all summer, hadn't even realized that her old upstairs neighbors had moved out, although now that she thought about it, their cars were gone. This was almost too exciting.

"Looks like it," said Julie.

"That's great!" said Wilhelmina. "Do you like Math in the World?"

Julie rolled her eyes and started laughing, and Wilhelmina started laughing too. Sometimes, when people laughed at what you said, you knew somehow, right away, that it was because they *liked* what you said. The laughter was like bells inside Wilhelmina, the joyful kind that ring out when something wonderful is happening.

"Want to see something funny?" said Julie.

"Yes," said Wilhelmina and Bee together.

Then Julie eased herself out of her giant hoodie and it became plain why she was wearing it: because it was the only long-sleeved garment that would fit over the cast on her right arm, which was exactly the same shade of purple as the cast on Bee's left arm. She held it out to Bee, laughing again. "Soccer accident," she said. "You?"

When Bee smiled, something cried out inside Wilhelmina. She could feel the sweetness of his smile, and also the sadness behind it. "Great color choice," he said.

"You too," said Julie.

"I also play soccer," said Bee. "Goalie. You?"

"Striker."

"That makes you my nemesis," said Bee, which got another laugh from Julie.

"Want to come inside?" said Wilhelmina. She extended her arms. "I can pour you both drinks."

O n the Monday five days before she stepped into her own, Wilhelmina had a dentist appointment.

It was a relief to leave the apartment early, because Delia was marching around in a state of high dudgeon. She wanted, quite desperately, to go to Pennsylvania with Wilhelmina and the aunts. The reason she wasn't allowed to—school—was not compelling to her. "It's virtual school!" she shouted. "I can do it from anywhere!"

"You can do it from anywhere *with Wi-Fi*, Delia," said Cleo, her nose clogged, her eyes swollen. Cleo was leaning against the kitchen counter, pulling boxes of cereal out of the cabinet with the hand she wasn't using to prop herself upright, trying to make Philip's breakfast. "The aunts canceled their Wi-Fi when they closed up the house."

"Eleanor and Madison can tell me what I miss!"

"Delia, we can't ask the aunts to take charge of all your needs."

"I bet Wilhelmina stayed with them for an entire summer when *she* was ten," shouted Delia.

"She wasn't in school!" said Cleo. "And the aunts were eight years younger then, Delia."

And there were three of them, thought Wilhelmina. Three had been the perfect number.

"It's not fair!" shouted Delia. "Wilhelmina gets to do everything!" Then she stormed away and slammed Wilhelmina's bedroom door.

Cleo stared at the ceiling, her upturned nose pink and chapped.

"It is certainly unfair," she said. "I can't argue with that. Where's Philip gotten to? Philip!"

Philip was in the living room, where Wilhelmina's barricade still stood. He knelt in the window chair by himself, having an animated conversation with the statue of Saint Francis.

"Wilhelmina gets to do *everything*!" she heard him say, in a cheerful but accurate mimicry of Delia's outraged tone. Wilhelmina slipped out the door.

OUTSIDE, the world was bright and chilly and the sun touched nearby houses with pink and gold. Wilhelmina turned to glance up at Julie's windows, but the Dunstables' curtains were drawn. She began the tromp down the hill.

Her dentist was in the Lupa Building, three stories above Alfie Fang's. Wilhelmina wore leggings striped in various shades of blue and a deep blue sweatshirt dress, plus a blue-and-purple scarf that looked sharp with her red coat and glasses. Sometimes the colors Wilhelmina wore made her feel more substantial as she moved through the world. She needed that this morning, because the majority of her attention was focused on an abstraction, and an absence: all the things that weren't happening on her phone.

Finally, *ding*!

Wilhelmina dug her thumb out of her glove and read while walking.

Okay, wrote Julie. *Sorry that took so long. I had to do a complicated runaround to get James's number so no one nosy would ask me nosy questions. Then I had to grill him. We video-chatted. I wanted to see his face while he answered my questions*

Okay, said Wilhelmina. *No prob*

Then I had to grill Eloisa about whether he was trustworthy. According to her, the answer is yes. She's known him a long time. Like, he moved here from Waltham junior year, but she knew him before that. I think their dads are friends?

Okay, said Wilhelmina again. *I didn't realize I was asking you to do so much work*

It's fine. Anyway, James is seeing the weird shit too

Wilhelmina walked to a bus stop bench and sat down hard, trying to sort out her reactions to this. Relief was among them, but her relief was muted. Mostly, Wilhelmina felt like Julie was very far away.

Oh, good, she wrote back mechanically. *Thanks*

Are you freaking out? said Julie. *About whether you're imagining my texts?*

No, I'm good

He seemed relieved. Like, to be asked. He's probably also been wondering if it's all in his head

Maybe we're seeing bizarre shit because the world is on fire and our minds don't know how to cope, Wilhelmina found herself saying, a bit randomly.

Or maybe weird shit actually is happening, because the world is on fire, said Julie. *You okay there, elephant? Where are you?*

On my way to the dentist

Fun. BTW he's definitely into you. He kept grinning whenever I said your name. Want me to ask Eloisa? We talked a long time. I trust her. Plus I think she's James's wingman

Yeah, I don't know, said Wilhelmina. *I need a minute*

You okay? You seem . . . distant

I'm fine, said Wilhelmina. *What do you mean, you talked for a long time? Like, about me and James?* Or maybe about you and Bee, she added to herself, suddenly wondering if that was even possible. If Julie and Bee were becoming, like, a thing, would they talk to other people about it before they talked to her? Maybe that was why Julie kept nudging her to be into James. Because she was into Bee, and that would be all neat and tidy.

No, don't worry, said Julie. *Mostly about college. She's looking at some of the schools I'm looking at. She wants to fly too*

Julie had been talking about college, about spreading her wings and dropping herself down someplace completely new, for years. It was among the reasons Wilhelmina had given her the elephant necklace with butterfly wings.

I'm sorry your year got delayed, elephant, said Wilhelmina, meaning it.

Thanks. Anyway, yours did too

I'm going to be late for the dentist

You go, said Julie. *We'll talk later*

Thank you, Julie. I owe you big time

You'd do the same for me, elephant. Bye!

AT THE LUPA BUILDING, Wilhelmina walked past Alfie Fang's, succumbing to the urge to peer through the windows. The light reflecting off the glass made it impossible for her to isolate anything beyond indistinguishable shapes, which was probably for the best. It was good that James was seeing the same odd things she was seeing, but that didn't make it normal. Nor did it leave her with the first idea of what to say to him.

She stood outside the building's main entrance, calling the dental office to check in. Elongated wolves sat on lintels above the giant doors, watching her while she answered the long list of Covid-protocol questions.

When she got the go-ahead to enter, she passed under the wolves. Inside, the lobby was made of marble and chrome; more wolves perched above the elevators. With a cheerful *bing*, an elevator opened and Mrs. Mardrosian stepped out.

"Mrs. Mardrosian!" said Wilhelmina.

The older woman was wearing the same black peacoat and flowered scarf she'd worn in the cemetery the day Wilhelmina had changed her tire. A crooked mask slipped down her face, revealing her nose. "Am I supposed to be a martyr?" she said, to the air apparently, because she wasn't looking at Wilhelmina.

"Mrs. Mardrosian?" said Wilhelmina. "How are you? Were you able to get your tire fixed?"

"What?" said Mrs. Mardrosian, turning toward the sound of Wilhelmina's voice, unfocused. "Oh, is that you again, Wilhelmina?" Her mascara was running on one side, a dark tear finding all her face's wrinkles. "Are you in this building too?"

Wilhelmina wasn't sure what to say to that, since the answer was obvious. She was standing right there. "I'm going to the dentist," she said.

"Right," said Mrs. Mardrosian, with a touch of sourness. "I was just there. Yes, I did get my tire replaced, but I still haven't found my keys. Probably turning to rust beside some grave somewhere. Well, have a nice day."

Mrs. Mardrosian wandered away toward the big revolving door, still muttering to herself. *Okay,* thought Wilhelmina, stepping into the elevator, glad to have it to herself. *Whatever.*

Upstairs, the dentist's office looked different from the last time she'd been there, mostly in the sense of partitions. A plexiglass wall separated Wilhelmina from the woman sitting at reception. A quick glance down the corridor showed her that plexiglass partitions divided some of the other sections of the office that had used to be open too.

Another difference was that the woman at reception was cradling a small owl in her lap.

Wilhelmina blinked, leaning in to stare. The owl lay on its side, draped in a blanket, staring back at Wilhelmina with big, yellow eyes. It was teeny. As small as a robin!

"Yes, hon," said the woman behind the plexiglass. "I know what you're thinking. But it's perfectly hygienic."

That wasn't what Wilhelmina had been thinking. "That's an owl, right?" she said, still staring. It had a round, pale face, and brown streaks on its tiny head. "I'm seeing an actual owl?"

"Yes," said the woman. "I live near that patch of trees above the stadium, you know it, hon? We get some critters there. I found this little one in my yard, lying on its side, just like you see. It has an injured talon. Anyway, I couldn't just leave it there, right? So I wrapped it in a blanket, and here we are. I've been on the phone with the raptor rescue center. They say it's a northern saw-whet owl."

"I see," said Wilhelmina. "Did they tell you to keep it in your lap like that?"

"No!" the lady said. "They told me to keep it in a box and avoid its feet, because its talons are dangerous. But every time I put it in the box, it starts making this heartbreaking chirping noise, and it doesn't stop until I put it back in my lap! I drove here with it lying in my lap too. I'm worried I'm ruining it for the wild! But I couldn't leave it in my yard, right?"

"You really couldn't," Wilhelmina agreed. "It would've died."

"Exactly!" said the woman. "So here we are. But I should let your hygienist know you've arrived. It's Wilhelmina, right?"

"Yes," said Wilhelmina, who was suddenly remembering the dream she'd had last night. She'd been sitting inside an old-fashioned car in a barn with an owl, who'd been in the driver's seat, staring straight ahead.

"Trust yourself, Wil-helm-ina," said the owl, who spoke in low, deep owl hoots that Wilhelmina understood, because Wilhelmina spoke owl. In fact, Wilhelmina spoke owl so fluently that she knew that the owl, speaking her name, was dividing it up with dashes. "Trust Ray," the owl added. "Your names mean 'protector'!"

Another patient stepped into the reception area, wearing a puffy sky-blue coat.

"Oops, I'm so sorry!" said the owl lady. "We're supposed to have this system set up so the patients never encounter each other. I don't know what happened." She indicated the distant side of the room. "Wilhelmina, hon, will you go sit down over there while I check James out?"

Of course Wilhelmina could go sit down over there, while of course the woman checked James Fang out. Because who else would have an appointment right now, at the same time as Wilhelmina's, at the dentist/owl rescue center? She dared a glance at James. He looked extremely cheerful to see her.

"Hi, Wilhelmina," he said. "Are you okay?"

"I'm great," said Wilhelmina, who was clutching her temples, trying to cling to that dream as it faded away. At least he was wearing a shirt today, which was not a helpful thought right now, actually.

"I talked to your friend," said James. "You know, Julie?"

"Uh-huh."

"Over there, please, Wilhelmina?" said the owl lady, pointing more forcefully.

"Right," said Wilhelmina, turning, aiming for a chair on the other side of the waiting room.

"Parliament," said James.

"What?" said Wilhelmina, wheeling back.

"Parliament," he said. "That's what a group of owls is called. I looked it up."

"James is the one who told me about the raptor center," said the owl lady. "I don't know what I would've done otherwise."

"I used to work there sometimes," said James, who was definitely grinning at Wilhelmina under his mask. She could tell.

"That'll be two hundred sixty-seven dollars for today, James," said the owl lady.

"Right," said James grimly, fishing a card out of his coat pocket. While he waited for his card to process, while he turned to glance repeatedly at Wilhelmina, while he said his goodbyes and left the office, Wilhelmina couldn't help but notice that James was slightly glowing at the edges, as if he were standing in front of a miniature sun.

When he'd gone and Wilhelmina was allowed to approach the desk again, she saw that the owl lady and the owl lady's owl were both glowing slightly too.

HER DENTAL CLEANING WAS NORMAL, except that she had to gargle with a vile antiseptic rinse beforehand, and also her hygienist, Liz, was dressed like an astronaut. But it was normal in the sense that nothing glowed that shouldn't, and no new owls appeared. Nothing solid vanished into thin air, and none of the signs on the walls changed.

When she returned to reception, the owl lady was on the phone.

"Yes, my name is Ellie," she said. "Ellie Saroyan. That's right. You'll find me on the fourth floor, but please call ahead. I'll have to ask you the Covid screening questions before I can let you in, I'm afraid. All right! Thank you!"

She hung up. "That was the raptor center," she told Wilhelmina. "They think she's a young female."

"Oh?"

"And possibly she's in the middle of her migration. They're going to come and pick her up! Isn't that great?"

"Yes," said Wilhelmina. "Only the most full-service raptor centers do house calls at the dentist."

The owl lady threw her head back and trilled a laugh that was surprisingly musical; she startled a smile onto Wilhelmina's face.

"Oh, you're so funny, hon," she said. "Now that she's going, I'll miss her. I hope she'll be able to return to the life she's supposed to be living."

Wilhelmina studied the owl's tiny face, which was staring at her sideways. The owl's beak was a small, dark, graceful hook, and her eyes were bright and steady. She looked both extremely silly and thoroughly dignified.

"Me too," said Wilhelmina.

ON THE ELEVATOR RIDE DOWN, Wilhelmina was thinking about the rest of her day, the shape of which would depend on whether the aunts received their ballots. She fished her phone out of her pocket and texted her father. *Mail? Ballots?*

He texted back immediately. *Mail came. No ballots.*

Well, then. Wilhelmina was driving to Pennsylvania today.

The elevator dinged and the door slid open. Wilhelmina stepped out under the wolves, expecting the lobby. Instead, the space transformed around her, the marble walls shrinking so fast that she ducked, shrieking, as the marble turned into glass blazing with light. Raising a hand to shield her eyes, she saw a familiar floor of black and white squares and a counter with a tiled mural of a forest behind it. The smells were familiar too: powdered sugar, yeast, honey glaze. Coffee. She was in a small, triangular doughnut shop. This was Alfie Fang's.

With the beginnings of a tired, familiar fury, Wilhelmina straightened and held her ground. No elevators opened into Alfie Fang's normally, but what could she do? This one had. She looked around, searching almost impatiently for whatever written message she was supposed to receive this time, wanting to get this over with. The shop was full of customers, who were alarming, because they were translucent. She could see *through* them, to the walls and the furniture, which only made her more tired somehow, more angry. See-through people felt like a hallucination cliché. They moved around her smoothly, not looking at her, as if some instinct told them she was there, but they couldn't actually see her. Their voices were cheerful but muted. The most noticeable thing about them was that no one was wearing a mask.

In fact, Wilhelmina caught sight of James in the kitchen doorway, peeking out into the front of the shop, not wearing a mask. James! There was no plexiglass along the counter, so Wilhelmina could see him clearly. He was smiling at someone. He had the most adorable dimple in one cheek when he smiled. Wilhelmina turned to see who he was smiling at and discovered that behind her was the shop door, opening and closing as customers came in. Her elevator was gone. She waved her arms in the air to get James's attention, but he didn't seem to notice.

Beside James, lights began to sparkle on the mural of the forest. Biting back a sigh, Wilhelmina waited for the sparkles to resolve into words.

HELP THE DOUGHNUTS! said the lights.

"What?" cried Wilhelmina. "What's that supposed to mean?"

The lights blazed so brightly that it hurt; then, all at once, they disappeared. Wilhelmina pulled off her glasses, dabbing her streaming eyes with her scarf, then waited for clarification, but none came.

Okay, fine, she thought, looking around at the spectral people nearby. *Is that it? Can I leave now?* If so, *how* did she leave? Her elevator was gone. Was she supposed to walk out through the door?

Wilhelmina moved toward the door, not sure what would happen when she touched it. But when she grabbed at the handle, she found it to be solid enough—so solid, in fact, that she swung around once more, expecting the people to have gone solid too. James was standing at the kitchen entrance again, looking straight at her. He grinned his dimpled grin at her.

But when she raised a hand, James's face registered no recognition— and then she realized she could see right through his body into the kitchen beyond. When his mother came up behind him, Wilhelmina could see the two of them superimposed.

It was creepy, which filled her with a burst of indignation. She didn't like the way this supernatural bullshit was using James and changing him into something creepy, when he was so nice. She turned back, swung the door open, and stepped outside.

ON THE SIDEWALK, people stood in a socially distanced line that extended down the block, wearing masks.

"Thank you," one of them said to a startled Wilhelmina as she held the door for him. When she spun back to look through the glass, she saw the plexiglass partition at the counter, and a customer at the register with a big pile of doughnut boxes in his arms. She squinted, trying to see through him. He was opaque.

Okay, then. It was over. Fine. Wilhelmina began to march down the street, taking long steps with her big Hart feet. "Leave me alone!" she shouted at the sky.

"Wilhelmina?" came a voice from behind her.

"Oh, what now?" she shouted, then turned.

It was James, racing after her, masked but wearing no coat. He ran with a doughnut raised over his shoulder in one hand, as one might carry a javelin. In fact, Wilhelmina had a memory suddenly of James throwing a javelin. She was sure she'd seen him do that before in the stadium, running on very nice legs, then, with very nice arms, hurling a giant, vibrating spear, which had soared forever across the sky.

Like a ray, she thought, sighing. She tucked her hands into her pockets and waited for him quietly. *Trust Ray.*

"Hi," he said as he neared her, stopping a few careful feet away.

"Hi," she said.

"I saw you through the window," he said. "I wanted you to have a replacement doughnut for the one that was stale."

"That's very nice of you," she said, her defenses fizzling.

"Honey cruller, right?"

"Yeah."

"That's one of my favorites too."

"All your doughnuts are delicious," said Wilhelmina, "and of course the portraits are amazing. But I think there's a kind of genius to the simpler ones, like the honey cruller and the youtiao."

She could tell James was smiling again. "My dad talks about them that way too," he said. "He'll be happy when I tell him you said that."

Then he stretched out toward her and Wilhelmina reached toward him. He'd enclosed the doughnut in one of those paper pastry pockets. She grabbed it, stepped back, and held it up to her nose. It was soft and sticky and smelled wonderful. *Help the doughnuts.* She was going to help this doughnut achieve its destiny.

"Thanks," she said. "If you could see my mouth, you'd know I'm smiling."

"Me too," he said.

"A parliament?" said Wilhelmina. "Really?" She was babbling, to detain him. Realizing this, she felt her ears turn pink.

"Yeah."

"That's cute."

"It *is* cute."

"I don't suppose you know what a group of snow geese is called?" she said. "Like, is it a gaggle, like with regular geese?"

"I don't know," he said. "But I'll find out."

WILHELMINA RETURNED HOME to an elevated level of up-roar. At the rolltop desk in the living room, Philip sat in Esther's lap having online storytime, which was normal enough, but a lot of noise seemed to be coming from the kitchen.

"I'm making egg salad!" she heard Theo shout, to a background of clattering dishes and the sound of chopping. "Do you like a touch of Dijon mustard in your egg salad? Cleo is picking up a nice bread and we have these lovely cheeses Wilhelmina got yesterday and I'll pack fruit. We have three thermoses! Should I make coffee? One black, one with cream, one with cream and sugar? Or would you rather I sent you with the coffee beans and put some cream in the cooler? And maybe you'd like to take the empty thermoses so you can fill them up in the morning, in case there are lines at the voting! Oh! I'll put the camping chairs in the trunk when Cleo gets home!"

As Wilhelmina entered the kitchen from one direction, Aunt Margaret entered it from the other, wearing her eye patch and rolling a small suitcase.

"I expect we have coffee in the house, dear," she said. "And thermoses. Hello, Wilhelmina."

"I'll pack them anyway, just in case," said Theo, frantically chopping. "Hi, honey. You don't want to be without coffee."

"Dad!" yelled Delia, bursting into the room behind Aunt Margaret. "I need you!"

"I'll be there in two minutes, honey," said Theo. "Please stop bellowing into your great-aunt's ear."

"I need you now!" yelled Delia. "You're the one who says school is so important!"

"I can help you, Delia," said Wilhelmina.

Delia turned a venomous glare upon Wilhelmina. "I don't want your help," she said, then spun around, ran back into Theo and Cleo's bedroom, and slammed the door. Next, behind Wilhelmina, Cleo entered the kitchen, holding a shopping bag and a pink box. She smelled of cold.

"Hi, honey," she said. "What does Delia need? I'll help her."

"She needs a more respectful means of expressing her feelings," said Theo testily. "But I gather she also needs something school-related, rather urgently."

"I'll check," said Cleo, moving around Wilhelmina, placing the box on the table. It was a doughnut box, from Alfie Fang's. "How was the dentist, Wilhelmina?" she said.

"Mom!" said Wilhelmina in confusion. "What are you doing?"

"I'm feeling a little better," said Cleo. "So I filled up the tires and topped off the gas."

"And you went to Alfie Fang's?" said Wilhelmina, studying her mother dubiously. Cleo didn't look better. Her eyes were bloodshot, and her nose was still puffy and raw. "We must've just missed each other!"

"We wanted you to have doughnuts for your trip," said Cleo. "Any idea what category of problem Delia's having?"

"No clue," said Theo.

"Okay, I'm going in."

This was definitely a different Cleo. As Wilhelmina watched her shrug out of her coat and march off to help Delia, she saw her other mother emerging from the fog. Her bright and alert mother. *Well,* thought Wilhelmina, with a small stab of resentment. It was about time.

"Wilhelmina, hon?" said Theo, sweeping in beside her. "You have masks? You have your phones? Don't forget a scarf, or something to make a pillow for your lumbar. Should you bring your sunglasses? You'll be driving southwest all afternoon. Do you have both acetaminophen and ibuprofen? Oh!" he said, patting his own head as if struck by a thought. "I want to check you have the spare tire, and a jack and a wrench. And I'll get you a flashlight. Have you downloaded any podcasts?"

"Dad!" said Wilhelmina. "We're going to Pennsylvania! Not the moon!"

"Stop and rest at least every two hours," continued Theo. "You promise, honey? Long drives are tiring. You know not to drive if you've taken metaxalone, right?"

Metaxalone was a muscle relaxant Wilhelmina took sometimes, and of course she knew that. *"Dad,"* she said. The chaos, or Theo's badgering, or *something* was making her emotional. She felt crowded, and also strange about the journey ahead, as if she wasn't sure it was a good idea. She wished everyone would leave her alone. She wished they could stop preparing, and just go.

She went to her bedroom and packed a bag.

ON A DAY WITH GOOD TRAFFIC, it was a drive of four and a half or five hours to the aunts' home in northeast Pennsylvania, and one Wilhelmina knew well, woven as it was into the earliest patterns of her life. But she'd never been behind the wheel before on that drive, or driven so far anywhere in one day. Anticipating the pain that would start in her neck, spread to her pecs and shoulders, then set fire to her hands, she began alternating acetaminophen and ibuprofen before they started.

The sun blazed relentlessly as they drove west on the Massachusetts Turnpike. When Wilhelmina had ordered new glasses, she hadn't ordered new prescription sunglasses. Now she regretted it, because after a few days of wearing her new glasses, her old prescription sunglasses were distorting her sense of space. Should a person with depth perception problems be directing a metal box along a path clogged with other moving metal boxes, at seventy miles per hour? Wilhelmina put her new glasses back on and suffered, hoping for cloud cover that never came.

In the back seat, Aunt Margaret gazed through the window dreamily. She'd asked to sit in the back so that she could let her mind wander, as she always did on car rides. She'd attached a pink button to her coat. In red and blue letters, it said JOE BIDEN. Under that in smaller print it said, I GUESS. Beside that button was another, bigger button showing a luminous painting of Kamala Harris, and under Kamala, the words I'M SPEAKING.

Beside Wilhelmina sat Esther, with the doughnut box perched on her lap. She wore a determined and slightly grim expression, and Wilhelmina wondered where that expression came from, because she had a feeling she'd seen it on Esther's face now and then recently. She tried to recall, had that expression always been in Esther's repertoire, or had she changed at some point? Aunt Margaret and Esther *had* changed, she remembered, when Frankie died. Their movements had slowed noticeably, as if walking and sitting down had become painful, or as if, very suddenly, they were old. For a while, their speech had also changed. They'd seemed to pause before every statement, as if something kept rising into their throats to stop them speaking. Wilhelmina had understood the pause, because her own life had become filled with new, swollen pauses. Every thought was suspended, stuck behind a sort of gluey mass. It was grief, she knew, filling her up like pus around a wound.

"Are you all right, Wilhelmina?" Esther asked gently.

"Yes," said Wilhelmina, shaking herself out of her reverie. "I'm fine."

"You had a very serious look on your face," said Esther.

"Did I?"

"I thought you might be worrying about the election."

Wilhelmina grasped for another, any other, topic. "Are the doughnuts safe?" she asked, wondering, with perfect awareness of the absurdity of it, if she was supposed to be *helping* them in some way.

"Certainly they are," said Esther. "Want one?"

"No," said Wilhelmina. "I just wanted to make sure they were . . . comfortable. Would you like to listen to a podcast?" she added hastily.

"Maybe in a bit," said Esther. "Right now I'm content to admire the sunlight on the leaves."

"Isn't it beautiful?" said Aunt Margaret from the back seat. "This might just turn out to be the best day of the year to go home."

"You read my mind," said Esther. "Wilhelmina, I guess you've never been to the house in early November?"

"I expect the yard will be a little overrun, but the trees will be beautiful," said Aunt Margaret.

"The house will be cold as a penguin's schmeckel," said Esther. Wilhelmina didn't know that word, but her best guess was that it meant "penis." Yiddish seemed to have a hundred words for "penis."

"I'm not altogether certain penguins have schmeckels, dear," said Aunt Margaret. "In fact, I rather think they don't."

"What?" said Esther, who seemed quite intrigued by this. "What do they do then, shoot their stuff out of their ear?"

"I'm remembering now," said Aunt Margaret. "I think most birds just have, you know, *openings*."

"Openings!"

"Yes. They press their openings together. There's a term for it. I can't recall what it is."

"You're pulling my leg."

"I'm not," said Aunt Margaret. "I read an article in *National Geographic*."

"Well," said Esther, shaking her head. "Mother Nature is a wonder. A polar bear, then?"

"Yes, I'm quite sure a polar bear would have a schmeckel."

"Then that's how cold the house will be," said Esther. "It takes a long time to bring up a big old house like that. By the time it warms up, we'll be leaving again."

"But what a treat," said Aunt Margaret, "to go home unexpectedly for a day. It's like seeing a shooting star, isn't it?"

"I hope it lasts longer than that," said Esther with a teasing smile.

"Our lives are as brief as shooting stars," said Aunt Margaret, "if you step back far enough."

On that philosophical note, the aunts subsided into silence. Wilhelmina's phone buzzed occasionally in her pocket as she drove. She hadn't told Julie or Bee where she was going. She couldn't have articulated why not, and it was starting to occur to her that when they found out, they might think it was strange that she hadn't said goodbye. In fact, they might not like it. None of them had gone on any trips since the start of the pandemic. Bee had canceled the college visits he'd been planning last spring, and Julie's family hadn't done their usual summer drive to North Carolina to visit her father's family. Now here she was crossing state lines, and she hadn't let them know.

Wilhelmina gripped the wheel harder, squinted into the sun, and instructed herself to do a thing she was doing a lot lately: quit thinking about it.

IN CONNECTICUT, when they stopped at a service plaza to use the restrooms, Wilhelmina was upset by the number of people wearing their masks on their chins.

"We'll see more of that at home, of course," said Esther, as they pulled back onto the highway.

"We'll see more of a lot of things," said Aunt Margaret cryptically.

Wilhelmina's neck was aching. Her eyes were aching, and the muscles all around her collarbone were aching. Every other driver in Connecticut seemed in top physical condition, perfectly able to speed, swerve, honk, and cross multiple lanes of traffic without signaling.

"If Massachusetts drivers are called Massholes," she said, "what are Connecticut drivers called?"

"Hm," said Aunt Margaret from the back seat. "I feel like we should be able to do something with 'Connecticut' and 'contemptible.' 'Contempticutible'?"

"That's awful," said Esther.

"I see the way they keep Connecticutting you off, Wilhelmina."

"Margeleh," said Esther, her mouth twitching into a smile that, in turn, caused Aunt Margaret to look very pleased with herself. "Por favor, stop before I have to kill myself. Wilhelmina, just hold on a little longer. Quite soon, we'll pass through a door."

"What?" cried Wilhelmina. "I have to drive through a door?"

"She doesn't mean a literal door," said Aunt Margaret. "For heaven's sake, Esther, don't scare the child."

"I apologize," said Esther. "I shouldn't be loose with my metaphors while you're driving in stressful conditions. I only meant a threshold. A place where things change. Do you ever pass through a sort of door, Wilhelmina, and noticed that everything on the other side feels different?"

"I guess."

"It *could* be a literal door, of course," said Aunt Margaret. "Like the door to our house. I confess a sense of peace comes upon me whenever I enter our house, Esther. Or it could be a revolving door, like to a department store. Or a bus door, or an attic door. But I also feel it when I step into any of Frankie's gardens."

"As do I," said Esther.

"Or when I walk into a lake, then switch from walking to swimming."

"I feel it sometimes when I put on certain clothes," said Esther. "Like I've stepped into a slightly different realm."

"I think a storm can be a door," said Aunt Margaret.

"But," said Wilhelmina, "you're just calling *everything* a door. I mean, you're talking about feelings and sensations. Like the way a soft sweater makes you feel different, or the way a house smells when you step inside it."

"It does involve feelings, yes," said Esther. "But sometimes the feelings are an indicator that you've crossed the threshold into a different kind of space. Maybe even a sacred space. It bears noticing. Sometimes there are opportunities behind doors."

"Esther is very sensitive to doors and thresholds," said Aunt Margaret approvingly.

"You have your own sensitivities, Margie," said Esther.

"Pay attention to it, dear," said Aunt Margaret, "the next time you reach for a dress and you're not sure why you know it's the one you need to wear that day. Or the next time you step out of an elevator."

Wilhelmina glanced at Aunt Margaret sharply in the rearview mirror. But she was gazing out the window again, wearing her usual placid car expression. Next Wilhelmina's eyes shot to the doughnut box in Esther's lap. It looked normal, just a box—not glowing, or turning into a bird, or sparkling with a badly punctuated message.

"There now," said Esther. "I think we've reached it. Do you feel the difference?"

What Wilhelmina felt was exasperation. She had no patience for Esther's doors; of course it felt different when you walked into a house, or a store, or a lake. Of course the driving would get easier as they passed out of the parts of Connecticut that fed New York City, into the more rural parts that led into New York State. She found herself not wanting the driving to be different, just to spite Esther.

But it *was* different now, and Wilhelmina couldn't quite figure out why. The traffic around them was the same, the number of lanes the same. The blaring sun, the autumn leaves, the boring gray road with its boring white lines. A car with Connecticut plates swerved across three lanes right in front of her without signaling, the same way all these drivers seemed to think it was okay to do, and Wilhelmina was unconcerned. Her neck still hurt; everything still hurt. But it was like she'd entered a zone of driving ease. Nothing rattled her.

I've just gotten used to it, she told herself. *I'm the one who's changed.*

AROUND THE TIME they crossed into New York State, the sun dropped behind the hills. Wilhelmina's relief was extreme.

They stopped again, this time for gas, and Wilhelmina stretched her aching arms against the outside of the car. Esther, who had arthritis, was stiff too; she went on a slow walk around the parking lot. Wilhelmina's shoulders and neck were turned in on themselves, composed of pain. She cleaned her hands with an alcohol wipe and medicated again. Then the aunts decided to break open the doughnuts before getting back on the road.

Nothing weird happened; the doughnuts were just doughnuts. Wilhelmina chose a youtiao, which was a long, airy, Chinese doughnut made with salt, baking soda, and baking powder, rather than sugar and yeast. Wilhelmina liked an unsweet doughnut on occasion. Hers was definitely not stale.

It was dusk as they crossed into Pennsylvania and exited the interstate. The roads narrowed and the traffic lessened. They began to see crossroads, farms, houses with lights in the windows, political signs in support of both candidates. Occasionally they saw dramatic displays of flags and absolutely gigantic banners, stretched across the tree trunks on the roadside.

The giant displays were always in support of the president, and Wilhelmina was unprepared for what they did to her. Why? Why was she unprepared? It was nothing she hadn't seen before. Maybe more of it than she was used to in the Boston area, where voters leaned left. But nothing new. And she'd guarded herself so well.

So why did it hurt so much? Why did every sign feel like a brand-new betrayal—and why was each one a surprise? She knew this already. She *knew* that they loved their bragging, racist, homophobic bully, that they hated the people she loved. So why did it feel like a new wound, every time?

"Why do the signs have to be so *big*?" said Wilhelmina.

"The weaker your argument," said Aunt Margaret from the back seat, "the louder you need to yell."

"My head hurts from all the yelling," said Esther.

"Oh, Esther," said Aunt Margaret, sighing. "My head hurts too."

BY THE TIME Wilhelmina pulled the car into the aunts' driveway, it was dark enough that the house and the yard, the gardens and trees were no more than inky, looming shapes. It was a comfort to Wilhelmina somehow, almost as if she wasn't really here yet, not quite. The house would reveal itself to her in stages so that she could adjust. She'd announced her intention to drive the aunts home in a moment of instant decision. She hadn't thought—hadn't let herself think—how it would feel to be here.

Wilhelmina's Pennsylvania summers had stopped a couple of years before Frankie had died. In fact, her last summer here had been the summer before the 2016 presidential election, the summer she was fourteen. The summer after that, instead of Wilhelmina going to Pennsylvania, Frankie had come to Boston, to take part in a clinical trial at one of the hospitals. The summer after that, Frankie had died. Wilhelmina had been to the house for short trips since then, but always with the rest of the family. Never just her and the aunts.

While Esther made her way down into the basement to turn on the breakers and the water, Aunt Margaret and Wilhelmina climbed the porch to the front door.

"We'll turn up the heat," Aunt Margaret said, fumbling for her keys, "and see if we have enough wood for a fire. Do you want to sleep downstairs, Wilhelmina? Your little attic room will be the last part of the house to get warm!"

"That's okay," said Wilhelmina quickly, alarmed at the notion of being kept from her room. "I'll sleep there anyway."

"All right, well, you let us know if you change your mind," said Aunt Margaret, pushing the door open. "It feels close to freezing out here."

Wilhelmina stepped into the house, thinking about Esther's thresholds. As Aunt Margaret passed through the foyer and into the kitchen, turning on lights and making small, happy exclamations at seeing this painting, that bookshelf; as she came out again and crossed into the living room, where she expressed her pleasure at the rack full of wood beside the fireplace, Wilhelmina stood still, letting the house illuminate itself in circles of golden light around her. She smelled long-gone wood-fires, and a familiar, faint scent like a mix of vinegar and herbs that she thought of as the Pennsylvania house smell. Before her, a staircase stretched up into darkness, the staircase on which she'd sat a hundred times, eavesdropping.

There was nothing to eavesdrop on now, because she was grown-up, and Frankie was dead. Wilhelmina wondered if she'd volunteered for this drive for a reason to do with Esther's doors after all. Not because she'd wanted to cross a threshold into a different space, exactly. More because she'd wanted to step into a different time.

WILHELMINA'S ROOM was colder than she'd anticipated, and dimly lit from weak bulbs in the old lamps on the desk and the small bedside bookshelf. The dimness suited her.

When she sat on the bed, she could feel the frigid outside air seeping through the glass of the dormer window. She sneezed, then wondered how much dust the room's darkness was hiding. Her hand reached instinctively for the thing her hand always reached for when she first entered this room and sat on the bed—the three blue stones in the windowsill. During her very first summer with the aunts, Frankie had given her these stones. She'd been five, and excited, happy to be here, not particularly homesick the way some children might be, and she'd loved her attic room. But she'd had a couple of nightmares her first few nights. When she'd woken from them, she'd felt very far from other people.

In the kitchen one morning after one of her nightmares, Frankie had pulled Wilhelmina into her lap. Wilhelmina had snaked her arms around Frankie's warm, soft body, resting her ear on Frankie's chest.

"You can sleep on the second floor like we do, dear," Frankie had said. "We have lots of bedrooms."

"Yes, Wilhelmineleh!" said Esther. "You can even sleep in one of our rooms if you want." But Wilhelmina had wanted her up-high room with the sycamore outside the window. It was all hers, and it felt like a tree house.

So Frankie had given her three blue stones. She'd told Wilhelmina that Aunt Margaret had found them on a secret beach and that one was Esther, one was Aunt Margaret, and one was she, Frankie.

"I can give you two more for your parents, if you like," she said.

"No, you aunts are enough," said Wilhelmina.

The next time she had a nightmare, she woke in the usual panic, then saw the stones in the windowsill, blue and opalescent in the moonlight. When she sat up and touched them, her breathing calmed, because she knew that her aunts were real and that the nightmare was not. She felt the aunts sleeping in their beds on the floor below hers. She went back to sleep.

Wilhelmina cupped the stones in her hands. Today they were small, curved oblongs of ice, so cold that a surprised squeak rose from the back of her throat, but they were also just as she remembered them. Beautiful, and blue wherever the light touched them. They calmed her.

As she grew calm, the reality of where she was filled in around her, infusing her with sadness. On instinct, she called Bee.

"Hey, elephant," he said.

"Hey," said Wilhelmina. "Guess where I am."

"New Zealand?" said Bee.

Wilhelmina snorted. "I'm at the aunts' house."

"What!" he said. "In Pennsylvania?"

"Yes."

"How did that happen?"

"Their ballots didn't arrive," she said. "So I drove them home to vote."

"Oh my god, Wil!" he said. "Pennsylvania is a swing state! You're a hero!"

It hadn't occurred to her to expect this reaction. "No, I'm not."

"Wait, when?" he said. "I saw you yesterday! You drove there today?"

"Yeah."

"Why didn't you tell me?"

"It all—happened really fast," she said, which made her obscurely unhappy, because it felt like a half-truth. She'd gone to sleep last night knowing she might be driving to Pennsylvania today. She'd gone to the dentist this morning. She'd texted with Julie, kind of a lot, and never mentioned it.

"Yeah, heroics often need to happen fast," he said. "It's, like, in the hero handbook. Does Julie know?"

"No," she said. "You can tell her."

"I'm really proud of you. Pennsylvania has like twenty electoral votes! It's like the swingiest swing state!"

"Elephant!" she said. "You're getting too excited. Anyway, Florida has twenty-nine."

"Does your neck hurt?"

"No," she said, because if she told him how much her neck hurt, he would say more about how she was a hero.

"Julie's going to love this," he said. "I'm texting her while we're talking."

"Bee, please stop," she said. "Please stop thinking so highly of me."

"But it's really fucking cool, Wil," he said. "Come on. You have to see it. The GOP in Pennsylvania's been trying so hard to suppress mail-in votes, which is obviously working if the aunts didn't get their ballots. So what are people doing? They're driving across the fucking land to vote! I can't help it. It makes me hopeful."

"Stop!" said Wilhelmina. "Please stop! I can't talk about hope!"

"Okay, sorry," he said, then added in a teeny, tiny, high-pitched voice designed to make her laugh, "But I'm hopeful, elephant."

Hope is ignorant, Wilhelmina didn't say. *I came here for myself, just for myself,* she didn't say. *I miss you, and I'm mad at you, and I despise myself for being mad at you,* she didn't say. All the things she wasn't saying were creating such a confusing barrier between her and her best friend, her oldest friend. She'd never felt cut off from him like this before.

"I saw Julie's necklace," she said, because the barrier of untruths was too painful. "A crow had it. It flew away."

"Oh! That sucks," he said. "Hey! Maybe I should get her a replacement. What do you think?"

Wilhelmina hated that idea so much that for a moment, she couldn't speak. The necklaces were from *her.*

"A crow!" Bee went on. "You know, I kind of like the idea of the crows keeping our necklaces for us. Like, hanging on to them for us. Maybe her necklace is having its own adventures. Kind of appropriate for Julie, don't you think? I mean, you did give her the elephant with wings."

Tears were filling Wilhelmina's eyes. Outside her room, she heard someone on the stairs. "Listen, one of the aunts is coming," she said. "I'll talk to you soon, okay?"

"I love you, hero," he said. "Sweet dreams!"

Wilhelmina dropped her phone into her lap, then noticed she was still holding the stones in her other hand. As she placed them back onto the windowsill, Aunt Margaret appeared in the doorway, a pile of bedding in her arms.

"Good gracious," said Aunt Margaret. "It's like the Arctic up here! We've got a nice, cheery fire downstairs if you'd like to join us, dear. Esther's throwing some dinner together from your father's supplies."

"I'll come down soon," said Wilhelmina, blinking hard to hide her tears.

"Good," said Aunt Margaret, collapsing on the bed beside her, catching her breath. "I'm sure I remember a time not too long ago when I could handle those stairs without huffing and puffing. Now, Wilhelmina, I've brought you one of Frankie's beautiful blankets, because I thought you might like that. But with a nod to reality, I've also brought you one of our good sleeping bags. You could sleep in the yard in the middle of winter in this thing and be warm," she said, placing the floppy sleeping bag and the blanket on the bed between them, then smoothing them with one hand.

"Thank you," said Wilhelmina, whose eyes were on the knitted blanket. It was thick and tightly woven, sky blue, with a pattern of flying black birds.

"There's not much light in this room, is there?" said Aunt Margaret, looking around critically. "I suppose there was never much need for light in the summer."

"No."

"I miss our summers," said Aunt Margaret. "You must always, always consider this your home, my dear."

"Thank you."

"We can't overstate how grateful we are for this," said Aunt Margaret. "I've lived through eighteen presidential elections before this one. Eighteen! Can you believe that? I was just counting them as I came up the stairs. None of them, not *one* of them, has worried me more than this one, Wilhelmina. Not Richard Nixon, not George W. Bush, not even the last one, when this monster came into power. Living in a swing state and not being able to vote—well. It would've broken our hearts."

"I really just—wanted a drive," said Wilhelmina weakly, pulling at Frankie's blanket and wrapping it around her shoulders, like a hug. Like a shield from all this praise.

"Well," said Aunt Margaret, speaking in a gentler voice. Aunt

Margaret was observing her now, one-eyed, with a softer expression on her face. "In that case, thank you for wanting a drive."

With a labored breath, she stood. Briefly, she rested one hand on Wilhelmina's shoulder. "Come eat," she said. Then she left the room.

Alone, Wilhelmina pulled her blanket tighter. It wasn't easy. Her palms were hot and stinging, and her shoulders protested with every movement. *Frankie,* she thought. *Help. I can't do this anymore.*

She remembered, with a flash of incredulity, that when she was young, the aunts had talked about how she would come to live with them for an entire year. A year between high school and college. *This* year; it was supposed to have been *this* year.

Wilhelmina fell back onto the bed, laughing. How many times had she looked forward happily to this year? The aunts "teaching her all their best lessons," and learning all of hers. *What lessons have you taught me this year, Frankie?* Wilhelmina asked her. *Huh? You died. And what lessons do I have to teach? Monsters can take over the world. They can steal everything for themselves, and laugh when people start dying. They can lie and people will believe them. They can be cruel and people will love them for it. People will* help *them be cruel, not just for one evil reason, but for an entire, endless range of evil reasons. People have so many justifications for being cruel.*

And my power to change any of it is so small, Wilhelmina thought to herself. *An entire day's painful drive will get us two votes in Pennsylvania.*

Her phone buzzed, then buzzed again, resting on Frankie's blanket, vibrating against her stomach. Wilhelmina knew it was Julie calling. She wanted Julie's voice, her laughter, her company. Her company for *real,* not through the phone. And she didn't want Julie's praise. While she was thinking about it, the call went to voice mail.

For a few minutes, she lay there, remembering how she used to be able to hear the voices of the aunts at night through her window. She couldn't hear anything now except the sycamore rustling outside.

Through some instinct of Wilhelmina's that she hadn't paid much attention to for a long, long time—maybe since the last time she'd lain here, listening for the aunts?—she sensed that Aunt Margaret and Esther were in the living room, eating bread and cheese and egg salad with hot tea, while huddled around the fire.

With her blanket still around her shoulders, she got up, went downstairs, and joined them.

The aunts had conversations that moved around Wilhelmina, as if they were tossing a ball one to the other and she was inside the circle. She could take part if she wanted, but whether she did or not, she knew she was included. Often she kept quiet on purpose, even as thoughts and questions mounted inside her, because of how it felt to be embraced by the conversation. And then eventually one of them would say, "What do you think, Wilhelmina?" and she would come out with her ideas while they listened, nodding and making exclamations of appreciation or surprise, the same way they did to each other.

During the summer Wilhelmina was eleven, the aunts returned often to a certain conversation. It was like they all kept it tucked in their pockets, so that any of them could pull it out when she wanted it. The conversation was about something that hadn't happened yet, but the aunts could see it coming.

It was the summer of 2013. It wasn't legal for same-sex couples to marry in Pennsylvania, but in some of its bordering states, the marriage laws had changed. And something had happened in the Supreme Court that very summer, a decision requiring the federal government to recognize any same-sex marriage that any state had approved. The plaintiff for that case had been a woman from Pennsylvania, Edie Windsor. The Supreme Court's decision had lit a fire under a lot of butts. Bills were introduced and lawsuits were filed all over, including in Pennsylvania, where advocates hoped to overturn a same-sex marriage ban that had been in place since before Wilhelmina was born.

Wilhelmina had noticed that the aunts' conversations tended to follow a certain pattern. First, someone, usually Frankie or Esther, asked the others if they'd noticed some piece of Pennsylvania-specific news. "Did you see that Brian Sims and Steve McCarter are planning to introduce a bill to the General Assembly?" (The General Assembly was the name of Pennsylvania's legislative branch, and Brian Sims and Steve McCarter were members of the House who supported gay marriage.) Or, "Did you see the ACLU filed suit?"

Next, some chatter would follow. Sometimes it was contemplative or analytical or hopeful. Sometimes you couldn't predict it, like Frankie having a crush on Brian Sims and Esther calling her a cradle robber. Wilhelmina googled him. She supposed he was handsome, for a politician who was like forty. But obviously Frankie wasn't a cradle robber if he was *forty*!

"Look at those bright eyes and those rosy cheeks," Esther said.

"Stop infantilizing the boy," said Frankie.

"You're the one who just called him a boy."

"He's like forty!" said Wilhelmina.

"He's thirty-four," said Esther.

"That's basically forty," said Wilhelmina.

"I defend my right to admire privately the appearance of a grown person who's fighting to make gay marriage legal in Pennsylvania," said Frankie.

Regardless of the shape of the conversation, the next step in the pattern was this: eventually, tears would begin to slide down Aunt Margaret's face.

"Oh, Margie," Frankie would say. At that point, Wilhelmina would move closer to Aunt Margaret, because she knew a group hug was coming and she wanted to be part of it.

She thought about it on her own for a while before finally asking one day, "Aunt Margaret, why does it make you cry?"

"Oh," said Aunt Margaret, her tears beginning anew. "It just hurts, my dear. As if now that things are changing, I can feel everyone's pain all at once, all of it that's ever existed. Does that make sense? I'm not sure how else to explain it."

It made a kind of sense that Wilhelmina could feel, even if she got muddled when she tried to understand the logic. It seemed that when a good thing was happening, one would expect to feel joy. But Aunt Margaret's grief had its place too in the summer they were all living, even though that summer was otherwise composed of happy things.

No group hug followed Wilhelmina's question this time, because Wilhelmina and the aunts were in the car. They were on their way to go camping for a couple nights. But Frankie, who sat in the front passenger seat, found a tissue in one of her bags and passed it to Aunt Margaret, who sat in the back with Wilhelmina.

"Of course," said Frankie, "if this change does happen, we'll have to discuss the practicalities."

"What practicalities are there for us to discuss?" said Esther, who was driving. "We are not a same-sex couple."

"No," said Frankie. "But it might make sense for one of you to marry *me*."

Wilhelmina felt the air in the car change. Beside her, Aunt Margaret was surprised; in front of her, Esther was agitated.

"We have paperwork," Esther said. "We've taken legal steps already."

"But this would add an extra layer of protection," said Frankie. "Simplify some things."

"And complicate others!" said Esther.

"Not now," said Aunt Margaret in a voice that was certain, but trembled with a new rush of tears. "We'll have this conversation, but not now. Not in the car. There's no *room* in the car!"

"That's true," said Frankie. "I'm sorry, love. It's not a car conversation."

Now Wilhelmina was the one who was surprised. Not by the rush of emotion that had risen so quickly; the aunts often rustled like trees with changing emotion. She was surprised by the realization that some conversations were car conversations and some weren't.

"Wait," she said. "What's a car conversation?"

"Now, that is an excellent question," said Esther, smiling softly as she drove. "There's no escape in a car. I suppose it needs to be a conversation everyone wants to have."

"It also needs to be about something you don't mind being completely surrounded by," said Aunt Margaret.

"So, a topic that isn't like someone else's tuna sandwich," said Esther.

"Or like a squirrel that's gotten out of its box," said Frankie.

"That sounds terrifying," said Esther. "Why would you have a boxed squirrel in the car?"

"You wouldn't. That's the point."

"Some conversations benefit from an open sky and a wide view," said Aunt Margaret. "So there's room for your feelings to expand. There's not much room in a car."

"So, are we having a car conversation now?" said Esther. "What do you think, Wilhelmina?"

"I think so," said Wilhelmina.

"So then we need to figure out what changed between the last conversation and this conversation," said Esther.

Wilhelmina thought about that for a bit. "The last conversation scared Aunt Margaret," she finally said.

"Oh, Wilhelmina," said Aunt Margaret, beginning to drip with tears again. "You're right. It did scare me."

"No scary conversations in the car, then," said Frankie softly, turning back and passing Aunt Margaret another tissue.

It was a busy summer for the aunts, busier than usual. Frankie had had another surgery for ovarian cancer in the spring, and it was taking her longer to get her strength back this time than it had last time. Or anyway, that's what everyone said; Wilhelmina couldn't remember last time. She'd been very young. Frankie seemed regular to Wilhelmina, aside from every four weeks or so, when she had chemo and felt sick for a few days. "I'm completely fine," she always said, in a voice Wilhelmina believed. She was just tired, that was all. But it did mean that Esther and Aunt Margaret were taking on more of the chores.

Also, this summer, the aunts were renovating, because Esther and Aunt Margaret were starting a new business that they intended to run from home. Esther had long been some kind of consultant and Aunt Margaret an accountant and bookkeeper, each of them working in a small office in town, right down the street from each other. They'd now retired, but not with the intention of ceasing to work. They wanted to keep working, and do so together.

Beside the house was the broken-down carriage house with a sagging roof and a bare cement floor. For years, Frankie had encouraged the lilacs, forsythia, and masses of thorny roses to grow wild and tall around it, to deter anyone, especially their young summer resident, from trying to find a way inside, because it wasn't safe. Wilhelmina had always looked upon that corner of the yard as impenetrable.

But now the flora was cleared, the old structure was torn down, and atop the strong concrete base, a team of men were building a small office. It was going to have running water and electricity and its own teeny bathroom. It was going to have a woodstove and a vaulted ceiling. It was going to have a sign beside the door, with Esther's and Aunt Margaret's names in lights: PÉREZ AND HART, SOULFUL CONSULTANTS.

The work was almost done. The men were now nail-gunning shingles to the outside, which was why the aunts and Wilhelmina were going camping for a few days, as they'd done a couple other times that summer too, whenever the noise had reached nerve-fraying propor-tions. They were driving to Hickory Run State Park, which had a lake for swimming, a waterfall Aunt Margaret adored, and a gigantic, flat stretch of land completely crowded with boulders. It was called the Boulder Field, and it wasn't like other places Wilhelmina had ever been. She loved to scramble across it on her sturdy, stompy feet. It was thought to be a relic from a time hundreds of thousands of years ago when a retreating glacier had dropped its load of boulders, the same way Wilhelmina's shoes, after a day at the beach, dropped clumps of sand around the house.

In the car as they drove to Hickory Run, Wilhelmina began to work her way through a few questions she was keeping to herself. If two of the aunts married, what would happen to the other aunt? If two of the aunts married, why did one of them need to be Frankie particu-larly? And why was Aunt Margaret scared?

She wondered if the questions were connected. Was Aunt Margaret scared because she didn't want to be the aunt who didn't get married?

She waited until the car had entered the narrow, winding roads of the park. She waited until they'd located the cabin in which they would be staying, which had a name she liked, written on a board above the entrance: RUFFED GROUSE. She waited until they'd parked and climbed out, because she understood that it wasn't a car conversation. She put the question to Esther after Frankie and Aunt Margaret had gone bus-tling into the cabin, because she considered Esther to be the most neu-tral party.

"If two of you marry each other," she said, "will the third one of you be . . . left out?"

"Oh, no, bubeleh!" Esther cried, with more passion than Wil-helmina had been expecting. "Nothing like that."

"What's that?" said Aunt Margaret, coming out of the cabin again. "What's wrong, Esther?"

"Wilhelmina asked if one of us would be left out, if the other two married," said Esther.

"Oh, no, dear!" cried Aunt Margaret, in such a perfect echo of Esther's tone that for some reason, tears pricked Wilhelmina's throat. "Never. It would only be a legal decision, a practical one. When people are married, certain rights become straightforward in the eyes of the law, like, oh, boring things like beneficiaries, or who gets to make medical decisions. It wouldn't change how we live, Wilhelmina. Is this conversation upsetting you? We don't need to talk about it in front of you if it makes you worry!"

"You can talk about it," said Wilhelmina. "That was the only part I was worried about."

"All right," said Aunt Margaret, coming to Wilhelmina and pulling her into a hug. Aunt Margaret was a good hugger, so Wilhelmina welcomed the hug, even though she was confused. Aunt Margaret didn't seem scared of being left out. So something else was scaring her.

While Frankie and Esther rested, Wilhelmina and Aunt Margaret went to the lake. It was smaller than the lake near the aunts' house and had no secret beach with blue stones, but its lack of familiarity made it interesting. Wilhelmina ignored the floating buoys that enclosed the designated swimming area and set out for an adventure on her own. She didn't rush; her progress was steady and deliberate, just as it was when she moved across land. Warm sun, cold water, and strong swimming set her body tingling with joy.

While she was lying on her blanket drying off, Aunt Margaret let her borrow her cell phone to call Bee and Julie. Bee wasn't home, which made Wilhelmina miss him with a sweet yearning, but at least his mother answered the phone, rather than his father. She sounded hassled, and tired. Bee had a new little sister that summer. So did Julie.

Julie answered on the first ring. "Hey!" she said. "Miss you."

"Miss you too," said Wilhelmina.

"We're driving home," said Julie, who was on her mother's cell phone.

"Soccer or chess?" said Wilhelmina.

"Chess," said Julie. "A tournament."

Wilhelmina knew that Julie gritted her teeth through chess tournaments. She always did well, but it wasn't fun. Also, at tournaments, she was usually one of few girls and often the only Black girl. "I always feel like I have to prove something," she'd told Wilhelmina and Bee. "You know?" But her parents wanted her to persevere, so she did. They told her it would look good on her college applications someday, which Wilhelmina found alarming, because her parents never talked about college applications. "Should I be thinking about my college applications?" she'd asked her father once. "What?" he'd said, startled. "No, Wilhelmina. You're eleven."

"I'm sorry I'm not home!" said Wilhelmina. "How was it?"

"Fine," said Julie. "Won three, lost one. I played against a five-year-old."

"What!"

"He's a child genius, apparently," said Julie. "It was my hardest win. But oh my god, Wil, it took him *forever* to write his notations."

"Was he writing different notations from everyone else?"

"No! Exactly the same! But he's five! He can't write yet!"

Wilhelmina's laughter felt like music. "I knew you would laugh like that," said Julie. "That's why I wanted to tell you. I miss you!"

"Me too," said Wilhelmina. "My aunts want you to come visit."

"I know," said Julie. "My parents say maybe next summer."

"Did you get the blue stone I sent?"

"Yeah," said Julie. "I keep it in my pocket."

For dinner that night, they had spaghetti with homemade meatballs and sauce that Frankie had cooked ahead of time and frozen, plus a salad Wilhelmina made with normal salad ingredients like lettuce and tomatoes, but also blueberries and mint. Wilhelmina thought that camping spaghetti made by Frankie, with a salad made of things Frankie had grown, might be her favorite meal. After dinner, she washed the dishes with Esther at the outside pump, then climbed into bed early, exhausted and happy, not too worried about the questions to which she had no answers. That night, it rained, a steady thrumming on the roof right above their heads. An owl found them, hooting its way into Wilhelmina's dreams.

In the morning, Wilhelmina and the aunts drove to the Boulder Field.

"Have you met the ranger?" asked Esther, who was driving again. "I ran into her this morning at the bathroom. She told me the attorney general refuses to defend the marriage ban in court!"

"Really?" said Frankie. "Are you okay with this conversation, Margie?" she added, glancing back at Aunt Margaret.

"I have no problem with news," said Aunt Margaret placidly.

"She says the ban is unconstitutional!" said Esther.

"Has the governor responded?" asked Frankie.

Esther snorted. "Not yet. I'm sure he's checking with his donors."

"You talked about all of this with the park ranger?" said Aunt Margaret, impressed.

"Sometimes you can just sense a kindred soul," said Esther.

"Yes," said Aunt Margaret. "That's true. On the other topic," she added. "The one we won't talk about in the car. I want to reiterate that I *will* talk about it. I just need some time." She was awash in a pool of sadness, but she was speaking bravely. Wilhelmina felt it.

"Thank you, Margie," said Frankie.

A long silence followed, during which Wilhelmina could feel a sort of desperate resistance coming from Esther. Esther was battling with something inside herself, something that was causing her great distress.

Finally, her tight grip on the steering wheel loosened, and a tear trickled down her cheek. She said, "I'll be willing to talk about it too."

"Thank you, Esther," said Frankie.

Wilhelmina knew that this was the moment to say, *What's going on? What is this about?* But something stopped her. It was partly a sense, unfamiliar and confusing, that she was on the outside of this particular conversation, that they didn't entirely remember she was there. No one was going to smile at her and say, *What do you think, Wilhelmina?*

But maybe it was also because she was beginning to guess what it was about. Yesterday, Aunt Margaret had talked about beneficiaries, about medical decisions. Those words had connected with Wilhelmina's understanding that Frankie had had surgery in the spring, and that every few weeks, she went in to the doctor for chemo. The surgery had gone well, and the chemo was routine. It was normal that Frankie was tired, and that the chemo was rough sometimes. Everyone said so. Her hair was different now too—her silver crown of braids was gone and instead she had a short arrangement of soft, white fuzz—but that was normal too, for people to change their hair.

Nonetheless, despite how normal everything was, Wilhelmina was beginning to experience a small blockage in the flow of her curiosity. She was inclined to look out the window at the trees instead.

At the Boulder Field, the aunts gamely commenced to climb among the cluster of boulders nearest the edge. Then, fairly soon, they found comfortable rocks to sit down upon while sharing a thermos of coffee, as they always did. The aunts liked to sit and survey the expanse of uneven gray rock, but they left the exploration to Wilhelmina, who had young ankles.

The field spread out for about sixteen acres, and Wilhelmina liked to hike all the way to the far side. It required a slow, careful pace. Some of the smaller boulders rocked when you stepped on them, and some of the hugest were too steep to climb. She liked to veer slightly to the right as she began, to visit the single spindly pine tree that had pushed its way up through an impossible terrain. The Boulder Field was surrounded by woodlands, but it took an unusual tree to grow in its middle. When she reached the tree, she patted its trunk. Then, steadily, she continued on.

Most of the rocks were gray and smooth, but occasionally she discovered one with a touch of color or sparkle. When she came upon a bluish boulder, she briefly enjoyed imagining that this was the pebbly beach with the blue stones and she'd shrunk to the size of a mouse. She wished she could tell Bee. Then she wondered what had created that pebbly beach. Another glacier? She wondered where lakes came from. When a noisy group of kids mostly older than she passed by, she wondered how to study them without them studying her.

There were seven of them: three girls and four boys. When she felt the eyes of one of the boys on her, a dark-haired boy with a weird, gangly-looking bird on his T-shirt, she changed her route subtly to discourage him from talking to her, and took care not to look into his face. They were just very . . . tight-knit and loud. One of the older boys, a blond one, wore no shirt. He had muscles she might expect to see in an underwear ad, which Wilhelmina found exquisitely embarrassing. She wished for Julie. It was funny, sometimes she wished for Bee and sometimes she wished for Julie. She just knew Julie would say something about that shirtless boy that would make her giggle and feel less weird.

Much to her relief, the group moved on. Once alone, she sat down for a bit. Something was tugging at her, something she wasn't sure she liked. She was thinking, for some reason, about Bee's sadness. Bee wasn't always sad, of course, but when he was sad, Wilhelmina could feel the force of it. And she never felt the need to guard herself from it. Bee's sadness wasn't threatening to her. It just *was*.

Same with the pain Aunt Margaret felt for the whole world, now that the marriage laws were changing. Wilhelmina could feel that pain too, but it didn't unbalance her.

The aunts' sadness when they talked about marrying Frankie was different somehow. It wasn't just their sadness. A deep-down part of Wilhelmina sensed that it was her sadness too.

She pushed up from the boulder she sat upon and continued to explore. With a decision that wasn't entirely conscious, she resolved to leave the topic out here on the rocks. She wasn't going to think about it anymore.

When Wilhelmina returned to the aunts, she had a scrape on one shin from bashing into a sharp rock, and she was ever-so-slightly grouchy.

"Does that hurt, bubeleh?" asked Esther, her face pursed in concern.

"It's fine," said Wilhelmina, more snappishly than she ever spoke to the aunts. She scrambled past Aunt Margaret and Esther, who were sitting together, and on to Frankie, who was sitting with a thin man with a ring of graying hair who looked slightly familiar to Wilhelmina.

"And that's Angela," the man was saying in a rumbly, singsong voice, "the one with blond hair who's waving her arms like a windmill. And Raimondo there at the back, the dark-haired boy, our youngest. It's his middle name, but it was my wife's brother's name, so he forebears and lets us use it. We call him our Ray of light."

"How nice," said Frankie. "You must love to have them all here at once."

"I wish it could happen more often," said the man, who had a sweet smile. "They live so far away."

"Allow me to introduce my great-niece Wilhelmina," said Frankie. "We have her all summer. It's one of the joys of our lives."

"Nice to meet you, Wilhelmina," said the man, who looked old to Wilhelmina, but younger than the aunts. Less gray, more boisterous. And more and more familiar. For some reason, Wilhelmina could picture this graying man on a blanket on a beach, at the lake near the aunts' house. She could see the golden light in the air around him, and feel herself wrapped in a towel, shivering in the sun. Was that weird? She spun back to peer at the kids out on the rocks, who were making more noise than seemed possible. Had she seen any of them before? They were too far away for her to isolate their features, and she didn't want to attract their attention.

"Nice to meet you," said Wilhelmina.

"How was your adventure, dear?" asked Frankie.

"Fine."

"Shall we head back for some lunch?"

"Okay."

"All right," said Frankie, pushing herself up with knees that crackled. "It was lovely to meet you, Rudy," she said to the man. "Enjoy your grandchildren." Then the aunts drove back to the cabin, where Frankie made tuna sandwiches with pickles and no celery, Wilhelmina's favorite way to eat a tuna sandwich. After lunch, she went swimming again with Aunt Margaret. The water felt strange on her scraped shin, but in a nice way, like it was numbing the sting.

The next morning, they visited the waterfall, then puttered around for a while, a sunny, lazy day. It was late afternoon when they began to pack the car.

Now that Wilhelmina was resisting certain topics inside her thoughts, it was, perhaps, fortuitous that Aunt Margaret had a low tolerance for the related conversations. Wilhelmina didn't need to think about her own low tolerance, because Aunt Margaret would always raise objections before Wilhelmina got uncomfortable enough to notice.

Nonetheless, it was a different mode of being for Wilhelmina. She wasn't a natural non-thinker. Not thinking about something required some defenses, and not thinking about the fact that she wasn't thinking required even more. Not just a tight web of vines, but maybe a few well-placed thorns.

On the car ride home from Hickory Run, Esther asked Frankie to remind her when her next chemo appointment was.

"About ten days, I think," said Frankie.

"It'll be nice when the renovations are behind us, and we have a routine of working from home," said Esther. "We'll be able to be more present and helpful."

"We should have done this sooner," said Aunt Margaret from the back seat.

"Well," said Frankie. "Your jobs were paying for our lives!"

"But we could have done it sooner," said Aunt Margaret.

Frankie paused for a moment. When she spoke, her voice was gentle. "We still have time."

Wilhelmina changed the subject. She was unpracticed, so she did it abruptly, and a little too loud. "How did you know that man you were talking to yesterday?" she said.

The aunts were startled. Frankie, who was in the front passenger seat, shot her a puzzled glance in the rearview mirror.

"The one with the grandkids," Wilhelmina said. "You called him Rudy."

"Ah," said Frankie. "I met him for the first time yesterday. He seemed to want to talk about his grandchildren, so I lent him an ear. Why do you ask, Wilhelmina?"

"I just wondered. He looked familiar. I thought maybe I'd seen him at the lake before."

"You mean the lake at home?" said Frankie, puzzled again. "You've seen him at our lake?"

"I mean, maybe. I don't remember."

"Well!" said Aunt Margaret. "I'll have to watch for him. Though I'm afraid I hardly paid him any attention."

"Me neither," said Esther.

"Next time I go swimming, I'll stand at a high point on the beach and bellow his name," said Aunt Margaret.

"Oh, yes, that'll make him eager to befriend you," said Esther. "You should do the same thing in grocery stores until you find him. Assuming it's the same person. Otherwise, you're just a woman bellowing a random name in a grocery store. Rudy, was it?"

"I'm sure it's Rudolfo," said Frankie. "Italian."

"Rudolfo," said Aunt Margaret. "That makes me wonder something."

"Yes?"

"What would Santa's other reindeer be named if they were Italian?"

"Hm," said Frankie, intrigued. "I can probably work that out. Let's see, Dasher. Like, as in, to rush? So, Affrettatore?" She pursed her lips, then nodded. "Yes, that works. Affrettatore," she said, the word drawn-out and musical, the *R*s rolling in her mouth, just like when Esther spoke Spanish. "Let's call Dancer Ballerina to keep things simple. Prancer. Huh. I don't know the word for 'prance.'"

"Vixen would be Isabella Rossellini," said Aunt Margaret.

"No! Gina Lollobrigida," said Esther. "Una tremenda manguita!"

"I always want to call people mangoes," said Aunt Margaret, "but I can never remember which fruit means a sexy person and which one means a vagina. I don't want to call someone a vagina by accident."

"'Papaya' means vagina," said Esther. Wilhelmina had heard this conversation before; it was about Cuban slang. "They're both three syllables long. Papaya, vagina. You can remember it that way."

"Oh! What a helpful mnemonic, Esther!"

"Okay, I'm looking ahead to Donder and Blitzen," said Frankie. "What do those words even mean?"

Wilhelmina was enjoying this new conversation thoroughly. While the aunts chattered, she watched the crescent moon through the window, pale in the sunlight, then turning to gold as the sky went deep and pink.

"I wonder how much they'll have managed to get done?" said Aunt Margaret as the car, now moving through darkness, neared the house.

When they finally pulled into the drive, it was too dark to tell if the builders had finished with the shingles. But they'd hung Aunt Margaret and Esther's sign beside the door, and turned it on.

"Oh," said Aunt Margaret, sighing with happiness. "Just look at that."

"Beautiful," said Esther. "Is that how you pictured it, Frankie?"

"Exactly," said Frankie.

"Do you like our sign, Wilhelmina?" asked Aunt Margaret. "It was Frankie's idea to use all those little bulbs. We told her it was impractical, but now I'm glad she convinced us."

"I see lights like those in my dreams," said Frankie. "Do you remember the old movie marquee from when we were little, Margie?"

"Barely," said Aunt Margaret.

"I get announcements," said Frankie. "In my dreams. Beautiful, sparkling announcements. 'Remember to water the cucumbers!' 'Your missing sock is in the dryer!'"

"*Was* your missing sock in the dryer?" asked Aunt Margaret, sounding impressed.

"Well, yes, but is that such a revelation?"

"I suppose not. But of course your dreams sparkle, Frankie."

Wilhelmina wasn't really listening. She was gazing at the sign, transfixed: PÉREZ AND HART, SOULFUL CONSULTANTS. Each letter was made of tiny little lights that glowed gold, suspended and sparkling, as if the names of her aunts were written in fireflies.

TUESDAY, NOVEMBER 3, 2020

On the Tuesday four days before she stepped into her own, Wilhelmina woke in her bed in her room at the top of the aunts' house in Pennsylvania.

She woke from a confused dream about swimming in a lake, with the moon casting a flat, cold light onto the water. On the shore was a waiting wolf. And then something scraped against her skin, something with hard, sharp claws. Wilhelmina woke up gasping.

In the air above her bed, she thought she saw dancing colors. Floating bits of paper? Her bleary morning eyes couldn't figure it out, so she groped for her glasses. When she shoved them on, the sun-sequined leaves of the sycamore outside her window came into focus. Propping herself on one elbow, she saw the blue stones on the windowsill. Next, Frankie's knitted blanket drew her eyes, black birds flying across a blue sky.

Wilhelmina remembered what day it was, and why she was here. With a sense of sliding panic, she remembered that before this day ended, she would be back in Massachusetts again. On the bedside bookshelf, her phone buzzed. When she saw Julie's name, she braced herself for Julie's praise. What a hero Wilhelmina was. How hopeful we should all be.

Instead, Julie wrote: *Hey, elephant. Bee told me about the crow that's "keeping" my necklace. Of course he thinks that's a deep thought, but let's face it, my necklace is gone. OMG! So sad! And I'm jealous too! You guys still have your necklaces!*

Wilhelmina's insides were filling up with something not very kind, in response to Julie believing *she* was entitled to jealousy. She imagined a little plumber inside her, installing a faucet up near her collarbone, then leaving it to run, a steady trickle of bitterness that seeped down past her heart and her lungs and pooled around her uterus and fallopian tubes, her kidneys and liver, rising up past her stomach. When it got to her throat, maybe she would choke on it.

Her phone buzzed again. *Thanks for telling us,* wrote Julie. *I'm glad you were there to see what happened*

Wilhelmina muted all notifications from Julie and Bee. Her phone stopped buzzing.

SHE TOOK OUT HER NIGHTGUARD and put on her necklace, chasing away all thoughts about why she was putting it on, or whether she should put it on. She went downstairs, wearing Frankie's blanket as a cape over her pajamas and holding a small handful of painkillers. She was almost afraid to start stretching. Her neck, chest, shoulders, and jaw felt immovable, like a marble bust of herself.

She smelled coffee, but she couldn't find her aunts. In the kitchen, beams of sunlight illuminated floating dust that made Wilhelmina sneeze.

Then she heard Aunt Margaret's voice, cheerful and bright, and another voice answering. She followed the noise to a front window, where a collage of trees around the house and along the road instantly dazzled her: the oaks and birches, the beeches, one ginkgo, and especially the maples—the sugar and red maples! Wilhelmina almost couldn't believe the assault of red, gold, pink, orange, yellow, green, brown. Needing to be closer, she opened the front door and stepped onto the porch in her socks and blanket cape, squealing a little as the cold cut through her sock bottoms to her feet.

"Is that Wilhelmina?" called a voice from the road.

Aunt Margaret was at the driveway's end with a rake in her hands, wearing her pale green winter coat with the political buttons, standing beside a massive pile of crimson leaves. Across the road at a respectful pandemic distance stood the aunts' longtime neighbor Mrs. Watchulonis, who lived ten minutes' walk away.

"Hi, Mrs. Watchulonis," said Wilhelmina, startled by the tears that sprang to her eyes. Mrs. Watchulonis was younger than the aunts, yet she was smaller and more white-haired than Wilhelmina remembered her. "Are you taking your morning walk?"

"Every day, rain or shine!" said Mrs. Watchulonis. "Imagine my surprise to find your aunt Margie raking leaves!"

Wilhelmina was wondering about that, actually. Should a person who'd just had eye surgery be engaging in an activity that stirred up infinitesimal pieces of leaf dander? "Did your eye doctor say anything about raking leaves, Aunt Margaret?" she said.

"Don't you worry, Wilhelmina," said Aunt Margaret. "I've been assured that my eye patch is up for the job."

Wilhelmina didn't want to know what that meant. Also, she was cold. "Good to see you, Mrs. Watchulonis," she said.

"You too, Wilhelmina," said Mrs. Watchulonis. "You've gotten so grown-up. I can hardly believe it. And what a wonderful thing, for you to drive your aunts home so they can vote."

BACK INSIDE, Wilhelmina wandered, not certain what she was looking for. In a kitchen cupboard, she found some breakfast cereal that wasn't as stale as she thought it should be, given that it had been untouched for—what was it now? Three, three and a half months? The aunts had held out together for most of the spring and summer, a little overwhelmed by the challenge of caring for a giant old house by themselves in a pandemic. They'd managed. Aunt Margaret was a gardener—not like Frankie, but she'd kept a few things growing, and Esther wasn't bad at house upkeep, as long as she could go slow. Neighbors helped. They'd managed—until a stretch in late July, when Aunt Margaret had sprained an ankle, and Esther had had a bad patch with her arthritis. Suddenly, they hadn't been able to take care of each other. Theo and Cleo had convinced them to come to Massachusetts for a bit.

What a strange house this was for Wilhelmina now, dusty and cold, empty, in the wrong season, and with the wrong views outside the window. But it smelled right. It felt the same. When Wilhelmina turned to look at the kitchen table, she could almost see herself there, writing a letter to Bee, three blue stones above the page.

She sat at that table now with her cereal, eating it in stages while beginning the process of trying to stretch the pain out of her neck. She took her first painkiller and poured herself some coffee. Then she closed her eyes and breathed, listening, waiting for some indicator of Esther's location.

Esther was in the carriage house.

Bemused about why she thought she knew that, Wilhelmina found some old garden shoes of Aunt Margaret's. Still wearing her blanket cape and carrying her coffee, she went outside.

AUNT MARGARET'S and Esther's consulting office had always seemed a little odd to Wilhelmina—or anyway, odd for a consulting office. Not odd as a space for the aunts. It did have office-ish things like a desk with a computer on it, a printer, a filing cabinet. But those items were tucked away in a corner near the entrance, while the centermost focus of the room had more the air of a well-lit kitchen with very high ceilings.

Or a chemistry lab, Wilhelmina thought now as she entered the sunny space and found Esther seated on a tall chair at the counter in the room's middle. The counter reminded Wilhelmina of the islands in the kitchens of rich people. Bee's kitchen in his house before his father had died had contained an island where his father had liked to stand, glass-eyed and bitingly jovial, making waffles and drinking scotch at random times of day.

The carriage house counter was a square. Each side had a different purpose. One side contained a deep, porcelain sink with a long, swan-necked faucet. One contained a small, glass stovetop with two electric burners, and cabinets underneath. One, the one at which Esther sat, was like a high tabletop for working. The last side was crowded with gigantic potted plants—all looking surprisingly alive and green to Wilhelmina's eye—with bookshelves underneath. The plant and bookshelf side faced a small area with a Persian rug, a rust-brown love seat, and a pair of upholstered navy armchairs around a glass coffee table. A woodstove stood in a nearby corner. The windows were many, and cast long blocks of golden light onto the scene. The few framed pictures on the walls were black-and-white photographs of forests, songbirds, and owls.

"Good morning, Wilhelmina," said Esther, glancing up with a small smile as Wilhelmina entered. Esther was wearing forest-green slacks and a sweater in a paler green, and her locs were piled up on top of her head, sticking out like branches; she looked like a forest.

"Good morning," said Wilhelmina.

"That blanket," Esther said, gesturing at Wilhelmina with a vague hand. Esther was doing something at the counter with candles, a bowl, pencil, and paper. She seemed distracted.

"Yes?"

"I think it's a sort of a . . . *something* for you," said Esther.

"Yes?" said Wilhelmina, with an edge of impatience.

"Not a shield, exactly," said Esther. "Not a comfort. But something in between. Maybe a kind of shelter. You should take it with you when we go."

Wilhelmina brought her cup to her face, the sleeves of her blanket cape rising as she lifted her hands. She remembered the robes of the priest at the funeral she'd gone to with Frankie so long ago, the funeral for Mrs. Mancusi, Frankie's empress. The priest had raised a round white disc of bread into the air and an altar boy had rung a soft, sweet bell. The priest's robes had hung from his hands the way Frankie's blanket was hanging from Wilhelmina's hands now, and she hadn't understood what any of it had had to do with Mrs. Mancusi. But when the bell had rung, she'd felt the whole room of people around her, united in their wish to pay tribute to the woman who had died.

Carefully, Wilhelmina raised her coffee mug into the air, for Frankie.

"I take it back," said Esther, in a different voice, focused and certain. "That blanket is your battle armor."

Wilhelmina was tired of obscure pronouncements. "What are you doing, Esther?" she asked, lowering her coffee cup.

"Oh," said Esther, who was jotting something down on a small slip of paper. "I guess it's a sort of . . . strengthening." Esther held the piece of paper to the candle flickering on the counter before her. When a flame began to curl the paper's edges, she placed the burning page into a shallow ceramic bowl that showed evidence of other burnt paper. Then she picked up her pencil again.

"You know how that man's been priming his followers?" said Esther. "To assume our side's cheating? So, if votes are taking a while to be counted, and the count is turning against him—like when that worm of his was elected governor in Florida—he starts shouting about forged votes? Votes appearing out of nowhere? And his people believe him? They can't—or won't—see what game he's playing?"

"Yes," said Wilhelmina, her throat suddenly dry.

"Well," said Esther. "It'll take a while for the votes in this election to be counted. I expect a lot of lies, from a lot of people. A lot of harmful noise. A lot of people are going to be under pressure to do wrong. A lot of people's integrity is about to be tested, Wilhelmina."

Esther jotted something down on another slip of paper. Then she held it up to the flame. "So I'm sending out a sort of prayer," she said. "To give courage to the people who'll need it."

Thoughts were stumbling over each other inside Wilhelmina's mind—hot, frustrated thoughts. Candles? Prayers? Had Esther subjected her consulting clients to this? Write your investment goals on this paper and then we'll burn them together? What use was it?

There was nothing she could say that wasn't sharp and mean. She spun around and went outside.

FRANKIE HAD HAD A NUMBER OF FLOWER BEDS, an herb garden, and a few berry bushes, some of which—the lilies of the valley and the raspberries in particular—had repeatedly attempted to take over the yard. And then, bigger than all the others combined, she'd had her vegetable garden. Every summer day, Wilhelmina could find Frankie kneeling in there, her hands in the dirt.

Her blanket snagging on broken stalks, Wilhelmina walked straight into the vegetable garden. She followed the paths between rows of dead-looking plants to the middle, where a tangle of dusty vines announced that tomato season was long over. She crouched, running her fingers along the vines and bringing them to her nose, hoping for that distinctive tomato-vine smell that had used to be synonymous with summer for Wilhelmina. She remembered pulling Julie into this garden once, a hand on her wrist, to share the tomato vine smell.

"Yeah, I know what tomato vines smell like," Julie had said, rolling her eyes at her friend, but letting herself be towed down the rows of Frankie's vegetables. It hadn't been the smell, really, that Wilhelmina had wanted to share; it had been something about herself.

"If you had to name what summer smells like," Wilhelmina had asked her, not sure how to explain, "what would you say?"

"I don't know about summer," said Julie, thoughtful. "Maybe that smell when you put a sparkler in water. But fall is my favorite season. Fall smells like fires in our fireplace." Next she'd put her fingers to the vines, then raised them to her nose. She'd smiled, delighted, and Wilhelmina had been happy.

Now Wilhelmina was looking for something in this garden. What? A door? On the other side of which she would find—what? A place where everything hurt less?

What she did find was Frankie's old gardening bench. One of Esther's many cousins had made it, oh, eons ago—Wilhelmina could remember that cousin, she thought it had been Ruben, hammering and sanding the little bench and offering it to Frankie with such shy kindness in his face. Frankie had used that bench always. And now here it was, planted in the garden in a spot between the tomatoes and the beans. Esther and Aunt Margaret had made a shrine of it. It was a kneeling bench, which meant it had a slanted surface, so the aunts hadn't tried to rest anything atop it. But they'd turned the space underneath into a little bird sanctuary with rows of wooden and ceramic birds, much like the birds the aunts had placed on the windowsill at home, but smaller. There was no snow goose with a bobbing head in this collection, but there were a lot of glazed ceramic owls. A veritable parliament of owls, and a few songbirds Wilhelmina couldn't identify, and at the bench's far right end, a handful of tiny black molded plastic birds that spilled out from under the bench and spread across the dirt beyond, as if they came and went as they pleased. Their heads were sleek, and their wings were sharp. Some of their beaks were open, as if cawing. They were crows. Wilhelmina supposed that the birds on her blanket cape were probably also crows.

A crack did open then, but Wilhelmina pushed it closed again. Esther and Aunt Margaret were wrong. There weren't any doors to anything in Frankie's garden, and Wilhelmina didn't want to think about crows.

"Well, Wilhelmina," said Aunt Margaret, coming around the corner of the house with her rake. "Shall we vote?"

WILHELMINA CHANGED into the only clothes she'd brought: a soft, loose, gray-brown sweater dress and brown leggings she'd chosen because they made her feel like a bear who at any moment was allowed to call it and go into hibernation.

Then she stretched again for a few minutes, or tried to. Sometimes Wilhelmina imagined a surgeon opening up her skin and reaching under her fascia, then easing her tight cords of muscle flat with warm, gentle fingers. Then applying some sort of ointment that would keep them soft and supple indefinitely, then closing her up again with no pain.

In the car, as Wilhelmina fastened her seat belt around her red coat, Aunt Margaret reached forward from the back, something golden and sparkly in her hand.

"This is for you, dear," she said.

Wilhelmina accepted the tiny item and inspected it, surprised, then completely unsurprised, to see an owl staring back at her. It had a round little body and big, taloned feet; steady eyes made of deep red stones; and a facial expression of apoplectic rage mixed with utter disdain.

"It's an ear cuff," said Aunt Margaret.

Wilhelmina saw then that the owl was standing on a thick, golden branch that curved almost into a circle. "Why are you giving me an ear cuff?"

"It was Frankie's," said Aunt Margaret. "I found it in my jewelry box this morning and knew she'd want you to have it."

With some ambivalence, Wilhelmina considered the owl, wondering if a person could have an owl saturation point. The truth was, she'd

reached her bird limit generally. She wanted to say to the universe, *I get it. Some message about birds. Now back off, okay?* But at least this bird looked pissed off, and it wasn't a crow. It wasn't an elephant either.

Carefully, using the rearview mirror, she slid the little owl around the cartilage of her left ear. Its deep red eyes worked well with her glasses. It sat there, nicely framed by wispy bits of her dark hair, looking nettled and ferocious.

"The stones that make its eyes are garnets," said Aunt Margaret. "Garnets are vessels for abundant love."

THE DRIVE TO THE FIRE HALL was both familiar and unfamiliar to Wilhelmina, because of the transformation of the trees. When they passed the lake where Wilhelmina had used to swim to the blue stones, she was startled by the birch trees surrounding it. Somehow she'd failed to notice all those birches, until now, when their leaves glowed like pale yellow suns.

"Just look at that," said Aunt Margaret dreamily.

"Oh my," said Esther, who was not beholding the birch trees. Esther was staring straight ahead, at a row of cars parked on the grass at the edge of the road. "That can't be the parking for the voting, can it? This far from the fire hall?"

Then a line of people came into view, standing in the grass on the side of the road opposite the cars. The line seemed to stretch on forever. The fire hall was nowhere in sight.

Coming abreast of the people, Wilhelmina stopped the car.

"Wilhelmina?" said Aunt Margaret. "You can't park in the middle of the road."

"She wants us to get in line," said Esther, releasing her seat belt and pulling her mask up. "Vámonos, Margeleh."

Wilhelmina was already jumping out and running around to the trunk, where the camping chairs were stored. "You two get in line

while I investigate," she said. "Maybe they have a shorter line for senior citizens."

A convoy of traffic was approaching from the opposite direction,
horns honking. Wilhelmina and the aunts crossed the road into the grass,
joining the end of the line, trying to get out of the way. Three pickup
trucks passed in succession, honking, flying MAGA and Blue Lives Matter flags. An armored truck followed them, a machine gun attached to its
roof. A banner hung below the gun. It said, COME AND TAKE IT.

Wilhelmina's car was still blocking the road. She helped the aunts
open their camp chairs, then ran to it and jumped back in.

FOR A FEW MINUTES AFTER THAT, Wilhelmina was alone,
inching along through a scene that would've been incomprehensible a
year ago: dozens of people—hundreds?—lined up at the edge of a rural
road, most of them wearing masks on their faces, most spread out six-
ish feet apart. With the windows closed and the sounds outside muted,
Wilhelmina's progress had the feeling of a slow, weird, amusement park
ride with an unidentifiable theme.

Eventually, she reached the fire hall, tall and gray-shingled, with
giant, fire-truck-sized doors. She noticed that the voting line seemed to
split into three or four branches at the hall, and that the parking stretched
on past the hall in the other direction. Wilhelmina kept driving.

When she got to the last parked car, she pulled over, tucking her
car into place. Then, climbing out onto the verge, she took a minute
to herself. Wilhelmina hadn't prepared for this. She'd known about the
possibility of lines, but not *this*—not a wait of, what, hours? With two
women, one of them Black, in chilly weather, in a place where the vast
majority of people were white and some people thought it was okay
to drive by with MAGA signs and guns. Wilhelmina's head, neck, and
shoulders had gone rigid, like a tightly clenched claw.

The car she'd parked in front of had two MAGA stickers on its front bumper. With a memory that felt more than a few days old, Wilhelmina reached into the deep front pocket of her coat. She pulled out the sheet of stickers that her fingers had known they would find there, the stickers Julie's little sister, Tina, had given her on Halloween. Then, on her own back bumper, directly facing each MAGA sticker, she affixed two Spells for Goblin Banishment.

As she straightened, she noticed someone in her peripheral vision walking toward her from the direction of the fire hall. The person was still a good distance away, but when he saw her, he stopped in his tracks. Then he began moving faster. His voice was sharp and incredulous. "Wilhelmina?"

Wilhelmina looked up into the dumbfounded face of James Fang.

"WHAT ARE YOU *DOING* HERE?" cried James.

"What are *you* doing here?" cried Wilhelmina.

"I'm going for a walk!"

"All the way from Massa*chusetts*?" cried Wilhelmina.

"My grandparents are here!" he said, gesturing back toward the fire hall. "I drove them here to vote!"

"I drove my aunts!" said Wilhelmina.

"This is unbelievable," said James. A mask hung from one of his ears, but he wasn't wearing it. Quick, astonished smiles kept illuminating his face, one bursting in after the other. He wore his puffy sky-blue coat with the zipper open. "Your family's from here?"

"My dad's aunts," she said. "They moved in with us because of the pandemic. They didn't get their ballots in time."

"Same," said James. "My mom's parents. I just can't believe this."

"I can't believe it either," said Wilhelmina weakly.

The sound of honking broke into their conversation. Wilhelmina, instantly alarmed, motioned for James to step closer to her, out of the road. "Come here with me," she said. "They're horrible."

It was a different convoy of pickup trucks, though the flags were similar. This time, the last truck in line was flying a Confederate flag. When Wilhelmina saw it coming, she almost cried out; she didn't want James to see it. She tried to get between him and it, but she was stuck in the place between the two cars, and anyway, there was no way to hide such an ugly thing. It passed in a spray of gravel, very close, very loud. *Esther,* she thought. *Julie.*

"Hey," said James, whose mouth had grown grim. "Are you okay?"

"Of course I'm okay," she said. "Are you?"

"Yeah."

They studied each other's faces. Wilhelmina didn't know what it was like to be a person whose appearance was noticeably mixed race on a Pennsylvania roadside where people made a special point of flying racist flags on their trucks, but what she saw, as James watched her with his head tilted, was that his eyes were soft with concern.

"I think you're a kind person," said Wilhelmina.

His eyes widened, as if she'd surprised him. "You're a magic person," he said.

"I'm not," she said automatically.

"Then how come I'm not as surprised as I should be to find you here?"

Wilhelmina was having a hard time keeping all of her doors closed. Little cracks were opening everywhere, letting in light.

"Listen," she said. "I kind of want to check on my aunts. And, like, see if there's a line for senior citizens."

"Good idea," he said, pulling up his mask. "I should do that too."

OUTSIDE THE FIRE HALL, they found a masked woman wearing an official-looking vest that said ASK ME QUESTIONS. The woman was pink and plump and extremely apologetic. Every time she said something unaccommodating, she reached back and grabbed her thin ponytail anxiously.

"There is a separate line for senior citizens and disabled people, yes," she said, tugging on her ponytail, "but I'm afraid it's also rather long at the moment. Please ask your family members to wait in the main line. Anytime the senior citizen and disabled line gets low, one of us walks the main line collecting people."

"Okay," said Wilhelmina. "Thank you."

The woman looked like she was trying to pull her head off her body by her hair. "We'll come get you as soon as we can!" she said.

Leaving the fire hall, James and Wilhelmina made their way along the lines of people. When they reached a small, masked woman who was watching the two of them with kind, curious eyes, James shot Wilhelmina an apologetic, *see you soon* sort of expression over his mask and broke off to join the woman. She had long, dark hair wound around her head in a braid. Wilhelmina supposed she must be the mother of James's mother, Alfie, the tall and graceful proprietor of the doughnut shop. Who'd grown up here? Wilhelmina had never wondered where Alfie of Alfie Fang's had grown up, but it nevertheless wrenched her sense of things sideways to try to picture Alfie young, and growing up here. A tall man whose hair was a wispy ring of white stood beside James's grandmother.

"Wilhelmina?" called Aunt Margaret, as Wilhelmina drifted along the line toward her aunts. Snapping to attention, she found them sitting together side by side, watching her with matching high-eyebrowed expressions that put her instantly on guard.

"Wilhelmina," said Aunt Margaret as she approached. "Who was that dishy young man we saw you walking with?"

"Oh my god," said Wilhelmina.

"Margeleh," said Esther firmly. "No one says 'dishy' anymore. They say 'fine,' or 'thirst trap,' or 'side of sauce.'"

"Oh my god!" said Wilhelmina, whose mind was now presenting her with the image of the wet, shirtless James of her dreams. "No one says 'side of sauce'! Where did you even hear that?"

"Sauce goes in a dish," said Aunt Margaret, "rendering it dishy. Who is he, Wilhelmina? You didn't seem like strangers."

Wilhelmina was pretty sure her face was bright pink. "He's from my class at school," she said. "He drove his grandparents here to vote today, just like I drove you."

Aunt Margaret's eye widened dramatically. "What an extraordinary coincidence!" she said. "Who are his grandparents?"

"I don't know," said Wilhelmina. "His family owns Alfie Fang's."

"The doughnut shop?" said Aunt Margaret. "This is astonishing. And his grandparents live here, but they're staying in Massachusetts?"

"We need to meet them," said Esther. "Friends from home!"

"They should be in our bubble!"

"Okay, calm down," said Wilhelmina. "The line is moving. Let's move the chairs up, okay?"

"Okay," said Aunt Margaret, "but then you need to go tell that nice young man that we want to meet his grandparents."

What followed was an awkward but surprisingly sweet set of introductions. First Wilhelmina moved ahead in line and met James's grandparents, the Cognettis. They were both very kind, as kind as two people can be when meeting someone at a distance while wearing masks, with a soft glow of joy in their faces every time they looked at James. His grandmother Rose, something about her manner, her straight shoulders and high chin, reminded Wilhelmina strongly of Alfie, even though Rose was much shorter. James's grandfather Rudy reminded Wilhelmina obscurely of someone she couldn't place. His name was familiar. Hadn't the aunts known someone named Rudy, years ago? She would have to ask them. His voice, a pleasant rumble, tickled something in her mind. She could hear someone with that voice talking to Frankie, but not in a memory, exactly. It felt like a memory from a dream.

Next, Wilhelmina brought James to meet the aunts.

"They may say something mortifying," she warned him as they walked.

"What kind of mortifying?" said James.

"They think you're dishy."

James snorted, then threw his head back and laughed. It was a wonderful laugh, warm and high-pitched, familiar, as if maybe it had been part of the ambience at school for the last couple years, and she'd never quite registered it.

As it turned out, the aunts didn't embarrass Wilhelmina. They made no comment on James's dishiness and said only kind and gracious things—about his family's doughnuts, his consideration in driving his grandparents all this way, the remarkable parallels between his family's situation and their own. Nonetheless, Wilhelmina was relieved when it was over. She knew Esther and Aunt Margaret well enough to imagine the conversation they were storing up to have later.

Next, the elderly relations all assembled at a midpoint while James and Wilhelmina held their places in line. Wilhelmina observed them pulling out phones and shouting numbers at each other across the six-foot gap. The next time James and Wilhelmina joined each other, they mostly just snorted and giggled for a while.

"My grandparents can't actually use their phones," said James. "My grandpa holds his like it's a baby he's afraid of dropping."

"My aunts aren't actually so bad," said Wilhelmina. "Which is funny, because I think they're older than your grandparents are. Don't you think so?"

"Yeah," said James. "Did they both grow up here?"

"Aunt Margaret did. Esther grew up in New York. They met in college. You're too late to meet my other aunt," said Wilhelmina. "Frankie. She grew up here too. But she died."

"Was she your aunt Margaret's sister?"

This sort of question always made Wilhelmina wary. "No," she said, trying to keep her voice from sounding automatically defensive. "They weren't like that. They were like a couple, but with three of them."

"Oh!" said James. "I see." He scrunched up his face. "Did I say anything obnoxious?"

"No," said Wilhelmina. "Why? Did my voice get deep and pissed off?"

"No," he said, glancing at her in surprise. "Are you pissed off?"

"No!"

"Oh, good."

"Why did you think you said something obnoxious?"

"Because it never occurred to me that you might've had three aunts who lived together as a throuple," said James.

"Well, it's pretty unusual," said Wilhelmina. "Maybe you've never encountered it before."

"Why did you think your voice was deep and pissed off?"

"It happens sometimes," she said. "When I'm preparing to get pissed off."

"Filing that under useful information," said James.

There was a small commotion behind them, from the direction of Esther and Aunt Margaret.

"Oh my!" cried Aunt Margaret. "Are you all right, Esther?"

James and Wilhelmina moved to them quickly. Esther was, indeed, all right, but the same couldn't be said for her chair. It had torn from the frame at one of the grommets and almost spilled her onto the ground.

"Hm," said James, dropping to one knee in order to inspect the damage. "Maybe we can fix it."

"It's okay," said Esther, who was standing. "It's not worth the fuss. I don't need a chair."

"You can have my chair, sweetie," said Aunt Margaret. "Your arthritis. I can stand."

Behind them in line, a woman spoke up. "Would you like a folding stool?" she said. "I have one in my car."

"Oh, no thank you," said Esther, glancing back at the woman, who was wearing a red mask with MAGA emblazoned across it. "No need for anyone to go to any trouble."

"It's no trouble," said the woman. "My car is close by. And I'll wipe it down with an alcohol wipe."

"But maybe you want it for yourself," said Esther. "Or maybe someone else would like to use it."

"Let me get it for you," said the woman, "and then you can decide."

As the woman moved away from the line toward her car, Esther looked after her, a quiet, almost grave expression on her face. When the woman returned with a small, black folding stool, then wiped it down thoroughly using a succession of alcohol wipes, Esther accepted it politely.

"Thank you," she said. "It's very kind of you."

"No reason to stand if you don't need to," said the woman.

Wilhelmina realized she was braced, but she wasn't sure what she was braced for. The MAGA woman to announce something in defense of the racist person for whom she was voting? Esther to decide she couldn't bear to sit on a MAGA stool? Nothing happened. The woman returned to her place in line, beside a man who was wearing a mask that covered his mouth but not his nose. Esther sat down. It was a low stool. Her long legs, bent at the knees in her green slacks, made Wilhelmina think of a grasshopper.

"I'll take the broken chair back to the car," she said.

"Thank you, dear," said Aunt Margaret. "How are your hands holding up?"

Wilhelmina's hands were burning, and she felt the pressure of something in her neck and chest, something that was trying to expand. "They're well enough that I can carry a chair to the car," she said.

"What's wrong?" said James. "I can carry the chair."

"But germs," said Wilhelmina.

"Hand sanitizer," said James, patting the pocket of his puffy sky-blue coat.

Wilhelmina let James carry the chair.

For most of the walk past the fire hall, then past the line of parked cars, they moved in silence. Wilhelmina was stuck in a rumination she got stuck in sometimes, when she found herself thinking about perfectly nice people who were MAGA voters. How could they be? What piece were they missing? Or was there something she was missing? Could she be the one who didn't understand? And then she wondered if they were trying equally hard to understand her. Did they too wonder whether they were the ones who were wrong? If not, was that the piece they were missing? Did all harm come from a refusal to consider whether one might be wrong?

Wilhelmina never came to any conclusions.

"The littlest things feel so full of significance," she finally said. "You know?"

"Yeah," said James. "She was really kind, but it was like she had no awareness of what a vile thing she had on her face."

"Yeah," said Wilhelmina. "Thanks for carrying the chair. I have this . . . pain problem. I'm supposed to be stretching, but I haven't really had a chance."

"Can you do it now?" he said. "What do you need? Like, a mat?"

"A tree," she said.

"Hm," said James, glancing into the field of golden grass that stretched out beside the road. "I'm guessing you mean a vertical tree."

"Are there horizontal trees?" said Wilhelmina, then noticed what

James had noticed: a fallen tree trunk in the field. "Oh. Hm," she said, thinking about her foam roller. Wilhelmina's foam roller was a thick cylinder, like a three-foot length of telephone pole, but made of firm red foam. In the time before the Delia Invasion, Wilhelmina had often set up the foam roller on her bedroom floor and reclined on it lengthwise, extending her arms, letting her shoulders drop, and feeling a massive stretch in her pectorals and the scalene muscles of her neck. She could even watch stuff on her laptop while she did this, if she stretched one arm at a time.

"You know foam rollers?" Wilhelmina asked James.

"Oh yeah," he said.

"Would it be too terribly weird if I went and lay down on that log for a while?" she said.

THIS IS DEFINITELY *one of my weirder days,* Wilhelmina thought to herself a few minutes later. Because not only was she lying on a log in a field in Pennsylvania, stretching her arms out like a crucifixion, but James Fang was lying at the other end of the log, telling her about how he wanted to work with birds.

"Birds?" said Wilhelmina. Her stretched-out arms suddenly felt less like arms, and more like wings. Maybe James was the person to ask about penguin penises? *Too soon,* thought Wilhelmina.

"Yeah," he said. "Like, I want to be the person on the other end of the phone when someone finds an injured owl in their yard. Or an albatross."

"An albatross?" said Wilhelmina, startled. Did people in Massachusetts find albatrosses in their yards?

"That reminds me," said James, sitting up. He was holding a long stick to manipulate his shoulders into odd positions that he'd told her were javelin stretches. This was the kind of day Wilhelmina was having. James Fang was teaching her javelin stretches with a giant branch in a field in Pennsylvania. "I haven't looked up the answer to your goose question yet," he said. "But I haven't forgotten."

"Oh," said Wilhelmina, remembering. "Thanks. It's not an emergency."

"How's your stretch?"

How was her stretch? The release in Wilhelmina's neck when she lay on this log felt like a bath of pure joy. Almost. Like a bath of pure joy if joy hurt. "It's a good stretch," she said.

"That's great," he said. "Hey, Wilhelmina, when do you want to talk about all the weird stuff that's been happening? We should talk, right? I mean, it was a huge relief to talk to Julie, but we're the ones it's happening to."

When James spoke Julie's name, Wilhelmina heard a tiny *ding*. A sweet little bell, to accompany the name "Julie." It wasn't her phone, which was still muted.

She sat up and looked at James. "Did your phone ding?" she said, even though she knew it hadn't.

"No."

"Did you hear a bell?"

"No," he said. "What's going on? Did something else weird happen?"

Wilhelmina had the need suddenly, like a symphony of bells rising up through her body and shoving the words out of her throat, to ask James about the habits of crows. "Crows," she said.

"Crows?" he echoed, holding his branch beside him like a walking stick and looking back at her. His mask hung from his ear again. She could see the quizzical look on his face. "Did crows happen?"

"I just want to know," she said, "where do crows live this time of year?"

"Where do they live?" he said, looking more and more confused. "Like, what part of the country?"

"Where would I *go*," she said, "if I wanted to find one? Like, at home?"

"Oh," he said. "Well, they fly all over. Like, they fly for miles every day, looking for food. And then at night they come back and roost in a tree, like, in groups, in the biggest, tallest tree they can find. Up high, so they can have a view of everything." He scrunched his face at her. "Is that what you're asking me?"

"I guess so, yeah."

"Why?"

Wilhelmina shrugged.

"Are you not going to tell me why?" said James.

"I guess not, no," said Wilhelmina, swallowing.

"And we're not going to have a conversation about all the weirdness either," he said. "Are we."

Something had changed in James's tone, though his expression remained even. Wilhelmina studied him with a touch of apprehension, obscurely alarmed when his eyes held her gaze unflinchingly. "Are you . . . annoyed at me?" she said.

"We need to talk about the weirdness," he said. "I'm getting the sense you don't want to talk about it. I'm even getting the sense you want to pretend it's not happening. But it *is* happening, so we need to talk about it."

"It's not happening," said Wilhelmina.

James's eyebrows rose. "Do you have any idea how much you were glowing when I first saw you today?" he said. "I thought one of the cars was on fire."

"It's not happening," Wilhelmina said, hearing her own voice drop to the register of a cello.

James stood up, his face flushed. Calmly, he placed his branch on the ground beside the fallen tree. "It's scary," he said. "I get it. But especially today, when we're here with this line of people, most of whom are probably going to vote for a racist fascist while swearing up and down and even believing in their own hearts that they're not being racist or fascist, I can't be with you if you're going to look straight at this and deny what it is."

"Wait, what?" said Wilhelmina, also standing, almost tripping. She righted herself against the tree trunk with one burning hand. "You think I'm like them?"

"I mean, I don't think you vote like them," he said. "But you're denying the truth like them, aren't you? To yourself and to me?"

Wilhelmina was absolutely winded with disbelief, and overcome with pain. She bent down over the tree, propping herself up on her hands, trying to catch her breath.

"Hey," said James, moving a step closer. "I'm sorry. It was a mean analogy."

Out on the road, another chorus of honking began. More trucks with flags. Wilhelmina had one searing need: to get away from James, who thought she was like them.

"I need to check on my aunts," she said, turning away from him, and running toward the road.

SHE COULDN'T FIND THE AUNTS. They weren't in line, no matter how many times she walked up and down it searching. Finally, it occurred to her to look for the MAGA woman who'd lent Esther the stool. When she found her, the woman was carrying the stool.

"Excuse me," said Wilhelmina, approaching her. "Did you see where my aunts went?"

"They've gone ahead to the senior citizen line, hon," said the woman. "Someone came to get them."

Which meant they were probably in the fire hall, voting. Good. They could leave soon.

"Thank you," she said, then set out for the hall, pretending not to see James, who was hovering nearby, watching her in obvious distress.

Outside the fire hall, she found a place to wait where no one else was waiting, with a view of the doors. Then James's grandparents emerged. She ducked and darted away before they could see her, spun around, and crashed straight into James.

"Sorry!" he said. "Sorry! Wilhelmina—"

"All right, my dear," said James's grandmother, coming up behind them. "We're done."

"We had to fill out provisional ballots," said his grandfather. "Took a bit longer."

"My Ray of light," said James's grandmother, reaching her hand up to touch the side of James's face. "You're upset. What's wrong?"

"I—" said James.

"I hope you have a nice, easy drive home," Wilhelmina interrupted, infusing her words with every drop of Politeness to Elders she possessed. "It was lovely to meet you," she said, backing away. "Pardon me while I go check on my aunts."

"Of course!" said Rose. "You have a safe drive too!"

"Bye now," said Wilhelmina, turning and walking off in no particular direction, just away. She didn't look at James. When she turned back some moments later, she was relieved to see them moving slowly toward the cars with their backs to her. Rudy had a hand on James's shoulder and was patting him gently.

When she turned around again, her aunts were walking toward her, exuding joy.

IN THE CAR, the aunts' chatter fell like leaves around her, comforting Wilhelmina with its lack of demands upon her.

"I wonder if Rudy is short for Rudolph," said Aunt Margaret. "Or maybe Rudolfo. 'Cognetti' is certainly an Italian name."

"I have sympathy for all Rudys these days," said Esther. "Imagine having to share a name with that shmegegge."

"You mean Giuliani?"

"I didn't like that man much when he was mayor," said Esther, "but can you believe him now? All along, he was looking for a bigger bully to worship! Pathetic."

"I'll never forget that he announced his marital separation at a press conference," said Aunt Margaret, "before ever telling his wife."

Esther hooted. "I forgot about that!"

"I'd be tempted to change my name," said Aunt Margaret. "Maybe to Rudyard."

"Or Ruby," said Esther. "Or Rumi."

Or one of the other reindeer, Wilhelmina thought, but didn't say out loud. Wilhelmina wasn't in a mood to draw attention to herself at the moment. Also, she was having some disorienting déjà vu. They'd had a Rudy conversation once before, she was sure of it. It had been about Italian names and reindeer, and it had taken place in a car. That was all Wilhelmina could remember about it, and the aunts didn't seem to remember it at all. Nor did they seem to find James's grandfather familiar. She was tired of memories she couldn't reach, like they were trapped behind a door that had closed without her noticing, a long time ago.

At the house, she went inside only briefly, climbing the stairs to her bedroom and packing her things. She left Frankie's crow blanket heaped on the bed. She ignored the blue stones in her peripheral vision. But she did reach into the drawer of the desk tucked under the hanging bookshelves in the corner, then pull out the bundle of cards that were wrapped in a dark cloth covered with a scatter of bumblebees. Frankie's tarot cards. She didn't know why she wanted them. She only knew that her primary goal was not to feel anything, and if she left them behind, she would feel something.

She jammed the bundle into her suitcase, zipped it closed, and rolled the suitcase out into the hall. There, she stopped for a moment, assessing. Turning back, she reentered the room. She grabbed the blanket and the stones. It wasn't easy to fit the blanket into her suitcase, but she managed it.

Navigating her suitcase down the stairs with aching arms and tight shoulders, she went outside to wait in the car.

ON THE LONG DRIVE back to Massachusetts, Wilhelmina was mostly quiet. She breathed through pain, counting down the minutes until she was allowed to medicate again. Fantasizing about the muscle relaxant she would take when she got home. She noticed Esther's door when they passed through it in Connecticut. The driving became more difficult, the tension in her head increasing. She clenched her teeth and kept breathing.

Her attention flitted sometimes to the aunts' conversation. "I don't think you've said his name out loud once," Aunt Margaret was saying. "Not once in his presidency."

"Names have power," said Esther grimly. "I'll never say his name. It summons a little part of him into being."

"A good argument for talking about all the people who make us hopeful instead," said Aunt Margaret. "Like Wilhelmina," she said, reaching forward from the back seat and touching Wilhelmina's shoulder lightly.

"You don't need to summon me into being, Aunt Margaret," said Wilhelmina. "I'm right here."

"Were you aware that Frankie chose your name, Wilhelmina?" said Aunt Margaret.

"What?" said Wilhelmina, startled. "No. What do you mean, she chose it?"

"More like she suggested it," said Esther. "And your parents liked it."

"It's not an Italian name, is it?" said Wilhelmina.

"No," said Esther. "German or Dutch, I think. I don't think it was a family name."

"She liked its meaning," said Aunt Margaret. "'Resolute protector.' Quite a lot for a baby, though not for the young woman you've become, Wilhelmina. She liked that it contained the word 'will,' and the word 'helm.'"

"Maybe she wanted you to be safe inside your armor," Esther said, then added, as an afterthought, "Our Wilhelmineleh."

Memories rushed into Wilhelmina's heart; she was five years old. "Esther," she said. "You haven't called me that in a long time."

"Haven't I?" said Esther. "My mother used to do that to names. I was 'Estherleh' sometimes. My papa called me his Estrella, or his Estrellita—his little star. Did you know 'Esther' means 'star'?"

"It sounds familiar," said Wilhelmina, "but I'm not sure I've ever thought about it."

"We don't think about the words we use all the time," said Esther.

"Are you . . ." Wilhelmina hesitated. "Are you *sure* my name came from Frankie?"

"Oh yes," said Aunt Margaret. "We were present at the time. Your father had the flu when you were born, Wilhelmina, dear, as I'm sure you've been told, and your mother had a difficult delivery. We three were all there, helping. Like fairy godmothers."

Esther snorted. "Except competent ones," she said. "None of that Sleeping Beauty bunk."

"Though you are a beauty, Wilhelmina," said Aunt Margaret.

"Yes," said Esther. "That's undeniable."

"And after what you've done for us, Wilhelmina," said Aunt Margaret, "no one's more deserving of a long, restful sleep. The good kind. The kind that gives you peace."

IT WAS EARLY EVENING when Wilhelmina stopped the car in front of the Hart home, but the sky was already dark and pricked with stars.

She saw lights on upstairs, in Julie's living room, and told the aunts to go ahead inside. For a few minutes, she sat by herself in the car. She rested her arms and watched Julie's windows, unsure what she was waiting for. She touched her necklace.

Not really wanting to, she pulled out her phone and checked her missed messages. Twenty-five from Julie. Twelve from Bee.

Instead of reading them, she sent a group text to them both. *Hey. Home safe. So so tired. Going to bed soon*

Julie replied almost immediately. *Hey! I'm at Bee's. We're gonna watch the returns. Want to watch with us over text?*

Hands hurt too much, said Wilhelmina.

Over video chat?

Sorry, said Wilhelmina. *Going to bed*

You have more self-restraint than we do, said Julie. *Listen, can I give James your phone number? He's texted me like three times*

Wilhelmina put her phone in her pocket. The Dunstable car was in the narrow driveway, and the winter overnight parking ban hadn't started up yet, so she left the car parked on the street, and went inside. When voices clamored to greet her, she did her best to respond the way a normal person would. When her father placed a bowl of soup on the table for her, she sat down and ate it. When Philip tried to climb into her lap, she told him she was too sore. When her parents made motions like they wanted to hover around her asking questions about the trip, she pretended to yawn, announcing that she needed to medicate and go to bed. When Delia ran out to the car, then came back inside rolling the suitcase Wilhelmina had left behind, asking her if she needed help unpacking, tears swam suddenly in Wilhelmina's eyes.

"Thanks, Delia," she said. "Maybe tomorrow."

"You go to sleep, hon," said Cleo. "We'll clean up."

In her room, Wilhelmina pulled the blanket out of her suitcase. She detached the little owl from her ear, but left her necklace on. Then she took some metaxalone, found her mouthguard, removed her glasses, and crawled into bed.

IN THE MIDDLE OF THE NIGHT, Wilhelmina came wide awake.

Groggy from the metaxalone, she sat on the edge of her bed, holding her head in her hands. Her neck needed stretching so badly that after a while, she felt around for her glasses, then used her phone's light to search for her foam roller among the mountains of clothing and other miscellaneous Delia detritus. Finding it half under Delia's bed, she carried it out of the room, past Theo's laptop on the kitchen table and into the living room. There, she placed it onto the floor and lay down upon it.

Through the window that contained Frankie's treasures, a fat pale moon shone. In its light, Wilhelmina could see the head of the plastic snow goose gently bobbing.

When the pressure of the foam roller on her back and butt began to hurt a little, Wilhelmina levered herself up onto her feet again. Locating her boots, she slipped outside. It was cold, and she had no plan for how to find what she was looking for.

She rounded the dark house to the uneven backyard, understanding, now that she was outside, that the light of the waning moon was not enough to guide her gracefully across dirt that dipped and mounded without warning. Stumbling, she made her way downhill to the tall trees that grew along the retaining wall at the border between this property and the drop to the property below.

There, she steadied her hand against a tree trunk. She craned her neck up. *Crow?* she thought into the tree. *Are you there? I changed my mind. I want the necklace back.*

Nothing happened, except that a muscle pulled tight in her straining neck, burrowing into her shoulder and embedding itself there, a new little hub for the rest of her pain to organize itself around. What was she doing out here? The rustling trees cast frightening shadows and she couldn't even see what was real. And it was *cold*. Wrapping her arms around her body, Wilhelmina climbed up to the house again and went inside.

On her way back to her bedroom, her father's laptop stopped her. Why did she do what she did next? What purpose did she think it would serve? She went to the kitchen table, sat down, and opened the laptop. The election returns flashed back at her. The monster was leading in almost every swing state. The map of the nation shone red and pink, projecting his victory. In Pennsylvania he was leading by thirteen percentage points. *Thirteen.*

Wilhelmina went back to bed.

The summer Wilhelmina was thirteen, she woke morning after morning from the same dream. It was a dream that everything in life was just as it should be—school, her parents, Delia, Bee, Julie, summers with the aunts—except that there was something important that she didn't know. Something she was missing, and whatever it was, it was always just a few steps ahead of her, out of her reach.

Then, when she awoke, it was hard to shake the dream off. Because something *did* feel wrong to Wilhelmina. Some worry nagged her at unpredictable moments, and she couldn't figure out what it was. She'd assumed it was a Massachusetts feeling, something about school, maybe, where things had been changing, social factions emerging all around her, and social expectations. Or maybe it was something about the trials of living with Delia, who was a five-year-old agent of chaos. Or maybe something to do with her mother's irritating therapy gaze. She'd thought she would leave it behind when she went to the aunts for the summer. But it was in Pennsylvania too.

It was hard to describe. It was like the world around her had shrunk in some places, or slowed down in others, and her size was wrong, her speed was wrong, everything took *forever*, and she was *so impatient*. But impatient for what? Wilhelmina didn't know what she was waiting for. Every morning a bright red cardinal flew into the aunts' yard, perched itself on the frame of the basement window three floors directly down from Wilhelmina's bedroom, and jabbed at its own reflection in the glass, hard. Pound, pound, pound, over and over; most days, Wilhelmina woke to the noise. Frankie said male cardinals were aggressive, that he was defending his territory from the other male cardinal he thought he saw in the glass. If Frankie said that, then Wilhelmina knew it was true, but it wasn't what she saw. Wilhelmina saw her own relentless but pointless impatience. The cardinal was trying to pound through to a different feeling he would never reach. When she heard his pounding, she felt better, like something was scratching her itch. Until the noise became annoying. Then she would fantasize about dropping a flagstone out her bedroom window.

She didn't always feel like this. She felt it the least when she was with Bee, Julie, or Frankie. She felt it the most with Delia and her mother, and more and more at school. Her father, Aunt Margaret, and Esther had mixed results, and solitude was likewise variable. Whenever Wilhelmina had an outing with the aunts, no matter whether it was fun or not, it always seemed to last too long and she would bolt for her bedroom the moment her feet hit the driveway. But then she would hear voices below. She would sense her aunts moving to and fro and she would want to know what they were talking about, what they were doing. She would find a book and bring it downstairs so she could sit somewhere, pretending to herself that she was reading. Really she just wanted the aunts around her.

Esther and Aunt Margaret worked from home now. Wilhelmina had expected this to be a big change from all her years of spending time alone with Frankie during the day, but it wasn't. Esther and Aunt Margaret mostly kept to themselves during business hours, occupying different parts of the house from Frankie and Wilhelmina, leaving Frankie to herself when she was gardening, and of course, spending a significant chunk of time in the carriage house. Then, in the late afternoon, the aunts would come together again, noticing each other, talking, laughing, planning as usual, with no fuss or comment, as if this was their natural rhythm. It was like three people could occupy the same space, yet, by mutual agreement, exist on slightly different dimensions. It fascinated Wilhelmina. It also made her wonder if that was what was wrong with her: she was stuck in a dimension half a step removed from the one in which she was meant to be.

Esther and Aunt Margaret's clients were interesting. Through her high bedroom windows, Wilhelmina spied on them as they stepped out of their cars and walked to the carriage house, wondering what they did in their lives when they weren't here getting advice from Esther and Aunt Margaret. Advice on what, exactly? She thought that they were a bit out of the ordinary when it came to style. A disproportionate number of them had hair dyed non-hair colors, like shades of purple, pink, and blue. A disproportionate number of them wore clothing that was noticeably and deliberately . . . *different* from what other people wore. Stranger? Funkier, maybe? Like they shopped in very specific stores that weren't at the mall? Wilhelmina wasn't sure of the right words for the styles she saw, because it was new to her, to notice how people adorned their bodies. To notice *bodies*. Wilhelmina had become ever so slightly obsessed with bodies and their adornments, actually. Her own body had changed, and though her parents and aunts talked about how beautiful she was, casually, as if it was a given, and though on one level she chose to believe them—not her parents necessarily, but she believed Frankie, and she also mostly trusted Esther on this topic— Wilhelmina was of course acutely aware of the message out in the world that beauty meant *thin* bodies. That health and strength also meant thin bodies, even though Wilhelmina could swim longer and farther than anyone she knew, even Aunt Margaret. Even though her newer, rounder body with thicker arms and legs was a *stronger* body. Even though her big, sturdy feet made sense now, supporting such a body. And she had breasts now too, and a butt that stuck out, and she was still rather short. She was shaped like Aunt Margaret, which she hadn't been expecting. It wasn't necessarily horrible; Aunt Margaret was quite pretty—Wilhelmina could see it for herself, and Frankie and Esther were always saying so—but it brought with it all kinds of realizations about how Aunt Margaret adorned her body in a manner that was fine for Aunt Margaret, with long, flowing skirts and shirts and scarves in blues and greens and with long, flowing hair—she was *Aunt Margaret*, which was fine, whatever, but Wilhelmina was someone else. She wanted to look like something else. Like *herself*. So—what did that mean?

The summer Wilhelmina was thirteen, she made a study of how other people adorned their bodies. She noticed that when women had very short, dark hair, she almost always liked it. She noticed that when women wore above-the-knee dresses, both loose ones and dresses that fit their bodies closely, she liked the fit, on all kinds of bodies, even if she didn't like a particular dress, which she often didn't, because she was picky. Wilhelmina liked solid colors more than patterns, but only particular hues, the ones that rang a clear, joyful bell inside her. When she liked a pattern, it was for the same inexplicable reason: she just *did*. When the aunts' clients stepped out of their cars, sometimes they set her ringing like the bell above a shop door, and other times, she became analytical but indifferent.

There was a woman who had a body similar to Wilhelmina's, short and fat—Wilhelmina was practicing using the word "fat" as a descriptive term free of judgment, which was hard, since most other people used it as a slur, but the aunts didn't, nor did her parents—it was a neutral word for all of them, and so, with a certain measure of belligerence, she was testing it out. Julie and Bee were testing it out in solidarity with her, or anyway, they were trying to. Sometimes they cringed a little when they said it, or shot her worried expressions, because they didn't want to hurt her feelings, which, if Wilhelmina was being honest with herself, made it worse, but she could feel their solidarity in their hearts. Which meant something. Anyway, there was a woman shaped like Wilhelmina who wore summery shirts in patterns Wilhelmina consistently liked. The shirts looked handmade. They were always sleeveless, and fitted to her torso perfectly, with backs composed entirely of delicate straps that exposed the gray-and-black wings tattooed on her shoulders. She wore these shirts with tight jeans, and Wilhelmina found it incredibly sexy. She imagined her own back tattooed with giant wings and wasn't sure if that was right, but it was certainly right for this woman.

There was a man whose short hair was sculpted into an angular wedge above his head, regular brown hair on one side but with a wide streak of reddish purple on the other. He wore big brown boots and tight dark jeans and Wilhelmina thought his legs, thick and muscular, and his thick torso, and the chest giving shape to his T-shirt, were incredibly sexy too. She wished Bee were here to see that man when he had an appointment with the aunts. Bee wanted to color his own hair. He *had* colored his hair, actually, last year at Christmas. Hot pink. His father had shaved his head afterward. Anyway, Wilhelmina called Bee to tell him about the man's hair, though she didn't tell him about the man's overall je ne sais quoi, because she couldn't figure out how to say it without it sounding like all she meant was her own lust. She did feel lust, sure, but that was separate—completely—from the thing about the man that she wanted to share with Bee. It was something about a feeling some people had. It was powerful, like magic. She sensed it the moment they stepped out of their cars, the people who'd figured out exactly who they were.

When Wilhelmina talked to Julie on the phone, she didn't bother trying to go into details because—Wilhelmina was inexpressibly excited about this—Julie would get to see it for herself, because Julie was coming. The Dunstables were driving to visit her father's family in North Carolina and they were going to stay a night with the aunts en route. Just a night, but they promised to arrive as early as they reasonably could and stay as late as possible the next day, so that Wilhelmina and Julie could have some time together.

For almost twenty-four hours that summer, Wilhelmina was completely happy. She showed Julie around Frankie's many gardens. She took her swimming at the lake, and pointed out the faraway beach where she found the blue stones. She pulled Esther's tía Rosa's sketchbooks down from the glass-fronted bookcase in the sitting room—Tía Rosa had died and left Esther her sketchbooks—and showed Julie pages and pages of delicate drawings of plants, animals, and sometimes objects, labeled in Spanish, with descriptors and dates. "Esther says she kept records of all the spirits she met in the world," said Wilhelmina.

"Wow," said Julie, who always *got* things, without Wilhelmina needing to explain. "I can feel their spirits coming through the pictures."

She brought Julie on a walk down the sidewalkless road as cars careened by—"We walk facing traffic," she instructed importantly—past the Dornblazers' cows and the Watchulonises' apple trees, and introduced her to every neighbor they saw. "This is my best friend Julie," she said to Mrs. Watchulonis, then to Mr. Ransom, then to Mrs. Storz and her four children. She showed Julie the old, teeny cemetery with mossy, fallen-over stones from the 1700s.

When they got home again, she asked Frankie to pull Julie a tarot card, because Julie had always been interested in Frankie's tarot cards, more interested than Wilhelmina herself.

"Would you like that, dear?" Frankie asked Julie.

"Oh yes, please," said Julie.

At the kitchen table, Frankie patted the chair beside her for Julie to sit down, then began shuffling her cards. It was the deck Frankie used most often ever since she'd given Wilhelmina her old deck. It was the same style of deck, with the same pictures, but the cards were brighter and crisper, less softened with age.

Once the cards were shuffled, Frankie set the deck on the table and asked Julie to cut it. When Julie did, Frankie turned the topmost card over.

"Ah," she said, handing it to Julie. "The Three of Wands."

The card showed a person from behind, wearing flowing clothing of many colors, standing on high ground, looking out at ships sailing across a bay.

"What does it mean?" said Julie almost reverently, tracing the three wands in the picture with her finger. Two were stuck in the ground like pillars, or like a door the person had just stepped through. The third was in the person's hand, held like a walking stick.

"This is the card of an adventurer," said Frankie, "and a card of ambition. You see that beautiful, broad view over the water, and all those ships heading who knows where? It's about setting off into the world, on a literal or a metaphorical adventure. It's also a good-fortune card—things will go well for you in your ventures—and you see that colorful outfit? It's a card for a nonconformist."

"Wow," said Julie. "I love it. It feels just right for me." Julie had a cell phone; it was new, and an object of great envy for Wilhelmina. She took about twelve photos of her tarot card before she gave it back to Frankie.

That night, they slept in sleeping bags on Wilhelmina's floor because it was more fair than one of them having the bed. Then, in the morning, they woke to the Pound! Pound! Pound! of the cardinal on the windowglass far below.

"What the hell?" said Julie, pushing herself up blurrily, her bonnet slipping off, a sleepy but incredulous expression on her face. As Wilhelmina explained, Julie cried out, "Every morning?" with such indignation that suddenly the cardinal was hilarious. They both started laughing. Somewhere far away in the house, Tina, Julie's two-year-old sister, began howling. Julie pulled her sleeping bag over her face and said, "It's amazing to be two floors away from Teeny."

"I wish you could stay longer," Wilhelmina said.

"Me too," said Julie. "I can't believe you have, like, the whole top floor of this house to yourself."

"Let's spy," said Wilhelmina.

That morning, the man with the red-purple streak in his hair had an appointment with the aunts. Kneeling on Wilhelmina's bed, they watched him climb out of his car. Wilhelmina was so glad he'd arrived. She wanted Julie to see all the most fascinating clients.

"I like his style," Wilhelmina said, not knowing how to explain to Julie what she meant, or why he mattered. Hoping Julie would just *get* it, now that she saw him herself.

"Everyone really is white here," said Julie musingly, peering at the man as he disappeared into the carriage house.

"What?" said Wilhelmina, because it wasn't at all what she'd wanted Julie to understand about the man. "No, they're not. Esther isn't white!"

The expression that Julie turned to Wilhelmina contained so much startled hurt that Wilhelmina heard her own words again, and was ashamed.

"I didn't mean literally everyone," said Julie. "You don't need to correct me, Wil."

"You're right," said Wilhelmina. "I'm so sorry, Julie. I don't know why I said that."

"Esther was even the one who said it first," said Julie, a tear, to Wilhelmina's horror, making a track down her face. "That's why *I* said it, because I was going to tell you what Esther said. Because it was really sweet, actually. She said that it might be different from what I was used to here, and she just wanted to acknowledge it. She said everyone is really kind, but I could always come talk to her, about anything. I mean, it was unnecessary, Wil," said Julie, with a mild glare at the window glass. Julie wasn't looking at Wilhelmina. "I don't need to hang out with, like, your great-aunt. But it was nice. I felt like she was trying to look out for me."

Julie had put the slightest emphasis on the word "she" in that sentence. Esther, unlike Wilhelmina, had been trying to look out for Julie.

"Oh my god, Julie," said Wilhelmina. "I'm so sorry. I should be looking out for you!"

"I mean, it's okay," said Julie, as another tear dripped down her face.

"It's not okay," said Wilhelmina, her voice growing squeakier and squeakier as she understood that she'd made Julie cry multiple tears. "It's just, I think that guy is really hot! I'm trying to figure out my *style!*" Her voice was disappearing into the stratosphere; Julie began to stare at her with her mouth forming an O. "So I was being completely self-absorbed! I should've listened to you, Julie, and not been racist!"

"Oh my god, Wil," said Julie. "Take a breath."

"Sorry," said Wilhelmina, trying to get ahold of her voice. "Forget about that guy, he doesn't matter. Can I tell you what I wish I'd said, instead of what I did say?"

The girls were still kneeling beside each other on the bed, propped in the window. Julie had gone rigid when Wilhelmina had first spoken, but now she was feeling more regular again to Wilhelmina, like maybe she'd decided she didn't need to brace herself. She sniffled once, and nodded.

Wilhelmina took a breath. "You're right," she said. "It's like a sea of white people here. I know that matters. Next time I'm going to be more supportive."

Julie watched Wilhelmina's face for a moment. Then she said, "Thanks."

"Of course, Julie. Are you okay?"

"Mostly," said Julie. "I think you surprised me, more than anything else. I expected you to just *get* it. Like, you of all people. You're my person, you know? I didn't think it would be a thing."

Through her shame, Wilhelmina was having a realization. "I think maybe I didn't want it to be true," she said. "This place matters so much to me, you know? I didn't want it to be anything bad, or anything that might hurt you."

"But denying it's true hurts me more," said Julie.

"Yeah," said Wilhelmina, who could see this too.

"Hey," said Julie, bumping her shoulder against Wilhelmina's. The contact felt like it was made of generosity and grace.

"Hey," said Wilhelmina.

"Are you going to tell me about this hot guy?"

When Julie's family left, Wilhelmina wasn't sure how she felt, about anything. She wandered the house and the yard, trying to find the place where she would never hurt someone she loved with her own carelessness. She took a solitary walk to the cemetery, where, with a small burst of dismay, it occurred to her to wonder what Julie had thought, looking at the graves of white people from the 1700s, when slavery had been legal.

She swam a lot. Sometimes the lake felt too small. Sometimes when she reached the faraway beach, the breeze was too cold, the pebbles were too sharp on her feet, and she couldn't find any blue stones. She wore a garnet-colored two-piece bathing suit that covered her torso and had shorts that reached partway down her thighs, because she liked it. It was comfortable, she liked how it looked on her, and she liked that it was a fuck-you to the pressure women felt to be nearly naked on beaches. But she worried sometimes that people who saw her in it thought she was trying to cover her body, because she was ashamed, because she was fat. Wilhelmina felt pressure to be nearly naked and pressure to hide her body in shame. Pressures could be opposites. When they were opposites, how could you ever possibly make a clear statement of resistance? Were there modest bathing suits like hers that had the words FUCK YOU in big letters on the butt?

She asked Julie this over the phone, because she knew it was an easy question that would make Julie laugh. Wilhelmina didn't know for sure how to talk to Julie about what she was trying to do with her style, partly because she didn't know what she was trying to do. Wilhelmina didn't know anyone her age who had a body like hers. "I feel weird trying to explain it," she said.

"Hey," said Julie, who was eating something crunchy on the other end of the line. "We can have weird conversations. I found a makeup channel on YouTube I like. Want the link?"

"What do you mean, a makeup channel?"

"People teach you how to do different looks," she said. "There are hair and clothes channels too."

"There are?" said Wilhelmina, amazed.

"Of course there are!" said Julie. "I'll send you the link."

Often, when Wilhelmina swam, Aunt Margaret swam too. Aunt Margaret had an array of bathing suits in bright jewel tones, and you never knew which one to expect when she pulled her shirt off. Once, she started swimming in a magenta bathing suit, turned around, came back to shore, carried her bag into the bathhouse, and emerged in a jade-green bathing suit. "I couldn't figure out which one was right for today until I was swimming!" she announced as she dropped her bag back onto her beach chair, then ran into the water again.

After swimming, Wilhelmina always wanted to go straight home and sleep, or anyway, she thought she did. She wanted to be doing whatever she wasn't doing. But Aunt Margaret would drive out of the parking lot and turn in the wrong direction with no warning, because she "just needed to pop to the hardware store for a flapper for the downstairs toilet," or Esther needed a prescription picked up at the pharmacy, or a neighbor was home from a trip to Montréal and she wanted to welcome them back, or anything else on a long list of activities Wilhelmina badly wished not to be doing.

One day, Aunt Margaret turned the car in the correct direction and Wilhelmina breathed an internal sigh of relief. Then, three bends in the road later, Aunt Margaret slammed on the brakes and started driving the car backward.

"Aunt Margaret!" cried Wilhelmina. "What are you doing?"

"Did you see that sign for a pottery studio, dear?" said Aunt Margaret, still haphazardly backing up with her head craned around on her neck. "Don't you just love pottery studios?"

"I love not having car accidents!" said Wilhelmina.

"Oh, the nearest car is a half mile away, I promise," said Aunt Margaret, then turned the car down a narrow dirt road Wilhelmina had never particularly noticed before.

The road sloped downhill through a forest of birch trees. It was a relief to be driving forward. "How do we know how far away this place is?" said Wilhelmina.

"Oh, this road isn't too long," said Aunt Margaret soothingly. "It can't be far."

"How can there be a pottery studio you don't know about?"

Aunt Margaret shrugged. "New neighbors? Old neighbors with new hobbies?"

Wilhelmina clamped her mouth shut, preparing to hate the pottery studio. She had that grimy, sticky feeling that came from thick applications of sunscreen plus dressing in wrinkled clothing pulled out of a sandy bag while one's body was not entirely dry, and her long hair, gathered into a thick, dark knot, was dripping steadily, forming a wet patch on her back.

But as it happened, Wilhelmina didn't hate the pottery studio. First, because it turned out to be a small barn built of mossy gray stone, set back from the road and surrounded by shoulder-high corn that stretched out to the edges of the birch forest, which was charming. Second, because it was empty, with no hovering proprietor to whom Wilhelmina felt obliged to be pleasant. And third, because the pottery was of such unparalleled revoltingness that Wilhelmina was captivated. Someone—someone skilled—had made these pots on purpose. This mug, nicely shaped and well-balanced, but glazed the unique yellow-brown of diarrhea, and with seashell shards affixed to its outside that had been used as canvases for tiny paintings of coiled intestines, was someone's deliberate style.

"Dear me," said Aunt Margaret, picking up a viscera-colored bowl. A sculptured bloodshot eyeball stared up from its bottom. Aunt Margaret poked at the eyeball with an enchanted expression on her face. "What do you think, Wilhelmina?"

"Gross," said Wilhelmina.

"Yes," said Aunt Margaret, turning the bowl over to look at its price tag. Thirty-five dollars. "Where does one pay, do you suppose?"

"Honor system," said Wilhelmina, pointing to an open tin and a sign near the door. "But you're not buying that, are you?"

"No, I think not," said Aunt Margaret. "It's a hair too horrific for me. Though I would like to serve Esther soup in it and be around for her reaction when she uncovered the eyeball. What's extraordinary is that *this* is beautiful," she added, setting the bowl down and reaching past a series of nesting dolls. The nesting dolls were anatomically correct hearts, five of them, standing upright on squat legs of veins and arteries, glazed with a weird slickness that sent a little shudder crawling down Wilhelmina's back. She badly wanted to test whether they fit together, as nesting dolls should.

Aunt Margaret touched a finger to a little teapot behind the hearts. It was glazed a pale eggshell blue, speckled with brown at its base. The handle on its lid was sculpted into a delicate songbird.

Taking the teapot in both hands, Aunt Margaret tested the lid. Then she held the handle and pretended to pour. "It's light and perfect!" she said. "The handle is comfortable! Doesn't it look as if a being from another realm reached through the veils of hell to deposit it here, Wilhelmina?" She turned it over to check the price. Sixty dollars. "It's an investment," she said, "but I think this is why we came. We must buy it for Frankie. She'll be able to tell us what kind of bird this is on the handle."

"Okay," said Wilhelmina. "But I want to look at everything before we leave."

"Understood," said Aunt Margaret, setting the teapot back behind the hearts. She touched a stoppered jug shaped like a stomach, glazed a stomachy pink, that proclaimed on the outside in a beautiful serif font, SELF-PORTRAIT. "Is the self-portrait trapped inside the stomach, do you think?" she said. "Or is it the stomach itself? Did another stomach make this stomach?"

Wilhelmina was beginning to have feelings about this barn. Those five slimy hearts were her own bad dreams and bad decisions, crawling out of her body and lining themselves up on the table, giving her a break from herself. She wandered happily from piece to piece. While she was studying a group of tall pitchers also shaped like stomachs with lengthy esophagus spouts, another family entered the studio. Wilhelmina turned her back; she didn't want to talk to anyone; she didn't want to have to be nice.

"That's the one," said a boy's deep voice. "Viv? You have the money?"

"Wow," said a girl's voice. "Who's the artist?"

"Not that one," said the boy, his voice cracking on the word "that," becoming younger. "This one."

A moment later, they were gone, and Wilhelmina and Aunt Margaret were once more alone. Wilhelmina's shoulders relaxed.

"Hm," said Aunt Margaret, who'd rounded back to the entrance. "How interesting."

"What is it?" said Wilhelmina.

"They purchased our teapot," said Aunt Margaret. Then she pointed to the hearts, behind which gaped an empty space. "I was wrong," she said. "The teapot is not why we came."

Wilhelmina flashed with annoyance. In her mind, that teapot already belonged to Frankie, which meant that those people had stolen it. She crossed to the door with a few stompy strides and barged outside. In the narrow gravel drive, a car was turning around. On its back bumper, a sticker said, JESUS WOULD USE HIS TURN SIGNALS. The driver had a ring of graying hair; a teenaged girl sat beside him. In the back seat was a boy who was lifting that beautiful eggshell-blue teapot up to the light. She saw long, skinny arms and a mess of dark hair. "Assholes!" she said under her breath as the car drove away. "Thieves."

"Did you find any other treasures, Wilhelmina?" asked Aunt Margaret from the doorway. "Anything it would pain you to leave behind?"

"Only Frankie's teapot, which they stole," said Wilhelmina.

"I'm tempted to commission a new one," said Aunt Margaret, in an unruffled tone that Wilhelmina found intensely aggravating. "Just to see what the artist creates."

"Can we go home now?" said Wilhelmina.

At home, Wilhelmina showered, then climbed up to her bedroom and lay on her bed for a while, hating the way her wet hair soaked her pillow. She and Julie had started sending each other links to hair-styling videos. Black-person hair and white-person hair, men's hair and women's, colored and bleached and extensions, whatever; it was making Wilhelmina even more impatient.

She wondered why she'd never tried short hair before. Then she understood, through some unexamined instinct, that it was because of Frankie. Frankie's hair was thin and wispy, but she'd used to have long hair. Wilhelmina remembered it from a long time ago. Silver and thick, wound into twisted braids that she wore like a crown around her head, like an empress. Like *the* Empress in the tarot, sitting in her garden, with her pomegranate dress and her crown of stars. Right? Hadn't she? Wilhelmina grew her hair long because Frankie was fine. Or something? It didn't make much sense, it was illogical really, and she was going to get her hair cut. Somewhere, soon. The next time one of the aunts' short-haired clients stepped out of their car, as long as it wasn't that hot guy, of course, Wilhelmina was going to learn where they got their hair cut, without humiliating herself. They would find her breezily loitering in the yard after their appointment and she would ask them casually, as if she couldn't care less, "Hey, where did you get your hair cut?" Or maybe she could pretend it was her job, a responsibility assigned to her by someone else, to conduct a survey about where people got their hair cut. Or she could blame Frankie. *Hi. Excuse me. I'm sorry to bother you, but my aunt wants to know where you got your hair cut.*

Hating all of these ideas, Wilhelmina went downstairs to look for Frankie.

She found her on the second floor, in her bedroom, lying on her bed, which was unusual for Frankie during the day. Frankie didn't go in to the doctor for chemo this summer; instead, she took daily pills. The medicine had side effects, but it wasn't as dramatic as the IV chemotherapy had been. She was awake, propped up slightly by pillows, shuffling her tarot cards in her lap.

"Frankie?" said Wilhelmina, standing in the doorway. "What are you doing?"

"Wilhelmina, love," said Frankie, turning to Wilhelmina with a radiant smile that made everything all right, because how could anything be wrong when there was someone in the world who was always so happy to see her? Frankie patted the mattress beside her. "Come in, join me," she said. "Are you okay? I want to hear all about you, dear."

"We were going to buy you a teapot," said Wilhelmina. "But someone else bought it before we could." She entered the room, then sat on the edge of Frankie's bed a bit shyly. Wilhelmina walked by the aunts' bedrooms every day, but she rarely entered them. It was strange to think of Frankie having an intimate space Wilhelmina hardly knew, where she spent a lot of time. It felt like a different house in here; the light was different, or the air.

Above the headboard of Frankie's bed were framed three prints that were different from each other, but also the same. One was a big print of the Temperance card from the tarot deck Frankie had given Wilhelmina, the angel with the funny triangle on his chest and the giant red-and-gray wings, pouring water from one golden goblet into another. Wilhelmina had that tarot card tucked into her mirror at home in Massachusetts. It was Frankie's favorite card, because it was about seeing the world clearly, both its harsh realities and its magic. The other two prints were also Temperance cards, but from different decks. One showed a person whose gender was unclear; Wilhelmina thought of him as a feminine man. He wore a tank top, jeans, boots, and makeup, and had glowing white wings on his back; that funny triangle was tattooed on his chest. In one hand he balanced the sun, and in the other hand, the moon. In the third Temperance card, the giant winged person was, in fact, a bird. A heron, dripping water—or crying salty tears?—onto a graceful orange flame at her feet.

Frankie shuffled her cards against her stomach.

"Will you pull me a card?" said Wilhelmina. She asked Frankie to do this for her from time to time, less because she cared about the cards, and more because it felt like touch. When Frankie pulled Wilhelmina a card and told her what it meant, it was like someone brushing her hair, or rubbing her back, or aiming a fan straight at her on a sweltering hot day.

"Of course," said Frankie, then began a rhythmic and repetitive series of shuffles that sounded lovely to Wilhelmina, like all her summers together. While Frankie shuffled, Wilhelmina peeked around the room. Frankie had hanging shelves on one wall that were crowded with figurines, mostly birds.

Once the cards were shuffled, Frankie set the deck on the bed between them and asked Wilhelmina to cut it. When Wilhelmina did, Frankie turned the topmost card over, then brought the card into her lap, where she could see it more clearly.

"The Moon," said Frankie.

"The Moon?" said Wilhelmina, glancing at the Temperance print above the bed, where the androgynous person held the moon in one hand, the sun in the other. "I don't think I've gotten the Moon before. Can I see it?"

The card Frankie passed to Wilhelmina was an odd one. A dog and a wolf stood on the shore above a lake, staring up at a sad-faced moon. Some sort of shellfish—a lobster? A crab?—climbed out of the water behind them, as if it was sneaking up on them.

It wasn't a very nice card. Everyone looked cold and unhappy. "Yikes," said Wilhelmina. "Why is there a lobster?"

"I think that's meant to be a crayfish," said Frankie, who was lying back with her eyes closed, smiling. "But it hardly matters. It's an interesting card, Wilhelmina. It comes up when we're in one of the darker parts of our journey. It's about fear, and bad dreams, and discomfort. It's about bumbling around in the dark, and not being able to tell what's real and what's an illusion."

"Oh," said Wilhelmina, cradling the card in her hands. Funny drops of fire were falling down from the sky into the lake. A winding path led to mountains in the distance. It was kind of an ugly card, honestly, random and disjointed.

"What do you do?" said Wilhelmina. "Like, if you're stuck in a place where everything just . . . feels wrong? And you can't figure out why, or how to fix it?"

"Mmm," said Frankie, a noise of deep appreciation, as if Wilhelmina had said something profound, rather than something ignorant, something that had come from a place that felt a little bit desperate. Scared. "I've felt that way many times."

"You have?"

"It's one of the great human feelings," said Frankie simply. "Discomfort. Uncertainty about what's going on, or what's going to happen. The sense that things around you are wrong. A lot of things around us *are* wrong, Wilhelmina. People make terrible decisions to get away from having to sit with how wrongness feels. They can't bear to be lost and afraid. They'll choose something bad for them, or bad for others, just to feel like they're in control of something. It's understandable, don't you think?"

Wilhelmina touched the dog on the card, then the wolf. She didn't touch the crayfish, because she didn't want to. It was her least favorite part of the card.

"But I think there's a lot of value in learning to bear being lost, Wilhelmina, love," said Frankie. "The discomfort won't actually kill you, you know. Sometimes it's just a feeling you need to feel. Different feelings will come, when they're ready. The sun rises in the morning, right? Maybe it'll bring some clarity. Maybe it'll show you a new beginning for your life. One of the best things to learn how to do is wait."

WEDNESDAY, NOVEMBER 4, 2020

Wilhelmina dreamed that she was a tiny owl, lying on her side in someone's yard. Her talon was broken and something awful was about to happen. She needed to warn the vulnerable ones, but she couldn't move, and when she tried to cry out, the sound stayed caught inside her, and the effort hurt her talon. Something horrific was going to happen, and she couldn't cry or scream; she was trapped. She tried again, opening her mouth, trying to press sound through her throat. It hurt. It hurt!

ON THE WEDNESDAY three days before she stepped into her own, Wilhelmina woke thrashing. She was in her own bed in Massachusetts. She was herself, not an owl, and her voice was working just fine; in fact, she cried out as she woke. Her neck, her shoulders. *Ow.*

Wilhelmina pulled out her mouthguard and grabbed for her glasses. Delia was gone. Wrapping herself in Frankie's crow blanket, she stood, then slipped into the boots she found at her bedside. She listened hard, but heard no one. So she snuck into the bathroom, then the kitchen, and crept out the back door.

In daylight, it was easier to locate the crows. A number of them were flitting around in the highest branches of the backyard's biggest tree, an oak with leaves still thick and green. Which meant James had given her accurate information.

She wished she'd thought to ask him how to supplicate to crows. Food, probably, or a replacement shiny object? She touched her throat, her own elephant, and knew suddenly that this was the one the crows should've taken, that they should've taken *hers*. She was the one who didn't fit. But what could she do about it? It wasn't like she was inside one of Aesop's fables. She couldn't walk up to a tree and make a deal with a crow.

"Wil?" said a voice behind her.

Wilhelmina turned around to find Julie watching her from her high bedroom window, kneeling in her window seat. A princess in a tower? No, more like a bird perched in a really great nest she'd made for herself, stocked with all her favorite books and games. A nest she would fly away from, when the time was right. Wilhelmina had never begrudged Julie for wanting to go far away for college. She'd understood it. She'd always believed that no matter where in the world Julie's plans took her, their friendship would adapt. "Julie," she said in a cracking voice. "I miss you."

"Well, hey, I'm right here, elephant," said Julie. "What are you doing?"

She looked tired, her eyes puffy from sleep, or maybe from watching the election returns. Did she also have something guarded in her face? Was Julie watching Wilhelmina as if she knew what Wilhelmina had done?

Suddenly, Wilhelmina couldn't pretend anymore. "I let the crow take your necklace," she said. "I did it on purpose."

"What?" said Julie, plainly confused. "What are you talking about?"

Wilhelmina's mouth felt thick with shame. "The crow dropped your necklace right where I could reach it," she said. "I could've grabbed it, easily. Instead, I waited. Because I knew it would take it back."

Julie's bafflement was turning to incredulity. "What?" she said. "Why would you even do that?"

"I don't know!" said Wilhelmina. "It just happened."

"No, it didn't!" said Julie. "You just told me you did it on purpose!"

"Yes, that's true," said Wilhelmina, who didn't want to lie, and badly wanted to explain, but didn't know how to. "I don't know why, Julie! I've been really lonely! You guys are doing the pandemic together, and I'm on the outside."

"You're never on the outside, Wil!" said Julie. "This is just the way it is right now!"

"But I want to be in your bubble. I want to *have been* in your bubble. I want, when this whole thing started, for you and Bee to have been like, *no, sorry, we're not doing this without Wilhelmina!*"

"But it was for our sisters!" cried Julie. "We didn't decide it ourselves! Our parents did, and your dad has asthma!"

"I know!" said Wilhelmina. "But you don't know what it's been like. You're always together. It's always the two of you, without me. I can't touch you. I can't hug you. I can't even see your faces most of the time. And you guys—" Wilhelmina needed a breath to get this next part out. It was hurting so much to crane her face up to the window. "Are you guys, like, into each other?"

"What?" squeaked Julie, almost in horror. "No! Where are you getting that?"

"You're not?" said Wilhelmina, so surprised and so relieved that she bent over and took a few more deep breaths. Her relief was short-lived. She knew somehow what she would see when she looked back up at Julie.

She straightened. Julie had an expression on her face like Wilhelmina was some terribly sad event she was watching happen in the distance, something that was breaking her heart.

"Wil," said Julie, in a funny voice. "Why did I find out from James that you two ran into each other in Pennsylvania? Why didn't you tell me?"

"I—wasn't using my phone a lot yesterday," said Wilhelmina.

"Why didn't you tell us you were going to Pennsylvania in the first place?" said Julie. "Please be honest, okay?"

Wilhelmina started to say the thing about how everything had happened so fast, then stopped. She thought it through, for real. She said, "I truly don't know."

Julie watched her for a moment, with tears sliding down her face. Wilhelmina had to put a hand back to hold up her own head. Her neck was in agony. "You can have mine," she added, meaning her own necklace. She reached for the chain, but Julie looked aghast.

"Are you breaking up with me?" she cried.

"What?" cried Wilhelmina, shocked. "Of course not!"

"I just can't believe that you, like, *offered* my necklace to a crow!" said Julie. "Like, pushing me out of our circle! You have a disappearing act you do when you're upset. I get it. Or actually, I don't get it, but I get that it's real, and not something you do on purpose, to be mean. But this is the first time you've decided to make *me* disappear."

"I—don't want you to disappear," said Wilhelmina desperately. "I would never want you to disappear."

Julie took a moment to pat her eyes with her sleeves, then dropped her arms back to the windowsill, truly dropped them, as if she was exhausted. New tears welled up to replace the ones she'd wiped away. "Well, that's how it feels," she said. Then she tucked her chin to her chest in that old, familiar gesture of worry, shrugged her shoulders, and shut the window. The ancient rusted pulley that was still attached to her windowsill shifted once, with a squeak and a low, quick moan.

Wilhelmina felt like her entire body was on fire. She climbed the steep yard to the back door, clutching Frankie's blanket and gulping air. Inside, she found her mother doing dishes in the kitchen, humming something cheerful that sounded like the main *Star Wars* theme.

"Good morning, Wilhelmina," Cleo said, breaking off in the middle of a series of *duh-da-da-duh*s.

"Where is everyone?" said Wilhelmina.

"Delia's having school in our bedroom with Dad, and the aunts are doing Philip's school in their room, bless them. They wanted to give you the day off."

Wilhelmina grunted.

"You've looked at the news this morning?" said Cleo.

"No."

"You haven't looked at the news?" said Cleo, turning to stare at Wilhelmina.

"No," said Wilhelmina, moving toward her room so that Cleo could stop reminding her of the existence of the news.

"So maybe you don't know that Biden's favored to win?"

"What?" Wilhelmina cried, instantly dizzy. "But he's behind by thirteen points in Pennsylvania!"

"Those numbers are changing, hon," said Cleo. "You remember all the mail-in ballots?"

"But the whole map was pink! Thirteen points!"

"He's favored!" said Cleo, waving one hand and sending a clump of soapsuds flying. "Even the betting sites are favoring him. If he keeps Nevada, Arizona, Wisconsin, and Maine," she said, dripping more suds as she counted on her fingers, "and if he gets either Pennsylvania or Michigan, he's going to win."

Wilhelmina needed to lean against the wall. "You're talking about Joe Biden," she said. "Kamala Harris and Joe Biden?"

"Yes," said Cleo, her face breaking into a tired smile. "Look for yourself. The percentage has been dropping like a rock in Michigan. They're only trailing by half a point there now."

Wilhelmina put a hand up, turned away. She staggered to her bedroom, where she slammed the door and crossed to her bed, bunching Frankie's blanket into a ball against her pillows and pressing her face into it. She breathed. Then she began to cry, muffling the sound with the blanket. As her cries turned to sobs, she felt like she was crying for all the sadness in the world.

IT WAS HER PHONE that finally stopped Wilhelmina's tears, not because it made a noise, but because she happened to look at it in the moment it lit up with Bee's name.

Yesterday, she would've let it go to voice mail. Today, she answered. "Hi."

He paused. "Hi," he said, in a voice that made it obvious he'd talked to Julie, though Wilhelmina had already known that, the moment the phone had lit up.

There was a long pause. "So?" said Wilhelmina. "Are you mad at me?"

He made an exhaling noise that sounded confused. "Maybe a little?" he said. "But mostly I'm just, like, so bewildered. I mean, I know it was Julie's necklace, not mine, but they all mean the same thing, right? Do you not want to be our friend anymore?"

"Yes!" she said. "More than anything!"

He made another series of confused-sounding noises. Wilhelmina kept thinking he was about to start talking again, then he would stop himself.

"I used to worry a lot," he finally said, "like, when we were little, that you would stop being my friend."

"What!" cried Wilhelmina. "Why? Did I do something to make you think that?"

"No," he said, "it was never anything you did. It was because you had two entire homes. You had two parents who were nice people, and you had the aunts, who were, like, the most comforting beings on the planet. I figured you didn't need me."

"Oh, Bee," said Wilhelmina. She was crying again, but this time it was for younger Bee. "That was never how it worked. I always needed you. Do you understand that now?"

"Yeah."

"I feel like right now, maybe you and Julie don't need *me*," she said.

"That's false," he said. "I . . ." He hesitated. "I sort of wish you'd kept me in the loop about that. Instead of performing a dramatic gesture with a crow. I mean, maybe I should've known? But I didn't."

"I know," she said. "I—I don't know why I didn't."

"I know it used to be easier for you to tell me your feelings," Bee said. "Before Frankie died. I know you're still grieving her."

Wilhelmina was crying harder. She couldn't hide the sound of it, and she couldn't respond to that.

"Are you mad at me?" said Bee. "For not realizing how you've been feeling?"

Since he'd asked, she couldn't pretend. "Yeah," she said. "A little bit."

He paused. Then he sniffled. Bee was crying. "That seems fair," he said.

"What should I do?" said Wilhelmina. "How do I fix this?"

"I don't know," said Bee. "But will you tell me whether we're still friends, even when we're upset with each other?"

Wilhelmina said that yes, of course they were, because she couldn't bear the answer to be no. But she wasn't sure what it meant anymore.

SHE FOUND HER FOAM ROLLER and did her best to stretch away some of her pain. The crying hadn't helped. Wilhelmina's body was winding in on itself tightly like an echidna, except echidnas were adorable.

She sought out her mother, who was still in the kitchen, chopping carrots and potatoes. "Does it work for me to not drive anywhere today?" she said. "It'd help a lot if I could take more muscle relaxants."

Cleo pursed her lips, then nodded. "I can do any driving that comes up. Why don't you take the day off from jobs, hon?"

"Thanks," said Wilhelmina.

Back in her bedroom, Wilhelmina dressed herself in a daze, reaching for clothing that felt right, not really paying attention. Soft things, comforting things. Also Frankie's owl, which was a small, enraged weight on her ear. She took off her necklace. Then she put it on again. Then she took it off again.

With one deep breath to gird herself, she went to the aunts' bedroom and tapped on the door.

Esther answered, tall and grave. "What can I do for you, Wilhelmina?" she said quietly. Behind her, Wilhelmina could hear Philip's teacher talking about the letter *S*. "Snakes!" she said. "Snores! Stars!"

"Esther," said Wilhelmina, "would you feel comfortable texting one of James's grandparents and asking them for his phone number for me?"

"Of course," said Esther, not waggling her eyebrows, or doing any of the teasing Wilhelmina had feared. "I like your blue."

"Huh?" said Wilhelmina, then looked down at herself. She was wearing a fuzzy cornflower-blue hoodie over navy-blue leggings. She noticed that Esther wore deep blue jeans and a long twilight-blue sweater, and blue stones in her ears. "You too?" she said.

Esther made a small noise of affirmation. "The last time people voted for him," she said, "we really couldn't know for sure what kind of president he would be. This time, we know, and look how many people still love him." She shrugged. "Often when I'm hurting, I wear blue."

WHEN THE TEXT with James's number arrived from Esther, Wilhelmina was lying on her foam roller again. It seemed to help her pain while she lay on it. But the moment she got up, the echidna effect would return.

She sat on her bed for a while, trying to figure out what to say to James. She finally settled on, *Hi. It's Wilhelmina.* Not exactly earth-shattering, she knew, and she was agonizing over what to say next when he replied.

Sorry I hurt your feelings yesterday

Please don't apologize, she wrote all in a rush. *You were right. I'm sorry.*

But I am sorry, he wrote. *It was a mean analogy*

It's okay, she said. *I shouldn't have run away*

How u feeling?

All over the place, she said. *Listen, do you know what happened to that owl from the dentist?*

No why?

I had a nightmare about the owl, she said.

A few minutes passed. *Sorry slow,* he wrote. *At the shop. U text wicked fast*

I'm dictating, she explained.

I had nightmare too. About a wolf

Wilhelmina lay back on her pillow, resting her phone on her stomach for a moment and remembering her dream. She wondered if the owl in her dream had been injured by a wolf.

Was it a mean wolf? she asked.

Not sure, he said. *It was hungry tho*

Wilhelmina took a breath, preparing herself. *Want to talk about it?* she said. *All of it?*

All of it, ALL of it? he said.

Yes.

Yes, he said. *Today?*

Today is good.

Noon?

Sure.

Library?

The library was a few blocks from the Lupa Building, a twenty-minute walk downhill from Wilhelmina's home.

Sure, she said.

Then she laid her phone on her stomach again, rested her stinging hands, wondering if she could convince her aching body to nap a bit. Just in case she succeeded, she set an alarm.

Before she closed her eyes, she turned notifications back on for Julie and Bee, trying not to think too much about why it mattered. She reached for her necklace, then remembered she wasn't wearing it today. Then, just once, she checked the news. The top headline was, "Biden Takes the Lead in Michigan."

SHE WOKE AROUND ELEVEN THIRTY, to the sound of Julie's cat Esther thundering across the ceiling above. Below, in the basement, someone was slamming the doors of the washing machine and the dryer.

"Daddy?" came Delia's muted voice. "After school, can I make a unicorn cake?"

"What?" came Theo's voice. "A what?"

"A unicorn cake!"

"Is that something you've done by yourself before, sweetie?" asked Theo, who sounded extremely harried, and also muffled, as if his head were in the dryer.

"Yes!" said Delia. "Basically. Almost. I need to make one for Eleanor."

"I'm working this afternoon, Delia," said Theo. "I don't mind if you make a dozen unicorn cakes, but your mother will become the arbiter of your fate shortly."

"Mom!" screamed Delia.

"Honey," said Theo, "you need to go into the room she's in, wait until she can give you her attention, then ask her in a respectful tone of voice. Oh my god. How can *four* different socks be missing? This is so stressful!"

In the living room, Wilhelmina found her mother lying flat on the floor with her eyes closed, taking noisy, deep breaths and speaking words as she breathed out. "Alaska," she said. "Arizona. Georgia."

"Mom?" said Wilhelmina, going to the coat closet. "What are you doing?"

"A relaxing meditation," said Cleo. "Maine. Michigan. Nevada."

"Are those the states that haven't been called yet?"

"Yes. North Carolina. Pennsylvania. Wisconsin."

"Is that really relaxing?" said Wilhelmina. "Wouldn't it be better to, like, name all the planets? Think about how far away Saturn is. The election doesn't matter on Saturn."

"Mm," said Cleo. "Very wise. Mercury. Venus. I might just skip over Earth."

"You do that," said Wilhelmina, who was trying to decide if she could bear a bright red coat today. "What's the weather supposed to be like?"

"High of fifty-five," said Cleo.

"Mom!" shouted Delia, bursting into the room. "Can I make a unicorn cake?"

Wilhelmina found a blue mask in one of her coat pockets. Then she settled on a faded blue jean jacket, with a blue hat and mittens and her purple and blue scarf, in case she was too cold. She set off down the hill, keeping her ears cocked and her eyes peeled for crows.

ON THE LAWN IN FRONT OF THE LIBRARY, a giant maple tree wore a colorful knitted covering on its trunk. It was like a tube dress, tree-sized, with striped sections, checkered sections, sections with tassels and flags. A knitted banner on the front read, BLACK LIVES MATTER.

Wilhelmina circled the tree, touching a stuffed heart that hung from a branch. Then she sat on the low wall behind the tree, trying to find a position that hurt her neck less. Across the street was a sandwich shop she'd once loved for its meatball sub, with meatballs and sauce that came the closest to Frankie's she'd ever been able to find. Theo had loved their Tunisian tuna sandwiches. The sign still hung above the windows, but if you pressed your face to the glass, you could see that the tables, the cash register, the fridges and the stoves were all gone, lost to the pandemic. The guy who'd owned it had always had a friendly smile for her, and sometimes his kids were in the shop. Wilhelmina wished she had a way to know if they were okay.

Down the street, James appeared, wearing his sky-blue coat and holding a small pink box. His mask was on his chin, so she could see his face.

"Hey," he said, stopping a good eight feet away. As he studied her, his eyebrows furrowed in concern. "How are you?"

"That bad?" said Wilhelmina.

He smiled. "You look unhappy."

There was a kindness to James Fang, one with which he seemed very free. It seemed the easiest thing in the world to him to care about how she was. It brought stinging tears to her eyes. "I'm in some pain," she admitted, "but I'll be okay. My meds will start helping soon."

"I'm sorry to hear that," he said. "I brought you some really ugly doughnuts." He sat on the wall right where he stood, opened the box, then stretched out and placed it on the stone between them. "My mom let me take the unsellables."

Wilhelmina leaned over and peeked into the box, which contained three doughnuts. One was misshapen, and the other two were delightful, a Ruth Bader Ginsburg with a collar that resembled a frantic squid, and a unicorn with a perfect sculpted horn of sugar glass, but a horrified expression on its face.

"What did you do to that poor unicorn?" said Wilhelmina.

"Nothing, I swear."

Wilhelmina extricated the unicorn from the others. "Thank you," she said. "How are you feeling? You got home yesterday with no problems?"

"Yeah," he said, taking the RBG. "We're all okay. A little hurty on the inside, maybe."

"You mean because I upset you?" said Wilhelmina in alarm.

"Nah," he said. "The election."

"Oh," said Wilhelmina. "Right."

"It's like, you keep thinking people'll realize what he is," said James. "And care. But I think maybe they know what he is."

"Yeah," said Wilhelmina. "That's what I think."

"This guy came into the shop this morning and told me we weren't going to get away with it. Like, while I was handing him his box. He was like, 'You people aren't going to get away with it,' and I was like, 'I'm sorry, sir?' and he was like, 'Stealing the election.'"

"Oh my god, James," said Wilhelmina. "I fucking hate that guy!"

"I was like, 'Oooookay, well, have a nice day,' and he made this humphing noise, and shook his head like he had me all figured out. He almost knocked over this little old lady while he was storming off."

"I hate him," Wilhelmina said again. "He's human garbage. I'm sorry you have to put up with that shit, James."

"Oh well, it doesn't happen a lot," said James. "But it's hard that I have to stay polite, you know? Because he's a customer. If he did that out on the street, I'd ask him a few questions. What does he mean, *you people*, exactly? People who make Kamala Harris and RBG doughnuts? People who look Asian? Did he order doughnuts from us just so he could insult us?" He glanced at her sideways. "Your voice really does get deep when you're mad," he said.

"Tell me if you see him," said Wilhelmina. "I'll accidentally kick him in the balls."

"I'm glad we have a plan," said James. He took a bite of his doughnut, then chewed thoughtfully for a minute. "So, listen, Wilhelmina. I feel like I should tell you some of the stuff that's been happening to me, like, when you're not around."

"Stuff?" said Wilhelmina, her heart sinking a little. "Have you been getting messages in lights?"

"No, nothing like that. I mean, I got that one in the cemetery that told me to trust you, but you were there for that. Why? Have you gotten more messages in lights?"

"Why don't you go first?" she said.

"Okay, well," he said, considering her doubtfully. "If you've been getting more messages, like actually written down, then my stuff isn't going to seem like much. But, I've just been getting these . . ." He shrugged. "Just these feelings, like I should do things. Like I should go somewhere. Like, that's why I went to the cemetery in that snowstorm, and it's why I went back the next day, and it's why I told my grandparents I'd drive them to Pennsylvania. It's like an itch, but, like—to *go* somewhere."

"Are you . . . hearing voices?"

He hesitated. "No. There are no voices. But honestly, it feels as scary as if there were voices. Like, it doesn't feel normal to be at home watching TV or birds or something, then suddenly you have this compulsion to go to the cemetery. Then once you get there, you have this compulsion to go walk in a specific place."

"That does sound kind of disconcerting," Wilhelmina admitted.

"And then, every time, *you* show up," he said. "Wilhelmina Hart from school, who's basically, like, who I would *want* to show up, if I were making the story of my life up in my head. So of course I can't help but worry that that's what I'm doing."

"Right," said Wilhelmina. "I get that, like, completely. I've been scared of the same thing." *I'm who you'd want to show up?* she didn't say, masking her feelings about that vague compliment by focusing on her unicorn doughnut. She popped the sugary horn onto her tongue and let it melt in her mouth. "I don't think that's what you're doing."

James nodded. "My grandmothers don't think so either," he said seriously. Then he shot her a sideways glance that was—something. Maybe a little embarrassed? "I've got grandmothers who maybe aren't like other people's grandmothers," he said. "They, um, practice the sacred arts. My great-grandma on my mom's side was basically Strega Nona—remember that story?"

"A little," said Wilhelmina, who was feeling kind of strange. Like she already knew where this was going.

"My dad's mom would call herself a practitioner of craft," he said. "Like, from a Taoist tradition. My mom's mom—that's the grandma you met, remember? She thinks my dead great-grandma—her mom—is sending me messages." He sighed once, shortly. "I know how it sounds. I get if it's too weird."

Wilhelmina took one a slow breath, so that her own sigh wouldn't be so audible. "No," she said. "It's really not."

"The thing is that it always feels a little bit like my great-grandma," he said. "Like, when I get those feelings. I always, I don't know, find myself remembering her. She used to tell me I had a gift. She called it the 'gift of istinto.' I mean, it sounds fancy, but it's just the Italian word for 'instinct.' But she said that *she* had it, that sometimes it just came over her that there was someplace she should go. That it would"—he glanced at Wilhelmina again, with that same flash of embarrassment—"'put her in the path of the worthy challenge.' She always thought it was her father sending her messages. From the afterlife. He, like, died in World War II. And she always said *I* had that gift, and I was always like, sure, okay, Nonna, because she never told my sister Viv that Viv had any gifts, and my sister always told me it was because Nonna was sexist, like, obsessed with her father and her male grandchildren and great-grandchildren. Viv thinks all old Italian ladies are sexist. And so then I would point out that she never told any of the other boy cousins that they had a gift, and she would say, well, that's cuz you're her favorite. And I always kind of liked that, honestly, even though I don't think it was true, because she was *my* favorite. This was a really long time ago. She died when I was like eight."

"I'm sorry," said Wilhelmina.

"Thanks," he said. "Anyway, I honestly think if I just had these urges to go places, it'd be fine. I mean, a little weird maybe, but I could chalk it up to, like, life stress or something. I could be like, *Hi, Nonna, thanks for visiting.* But the thing is that every time, *you're* there, and something weird happens. And I swear, you're always glowing like the *sun.*"

"Am I glowing now?"

"No," he said. "You're just really pretty right now. You look like a blue-gray tanager."

"I don't know what that is," said Wilhelmina, who felt herself warming up.

"Sorry," he said. "I talk about birds too much. I like to check on this live bird cam in Panama. There's this bird that's all these different shades of blue. It makes me think of the sky."

"Your coat makes me think of the sky," said Wilhelmina.

James flapped his hand. It seemed like a gesture of defeat. "It's my dad's coat," he said. "It's too big for him now. Anyway, will you tell me about your messages? Are they, like, street signs or something?"

Wilhelmina wanted to keep talking about birds. Or his great-grandmother, or coats, or anything, really. "I don't know why it freaks me out so much to have to talk about it," she admitted. "I start to feel panicky."

"I mean, don't you think this would freak most people out? I think that's normal."

"You don't seem to have a problem talking about it."

"I talk when I'm upset!" he said. "Maybe you get quiet."

Wilhelmina thought this might be an understatement. "Anyway," she said. "There was that time you were there, with the sign that told you to trust me, except my name was wrong."

"Right," he said. "You object to dashes."

"And I already told you that I got that, um—*prophecy* that my doughnut would be stale."

"Which it was," said James, nodding.

"Right. Although that one was a voice, not a sign in lights. There was a sign, but it only said my name."

"With dashes?"

"Yes."

"Don't you feel like that's the weirdest part?" said James. "Like, if there's some supernatural force at work here, why is it being weird with your name?"

Wilhelmina swallowed. "I think that's one of the weird*er* parts," she said. "But after my dentist appointment on Monday, I took the elevator down to the lobby and it opened into the doughnut shop."

"Wait, what?" said James, staring at her. "You mean, like, one of the elevators in the Lupa Building? It opened into the doughnut shop?"

"Yeah. And the people were, like, transparent, and no one was wearing masks, and you were there, but you couldn't see me even when I waved my hands in front of your face, and I was *really there*, James, because when I opened the door and stepped onto the sidewalk, I was really outside your shop. And the people were solid again and everything was normal. You came running after me with a doughnut, remember?"

James's eyes were very big. He seemed to need a minute; he took a couple bites of his doughnut. James was cute while eating a doughnut. He had a distracting crumb on his lower lip. "Okay," he said. "Wow. That's a lot."

"What did you see?" said Wilhelmina. "Did you see me walking by, like, as if I'd come from the lobby?"

"No," he said. "When I saw you, you were already walking away, like down the street. But I was busy; I wasn't really looking. You may have walked by."

"A lot of weird shit has happened," she said. "But I think that was the weirdest."

"It definitely beats anything that's happened to me. Was there a message in lights?"

Wilhelmina sighed. "Yes. 'Help the doughnuts.'"

James froze. "Oh," he said. "That one might actually make sense."

"Wait, really?"

"The shop is in trouble," he said, glancing at her again, then shrugging.

"It is?" said Wilhelmina, who was surprised. Everything at the shop seemed normal. The lines seemed long, though it occurred to her now that any line might seem long, if people had to spread out for social distancing. And she could remember longer lines, in the beforetimes, if she pushed her mind back. Plus, her doughnut had been stale.

"Yeah," said James. "It's in a lot of trouble, ever since the pandemic started and my dad got sick. Business is down a lot, we've dropped our breakfast menu, and the lunch crowd is gone. And the medical bills are rough. We've had to let practically everyone go. We got a grant, then we got a loan, and there's been an eviction moratorium, which helped. But now it's expired for small businesses. We have so much back rent due. The management company has started pressuring us to pay up."

"But that's terrible!" said Wilhelmina.

"Yeah," said James. "My dad got diagnosed with colon cancer a few months back."

Wilhelmina needed just a moment to go still and breathe. "I'm so sorry, James. That's terrible."

James nodded, carefully eating the last piece of his doughnut. "Thanks," he said. "It's been a hard year. We've had to change a lot of plans. But I guess everyone has, right?"

"Some people more than others," said Wilhelmina, who was feeling a little ashamed of herself for minding a house crowded with aunts, and a life crowded with other people's errands.

"What are you doing about college?" he asked.

"Deferring for a year," she said. "From UMass Amherst."

"Oh, that's cool," he said. "I was going to go to Amherst. We would've been neighbors." He glanced at her. "I like thinking about that."

Amherst College was really hard to get into, and really expensive. Wilhelmina wondered if James was telling her he'd had to give up his place there entirely.

Then he smiled, a real smile, though he also looked tired. "The doctors say my dad's responding well to treatment."

"That's great," said Wilhelmina with fervor. She paused. "Are any of them named Ray?"

"What?" he said, confused. "The doctors?"

"Yeah. Or do you know anyone named Ray? The other message I got said 'Trust Ray.' It was written on a tarot card."

"Oh!" he said. Then he smiled again, true delight shining through the weariness in his face. "That's me," he said. "I'm Ray."

"What!"

"My middle name is Raimondo," he said. "It was my grandma's brother's name. My grandparents call me Ray, and so did my nonna."

"Hang on," said Wilhelmina, who was dizzy. She peeked into the box at the remaining doughnut, which was a funny stretched-out shape, then examined James closely. "I'm having some weird déjà vu," she said.

"No problem," he said. "My nonna was always reading my tarot. I mean, it's not an explanation. None of this makes sense. But maybe that's why you saw it on a tarot card."

"Maybe."

"What do you think we should do?"

"Do?"

"Don't you feel like—I don't know, like someone wants us to do something? Hey," James said, leaning toward Wilhelmina suddenly. "Hey, are you okay?"

Wilhelmina felt a hot tear sliding down her face, though she didn't know why. What did one tear mean, when so many things were wrong? "Frankie used to read my tarot too," she said. "My aunt who died."

"Hey," he said. "I'm really sorry."

"It's okay," she said, wiping at the tear. "I keep having these dreams where she almost appears, but we keep missing each other."

"That sounds really upsetting," he said. "Like, you don't actually need nightly reminders from your unconscious that she's gone."

"Right," said Wilhelmina, who was ready to change the subject now. "Anyway. So you dreamed about a wolf?"

"Yeah," he said, watching her uncertainly. "Not for the first time. Do you think it's because the shop is in the Lupa Building? Doesn't 'lupa' mean wolf, like, in Italian?"

"There are wolves above all the doors," said Wilhelmina. "If the management company is pressuring you for money, no wonder you're having wolf dreams."

"Wolves at the door," said James dryly.

"What happened in your dream?"

"I think I was a bird," he said. "An injured bird on the ground, and a wolf could smell me. She was looking for me, and I was really sad, because I knew it was the way of nature that strong animals eat weak animals, but I wanted to live."

Wilhelmina thought about her own dream, about the hurting owl whose voice was trapped. "I dreamed I was a tiny owl with an injured talon," she said, "just like the one at the dentist. That lady, Ellie Saroyan—she said it was a northern saw-whet owl. I needed to warn someone of something, but my voice didn't work. Were you an owl in your dream?"

"I don't think so," he said. "I might've been a wren. Wrens are the best, you know? They have little fat bodies and pointy beaks. They look like narwhals. It's funny how your mind works in dreams. I was lying in a yard near a dark green house, maybe I was a wren, and all the colors looked the way they would to my human eyes. And in the dream, I thought that was strange, because birds can see colors humans can't see. Like, most of them can even see UV light."

A dark green house. As James spoke, Wilhelmina could picture that house. Its balconies, its black roof with missing shingles, its white window frames: it was like the house sprouted, and grew in her mind. She knew, suddenly, that the owl in her own dream had been lying in the yard of that house.

"The house," she said. "What do you remember about it?"

"Um," he said, "it was forest green, and huge. It had gingerbread, and white balconies—"

"Did it have windows up high with stained-glass edges?"

"Yes!"

"My owl was lying in the same yard," Wilhelmina said, sitting up straighter. They stared at each other, perfectly still, for just a moment.

"Huh," said James. "Well, it looked like one of those fancy houses on Oliver, or Pearl, or Marion. You know those giant houses?"

Bee had used to live in one of those giant houses; Wilhelmina knew those streets well. "The ones near that little patch of forest, south of the stadium," she said.

"Yeah," said James. "Feel like taking a walk?"

AS THEY WALKED, James ate the last doughnut. "You're sure you don't want it?" he said.

"You go ahead," said Wilhelmina. "It's hilly. You should carb load."

"I feel like you get me."

"None of these houses look right to me," said Wilhelmina. "You?"

"Nope."

They were climbing up Oliver Street, which was shaped like a horseshoe, with its round end abutting the little forest. A dirt walking path started there, leading through the trees to streets on the other side that were also crowded with fancy houses.

"Want to take the path through?" said Wilhelmina.

"Sure."

It was a short, downhill path, traversing the forest's edge, but even still, you got the sense, almost immediately, of stepping into a different kind of world. *A door,* thought Wilhelmina. *To what?* Trees surrounded them, slender gray beeches and tall, craggy oaks, with masses of fluttering green leaves just starting to turn gold.

On a sharp intake of breath, James went still. He stretched a hand out to Wilhelmina, almost seeming like he was going to grab her arm, then he remembered the pandemic. He pointed at something with his chin, and whispered something she couldn't hear through his mask.

"What?!" she whispered back. "What's happening?!"

He pulled his mask down. "Pil-e-a-ted wood-peck-er!" he whispered, his eyes bright and his nose poking the air repeatedly in the direction he wanted her to look. Not unlike a woodpecker, Wilhelmina found herself thinking, with a rush of fondness for this person who got so excited about birds.

Then she saw it, clinging vertically to a nearby tree. It was big, with a slender, black body and a long, thin neck. It had a white-striped face and a giant beak, shaped and positioned like every picture she'd ever seen of a pterodactyl. It had a bright red crest of feathers atop its head, like the ridge on the back of a stegosaurus. Wilhelmina had a sense of the age of the world.

It turned its head to them, then gazed at them with such intensity that she grew a little nervous. Then it burst suddenly from its tree and flew away. Not two seconds later, Wilhelmina heard the hammering of its beak on some tree farther away.

"I've never seen a pileated woodpecker in these trees!" said James.

"It was beautiful," said Wilhelmina. When they started walking again, she asked him, "Will you go to vet school, or something? How does a person work with birds?"

"Well," he said. "I'm not sure."

He said it in a funny tone, like "not sure" meant something specific, which made her wonder if it was about his family's finances. "I'm sorry," she said. "Was I just insensitive?"

"No," he said. "I have a math thing."

"A math thing?"

"I'm crap at math," he said. "Certain kinds of it, anyway. Arithmetic, algebra. And you need lots of math to get into vet school."

Wilhelmina was immediately, almost irrationally, indignant on his behalf. "What?" she said. "Why? Why should you need math to care for birds?"

"Well, you need math to *medicate* birds, for one thing," said James.

"Someone else can medicate the birds!"

James laughed, high-pitched and surprising, like his laugh always was. "Thank you for not trying to convince me I don't have a math thing," he said. "I can't tell you how tired I am of people who think I just haven't had math explained to me adequately yet."

"Of course you would know if you have a math thing!" said Wilhelmina. "Could it be something schools are required to accommodate?"

"You mean, do I have a diagnosed learning disability? Yes. It's a mild kind of dyscalculia."

"Then vet schools should accommodate that," said Wilhelmina.

"I don't even know if I *want* to go to vet school," James protested mildly.

"Sorry," she said. "I got carried away."

"When you get passionate, you start to glow," he said.

"When you're being sweet," she said, "you sparkle."

They both seemed rather surprised by these revelations. They stepped out of the forest onto Marion Road. At that border place, standing on leaves, dirt, and asphalt, they paused, watching each other for a moment. He was a nice height, thought Wilhelmina. His hair was messy and adorable, and she wondered what it felt like. She wondered about the shoulders he was hiding under that puffy sky-blue coat.

"I wish you were in my bubble," said James.

An immense shyness rose up inside Wilhelmina. "Me too."

"Look," said James, pointing over her shoulder. A few lots away was a forest-green house. The mailbox at the base of its driveway said SAROYAN, like Ellie Saroyan, the owl lady from the dental office.

Wilhelmina was unsurprised, but it wasn't as if everything made sense now. Every time a piece of the puzzle clicked into place, it was like the table the puzzle sat on turned into a bird and flapped away.

"What do you think we're supposed to do?" said Wilhelmina. "Spy?"

"I think we should ring the doorbell," said James. "If someone answers, we'll say we wanted to check in on the owl."

"Okay," said Wilhelmina. "I mean, I do actually want to check in on the owl."

Ellie Saroyan herself answered the door. "Oh! Hello!" she said, hastily reaching toward a small table in her entranceway, pulling on a mask. "It's James and Wilhelmina! Right?"

"Yes, that's right," said Wilhelmina. "We're so sorry to bother you at home. You said you lived near here, and then we saw your mailbox."

"No one ever visits," she said. "I assumed it was a package!"

"Of course," said Wilhelmina.

"We were just walking by," said James. "We wanted to check in on the owl."

"Oh, that sweet little owl!" said Ellie. "I just talked to the raptor center this morning. She's doing well! They said her talon should heal, and then they have a process for releasing her back into the wild. Isn't it wonderful?"

"That is wonderful," said Wilhelmina, relieved. Her dream had felt so real.

"Would you like me to show you where I found her?" said Ellie.

Wilhelmina had the sense that even though she'd never seen Ellie's backyard, she already knew exactly where Ellie had found the owl. She could feel the cold dampness of the grass against her face, and picture the little hollow in the lawn, just beside a garden bed where lettuce was still growing. "Sure," she said.

"Before we do," said James, in a slightly strangled tone that made Wilhelmina glance at him, "may I ask about the . . . lovely art in your entranceway?"

"Oh!" said Ellie, with a delighted trill of a laugh. "You must mean my obelisks!"

Wilhelmina saw then that Ellie had three tall paintings hanging in her entranceway, and each painting contained an obelisk. In fact, each painting contained exactly the same obelisk, positioned in exactly the same part of the canvas. The same sunset stained the same pink sky, reflecting the same rose and gold on the obelisk's surface. At the bottoms of the canvases, where night crept in, the same fireflies hung suspended in the same positions. Ellie had three identical paintings in her entranceway, framed in three different frames. And the fireflies were sparkling.

"My children did a Zoom painting party a few weeks ago," she said. "One of those ones where you all paint the same picture. Then, I guess without consulting each other, they each decided to frame it and send it to me as a present. You can imagine how surprised I was as the packages began to arrive. What do you think? Don't they look charming together? The fireflies sparkle like that at this time of day, when it's sunny."

"I see," said Wilhelmina. "So, *you* can see that they're sparkling?"

James shot her a sideways look that said, *That was a weird question.* "They remind me of the Bunker Hill Monument," he said hastily.

"Yes!" said Ellie. "I think that's why my kids thought of me! I used to take them to the Bunker Hill Monument all the time when they were little. We would climb to the top. Two hundred ninety-four steps! It's like a little bit of home for them, you know? Anyway, here, come around to the back. I'll show you where I found that little owl."

In the backyard, which looked much as Wilhelmina had expected, nothing glowed, nothing sparkled. Ellie showed them the flattened tuft of grass where the owl had lain, and Wilhelmina felt her dream owl again, cold and frightened.

"Well?" she said to James afterward. "Are you having a compulsion to go to the Bunker Hill Monument?"

"No," said James, shrugging. "Plus, I doubt it's open to visitors these days, right? But maybe we should look into it?"

WHEN WILHELMINA GOT HOME, Delia was making a unicorn cake.

From the state of the kitchen, Wilhelmina surmised that a unicorn cake was similar to other cakes, except that its cake to icing ratio was about one to nine. Philip ran up to her with an eggbeater held upright in both hands. It was covered in lavender icing.

"I only licked it a little!" he yelled, bursting with his own generosity. "You can go first!"

"Wow," said Wilhelmina. "No thank you, Philip, you can have it." At the counter, Delia was spreading lavender icing onto a series of pointy ice cream cones, wielding her knife with intense concentration. "Delia?" said Wilhelmina. "Is that part of the cake?"

Delia turned away from her task just long enough to roll her eyes at Wilhelmina contemptuously. "It's the horn," she said. "And all the backup horns."

Wilhelmina decided that someone in the household was probably in charge of supervising this operation, but it wasn't her. She went to her bedroom and shut the door. Through the wall somewhere nearby, she heard her father yell, "That fleabite is demanding a recount in Wisconsin? They haven't even finished in Wisconsin!" A moment later, he yelled again. "What are they even doing in Nevada? Cleaning out their belly buttons?"

Wilhelmina reconsidered her location. The kitchen and the bedrooms were on one end of the apartment and the living room on the other, or at least that's how it felt, by virtue of the short corridor that connected the living room with everything else. The bedrooms seemed to be her parents' workplaces today. The aunts seemed to be out. Wilhelmina had a feeling that her father was working in his bedroom and her mother was working in the aunts' bedroom. When Theo yelled, he was yelling through the wall to Cleo.

A moment later, she heard Cleo open a door, shout, "Okay, I have a session!" then slam the door. This supported Wilhelmina's theory. "Okay!" yelled Theo. Her parents weren't usually so shouty. She wondered if the election was bringing out everyone's more fundamental self.

Then she decided that since everyone was preoccupied, they might not notice if she did something weird. With tired arms, she carried Frankie's crow blanket, her laptop, her foam roller, and her phone past Delia and Philip and into the living room. There, she dragged the coatrack and the drying rack side by side in front of the armchair in the window near Frankie's treasures. She hung the blanket across both racks so that it made a kind of barrier. Then she sat in the chair, divided from the rest of the room by the scene of flying crows, comforted that she was as far away as possible from any other human.

Now what? she thought, trying to decide how much it would hurt to watch a makeup or hair video. Hurt her heart, she meant, because she and Julie often shared those videos with each other. Was there anything she ever did that was unconnected to Julie and Bee? Again she reached for her necklace. Again it wasn't there.

She could research the Bunker Hill Monument. First, though, she checked the returns. Biden had won three of the four electoral votes in Maine. That meant that if he kept Arizona, Nevada, and Wisconsin, he would need only Michigan or Pennsylvania to win.

As she was opening a tab to google the monument, a new headline popped up: "Biden Wins Wisconsin."

IN LATE AFTERNOON, Biden won Michigan. No news was coming out of Arizona or Nevada. On Twitter, the monster tweeted about his victories in Georgia, North Carolina, and Pennsylvania, three states where he was leading but had not, in fact, won yet. He also tweeted about a "large number of secretly dumped ballots" in Michigan, for which he had no evidence. And announced a lawsuit in Michigan, to demand the vote count be halted there; and announced a lawsuit in Pennsylvania; and asked the Supreme Court to intervene in the Pennsylvania vote count. Wilhelmina did a few calculations and discovered that the monster couldn't win the election unless he won Pennsylvania. It was going to be days, people were saying, until all the votes were counted there.

At dinner, the room felt crowded with everyone's feelings.

"Nice stew, Cleo," said Esther, who was one of the few calm presences at the table. "Was your phone ringing off the hook today?"

"I've got about twenty-five voice mails I haven't even listened to yet," Cleo admitted. Her eyes were puffy and rimmed with red and she felt exhausted to Wilhelmina. Theo reached a hand out and gave her an impromptu neck rub, which briefly brought a tired but blissful smile to Cleo's face.

"Did everyone see my unicorn cake?" demanded Delia. "It's for Eleanor. Don't eat any."

"It's a work of art," said Esther. "A visit from a unicorn is a blessing."

"Yes, beautiful," said Theo, who was watching Philip anxiously. "How much icing would you estimate Philip consumed?"

"He was my taster," said Delia.

"Mm," said Theo. Philip, who'd eaten very little dinner so far, was uncharacteristically subdued, which often meant he was going to vomit. Wilhelmina could see the wheels turning in Theo's head: Was it the icing? Or could it be Covid?

"Esther and I had such a nice walk today," said Aunt Margaret. "And a nice sit among the trees. It was one of those days when you don't want to be confined."

"How was your day, Wilhelmineleh?" said Esther. "How's your pain?"

"Okay," said Wilhelmina, who had no intention of reporting on most of the parts of her day. "I researched the Bunker Hill Monument. I've been wanting to go, but the tower's closed."

"I can get you into the Bunker Hill Monument," said Delia.

"What?" said Wilhelmina. *"What?"*

"I can get you in," said Delia, shrugging.

"What do you mean, *you* can get me in?" said Wilhelmina. "You're ten!"

"My friend Madison," said Delia, shrugging again. "Her mom, like, owns it or something."

"No one owns the Bunker Hill Monument! It's part of the National Park Service!"

"Whatever. I can get you in, but you can forget it if you're just going to yell at me."

"I was present for the conversation that illuminates this mystery," said Aunt Margaret, with a gentle cough. "I believe Madison's mother, Sue, who's a park ranger, manages the Bunker Hill Monument. We met her just a few days ago when we were out walking in the rain. She did, indeed, say she'd be happy to arrange a private tour for Delia, Eleanor, and one or two others in their friend group. Masked and socially distanced, of course. I'm sure that could include you, Wilhelmina, if you've been wanting to go."

"Well, *I'm* not sure," said Delia loudly.

"I know the Petrosians," said Theo. "I don't mind calling Sue after dinner."

"It would be me and a friend," said Wilhelmina. "If you wouldn't mind, Dad."

"Of course, honey," said Theo.

"Oh, first you didn't believe me and now you want to bring a friend?" said Delia. "Julie or Bee?"

"A friend of my choice," said Wilhelmina.

"What's that supposed to mean?" Delia demanded, in the very moment Philip shifted position significantly and Theo and Cleo, springing into action like the seasoned team they were, swept him up together and rushed him out of the room.

"Poor Philip," said Aunt Margaret. "He was looking a little green."

"I bet his puke is lavender," said Delia.

AFTER DINNER, Wilhelmina retreated to her blanket fort again. Outside the window, stars were beginning to prick the sky. When Philip found her, she helped him climb up into her lap. He seemed perfectly fine, and sweet-smelling from the bath someone had given him.

"What you doing?" he asked her.

"Nothing," she said. "Just sitting."

"I threw up," he said.

"Yes," she said, smelling his wispy hair. "Do you feel better?"

"Yes," he said, then went quiet, leaning against Wilhelmina's chest, watching Frankie's figurines in the window and drowsing.

Wilhelmina had a heightened consciousness of her phone, and of the messages no one was sending her. With her one free hand, she unlocked it and checked the news. The monster's lead in Georgia was shrinking, so he'd filed a lawsuit to stop the counting there. That made lawsuits in Pennsylvania, Michigan, and Georgia—where the uncounted votes were mostly in the cities of Philadelphia, Detroit, and Atlanta. Three cities with high Black populations. In fact, the monster was suing to stop *Black* votes from being counted.

In the meantime, in Arizona, a group of people had gathered outside a Phoenix counting center, shouting, "Stop the steal." Which seemed to Wilhelmina like a good thing for them to be shouting, until she understood that it was Biden they believed to be the thief. Biden, who was patiently waiting for the votes to be counted, while the monster made shit up about voter fraud. Oh, and also, the mob was armed with guns.

Wilhelmina began to wonder, could a person—could *she*—lose her mind, if other people kept persisting in yelling lies? Like, could a person truly lose her ability to cope? She'd watched a video of Cleo giving a talk once, at some event for destigmatizing mental illness. Cleo had said that many of the behaviors classified as symptoms of mental illness were in fact rational, normal, and healthy responses to unhealthy environments—the body's attempt to help the suffering human survive an onslaught of wrongness. If Wilhelmina kept being shocked to the point of numbness by how people were behaving, if she kept feeling herself spinning into what felt like a crazy place, because of the magnitude of her disbelief that people could be so passionately, violently wrong, did that mean she was healthy?

Her phone buzzed. She jumped for it, almost waking Philip. But it was James.

How ru? he wrote. *Bh monument closed*

I think I have an in, she texted back, dictating in a low voice. *Details soon*

U have an in to the bhm?

Apparently my annoying and possibly sociopathic ten-year-old sister is friends with the daughter of the manager

Ur magic, he wrote.

Wilhelmina didn't feel like magic. She felt like a heartsick weirdo, currently with no friends, hiding in a dark room behind a blanket. She didn't know what to say, so she let herself sit there in confusion, holding on to Philip.

Two things, he wrote. *1) I like the owl on your ear*

Wilhelmina smiled. She couldn't help it.

2) Group of snow geese is gaggle. But when flying, they r a wedge, skein or team—AND

If they fly in a big crowd all close together, they r a plump

Wilhelmina squeaked a little in her chair. *A PLUMP?* she wrote.

Yeah

A PLUMP of snow geese?

Yeah

She pictured a flurry of round-bellied birds with big, sturdy feet, black tips to their white wings, flying together across the sky. A plump. Laughing, she reached out and set the snow goose's head bobbing. *I love that,* she said.

Me too

Hey, he added immediately. *Blue-gray tanagers rn.* Then he sent her a link.

When Wilhelmina clicked on the link, she saw trees and green leaves, a sunny, tropical scene. At the bottom of the frame was a log crowded with bananas, and above it, a row of orange halves suspended from the branch of a tree. A hummingbird feeder hung on the right. "Panama Fruit Feeder Cam," said the description.

Three small birds sat on the oranges, spinning in circles as the oranges themselves spun, reaching their beaks down to the meat of the fruit. She recognized them as blue-gray tanagers instantly, because they were just as James had described: the streaky pale blue of a winter sky.

They were breathtaking. *Wow,* she texted to James. Then the picture changed, switching suddenly to a scene in black and white. *What just happened?* she texted him.

Night cam, he said. *Till morning. Not as pretty, but opossums visit. I saw owl once. Plus bats come to the hummingbird feeder*

Thank you, she said.

Yw. Lmk re bhm?

Will do

The pain of holding a device up one-handed was too great. Wilhelmina let her phone fall. Then, carefully, she lifted Philip into her arms and carried him through to the kitchen. Theo sat at the table, typing on his laptop.

"Asleep?" he whispered, standing. "I'll take him, hon. How's three tomorrow for the Bunker Hill Monument?"

"I'll check," she said.

Back in her chair, she texted James. *3PM tomorrow, Bunker Hill?*

He sent a thumbs up and another *Ur magic.*

3PM works, she texted to Theo. *Thanks Dad.*

Then Wilhelmina lay on her foam roller and propped her laptop on her belly. Frankie's blanket, suspended very near to her side, make her feel like she was in a tent in the woods somewhere.

She opened the bird feeder live cam and turned on the sound. The chirping of crickets, from a rainforest thousands of miles away, filled her blanket fort. As she stretched first one arm, then the other, a fat opossum with a long tail lumbered onto the scene. The opossum chose a banana carefully, then spent a long time consuming it. Every time it glanced at the camera, its eyes glowed like little suns.

It was different to be at the aunts' house while possessing a cell phone. It felt a little like Wilhelmina had tied a long silk thread to herself before leaving Massachusetts, and handed the other end to Julie and Bee. As she moved through each warm, sweet day, she collected walks and swims, sunlight and stars, to pass back along the thread to them.

The summer Wilhelmina was fourteen, the cardinal returned, pounding at the window glass. Or maybe it was a new cardinal; maybe aggressive dissatisfaction was endemic in Pennsylvania cardinals. The cardinal chose a different time of day (later) and a different basement window (farther from Wilhelmina's bedroom), and his behavior struck her differently too. Wilhelmina wasn't that cardinal anymore. No more senseless pounding. She'd figured some things out.

In the fall, she would start high school with Julie. She'd begun playing with eye makeup, with lipstick, and she wore glasses now. She liked her glasses, which were chunky, and bluish gray. She'd begun frequenting thrift stores with Bee, who himself had a bit of a thrift-store aesthetic. It wasn't easy to thrift for clothing long enough to fit Bee's increasingly tall frame, and it was even harder to find adornments for Wilhelmina's short, round body. But they persisted, like astrophysicists searching the galaxy for habitable planets. Gradually, Wilhelmina collected dresses that worked over leggings, over long-sleeved shirts, above boots, under belts. Wilhelmina was nervous about high school, sure.

She'd figured *some* things out—not everything. But at least she would march down its halls feeling right in her clothes.

Her long hair was gone. She'd taken a bus into Harvard Square after Christmas and told an embarrassingly hot man whose own hair was pink to chop it down close. It had cost her all her Christmas money plus one month's allowance, and ever since, she'd trimmed it herself. The first time she'd held a pair of craft scissors to her head, her heart had started pounding just like the cardinal in the window, but she'd thought of something Cleo liked to say—Cleo of all people, who was always therapizing when no one wanted to hear it, but who'd said: "Think about scary things as experiments. You'll try them out, and then afterward, you'll decide what you think. It'll make you feel like you have some power." Wilhelmina had cut some hair off, as an experiment. The experiment had gone well enough. So she'd bought some hair shears after that, which had been a lot less expensive than a haircut in Harvard Square.

High school, Wilhelmina thought to herself while she gardened with Frankie or swam across the lake. *After high school, a year with the aunts.* She imagined learning from the aunts—she didn't know what. How to run a business, like Esther and Aunt Margaret did? Running a business didn't sound too interesting to Wilhelmina, but she liked learning how to do things, and she liked the idea of skills that might one day lead her to a job she didn't hate. *Not* a librarian, not a therapist, not an emergency room doctor, and not a grade school teacher. Not someone with an unreasonable boss like Mrs. Mardrosian, who was, from Wilhelmina's way of looking at things, the foremost source of stress in Theo's life. Wilhelmina was quite certain about the things she didn't want to do, which was enough for now. Maybe in a year with the aunts, she could learn how to have . . . this quality they had. Not happiness, exactly, because the aunts often felt sadness. And anger, and worry; in that summer, which was the summer of 2016, all three aunts carried a deep and profound well of sadness and worry about the way the upcoming presidential election was shaping up. In moments of stillness, if she looked for it, Wilhelmina could feel it stirring inside them. But there was some other, fundamental quality the aunts had that she wanted to learn. It felt to her like strength, but it had nothing to do with muscles. It had everything to do with . . . being able to contain the whole world yet remain steady? Was that a quality a person could have? Wilhelmina felt it when she was with them. That there was room for everything here, and a sense of balance.

Wilhelmina's favorite time to talk to Julie and Bee was after a long swim at the lake. Not immediately; after she'd shivered herself back to warmth while wearing a towel as a blanket, drinking whatever tea or soup Aunt Margaret or Esther handed to her in the thermos. When the sun on her skin made her tingle with contentment, she would call them individually, or text them together. It depended on whether either of them was having a crisis. Bee's summer was composed of frequent small crises, because his dad was being even more touchy and erratic than usual and his irregular work hours made encounters with him unpredictable. Bee never wanted to text about it, because he didn't trust his dad not to read his texts. Actually, he spent a lot of time at Julie's, so sometimes, if Wilhelmina called one of them, she got to talk to both of them. Once, out of an irritated sense of obligation, she'd returned a call from her mother. Cleo was extremely pregnant that summer, and beset by constant, agonizing itchy rashes. It was a condition called PUPPP, which was way too many Ps and stood for "pruritic urticarial papules and plaques of pregnancy," which was a gross name. When Wilhelmina had called, Cleo had been itchy; Delia, who was six, had been impersonating an air raid siren in the background; and Cleo's voice had grown increasingly harassed, until finally she'd said, "Wilhelmina, hon, why don't you talk to Bee?"

"Hi," Bee had said, in his new, uneven, thirteen-year-old voice.

"Oh, hi!" Wilhelmina had said. "I didn't know you were there."

"My dad . . ." Bee said, sounding as if more words were coming, but then not saying them. It made Wilhelmina's heart begin to thump.

"Did he hurt you?"

"No! Just—you know. Stuff."

"Okay."

"Where are you?"

"At the lake."

"Find any blue stones?"

"The beach was sparkling with blue stones today," she said, because that's how it seemed on the beach this summer, now that Wilhelmina wore glasses that she took off to swim. Her uncorrected vision was good enough for most purposes, but she understood now that the world was sharper than she'd previously thought. She would pull herself from the water and look out upon a great expanse of pebbles that seemed soft at the edges, her peripheral vision sparkling with points of blue. "But I didn't take any. Should I go back and get you one? Or I could signal to Aunt Margaret," she said, because Aunt Margaret was swimming, in a bright yellow bathing suit Wilhelmina could spot even with her glasses still off.

"No. Next time," he said. "Do you think . . ."

Wilhelmina's hand was hurting a little, weird stinging in her palm. She switched the phone to the other ear. "Yeah?" she said. "What?"

"Do you think Frankie could pull me a card sometime?"

"Sure," said Wilhelmina. "I'll ask her later."

"Thanks," he said. "Have you talked to Julie today?"

"Not yet."

"She's having . . ." Bee's voice got low and whispery. "A problem with a guy."

"What? What guy?"

"I can't tell you now."

"Should I call her?"

"She's not answering. I think she's at chess."

"Can I text about it?"

"Yeah," said Bee. "That's fine."

"Okay. Stay tuned," said Wilhelmina. Then she set her phone on the blanket beside her for a few minutes, because holding it was making her hands feel tingly and weird. She rubbed at her palms.

"Everything okay, bubeleh?" said Esther, who sat in a beach chair nearby, reading an issue of *The Atlantic*. Esther wore a filmy, silver-gray wrap that reminded Wilhelmina of a rainstorm, big sunglasses, and a giant sun hat with a black ribbon. She looked like a movie star trying to go incognito.

"Yes," said Wilhelmina. "I called home, but Bee was there." She stopped, twisting her mouth up. Wilhelmina was never sure how much to say to her aunts on the topic of Bee. She had the sense that they knew he had troubles at home, but her loyalty to him always stopped her from providing details.

"Are you worried about Bee?" asked Esther.

In that moment, a door opened, and Wilhelmina realized she was always worried about Bee. Always. "Yes," she said.

Esther seemed to accept her brief and nondescriptive response. She lowered her magazine into her lap and pursed her lips thoughtfully.

"I think you see through Bee's father," she said. "Straight through his own self-deceit."

Wilhelmina sat up straighter and stared at Esther. "Do you know Bee's father?" she asked in surprise.

"He called a few times," said Esther, "the summer Bee was here. He gave me a funny feeling, so I googled him. Watched him give a speech about how wonderful he was. It was enough. Anyway, I know you, Wilhelmina. You can see into people. I trust your mistrust of that man."

Wilhelmina pulled her towel blanket tight, thinking about that. "I hate him," she admitted. It was something she'd never said out loud before. "I worry about Bee all the time."

Esther nodded grimly. "There's a special torture in being able to see the truth of a dysfunctional situation that others can't see."

"His mom can't see it," said Wilhelmina. "She pretends everything's fine."

"I expect that's another thing you see clearly," said Esther. "It's a power, you know. Seeing the truth of a situation makes you powerful. Unlike everyone else, *you* can make realistic plans."

Wilhelmina knew that this was wrong. "I can't make a plan for Bee," she said. "I can't save him."

Esther grunted in affirmation. "*Realistic* plans," she said. "Not plans that magically make everything better. Anyway, you've already set your plan in motion, bubeleh. You're Bee's friend. The kind of friend who acknowledges what he's going through."

Far at the other end of the beach, some kids were playing with a volleyball. Finding her glasses, Wilhelmina watched a dark-haired guy in sky-blue bathing trunks prop the ball on his hand above one shoulder, then run with it, then hurl it as far as he could across the sand, where it landed near a guy and a girl who seemed to have the job of marking its landing place. She heard a few cheers. Apparently, whatever he'd done, he'd done it well. They were too far away for Wilhelmina to see the details.

"Sometimes it doesn't seem like much," she said. "Just to be someone's friend."

Esther made another affirming noise. But she said, "A lot of bad situations don't have easy solutions. We care for each other as best we can."

At home, Aunt Margaret puttered around the kitchen, throwing beans, tomatoes, and carrots into the slow cooker that was her new toy. Now that Aunt Margaret and Esther worked from home, they seemed to like to do more of the cooking—"As long as I can throw it all in there and forget about it," Aunt Margaret said. Esther was different. She liked to cook complicated things and take her time doing it, often with her sister or one of her cousins on speakerphone if she needed advice. Once, her cousin Sofia visited, and brought some nice ripe plantains—hard to find in rural Pennsylvania. Wilhelmina feasted on platanos maduros for days. Esther could cook anything, really. Her pastas were almost as good as Frankie's, and she made a tofu with peanut butter, soy sauce, and ginger that was so delicious that Wilhelmina would volunteer for dish duty so she could eat the leftovers out of the pot.

Frankie still cooked too, of course, though she seemed just a bit tired out when it came to cooking this summer. When she did cook, she would make large quantities of soup, or massive vats of meatballs and her homemade sauce, then freeze the extras. Zucchini cakes with zucchini from the garden—mountains of them. Bread—four loaves instead of two. The aunts had a freezer in the basement down to which Frankie would send Wilhelmina with bags of bread or containers of soup. Then send her down again a few weeks later to retrieve some treasure that only needed defrosting in order to become a delicious meal.

Through the kitchen window, Wilhelmina saw Frankie in the garden, sitting on her bench, holding a hose to the cucumbers. "Hi, Frankie," she called through the screen.

"Hello, my love," said Frankie, turning to the window. It was hard to see her expression because she wore a giant cloth sun hat that had once been coral, but was faded now from the sun. It cast her face in shadow and made her look tiny, like a woman composed of bird bones. And still, her smile glowed.

"Later," called Wilhelmina, "could you pull a card for Bee?"

"Certainly," said Frankie.

Up in her room, Wilhelmina tucked herself against the wall on her bed and texted Julie and Bee. *Something happened w a guy, J?*

Oh hi, said Julie. *Just left chess. Heading home. B tell u?*

No details, wrote Bee.

Its Quinn Carter, wrote Julie.

Something twisted inside Wilhelmina: a flicker of misgiving she'd never realized she had for Quinn Carter, who was one of those guys who was universally liked on the basis of being excellent at all sports and never saying much. It hadn't occurred to Wilhelmina to think about him before. *Did he hurt u?* she wrote, surprised by her own suspicion.

No! said Julie. *Hes into me*

Super into her, said Bee.

Oh, said Wilhelmina, considering. You never knew with someone who didn't talk much. It created an air of wisdom, but it could also be a sign of moral cowardice. Regardless, if Julie might be about to start something with him, then she needed to support Julie. *Ru,* she typed, then erased it. Her palms were stinging again. She wrote, *How u feel abt that?*

OMG, said Julie. *TY for asking me that. Its like theres no room for me to feel how I feel cuz everyones acting like its a miracle and Im so lucky and of course I must be into him but I feel a big nothing Wil. I got nothing. I mean hes fine hes nice whatever. But I do not want to hang out w him I have other shit to do and I dont appreciate the pressure or the assumptions*

U dont have to hang out w him, Julie, said Wilhelmina.

TY!!!

U don't have to do anything

Anyway, Julie wrote, *the way Bethie Ramona and Hannah talk it sounds like those boys all expect bjs*

WHAT? wrote Wilhelmina, who was suddenly, unexpectedly floored. *WHAT?*

Yeah

What do u mean, EXPECT them

Its just what they do, wrote Julie. *Like Bethie is w Connor and Hannah is w Jeremy and they all hang out at someones house and the night isnt over till b&h give c&j bjs*

Like in front of everyone???!!!

No! Like theyll be at Ramonas house. She has her own bathroom

Theyll do it in Ramonas bathroom? Wow! Romantic! Wilhelmina searched for the puke emoji and added it five times. Then she sent it another five times. Wilhelmina was really upset. Honestly, she was confused by how upset she was.

I know, wrote Julie. *But anyway. It seems*

GROSS? wrote Wilhelmina.

Really one sided, Julie wrote.

Yeah, wrote Wilhelmina, who understood then, finally, why she felt a little out of control. It was because she was angry. *Yeah,* she wrote again, calmer now. *It sounds really selfish.* Her hands were weirdly burning, but this was important, so she kept typing. *It sounds like those guys are really selfish Julie*

Thats what I think too. And Quinn is in that group

Yeah, said Wilhelmina.

It doesnt mean hes like that

True

The girls act like its funny

Now Wilhelmina needed a minute to figure out a new feeling. Sadness. For everyone. That was how it made Wilhelmina feel, that those girls would find it funny, instead of unfair.

That makes me really sad, she wrote. *It's not funny*

I agree, said Julie.

What do u want? she asked Julie, badly hoping Julie wanted no part of this. *I support u, whatever u want*

I want to have my summer and forget abt Quinn

U get to, Wilhelmina wrote.

TY, wrote Julie. Then she added a crying emoji, which jarred

Wilhelmina out of her own feelings. She wished she could hug Julie. She sent her a string of blue hearts instead.

U got quiet B, Julie wrote. *Too much bj talk?*

Just listening, said Bee.

Like in a creeper way? said Julie.

No! said Bee. *Ouch!*

I know, said Julie. *Sorry.*

Connors in soccer. Central midfield, he said. *Nice guy when ppl r around but*

We did a drill alone once and he called me fag

Wilhelmina's jaw dropped. *OK,* she wrote. *Wow*

Shit, wrote Julie. *What u do?*

I told him apologize or hed become invisible to me on the field

He didnt. So I stopped passing to him

Pretty sure he hates me. U can c him going red at penalty kick drills w how bad he wants to get the ball past me but Ive decided he never gets it past me anymore

Wow, wrote Julie. *Thats a long game ur playing*

Hes in high school now, wrote Bee. *Gets a new goalie to b a douche to, for exactly 1 year*

Lol, said Julie.

Now Wilhelmina was giggling. *Hands hurt,* she wrote. *Cant type. B, F sez shell pull u card*

TY, said Bee.

TTFN

TTFN

TTFN

Alone in her room, Wilhelmina rubbed at the base of her palms again, not sure whether they were stinging or itching. It was weird not to be able to tell. They felt better when she wasn't typing. She could hear the muted voice of Aunt Margaret downstairs, speaking to someone who was too quiet to be heard. It was Frankie; they were in the kitchen together; water was running. Then Frankie moved to the stairs and climbed them slowly, then went to her own room.

Wilhelmina waited, but Frankie didn't come out. Getting up, she crossed to her desk and unearthed Frankie's old tarot cards, wrapped in the dark fabric with the scattering of bumblebees. Then she brought the deck downstairs and walked along the corridor, nonchalantly peeking through Frankie's open door. Frankie was lying on her bed with her eyes closed. She looked very small.

"Wilhelmina?" said Frankie.

"Yes," said Wilhelmina, not sure why she was whispering.

"How are you?"

"Fine."

"Would you like to come in?"

"Yes," said Wilhelmina, relieved when Frankie opened her eyes and turned to her, smiling.

"My old cards!" Frankie said, patting the bed. "Shall I pull one for Bee?"

"Okay," said Wilhelmina. "But the Temperance card is missing. I keep that one in my mirror at home."

Frankie turned her smile briefly to the three Temperance prints above her bed. "Temperance is a good focus card for any reading," she said. "We can just pretend it's already on the table." Then she reached a hand for Wilhelmina's cloth-covered bundle and began to unwrap it. "I haven't touched these cards in years," she said, with obvious pleasure. As she removed the fabric and smoothed it out onto the bed beside her, Wilhelmina felt how she imagined it might feel to be a cat someone was scratching behind the ears.

"Sit down, dear," Frankie said. Then she began to shuffle the old, weathered cards. Her hands were brown from the sun, and quick. Stroking the bumblebee fabric with one finger, Wilhelmina sat.

"Do you remember going to Mrs. Mancusi's funeral with me, Wilhelmina?" said Frankie. "Oh, some six or seven years ago? She was my math teacher in high school, and my mentor. She was like a mother to me."

Wilhelmina remembered a church interior, and a priest's even voice. She remembered a boy throwing pieces of tissue paper into the air that caught the colored light streaming through the windows. "I think so," she said. "Did you call her your empress?"

"Probably," said Frankie, smiling. "She was my empress. She even wore her hair in a crown."

"Like you used to do," said Wilhelmina, then wished she hadn't said it, because it broke some sort of spell inside her. She was anxious and cold.

But Frankie only laughed, running a quick hand over her short, wispy hair. "I did, indeed," she said. "It's lighter now. A crown can be a burden. These were Mrs. Mancusi's cards, Wilhelmina. She taught me tarot, and she gave these cards to me. I gave them to you, because—well, I'm not sure why. Because I love you, and because it felt right. I can't imagine that I could ever be for anyone what Mrs. Mancusi was for me, but I wanted to share some of her goodness with you."

"You're everything to me," said Wilhelmina.

Frankie stopped shuffling and looked at her hard. Wilhelmina was surprised by the surprise that sat in her face. Could Frankie truly be ignorant of how important she was?

Reaching out, Frankie touched Wilhelmina's cheek with her warm palm. "Your love is very powerful, Wilhelmina," she said. "Thank you for it."

"You're welcome," said Wilhelmina, who wasn't sure how else to answer.

"Now, a card for Bee," said Frankie. Wilhelmina cut the deck, as usual. Then Frankie turned over a card that brought an unmistakably sad expression to her face.

"What is it?" said Wilhelmina anxiously. "Is it something bad?"

"It's something true," said Frankie, handing Wilhelmina an unfamiliar card. It showed a man in a long dark robe, contemplating three overturned cups at his feet. Behind him, two more cups stood upright. In the background, a bridge led over a river to a building surrounded by trees.

"The Five of Cups is about loss," said Frankie. "Those cups have spilled over. Something that should've come to pass will never come to pass; it's missing. The pain of that is bone deep."

Wilhelmina had tears running down her face. "Bone-deep pain?" she said. "For Bee? Is that, like, a prediction?"

"Not a prediction," said Frankie. "Just a comment on his current situation. When I pull a single card like this, I'm not making predictions, Wilhelmina dear. Just presenting a framework for thinking about things. But, sweetheart, look. This card also shows a beginning. Look behind him. You see those two cups that are still standing?"

"Yes."

"That man is going to turn around," said Frankie. "You see? He'll turn around and see that not everything is lost. He has two cups standing upright. Those cups are filled to the brim with the love and support he needs. They're, like, his support cups."

Wilhelmina snorted. "That makes them sound like a bra!"

"And there's a path too—you see that?" said Frankie. "A path across a bridge, to a home."

"Do I tell Bee?" said Wilhelmina. "Won't it upset him?"

"I think Bee already knows about the pain," said Frankie. "Maybe it'll make him feel understood. And he might like to hear about the rest of it, you know? The full cups, and the path."

One morning a week later, Wilhelmina woke to a phone ringing somewhere far away in the house. She came very awake, very fast, which was strange. She sat gripping her sheets, and waiting for something.

When, soon after, there was a knock on her door, Wilhelmina shot across the room and yanked the door open. Aunt Margaret stood in the hallway, tears brimming in her eyes.

"Bee?" said Wilhelmina.

"His father is dead," said Aunt Margaret.

Wilhelmina needed to grab on to the doorframe for balance. "Dead!"

"Yes," said Aunt Margaret. "There was an accident of some kind, dear."

"Accident!" said Wilhelmina. "Was Bee in the accident?"

"No, no! Bee was safely asleep in his bed."

Behind Aunt Margaret, Wilhelmina saw Frankie and Esther making their way up the stairs, Frankie leaning on Esther for support. Their faces were suffused with concern. "Bee is okay?" said Wilhelmina.

"Bee is okay," said Aunt Margaret.

"Bee is okay?" said Wilhelmina, trying again.

"Bee is safe," said Aunt Margaret, "and his father is dead."

As Frankie and Esther made it to the top of the stairs, Wilhelmina burst into tears.

"There, there," the aunts said, surrounding her with their hugs and their warmth. "There, there, dear. You're safe. Bee is safe."

"I need to go home," said Wilhelmina, even though it was only mid-July.

"We did wonder if you would feel that way, bubeleh," said Esther.

"I don't want to leave," she said. "But I need to go home. Bee needs both of his support cups right now."

On the Thursday two days before she stepped into her own, Wilhelmina woke remembering that when Bee's dad had died, she'd known what to do. She'd known how to be Bee's friend. Her thoughts hadn't been hidden from her in the back of a closet somewhere, muffled by blankets. Her actions hadn't been secretive, or unconsidered, or strange. Nor had she felt that if she stepped into the light of the situation, cracks would begin to form in her convictions until she fell to pieces.

As Wilhelmina lay on her back staring at the blurry ceiling, the memories coursed through her the way memories do sometimes, a whole summer in a matter of seconds. When she'd gotten the news about Bee's dad, she'd gone home to Massachusetts and taken her place at Bee's other side, the side opposite Julie. She'd learned pretty quickly that it was like nothing else to lose a hurtful parent. Like nothing else to do so when you were thirteen, to a drug overdose, while the parent was an ER doctor who should've known better, while the other parent was in strident denial about who the deceased parent had been and how he'd died. Every section of Bee's experience made it unlike any other experience, and Bee was obliged to absorb the whole of it all at once.

They'd spent a lot of time that summer talking about a lot of things. Often lying on their backs on the floors or beds in their bedrooms, usually Julie's or Wilhelmina's, because Bee hadn't wanted to be in his giant house. Sometimes they crowded together in Julie's window seat. It was the window where a ten-year-old Wilhelmina had gouged holes into the outer sill with Mr. Dunstable's drill; it faced the backyard, and had a long view over the land that dropped steeply, speckled by dozens of other houses shored up by retaining walls, thick with trees. The sunsets from Julie's window were different every night, and sometimes quite beautiful. It'd been strange for Wilhelmina to be home, but not in school. The summer days had stretched out long and weirdly empty, and she'd missed the aunts, who were pretty terrible at texting. Days would go by before they responded to her texts, and the responses betrayed labor. She would call them and talk, but the calls would leave her missing them more.

That was the summer Philip had been born. The sink was always full of the bottles and rubber nipples and other claptrap that went with breast-pumping, Wilhelmina learned to change diapers and position a car seat, and her parents were always exhausted. Philip's cries became part of the soundtrack of her life, and she was surprised by how little she minded. She loved supporting his wobbly little head, and soothing him. She liked feeling needed by him.

It was also the summer her hand pain had started. By September she'd gone to her doctor, who'd sent her to a neurologist, who'd diagnosed her with something called thoracic outlet syndrome. It was a mechanical problem whereby the nerves and blood vessels that ran down her arms into her hands were constricted by pressure in her neck and shoulder area. The neurologist sent her to a physical therapist, who set her up with stretches and exercises that reduced the pain significantly, as long as she limited her typing. She'd discovered dictation, which Julie had also taken to, despite not needing it. Their texting had gotten much more grammatical and sophisticated. With everything that had been strange and hard about that summer and early fall, Wilhelmina remembered that she'd also had a hidden core of excitement, because of the likelihood that November would bring the election of the nation's first woman president.

She remembered the couple of rough days she'd had, late that

September. Julie and some of the soccer girls had been planning a weekend outing in downtown Boston, which wasn't unusual—Julie did things sometimes with her teammates—but then it kept growing in participants. Someone wanted to see a movie, and other people wanted to go. Someone else wanted to go to the aquarium. Someone else wanted to mob the merry-go-round on the Rose Kennedy Greenway, which, instead of horses, was crowded with animals native to Massachusetts, like peregrine falcons, lobsters, grasshoppers, and barn owls.

As the number of people grew, Wilhelmina had begun to feel a little confused. It wasn't that she wanted to be part of it, exactly; group activities were fine, but Wilhelmina didn't generally have the *Oh, fun!* response that she'd noticed so many other people seemed to have. Her preference was for smaller groups. *Much* smaller groups, really. Julie knew this, which was almost certainly why, as the exclusive soccer outing turned into more of a spread-out throng, she continued not to ask Wilhelmina if she wanted to come.

But Wilhelmina's mind had snagged on the barn owl at the Greenway Carousel. She was fourteen, so her wish to ride a barn owl on a carousel was maybe a little bit embarrassing, but that didn't mean she didn't want to be invited. She definitely wanted to sit on a barn owl. She was confused enough about it that when the morning of the outing came and she heard Julie head out of the house to catch the bus—Julie even texted her a heart and a *Cu l8r Wil*—she still hadn't said anything to Julie about it.

Bee wasn't going. Wilhelmina didn't know if Julie had invited him or not, but either way, he had to babysit his sister, Kimmy, that morning while his mom worked. Bee texted with Wilhelmina a little. *Come over l8r?* he asked her.

Sure, she said, but then she opened a fashion video Bee had sent her. Julie and Wilhelmina shared videos like this all the time, but Bee got into it occasionally too.

It was a video about hats. Wilhelmina didn't own any stylish hats, but it was fun to think about them, and she liked how this woman combined color, an olive-green cloche and an olive belt blending beautifully with the deep plum jumpsuit she wore. The jumpsuit was adorable on this woman, who was shaped like Wilhelmina, and had short hair like her too. In fact, Wilhelmina was starting to consider jumpsuits and hats quite seriously when the woman said, "Now, listen, nothing mean in the comments, okay? You know I'm still working on my postbaby fat. Send encouragement, not shame! Next month, no more giant jumpsuits!"

Wilhelmina slapped her laptop shut, the way you might raise a hand to your face to protect a place that's already been hit. Then she blundered her way through one terrible, upside-down day and night before finally approaching Bee and Julie.

"Oh no!" Julie cried, immediately and obviously dismayed. "I'm so sorry! I thought you would hate the big group! Of course you could've come!"

"I mean, you were right," said Wilhelmina, sniffling. "It was a reasonable assumption. I'm not really upset, Julie. I don't know what I am."

Bee's eyes, in the meantime, were growing wider and wider. "I watched that video with the sound off!" he squealed. "Kimmy was making me listen to a horrible kazoo concert! Oh my god, Wil, I'm sorry. I always screen the skinny people for shit like that. I should've known to screen the fat ones too."

Wilhelmina had begun to cry. "I'm so relieved."

"Oh, Wil," Julie had said, hugging Wilhelmina. "I'm really sorry."

"It's okay. You were right."

Bee joined in the hug. "Was it awful? I'm so sorry!"

"It's okay! It was an accident."

"But you've been carrying this around!"

"I'm sorry I didn't tell you both sooner," Wilhelmina had said. "I was just so confused."

On her back in her bed, a tear ran down Wilhelmina's face. She reached for her glasses and her phone. Neither Julie nor Bee had texted. *I'm afraid to push myself on you,* she wrote to Julie. *I'm not sure of the helpful thing to say. But I wanted you to know I'm sorry. I would be so hurt if you gave my necklace to a crow. I was scared I was losing you. I don't know why my actions were the opposite of my feelings. Maybe I was a little angry that you didn't realize how lonely I was. But how could you have known? I didn't tell you.*

She hit send, then added, *I'm sorry I didn't tell you sooner. I was just so confused.*

WHEN THEO GAVE WILHELMINA the choice of supervising Delia's school or Philip's, Wilhelmina chose Philip. When, next, he gave her the choice of his bedroom or her own, she chose her own.

Supervising Philip's school meant setting him up at the desk, staying out of sight of the camera but close by, paying half attention, and feigning enthusiasm and good cheer. The enthusiasm and good cheer were exhausting, but less exhausting than being stuck in a room with a ten-year-old who hated you and wanted help writing an essay about Alexander Hamilton, for example.

Wilhelmina spent Philip's storytime lying on her foam roller, letting her arms drop like weights, willing the muscles in her neck and chest to release. When the teacher began a very chipper discussion about the letter *T*, she moved to her bed and checked the driving directions to the Bunker Hill Monument, which was in Charlestown, where driving was never fun. *It'd better be worth it,* thought Wilhelmina. *We'd better get some nice, clear answers.* Then she took a long, slow breath and, finally, checked the news.

The electoral vote tally stood at 253–213, Biden–Monster. The races in Arizona, Georgia, Nevada, Pennsylvania, Alaska, and North Carolina were still too close to call. Alaska and North Carolina were lost causes, and Georgia probably was too. The states Wilhelmina cared about were Arizona and Nevada, where Biden was leading, and Pennsylvania, where he was not. And Biden's lead was narrowing in Arizona.

This morning, in reaction to armed protesters in Phoenix shouting, "COUNT THE VOTES," the Secretary of State of Arizona had said, "I don't understand the objective of these protesters. Of course we're going to count all the votes. We are legally obligated to do that." It seemed like such a sensible thing to say. But what was the use of saying sensible things? Other sensible people would nod their heads knowingly, but how did that help? The problem was the hordes of people to whom sense didn't matter.

The monster's lead was narrowing in Pennsylvania. Her heart rising into her throat, Wilhelmina nudged herself to do something she hadn't had the wherewithal for yet: focus on the hard numbers there. Today, on Thursday morning, the monster held 50.7 percent of the counted votes in Pennsylvania; Biden, 48.1 percent. There were about 140,000 uncounted ballots remaining.

Wilhelmina dug up the equivalent figures—the vote spread and the number of uncounted votes—from Tuesday night, Wednesday morning, and Wednesday afternoon. Then she did some math in her head. She figured out the rate of change of the vote spread across time. She factored in the votes still left to count.

Then she needed to go lie on her foam roller again, because if her math was correct and if the pattern held, Biden was going to win Pennsylvania.

"What words can you think of that have a *T*?" asked Philip's teacher. "Anyone? Philip?"

"I puked!" Philip announced.

"I'm so sorry to hear that, Philip," said his teacher. "Can you think of a word with a *T* sound?"

"Not really," said Philip.

T *is for tarot,* thought Wilhelmina. She glanced across the room at her mirror, which was still covered by her shirt. The angel in the Temperance card was having a nice long sleep, maybe, like when you threw a cloth over a birdcage. T *is for Temperance.* Levering herself off the foam roller again, she went to her bedside table and attached Frankie's owl to her ear. Then she extricated Frankie's cards from the drawer. She held the little bumblebee-covered bundle in both hands, wondering if she should pull a card for herself. Find out whatever she needed to know about whatever part of her journey this was. Was she the Fool, making a new beginning? Was she the Magician, learning how to use her tools? Was it time to meet the Devil? Was it time for her Tower to come tumbling down? Was she stumbling around under the light of the Moon? Frankie had always made it seem okay, whichever card she pulled. Frankie had always seen endings as new beginnings. But what was the point of pulling a card for herself? Unless she pulled one of the very few cards with which she was familiar, it wasn't like Wilhelmina would know what it meant. Frankie had been the one with the meanings.

Again, she checked her phone. *Morning!* said James. *CU in a bit* *Morning,* she wrote back. *See you soon.*

No one else had texted. Lightly, she touched her elephant necklace, which sat on her bedside table, standing pertly inside a curved enclosure created by the chain. Its trunk sprouting lilies made her think of spring.

Not sure if it was right, she put the necklace on.

WILHELMINA AND DELIA WERE LATE for their appointment at the Bunker Hill Monument, on account of a cake delivery Delia had scheduled into the proceedings without informing Wilhelmina.

She resisted a strong urge to speed as they drove down the hill to Eleanor's house. "Seriously," she said, "all you needed to do was *tell* me we were bringing the cake to Eleanor. You're old enough to know—"

"Everybody always starts insults with 'You're old enough to know,'" Delia interrupted loudly from the back seat. "I figured you were smart enough to know that if the cake was for Eleanor, then we needed to bring it to her."

"I thought she was coming to the monument!"

"While her grandpa's in the hospital with Covid?"

"Oh," said Wilhelmina. "I didn't know about that."

"It's why I made her a unicorn cake!"

Wilhelmina was feeling a little chastened. "I'm sorry to hear that," she said. "Is he okay?"

In the rearview mirror, Wilhelmina watched Delia wrap her arms tightly around herself, which was alarming, because the unicorn cake was balanced precariously on her lap, its horn swinging wildly with every pothole Wilhelmina drove across. The unicorn had giant eyes made of peanut butter cups, with maraschino cherry irises positioned at the edge of each brown eyeball. Whenever Wilhelmina was near it, she had the sense that she was being surreptitiously watched.

"He's on a ventilator," said Delia, glaring out the window with her face turned away.

"How old is he?" Wilhelmina ventured.

"I don't know, okay?" said Delia. "He's like the aunts."

They drove silently to Eleanor's house, which was nowhere in the direction of any route that would take them to Bunker Hill, but Wilhelmina kept her mouth shut about that. At the intersection where the man usually stood with his flag, they spotted him holding a new cardboard sign that said STOP THE STEAL.

"The world is full of jerks and ignoramuses," Delia said. She was holding the cake now, lifting it up protectively whenever they rounded a curve or approached a bump. Her voice shook a little.

"It was really nice of you to make Eleanor a cake," said Wilhelmina. When they reached Eleanor's house, which was the left side of a dark blue duplex, Delia scrambled out with the cake and carried it up the steps, where she placed it on the front porch. Then she seemed to change her mind about the positioning, carefully moving it six inches to the left, rotating it so that its gaze faced the door. Her head was bent and her expression very serious. She rang the doorbell and ran back to the car.

When Eleanor stepped out onto the porch, the two girls waved at each other wildly and shouted *hello*s and *I miss you*s. "You're a unicorn genius!" Eleanor shouted. "Thank you!"

"Okay," said Delia, getting back into the car and slamming the door. "We can go."

She was crying. Wilhelmina fumbled through her pockets for a tissue.

"I thought we were late and everything," said Delia roughly. When Wilhelmina passed back a tissue that was wrinkly, but clean, she added, "Gee, a snotty tissue? Thanks."

"I'm really sorry, Delia," said Wilhelmina. "You're a good friend, you know that?"

Delia took the tissue. "Whatever," she said.

CLIMBING the two hundred ninety-four steps of the Bunker Hill Monument with James, Delia, Delia's friend Madison, and Madison's mother, Sue, was a strange endeavor.

They wore masks as they climbed, each family group distanced twenty-five steps from the next. The Harts went first, then James, then the Petrosians. Every twenty-five steps, a stone marker proclaimed how many steps they'd climbed. Whenever Wilhelmina and Delia reached one, Wilhelmina called it out, so that the others below would know to position themselves one marker back from whomever was in front of them.

The steps were circular, dark, and cramped. Going first and with her mask smothering her face, Wilhelmina had the sense that she was the vanguard of an exploratory mission and it was her responsibility to confirm that the air was breathable and the structure sound, then warn the others below. Maybe this was an obelisk on an alien planet. A tropical planet? It was hot today, seventy-one degrees outside. In November! Hadn't it just snowed last week? Wilhelmina was dressed wrong, her leggings and long-sleeved hoodie making her feel like a cannoli someone was frying, probably the alien creators of this obelisk, which would turn out to be a clever construction wherein you tired yourself out by climbing, then, when you reached the top in a state of exhaustion, they ate you. *Push. Push!* Her legs were tired, but Wilhelmina kept flinging her Hart feet up onto the next step and pushing.

"Wilhelmina?" said James, his voice rising from below, echoey and deep. "You are seriously booking it."

"I am?" said Wilhelmina, stopping in surprise.

"I'm dying here," said Delia, leaning on the wall and gasping. Delia had a pair of binoculars hanging around her neck, which Wilhelmina hadn't realized the family owned.

"We're way behind!" came the tiny, faraway voice of Madison. "You can slow down, James!"

"Oh!" said Wilhelmina. "Maybe that's why I'm so hot! I'm sorry. I think my feet were trying to keep pace with my thoughts."

"Think about a sloth," said Delia.

"Or a penguin," said James, who could apparently hear them well, even though he was some distance below. "The walking kind, I mean, not the swimming kind."

"Or a giant tortoise," said Delia as they started up again.

"Or a manatee," said James.

Beside her, Delia was swelling with happiness. Delia hated Wilhelmina, but loved Wilhelmina's friends; it had long been thus. And James was new. When Wilhelmina and Delia had run up the hill, scurrying to join Sue, Madison, and Wilhelmina's "friend of choice" at the base of the monument, apologizing for their lateness, James had been a surprise to Delia, who'd expected Julie or Bee. Her eyes had widened. Then she'd tried for an air of nonchalance, but she'd turned almost pink with her yearning to interact with this new, older person.

"Or a starfish!" Delia almost yelled.

"Good one," said James.

Delia looked about to pop with glee. "How did you meet Wilhelmina?" she shouted down to James.

"School, I guess," said James.

"Why haven't I ever seen you before?"

"Fate has recently thrown us together," said James.

"James's family has the doughnut shop," said Wilhelmina hastily, to stop Delia from asking nosy questions about fate.

"You mean Alfie Fang's?" said Delia in amazement.

"That's right," said Wilhelmina.

"That means you're, like, famous!"

"Thank you," said James politely. "But mostly it means I spend a lot of time covered in sugar."

An image intruded upon Wilhelmina's mind, or maybe it was more of a feeling. James, covered in sugar. His mouth sweet, like a collapsingly soft doughnut—

"Oh, for Chrissake!" she cried.

"What?" said Delia.

"Nothing," said a flustered Wilhelmina, as the final step came into view. "Geez, finally! Two hundred ninety-four." She climbed into a round room that was smaller than she remembered, with dirty plexiglass windows that made everything feel too near. A narrow wire screen striped the top of each window, but not much air was moving.

"Yikes," said James, coming up behind them. "I remembered it as open air."

"Me too," said Wilhelmina, trying to move away from him. She was too warm, and he felt very close. "I guess we should spread out. And make this quick?"

"Yeah. Have you seen anything . . . *interesting* yet?"

Wilhelmina snorted. "Nothing. You?"

"Nope."

"So!" said Sue Petrosian, stepping into the room behind them with Madison. "Welcome to the observation deck! We can take turns at each window and move in a clockwise direction. How does that sound?"

"Great," said Wilhelmina. "Thanks again, Sue."

"Of course," said Sue. "It's too sad for the monument to stand here unused. We bring tiny groups up whenever we can, if people express an educational interest. Now, girls, you know you have to stay six feet apart!"

Sue moved toward Madison to pull her away from Delia, and Wilhelmina studied James, because she couldn't help herself. He was dressed appropriately for the weather, in a RailRiders T-shirt. The Rail-Riders were the minor-league baseball team in Pennsylvania whose games she'd used to go to with Frankie. They were also a Yankees affiliate, which made James a bit brave here in Red Sox Nation, assuming anyone besides her recognized the team logo. She wondered now, had they ever been at the same game? Also, did he know how he looked in that T-shirt? Wilhelmina's dream world had not done James justice. The arms and shoulders he'd been hiding inside his puffy sky-blue coat for these last few days turned out to be several tiers of attractiveness above and beyond what she'd dreamed. She had a feeling that the main difference was that this James was real.

"How do you feel about cannolis?" she asked him.

"What?" he said, instantly grinning. "Who doesn't like cannoli?"

"Don't you two even care about the view?" said Delia. "Come on, you're ruining the plan."

"Right," said Wilhelmina, moving toward Delia's window. A low, bulbous sun cast peach-and-gold reflections on Boston's skyscrapers. "It's very pretty."

"The city looks like a toy," said Delia, peering through her binoculars. "Look, the bridge looks like a ship!"

At a different window, James cleared his throat. When Wilhelmina glanced at him, he nudged his head at his own view.

"What?" said Delia. "What is it?"

"I guess we'll see when we get there," said Wilhelmina.

"You guys are being weird," said Delia. "Let me see!"

Wilhelmina moved to James's window with Delia and saw a long view to the west, which was the direction they'd come from today. Everything was very small, but Wilhelmina could recognize some of the tall towers of Harvard, especially Memorial Hall, a soaring red-stone building that looked like someone's wedding cake gone wrong. She could also see an enormous, castle-like office building she knew was on Mount Auburn Street in Watertown. She was looking at Cambridge and Somerville, with Watertown, Belmont, and Arlington behind them. Home.

Somewhere near the Cambridge-Watertown border, a small patch of land glowed. Not pink and orange in the setting sun; it glowed in that white-golden way that Wilhelmina, biting back on her weary impatience, recognized. And really, this was too much. It wasn't exactly quick or easy to get to the Bunker Hill Monument. It required a lot of fast driving, on roads that winged you away in the wrong direction if you weren't careful, while other drivers honked and cut you off. Plus, it was a headache to find parking around the monument, and her arms still hurt, and then all those steps. All so she and James could receive a message to head back toward home?

"If I'm being honest," said James, who'd moved to another window, "my sense of direction is crap. It's part of my math thing."

"Oh!" said Wilhelmina. "I'm sorry, I didn't realize. Did you have trouble getting here?"

"I left myself like an hour and a half," said James. "No worries. But where do you think that is? I mean, where exactly?"

"You mean . . . that?" said Wilhelmina, trying to sound blasé while indicating the glowing patch of land.

"Yeah."

"What?" said Delia. "It's, like, Harvard. Who cares?" Delia was glaring from one of them to the other the way she often did with Theo and Cleo, like their behavior was not just mysterious, but suspicious, and probably nefarious.

"May I borrow your binoculars, Delia?" asked Wilhelmina.

"No," said Delia, but she handed Wilhelmina the binoculars.

Through the round lenses, the view leapt into sight. "Well, it's on the border of Cambridge and Watertown," said Wilhelmina, trying to isolate the precise location of the glowing land. It sat beyond most of Cambridge's recognizable landmarks. "I see Memorial Hall, which nails down Harvard Square, and I think I see the business school across the river. I think I see Mount Auburn Hospital. Then, near that, I think I see . . ." Yes. Wilhelmina, who had an excellent sense of direction, was pretty sure she'd identified it. "It's Mount Auburn Cemetery."

James's eyebrows shot up. "Do you ever feel like you're going around in circles?"

"What's that supposed to mean?" said Delia. "I don't see the cemetery. What's going on?"

"We're just curious how far we can see," said Wilhelmina, handing the binoculars back to her. "What's the farthest thing you can identify, Delia?"

Delia's face flushed. "I'm not stupid," she said. "I know that's not what you meant. Hey, Madison, want to go outside?" Then she threw one mortified glance at James and ran for the stairs. They could hear the slaps of her footsteps, echoing like blows.

"Okay," said Sue. "Don't you worry, Wilhelmina, I'll keep an eye

on her. If you'll just start making your way down in the next ten minutes or so?"

"Yes, of course," said Wilhelmina. "Thank you."

While the steady footsteps of Sue and Madison receded, Wilhelmina and James stood across from each other, studying each other.

"Hey," said James gently. "My bad."

"No," said Wilhelmina, "I'm the one who lied to her."

James shrugged. "I set you up."

"It's okay," said Wilhelmina. "It's an impossible thing to talk about
without being weird."

As they watched each other for another moment, Wilhelmina had
a sense suddenly of the form of things. She and James were alone, in a
small, circular room, at the top of a high tower, with Sue Petrosian as
good as a guard at the door below. And they had ten minutes.

Conscious suddenly that she was supposed to be enjoying the view,
she spun around and looked out the window.

"Nice," she said, then heard her own inane comment, and had to
stop herself from snorting.

Across the small room, he'd turned to his nearest window too.
"Mm-hm," he said agreeably. Then he moved clockwise to the next
window, so she did as well. The view was lovely, really, soft and colorful
as the sun sank lower, yet Wilhelmina and James kept turning to look
over their masks at each other, like two people at the far edges of a clock
face. Whenever he moved around the circle's edge, it tugged her along
too, so that the room was always between them. If she moved first, her
movement nudged him along. It seemed they were destined to keep
circling from window to window, never catching up to each other.

Then he stopped moving. His shoulders rose and fell in a quiet
sigh. He turned to face her, leaning back against a windowsill with his
arms crossed.

"Yes?" she said, stopping too.

"Nothing," he said. "I'm just done pretending I care about the view. I'm interested in *you.*"

"Yeah," she said, putting her back to the wall behind her and allowing herself to focus on him. It was a relief. The light was painting his skin gold, and burnishing the tips of his hair. "How much time do you think we have?"

"I don't know," he said. "Five minutes?"

"I wish I could see your face."

"Yeah," he said. "I wish I could see your beautiful face too."

Wilhelmina's beautiful face was flushing with heat. She was too shy to voice the question she was thinking: Someone or something was trying to lead them around, and was this part of the reason why? A private moment in a tower, with James?

"Any ideas about the glowing cemetery?" she asked instead.

"No," he said. He had a nice voice. Its timbre was deep, and soft. "Maybe we missed something when we were there?"

"Whoever's trying to lead us around could be a lot less vague," said Wilhelmina.

"No kidding," he said, with a breath that was almost a laugh. Wilhelmina wanted him to laugh. She thought the sound might draw her right across the room.

"I asked my grandma to read my tarot last night," he said. "I haven't liked to do that, ever since my dad got sick, but I figured I could ask a really specific question, you know? I asked, 'What are Wilhelmina and I not seeing?'"

Wilhelmina tilted her head. "Did you get an answer?"

"It was a two-card reading," he said. "I got the Empress and the Magician."

Wilhelmina breathed out. "Frankie was my empress," she said.

James watched her with soft, dark eyes. "My nonna was my magician," he said. "But I thought maybe the cards represented us. You're the Empress and I'm the Magician. Or I'm the Empress and you're the Magician?"

"What?" said Wilhelmina, thinking of the Empress. Her beauty and power; her dress of pomegranates and her crown of stars. "*I* can't be the Empress!"

"When my nonna died," he said, "I wanted to burn paper for her, the way my nai nai does, my Chinese grandma. Do you know that tradition? You burn paper versions of the things you want the person to have in the afterlife. It's, like, how you deliver the things to them in the afterlife. Mostly fake money, but I wanted to send her other things."

"That's beautiful," said Wilhelmina, instantly picturing paper birds, paper flowers. Paper teapots and paper tarot decks, to send to Frankie.

"I wanted Nonna to have a tarot deck," he said. "I cut little cards out of tissue paper and drew pictures on them, like the Magician and the Chariot, the angel on the Temperance card. The Tower," he said, flinging a hand up to indicate the room around them. "Every one I knew. I wanted to burn them for her, but my parents wouldn't let me, because we were at my grandparents' house in Pennsylvania, I mean my Italian grandparents, and everyone was upset and had a hundred more important things to do. So I brought them to the church for the funeral. I kept trying to throw them into the air, like, during the Mass, which made my parents crazy, but anyway. I guess I was mixing my traditions, you know? In the Catholic Church, she'd risen to heaven. So I was trying to throw them to her."

Wilhelmina stared at James, seeing something else. She was in a church, watching floating pieces of tissue paper turn purple, blue, and gold. Beside her, Frankie had tears streaming down her face.

Wilhelmina's head was reeling. She fell to her knees.

"Wilhelmina!" cried James, running straight to her across the circle, dropping down beside her. She was gasping; she couldn't get any air.

"Wilhelmina?" he said, his voice sounding far away. "I'm going to touch you, okay?"

She felt herself nodding. His arm was around her, supporting her. His hand was holding her other hand, his skin was touching her skin, and he was coaching her to breathe, one slow breath in through her nose, one faster breath out through her mouth. Then another, and another. She felt her mask hot against her face, and pulled it off. Wilhelmina was breathing again.

"What happened?" said James, his voice close to her ear. "Are you in pain?"

She shook her head, though she was in pain, her grief very near. She leaned against him, feeling hot tears on her face. She pulled her glasses off and felt his chest against her cheek, her tears soaking his T-shirt. She found her arms, and put them around him.

"I was at your nonna's funeral," she said. "When I was little. I saw you."

"What?" cried James.

"Was her name Mancusi?"

"Yes!"

"I was at her funeral, with Frankie," she said. "She was Frankie's teacher in high school."

"That's amazing," said James. "Wilhelmina, that's amazing."

"Your nonna saved Frankie's life," said Wilhelmina.

IT WAS DIFFICULT TO EMERGE from the monument into the light, acting as if everything was normal. The world was too loud and the sun was too bright. As they walked down the broad outdoor steps toward the others, Wilhelmina's eyes kept tearing up, and James wore a dazzled expression that shifted to concern every time he glanced Wilhelmina's way, which he did often.

It helped that they wore masks that covered half their faces. Sue didn't seem to notice anything strange, nor did Madison. But Delia kept peering at them sharply, and her conversation grew louder. She and Madison sat on the steps sharing their worries about Eleanor's grandpa, but there was a different message in Delia's increasing volume: *What is going on with you, Wilhelmina?*

James and Wilhelmina spaced themselves a small distance from the others. Wilhelmina wanted to leave, but Delia and Madison didn't seem like they had any intention of wrapping their conversation up soon. So she sat on the steps.

"I—I know you probably want to talk about this," she said quietly. "You have questions."

"I do," he said, sitting nearby, "but you just fell over. I think that's an indicator we should go slow."

"I just—I have a lot going on right now," she said, "and I need a minute."

"Of course," he said. "Are you feeling okay?"

Wilhelmina felt like her sadness was right below her skin; like she was made of it. It was leaking out of her eyes. "It's like something's opened inside me," she said, "and all this feeling is just pouring out. Does that make sense? It feels a little—out of control."

He nodded. "I wish I could hug you again."

She said, "Can I see your face?"

James shifted a bit farther away and pulled his mask down over his chin. As he turned his worried eyes to her, the falling light touched his nose, his mouth. Places Wilhelmina realized she wanted to kiss.

"What are we going to do about this?" she said.

"About what?" he said. "I mean, which part?"

"The pandemic," she said, "and the not being able to touch."

"Yeah," he said, scratching his head, beginning to smile. "I'm feeling motivated to figure that one out."

"Add it to the list," said Wilhelmina with a small sigh.

"Added," he said. "Want to go for a walk with me in the cemetery tomorrow?"

WILHELMINA DROVE THE CAR HOME through relentlessly mean traffic, not talking to Delia, focused on a simple plan: Once home, she would go inside. She would spend the rest of the day in the proximity of others as little as possible. She wouldn't think or feel, or check the news. She would try not to hover over her phone. At night, she would sleep, then tomorrow she would walk with James in the cemetery, where nothing weird would happen.

Then, near home, as she pulled the car onto the long hill that climbed to their apartment, she got a feeling. The feeling made her stop the car in the middle of the road.

"Why did you stop?" said Delia.

On the sidewalk on the right, Julie and Bee came into view, walking down the hill together. As soon as she saw them, Wilhelmina hit the gas, surging the car forward noisily in her confusion. The roar attracted their attention, which was the last thing she'd wanted to do.

"Hey!" shouted Delia, waving. "Hi, Julie! Hi, Bee!" But her window was closed, and by the time she got it open, the car had already passed them in a whirl of dust. Julie and Bee watched them go, bewilderment plainly written on their faces.

"What are you *doing*?" Delia squealed. "Didn't you *see them*?"

"I saw them," said Wilhelmina, speeding up the last block and pulling the car to an abrupt halt outside the apartment.

"What is *wrong with you*?" cried Delia. "How do you even have a *driver's license*?"

"Delia!" cried Wilhelmina, her voice louder and sharper than she intended. "Back off!"

Delia's face crumpled. She pushed out of the car and slammed the door, running for the house.

Left alone, Wilhelmina sat for a while, hot with shame. If only she'd kept driving at a regular pace, it would've been such a normal thing to do. It was too late now. She'd driven like she was afraid of them, or at any rate, like she was trying to avoid them. Their faces had been worried and grave—until she'd started driving like it was the Indy 500. Bee's fingers had been working at something anxiously in his pocket. Wilhelmina knew, from long experience, that it had been the blue stone he kept there always. They were upset, and she'd blown past them.

A phrase was running on a loop through her head. It was something Esther had said once, long ago: "That which you water, grows. That which you don't water, dies." Why did Wilhelmina keep starving her garden?

AT DINNER, the conversation felt like it was lurching and crashing around her. She ate fast and tried to ignore it.

"Biden's catching up in Pennsylvania," said Cleo. "Did you see? And Georgia, did you see Georgia's getting interesting?"

"It doesn't matter!" said Theo. "Anything could happen! Stop trying to make me hopeful!"

"And judges threw out those lawsuits," said Cleo. "And his lead is growing in Nevada—"

"Nevada," said Theo scornfully.

"I did the Pennsylvania math," said Aunt Margaret. "I think Biden's going to take the lead there sometime tomorrow."

"Oh my god," said Theo. "Stop it!"

"I wonder if we'll feel it," said Esther.

"Feel it?" said Aunt Margaret.

"The moment Biden and Harris take the lead in Pennsylvania by exactly two votes."

"Ah," said Aunt Margaret. "Good question. Let's make it four votes, though, for Rose and Rudy."

"Who are Rose and Rudy?" demanded Delia.

"The grandparents of Wilhelmina's friend James," said Aunt Margaret.

"They voted in Pennsylvania?"

"Yes, at our very own fire hall. James drove them there to vote, just like Wilhelmina drove us. We met them Tuesday."

"You did?" said Delia, in a voice that squeaked at the end. "No one tells me anything!"

"Delia," said Esther. "Did you know your name means 'heart of a lion'?"

Delia's mouth fell open. "What?"

"Cordelia," said Esther. "In French, 'coeur de leon' means 'heart of a lion.'"

Delia's cheeks were tinged with pink. "I guess that's accurate, actually."

"Mm-hm," said Esther. "I think so."

"We were considering an evening walk," said Aunt Margaret, "if anyone's interested."

"I'm interested," said Delia.

"I'm interested!" shouted Philip.

"The other night, we heard an owl on our evening walk," said Esther.

"That reminds me," said Theo to Delia. "Someone told me you talk like an owl."

"What?" cried Delia. "Who?"

"Oh my god, they were right," said Theo.

Standing, Wilhelmina said, "I can do the dishes." Then, because

Cleo was studying her with that compassionate diagnostic expression she hated, she pushed away from the table.

"Mom and I can handle it tonight, honey," said Theo. "Why don't you rest your arms?"

There was something careful in his tone that told her what she would've preferred not to know: that Theo, and probably everyone, could tell something was wrong. She went to her room and shut the door. On a whim, she googled the Tower card, because she'd been remembering something about it, ever since James had mentioned it. It was a card about reality breaking. About the tower crashing down around you while you suddenly, almost violently, saw truths that had been hidden from you all along. It was about rising from the rubble with those new, painful truths, and moving on.

Wilhelmina, who was so surefooted, had fallen to her knees in the tower. What was going on?

SHE STAYED IN HER ROOM until the aunts and siblings departed for their walk and her parents removed themselves to their bedroom. Then, with her laptop and phone, she crept out again.

In the window inside her blanket fort, Frankie's snow goose bobbed its head at Wilhelmina gently. She touched its long neck, then touched it again, swinging it from side to side. Delicately, she touched the birds sitting on Saint Francis's shoulders and at his feet. She touched the parliament of owls. *Help me, birds.*

Her phone buzzed. Somehow she knew, without looking, that it was Julie.

I miss you, wrote Julie.

Wilhelmina's tears were back, pouring down her face.

I don't mind you texting, wrote Julie. *I'm just really sad, maybe a little mad. Is that okay?*

Wilhelmina couldn't dictate fast enough. *Yes. Anything you are is okay. I'm sorry I made you sad and mad. Also, sorry I was weird with the car*

It's okay about the car, said Julie. Then, before Wilhelmina could respond, she wrote again.

I think you're right, she said. *I should've realized how hard this was for you*

Wilhelmina was holding her breath. *Really?*

I think I did realize, said Julie. *But I didn't want to bring it up. Because I felt so guilty*

A release valve was opening inside Wilhelmina. All her generosity was pouring through. *Oh, Julie,* she wrote. *Don't feel guilty*

Julie didn't respond to this, but some explication came from above. Wilhelmina heard Tina shouting something, then Julie's mom, Maya, calling for Julie. Footsteps. Then the scurrying feet of Esther the cat, followed by a crash, then Maya yelling, "You cat!"

Wilhelmina, left at loose ends, made the questionable decision to check the news. The petulant pustule had just given a press conference.

"If you count the legal votes," he'd said, "I easily win. If you count the illegal votes, they can try to steal the election from us."

Wilhelmina couldn't bear it. She shoved her phone down into the crack at the side of her seat cushion. Opening her laptop, she clicked on the Panama live cam. A funny brown-gray bird with long pink legs and twitchy tail feathers was trying to negotiate a banana that kept swinging past its face in a wide arc. It was a thousand times better than anything in the news. Except that then her phone buzzed again.

"Agh!" she cried, digging for it, half-wild, but knowing it was James. *How u feeling?* he wrote.

Kind of . . . discombobulated, she said. *Sorry*

Dont apologize, he said. *Im here if you want to talk*

I mean, I kind of do, she said. *I mean, I don't*

?

I mean, there's a lot, and I don't actually want to be alone right now. But I don't think I can talk! I think I'm too . . . confused. Maybe a little numb. There's too much going on

I know numb, he wrote.

You do?

Yeah

How do I make it go away?

That I dont know, he said. *I always just ride it out*

Ride it out? she said. *How?*

K well. Im worried ull think I try to solve everything w birds, he said. *But its albatross egg laying season in New Zealand*

Do they have a live cam? wrote Wilhelmina.

Yeah, said James, *and its good rn. Want to watch w me?*

Yeah, she wrote.

While she waited for James to send the link, she listened for more noises from upstairs. Things seemed to have settled down up there, but Julie wasn't texting. Idly, Wilhelmina considered the rolltop desk outside her blanket fort. Wedged between a low bookcase and the fireplace, it was a desk she'd always liked. She liked the way the top rolled open, and the orderly pigeonholes it revealed. Theo and Cleo kept important papers in there, like tax stuff, bills, passports. Also some old letters.

Wilhelmina wasn't sure why she stood, then squeezed past the racks that held up her blanket fort. She rolled the lid of the desk open. As dust floated, she sneezed.

"Gesundheit, honey!" came her father's muted voice, from somewhere far away. The basement? What was the point of ever trying to find a private place in this apartment? Wilhelmina shuffled through the pigeonholes, uncertain what she was looking for. Her fingers found an old card, filed alongside a bunch of other old cards, with watercolor flowers on its front: lilies, tulips, dahlias. The flowers were a messy riot of color. Opening the card, she recognized Frankie's uneven handwriting.

"April 3, 2006," it said. A few days before Wilhelmina's fourth birthday.

"Spring greetings from all of us," Frankie wrote. "Enclosed are some sunflower seeds, and some birthday cookies I made specially for our darling Wil-helm-ina."

The summer Wilhelmina was fifteen was her upside-down summer. Instead of Wilhelmina living with the aunts, Frankie came to Massachusetts for a clinical trial of some cancer drug that someone had decided was a good idea, but that seemed, from Wilhelmina's perspective, mainly to make Frankie nauseated and tired.

She lived in an apartment near the hospital, which was in Boston. This arrangement had surprised Wilhelmina, who'd imagined Frankie living with them, probably taking Delia's room while Delia slept on the couch.

"Why do *I* have to sleep on the couch?" Delia had said when Wilhelmina had proposed this. "*You* sleep on the couch!"

"No one needs to sleep on the couch," said Cleo, who was, during this conversation, alternately nursing baby Philip and sneezing. Every time she sneezed, Philip's tiny mouth froze in place and he stared up at her, wide-eyed with amazement. "It's better for Frankie to be close to the hospital."

"Alone?" said Wilhelmina. "I could live with her."

"Esther and Aunt Margaret will be coming up a lot, and we'll be in touch with her every day. We'll bring her here for dinner all the time."

"But she might not want to live alone."

"She might not want to live in a chaotic home with a baby, far from where she needs to go for the trial, hon," said Cleo. "This Boston apartment is frankly a miracle."

"That's not what Dad says."

"He knows it's a miracle," said Cleo. "Grace Mardrosian can be difficult, and she tires Dad out. That's all."

Grace Mardrosian was Theo's boss at the library and, with her husband, the owner of the Boston brownstone containing the apartment in which Frankie would be staying. The Mardrosians' son lived in the apartment normally. Felix Mardrosian, a graduate student in archaeology, would be spending the summer at a dig in Iceland that his mother disapproved of, because Felix was in a relationship with the director of the dig, whom his mother also disapproved of, for reasons Wilhelmina didn't know. Thanks to Theo, Wilhelmina knew a lot of details about Mrs. Mardrosian's attempts to control the people around her, but she didn't know everything. What she did know was that Mrs. Mardrosian had let it slip in a conversation with her son Felix that one of her librarians who was constantly requesting time off was most recently requesting time off in order to drive his aunt into Boston repeatedly for a clinical trial. And Felix had asked who, and Mrs. Mardrosian had said, "Theo Hart." Felix had asked which hospital, and Mrs. Mardrosian had told him. And Felix had said, "That hospital is right near me. Maybe I'll ask Theo Hart if his aunt would like to house-sit while I'm in Iceland. She could feed my cats. You don't mind if I let her use the apartment, do you, Mom?"

Hence, every day at work, Mrs. Mardrosian hovered over Theo's desk, dropping weird, vague hints that she blamed Theo for her son's unsuitable relationship, and intimating that once Felix got his head screwed on straight, he would leave the dig and need his apartment back.

"I just hope the apartment doesn't turn out to be like a frat house," said Cleo.

But Felix Mardrosian's apartment was not like a frat house. It was, in fact, bigger than the Harts' apartment, despite being located in a pricey part of the city and occupied by only one man and two cats;

it was the first floor of a beautifully maintained building with a tiny back garden; and the decor was consistent with what one might expect from an aspiring archaeologist. Old stuff. Little bits of metal and clay that had probably lived aboveground for a brief flash of time long ago, then slept inside the earth for eons, until some patient human with an aching back had dug them out again. Books. Dark wooden tables and leather chairs. Lamps, everywhere; Felix really had a thing for pretty lamps. Weird random stuff, like an array of taxidermied animals that included a fox, a chipmunk, and a wolf. African violets in the windows.

"This will do very nicely," said Frankie on the day they all helped her move in. She rested in an armchair while Theo and Wilhelmina carried things and Esther and Aunt Margaret unpacked and made up the beds.

"There is, for sure, a feeling to it, the minute you walk through the door," called Esther from Frankie's bedroom, where she was hanging Frankie's shirts beside Felix's in the closet. The cats were in there with her; they followed Esther wherever she went. "Some of it feels like 'powerful young man of means,' but I don't think it'll hurt you."

"A lot of the objects in this apartment will steady you, Frankie," said Aunt Margaret, surveying the living room with her hands on her hips. "The lamps are very healing, and the violets, of course. These old things have a low, steady power. Very balancing." Aunt Margaret touched a series of small triangular stones arranged in a row on a shelf.

"The taxidermy is too bad," said Esther, coming in from the bedroom. The cats came with her, pressing themselves against her ankles and watching the rest of the group suspiciously. "How does it feel to you, Margeleh?"

"Mm," said Aunt Margaret, going to the wolf that stood snarling in a corner near an old-fashioned record player. "The most steadying objects are the ones best able to resist Felix's belief that he owns them. This wolf is confused, I'm afraid."

"I will try to befriend her," said Frankie. "I'm often confused."

Wilhelmina was letting this peculiar conversation wash over her the way she often did with the aunts, because she was focused on her own perceptions. Namely, that it was deeply, deeply strange to imagine Frankie living in this home that was brimming with someone else's objects—and also something more unsettling. The aunts were passing a feeling back and forth, from one to the other. They were scared.

Wilhelmina had a job that summer. She made sandwiches at a sandwich shop on Main Street a few blocks from the library. She liked it well enough. Her boss was easygoing, nothing like Mrs. Mardrosian, and she could get into a zone, layering sandwich ingredients or mixing capers into tuna and forgetting about how upside-down she felt. It hurt her hands and neck sometimes, but she was allowed to stop and stretch. Occasionally she worked a shift that ended at a convenient time to walk up Main Street to the library and deliver a sandwich to her father.

The walk took her past the Lupa Building, a building she liked because of its stylized wolves and the glimpses of chrome and marble through the tall glass windows. Also the doughnut shop, of course, Alfie Fang's, which had a black-and-white checkered floor and a mural of a forest on the wall and, occasionally, a cute boy cleaning the tables with a wet rag. She didn't know him. She figured he must go to a school somewhere besides Watertown High School. Wilhelmina had a heightened consciousness of cute boys that summer. A cute guy at school named Thomas had fallen hard for her last winter. It had been . . . educational. He'd seemed very sweet, and she'd liked being liked. Until they'd kissed, and it had felt like having her mouth excavated by a hagfish. Before kissing Thomas, Wilhelmina had never even heard of a hagfish, but the kissing had eventually inspired her to google "slimiest thing on Earth," which had led her to the hagfish, an eel-shaped fish that exuded large quantities of a milky and fibrous slime.

She'd tried the kissing a couple more times with Thomas. She'd tried to make alterations to the approach, the point of contact, the follow-through, et cetera, but it had been the same. Thomas, who was very enthusiastic, hadn't seemed aware of the problem, or of her attempts to solve it. So then she'd tried to talk to him about it, which was when his sweetness had turned sour.

"If you don't like it, maybe there's something wrong with you," he'd said with a new, hard set to his jaw. At which point Wilhelmina had decided that this educational opportunity had run its course, then done the googling that had led her to the hagfish. Julie hated Thomas now, like *despised* him, and Bee wanted to talk to him sternly about how to respect people. Her elephants. Wilhelmina had had to ask them both to stand down, which they'd done, of course. Their anger on her behalf was a comfort to her. It made her feel loved. But it didn't soothe her worries. *Was* there something wrong with her? This was one of the questions Wilhelmina was sometimes able to stop asking herself when she was in the sandwich zone.

Another was: What was wrong with everyone else? It wasn't just an upside-down summer; it was an upside-down world. Since the inauguration of the new president in January, a part of Wilhelmina was always dizzy. It was the part of her that processed cruelty and lies, and it was overwhelmed. It couldn't keep up. Wilhelmina, Julie, and Bee went to protests now regularly; they sought them out, because surrounding themselves with other people who also saw through the lies and hated the cruelty made them feel a little less crazy.

Often Julie and Bee came with her to see Frankie, the three of them taking the bus to the train into the city and going to the bookstore on Newbury Street first, or, on hot days, a movie. Once, they dressed up, made their makeup extra spectacular, and had high tea at the library.

Sometimes when they got to Frankie's, Esther or Aunt Margaret or both were visiting, and sometimes it was just Frankie. Either way, the visits always involved a certain amount of amazed poking at Felix

Mardrosian's eclectic treasures. Entire shelves in his living room were full of small shards of pottery, or those triangular rocks, or short metal rods.

"He should label his stuff," said Julie, with her nose to a piece of petrified wood.

"I know, right?" said Wilhelmina. "For those of us who feel like we're in a museum."

"Museum labels are boring," said Bee, who lay on the floor, communing with the taxidermied wolf, one of the cats climbing around on top of him. "I like it better without them. If a volcano erupted and our bodies were petrified in lava, like, until archaeologists dug them out centuries later, what activity would you want to be found stuck in?"

"Hm," said Frankie. "Picking tomatoes."

"Reading a really excellent book," said Julie.

Protecting Frankie, Wilhelmina thought but didn't say.

"Hanging out with you guys," said Bee. "Do you have a favorite treasure in this apartment, Frankie?"

"It depends which room I'm in," said Frankie. "In here, I love the lamps. Sometimes if I'm up in the night, I'll come in and turn on every single one and just sit for a bit in their glow. It's soft light, you know? Nothing harsh, just a lot of little warm suns."

"It doesn't keep you awake?" said Bee.

"It makes me sleepy," said Frankie, "like a bath."

Julie was counting. "Wow. There are twelve lamps in this room."

"Yes," said Frankie. "In the kitchen, I love the violets."

"Can we do anything for you?" said Bee. "Water the violets?"

"I'm perfectly content, but thank you, dear," said Frankie, smiling across the room at Bee. Frankie's smile had lost none of its power, but Wilhelmina wasn't sure what was fueling it. No, that wasn't quite right; she could feel the well of power inside Frankie burning strong. But Frankie's body, the container around the well, felt thin-walled and tired. Old. Her inner heat was too hot, too close to the surface.

Whenever it was time to leave and the other aunts weren't there, a fear would grip Wilhelmina that Frankie wouldn't be okay on her own, that she would burn herself up.

Frankie seemed to know. "You don't need to worry about me, Wilhelmina," she would say, reaching a hand up to Wilhelmina's face. "Want to go for a walk sometime, just you and me?"

"Here?" said Wilhelmina, who was having trouble picturing this version of Frankie walking extensively anywhere. "Around your block?"

"Oh no, somewhere beautiful," said Frankie. "Next time I come to your house for dinner, let's go to Mount Auburn Cemetery."

"Okay, but I can't drive yet," said Wilhelmina, who couldn't picture this version of Frankie taking the bus from the Harts' apartment to the cemetery.

"*I* can drive, Wilhelmina," said Frankie. "Have you forgotten? I'm sure your parents will lend us the car."

It was, in fact, a great comfort to drive the short distance from home to Mount Auburn Cemetery with Frankie in the driver's seat, then get out and walk. Frankie seemed strong the day of their walk, maybe not eager to aim for the highest hill, but not frail either. She seemed like Pennsylvania Frankie, gardening Frankie. Maybe there was nothing different about her and it was all Wilhelmina missing Pennsylvania?

"Ah, that beautiful sun," said Frankie, closing her eyes and stretching her arms out, like a flower opening its petals to drink in the light.

All the birds came out for their walk. They saw robins and sparrows in the trees, blue jays and cardinals, crows and ravens (Frankie knew the difference), turkeys, ducks. A hawk soared above, then dropped like a stone, then climbed and dropped again. Frankie chattered, mostly naming the trees, exclaiming over the flowers. Finding shapes in the clouds. Wilhelmina was quiet, because she had too many different things she wanted to say.

"How are you coping with all of your pressures, dear?" asked Frankie.

Surprised tears sprang to Wilhelmina's eyes. "I don't have any pressures," she said.

"Oh, everyone has pressures," said Frankie. "And I remember being fifteen, Wilhelmina, and I see the shape of the world around you."

The shape of the world, thought Wilhelmina. *I've gotten more political? I'm going to protests? I have a job? I'm worried about you?* "I'm worried there's something wrong with me," she said, a tear sliding down her face.

Frankie made a sympathetic noise and nodded, as if this was a normal thing to say and people were saying it to her all the time. "I know that feeling," she said. "What do you think is wrong with you?"

Wilhelmina's face was hot and pink. "Do you promise not to tell anyone?"

"I do," Frankie said, with such simplicity that Wilhelmina felt safe suddenly, like this conversation was possible.

"I kissed this guy," she said. "It was disgusting."

"Oh, I'm sorry," said Frankie. "That sounds very unpleasant!"

"But," said Wilhelmina, "I like guys. I liked *that* guy. So, wasn't I supposed to like it?"

Frankie stopped, then turned to face her niece. "There is nothing you are supposed to like," she said. "Not one single thing. That's a myth, and an unfair expectation. Do you hear me?"

Frankie wasn't usually this fierce. It helped. "I do hear you," said Wilhelmina. "But—" Another tear slid down her cheek. "What if I *wanted* to like it?"

"Oh, Wilhelmina," said Frankie, pulling her into a hug. "Then I think you probably will like it, some other time, with some other person." She paused, then smiled an inward smile, as if remembering something inside herself. "Tell me," she said, "this boy you kissed. Did you talk to him about it?"

"I tried," said Wilhelmina, who felt like she was hugging a bird. She didn't want to squeeze too hard. "I was as nice about it as I could possibly be. He's the one who told me there was probably something wrong with me."

Still hugging Wilhelmina, Frankie snorted. "Sounds like a classic bad kisser to me. A good kisser is going to be someone who *cares* whether you like it, Wilhelmina. Among other qualities, like not blaming you. Like *wanting* to communicate about it."

"Okay," said Wilhelmina. "I guess that makes sense."

Frankie took a step back so she could look into Wilhelmina's face, still clutching her arms. "Do you talk to Julie and Bee about these things?"

"Yes," said Wilhelmina. "They call him Hagfish."

"Hagfish?" said Frankie. "Is that an animal?"

"It's an eel-shaped fish that secretes a milky and fibrous slime."

Frankie let go of Wilhelmina and hooted so loudly that a bird burst out of a nearby tree. "Good heavens," she said. "*Fibrous* slime? Wilhelmina, you poor dear!" As she howled with laughter, she was luminous, and bigger somehow, ferocious and strong. A honking noise interrupted her. Together, they turned.

"Oh!" whispered Frankie. "Wilhelmina, it's a snow goose!"

The bird was standing with its feet submerged at the edge of a pond, watching them and honking, as if it wanted to join in the laughter. Its honk was so long and silly-sounding that Wilhelmina did begin to laugh.

"Let's back up," said Frankie. "Give her room."

Wilhelmina was happy to back away. The snow goose was a beautiful bird, long-necked and white with black-tipped wings, but geese were big, powerful creatures, and they could bite. It opened its wings and flapped, showing off its dark inner feathers. Then it lifted into the air and drops of water rained down, sparkling like sequins.

That summer, it was hard for Wilhelmina not to tether herself to news headlines. In August, a rally turned deadly in Charlottesville, Virginia. It was called "Unite the Right." The participants were openly neo-Nazis, white supremacists, white nationalists, members of the alt-right and of the Ku Klux Klan, marching together in protest of the removal of a statue of Robert E. Lee. As they marched with their torches, weapons, shields, and Nazi and Confederate flags, they met counterprotesters. Fights erupted. Then a rally participant plowed his car into a crowd of counterprotesters, killing a woman named Heather Heyer and injuring lots of other people. "Some very fine people on both sides," said the president.

In Boston, a public event was planned for the following weekend, called a "free speech" rally, but really a gathering of members of the far right. One of the scheduled speakers was a Holocaust denier. Another was the founder of the Proud Boys. When Wilhelmina heard that a counterprotest was planned, she knew she wanted to go.

Frankie was at dinner with the Harts when Wilhelmina told Theo and Cleo her intention.

"Oh," said Cleo, putting her fork down and looking across the table at Theo. "I have an event that day, and your father needs to care for Philip."

"What does that have to do with it?" said Wilhelmina. "I can get there on my own."

"What is it?" said Delia, who was seven. "Can I go?"

"Oh, honey," said Cleo to Delia, then stopped, looking sad and tired.

"Actually, Delia," said Frankie, "that's the exact day I was hoping you would come visit me in my apartment."

Delia considered Frankie suspiciously. "You mean *just* me?"

"Yes, you, and only you," said Frankie. "And the cats, of course."

"I want a cat," said Delia.

"Let's ask your parents, shall we?" said Frankie. "Theo and Cleo, could Delia be my special guest on Saturday?"

"Wilhelmina, hon," said Cleo, not even looking at Frankie. "This one feels different from the others."

"You mean because of Charlottesville?" said Wilhelmina.

"Yes."

"But if anything were to happen at this one," said Wilhelmina, "the chances of it happening to *me* are infinitesimal."

"What's Charlottesville?" said Delia.

"I'll explain to you about Charlottesville, dear," said Frankie. "Are you done eating? May I have the honor of doing your bath?"

"You don't have to do that, Frankie," Theo interjected. "You're our guest."

"I want to," said Frankie.

"Can I visit Frankie?!" shouted Delia.

"Yes, honey," said Theo. "You can visit Frankie."

"Yay!" shouted Delia. "Can Frankie do my bath?"

"We can't stop her if she wants to, can we?" said Theo.

A moment later, Theo, Cleo, and Wilhelmina were alone.

"Wilhelmina," said Cleo. "I'm glad you want to go, and we can't argue with your math. But I'm not sure how I feel about this one, especially since we can't go."

"Your mother and I may need to have a conversation, honey," said Theo.

Wilhelmina swallowed a series of sharp retorts. *What am I, eight? Since when do I need a babysitter?* She was ready to sneak to the protest if she needed to, the way Bee snuck to every protest, telling his mother he had soccer, or babysitting, or something; the way Bee snuck to therapy. Cleo herself had helped Bee find a mental health counseling center he could get to on his own. She'd told Bee to dig up his family's insurance card. "If your mother sees the mail from the insurance and asks you about it, let me know and I'll talk to her," Cleo had said, but Bee's mom never asked about it.

Wilhelmina had observed that Bee's first step in sneaking was to act like he didn't care too much about what he did. "Okay," she said with nonchalance.

Almost visibly, Theo and Cleo closed ranks. Their expressions sharpened and their backs grew straight. "I'm sensing you're very motivated about this," said Theo. "Is that right?"

Dammit. Too much nonchalance. "Do you know they were carrying Confederate flags?" said Wilhelmina. "They were chanting Nazi slogans!"

"Are Julie and Bee going?" said Cleo.

"They want to."

"Let's find out if Maya and Daniel are going," said Theo to Cleo.

"Oh my god, Dad, seriously?" said Wilhelmina. "You need to talk to Julie's parents? Like it's a playdate?"

"We need to talk to Julie's parents like it's a protest where things could turn violent," said Cleo firmly. In a distant room somewhere, Philip began to wail. Cleo stood. "Now, Wilhelmina. Are your hands well enough to do the dishes?"

The day of the protest, Wilhelmina woke to a feeling like her lungs were smaller, her instincts more electric. It was strange. She'd never been nervous about a protest before.

Julie's parents were going to the protest. Theo and Cleo had found a babysitter for Philip so Theo could go too, a decision Wilhelmina had been grouchy about when her parents had told her. It was fine he was going, but did he have to go with *her*? This morning, she came yawning into the kitchen and found him filling water bottles. When he turned, gave her a delighted smile, and asked her if she'd remembered to put on sunscreen, she rolled her eyes. But she was glad he was coming along.

The plan was for Bee to take the T into the city with Julie, Maya, and Daniel while Theo and Wilhelmina drove Delia to Frankie's apartment, then parked and took the T to meet up with them. Wilhelmina walked Delia to Frankie's building while Theo circled the block. When Frankie answered the door, she looked tired, and a little unsteady.

"Frankie?" said Wilhelmina. "Are you okay?"

"Just a little nausea, dear," said Frankie. "It comes and goes. Delia, I am ever so happy to see you. Come in, say hello to the cats!"

Delia bolted into the apartment. "Wilhelmina," said Frankie, still standing in the doorway, "I just talked to Esther and Margie. We want to go to the protest too. Will you carry us in your heart?"

That day in Boston, a few dozen right-wing ralliers were met by tens of thousands of counterprotesters, though Wilhelmina didn't know this while they were marching. It was one of the funny things about a protest. You knew who was around you: Bee, Julie, Julie's parents, your own father, and hundreds, maybe thousands, of unfamiliar faces. You felt the energy of those people, hot and strong. You shared their anger and their grief. You saw the helicopters above, and you knew you were a small part of a larger organism. But you also remained in your own body, your own thoughts. Inside Wilhelmina's body was Wilhelmina, her sadness, her confusion, her delight at being here with Julie and Bee. Her secret delight at being here with Theo. Her relief that such a massive number of people, more massive even than she realized at the time, had poured out of their homes to be here, regardless of, or maybe because of, what had happened in Charlottesville. And every time she saw a small, smiling woman, or a person with tanned skin and a generous nose—or someone plump like Mrs. Claus, or someone tall with locs—or anyone fashionable, or anyone in sparkly earrings, or a bird— she remembered her aunts. She remembered them over and over again, and brought them along.

FRIDAY, NOVEMBER 6, 2020

On the Friday one day before she stepped into her own, Wilhelmina woke from a dream about albatrosses. They were floating above a green, grassy shore, letting the wind fill their unbelievable wings, wings you would never imagine they possessed if you saw them first on land, big-bodied and bulbous and clumsy at walking. They would waddle, laboring to the edge of the rise, their chests massive and their beaks smiling, their wings looking like little stubs pressed against their bodies. Then they would unfold those wings on a series of hinges, and Wilhelmina couldn't believe how long the wings were. Or how quickly the wind caught them, hoisting the birds into the air.

In the dream, it was egg-laying time. A father and mother were building a nest. Once the mother laid the egg, the father and mother would take turns sitting on the egg and bringing food to the sitter. The father was frightened. The egg might break. The nest might become infested with flies. He or the mother might be drowned at sea in a storm while trying to hunt for the other. *Sometimes it is hard to feel hope,* he said.

The mother pooh-poohed this. *Hope can be a feeling you sit around waiting for,* she said, *or it can be the nest you build and the hunting you do.*

Hope is the nest you built, Wilhelmina, said the father. *And the hunting you do.* The dream had changed. The mother had climbed into the nest, ready for the work of laying her egg, and the father stood on the rise, unfolding his wings, letting the wind lift him out to sea.

Wilhelmina was kneeling in the grass before the mother, who spoke to her in albatross, with screeches and clicks that Wilhelmina understood.

I won't be able to talk with you like this always, Wil-helm-ina, said the albatross mother. *I won't always be near your door.*

Grief swept through Wilhelmina, as harsh as the wind that was trying to knock her over. *I miss you,* she said.

I'm in your heart, said the albatross mother. *Help the people who helped me.*

Who helped you? said Wilhelmina, then felt the wind lifting her, Wilhelmina, pulling her away.

You know, said the albatross.

I don't want to leave! cried Wilhelmina, trying to close her fingers around the grass, a tree, anything, but grasping only air.

I'm in your heart, the albatross said again, as Wilhelmina swirled away.

"Wilhelmina?" said a voice. "Wilhelmina? Wilhelmina! Geez! You sleep like you're dead!"

"What?" said Wilhelmina, groggily coming awake. Her mouth felt like she'd eaten a Muppet. "What time is it?"

"Early!" said Delia.

Wilhelmina hated talking to people while she was still wearing her nightguard. "Then why are you waking me up?"

"Because I just felt it!" said Delia.

"Felt *what?*"

"Biden and Harris taking the lead by four votes in Pennsylvania!"

THREE HOURS LATER, the news reports caught up with Delia's feeling.

"Biden and Harris take the lead in Pennsylvania," the headline said. And they'd taken the lead in Georgia too, which hadn't even been on

Wilhelmina's radar. "The sitting president won't have a path to 270 if he loses Pennsylvania and Georgia," said another headline.

Next came the news that he had no plans to concede.

It was still morning when Wilhelmina parked inside the cemetery, early for her meeting with James. It was another warm day.

I'll listen to the birdsong, she thought, opening her window. *I'll look for crows. I won't look at my phone. I won't look at my phone!* Reaching for her phone, she reread Julie's texts from yesterday. As she was doing so, Bee texted. *Hey,* he said. *How ru? How r we? Could we talk today?*

James tapped a finger on the side of her car.

"Hey," she said, clambering out, disoriented by the sun, by the interruption. James was wearing another T-shirt, this one gray with a barn owl in the middle of his chest. It was a close-fitting T-shirt, and he looked the way he always did, increasingly attractive with each passing moment. "Nice T-shirt."

"Thanks," he said. "You look great."

Wilhelmina, who was always confused by unseasonable weather, had decided to wear a blue dress that had a short, swinging skirt and a rainbow belt and collar, plus her boots—then pack the car with leggings, a hoodie, a coat, a scarf, arm warmers, sandals, a sun hat, and an extra mask, just in case. She was also wearing her elephant necklace—also just in case—and Frankie's owl. "Thanks," she said shyly. "You do too."

"I like your elephant and your owl," he said.

"Thanks."

"Where do you think we should go first?"

"I don't know," she said, still feeling like she was elsewhere, worried, on her phone. "Should we re-create our route from that first time we met?"

"Makes as much sense as anything," he said, shrugging. "I parked here that day and walked."

312 · FRIDAY, NOVEMBER 6, 2020

"I drove farther in and met Mrs. Mardrosian before I saw you. My neighbor," she added, when James looked puzzled. "She used to be my dad's boss. She needed help with a flat tire."

"Got it," said James. "Do you remember where that happened?"

"I think I could figure it out."

"I'm not sure I could re-create my route, so maybe we should focus on yours?"

"Okay," said Wilhelmina. "Let's walk."

The cemetery had a masking rule, so they pulled theirs on. Stone steps nearby led up through an expanse of low monuments to the road Wilhelmina remembered driving along that day, under tree branches heavy with snow. Today, the branches overhead seemed light and easy, rustling with leaves, blazing with color. Wilhelmina felt her feet connecting with the ground.

"How are you?" asked James.

"All right, I guess," she said. "I dreamed about albatrosses."

"I checked the live cam and their Twitter this morning," he said. "No egg yet."

"Something weird happened yesterday evening," said Wilhelmina. "I got it into my head to look in this desk in our living room. Like, it was calling to me. And I found a card from one of my aunts, Frankie, written when I was four. She'd written my name with dashes."

"Wait, what?" said James, stopping beside a gravestone topped by an angel. Wilhelmina could see the angel towering behind him, unfurling her wings. "Like in the messages you've been getting?"

"Yes," said Wilhelmina. The card had upset her. She'd brought it to Theo, demanding an explanation he'd been unable to give. "She wrote it that way sometimes, honey," he'd said, plainly puzzled, and worried, by her agitation. "Maybe she liked the 'helm' in the middle?"

"That's the aunt who knew my nonna, right?" said James. "Frankie?"

Wilhelmina hesitated. "Yes."

"So," said James, "whoever's been sending us messages calls me Ray, like my nonna did, and spells your name with dashes, like Frankie did."

Wilhelmina wasn't ready for whatever she would be confirming if she confirmed this. She studied her own boots for a moment, then raised her eyes to James, squinting into the sunlight. The angel's wings were spread out behind him, as if they were his own wings. *Trust Ray,* she thought. "Listen, James," she said. "I know we need to talk about that. And I will, I promise. But I don't have the space for it yet, like, in my heart. Is that okay?"

"Of course it's okay," he said.

"Frankie is gone," Wilhelmina said. "If I risk thinking about her any other way . . ." She stopped, wiping furiously at a tear.

"Hey," said James, his voice gentle. "Let's focus on the what, okay? What we're here for, what we're supposed to do. We can talk about the why another time."

"Okay," said Wilhelmina. "Thanks."

"Should we walk?"

"Yeah, let's walk."

She led him away from the angel statue, then up the hill she remembered driving. They moved in silence, Wilhelmina glancing at him frequently. His attractiveness was becoming frustrating. Even the way he walked was attractive, his arms swinging attractively at his sides and his legs bending attractively at his knees, which was ridiculous. What could be more unremarkable than legs bending at knees? She tried to refocus, tried to surrender to the act of waiting for something weird to happen. Something that would lead them one step closer—to what? To helping the doughnut shop? A cardinal flitted by, brighter even than the brightest maples. Far above, a tiny, soaring shape was a hawk; they watched it drop into a dive. As the road curved, they came upon a group—a rafter?—of turkeys pecking at the ground.

"Seeing anything yet?" said James.

"No. You?"

"Nope."

"Here, let's turn here," she said, leading them onto a narrow road that climbed toward a giant maple stretching out above them, like fire thrown against the sky. They stopped on its carpet of leaves, admiring the colors. Wilhelmina swished her boots through them, loving the papery sound, the earthy smell.

"Check it out," said James. "This family's name is Drown."

"I love the names in this cemetery," said Wilhelmina.

"Here's a Chang. You don't see a lot of Chinese names here."

"That's true. Let's turn onto this one," said Wilhelmina, who saw a familiar willow down a road on the right. The last time she'd seen this willow, it had been heavy with snow, and Mrs. Mardrosian had been standing beside it. Now, as they approached it, its limbs swung with pale green leaves.

"This is where I met Mrs. Mardrosian," Wilhelmina said. "She was looking for her keys in the snow."

"Anything weird about it?" said James. "Was she glowing?"

Wilhelmina scrunched her face. "That's a really good question. This was at the beginning of the weirdness, so I wasn't finely tuned to the glowing yet, but actually, I think she might've been glowing."

"Okay," said James. "Should we, like, re-create your interaction? You be you and I'll be Mrs. Mardrosian. Tell me what to do."

"You wander around the graves near the willow, digging in the snow with your ice scraper, wailing about your husband."

"Okay. What's his name?"

"Levon."

"Got it," said James, then found a stick and began poking at the grass around a gravestone topped by yet another angel. "Oh, Levon!" he said. "How could you leave me while I'm pregnant with twins?"

"She's old," said Wilhelmina, snorting. "He left her by dying."

"Oh, Levon!" said James, moving to another gravestone. "How could you leave me alone in a cold, dark world?"

"That's more like it. Now I'm driving by," said Wilhelmina, holding her hands up in a steering-wheel position and gliding past him along the road. "I see you have a flat, so I pull over. I get out of my car and ask you what's wrong. You tell me you've lost your keys."

"Hello! I've lost my keys, beautiful Wilhelmina Hart from school," he said, moving to a gravestone topped by a howling dog. "Will you rescue me?"

"I didn't know you felt that way about me, Mrs. Mardrosian," said Wilhelmina, "but I'm not going to leave an old lady alone in a snow-storm."

"My rheumatism!" said James, jabbing the grass with his stick. "My corns! Hey. Wilhelmina?" he said, his voice changing suddenly. "Look."

"What?"

James was digging around in the grass near the grave with the howling dog. He held something up, a glinty thing covered with mud. As he wiped it clean with his bare hands, it jingled.

Wilhelmina was speechless. She stared with her mouth ajar.

"Mercedes," said James, flipping through the keys. "A bunch of house-ish keys. Also a bathtub Mary," he said, indicating one of those charms of the Virgin Mary that showed her standing in an oblong blue enclosure. "Is she Catholic?"

"I don't know," said Wilhelmina. "Her name sounds Armenian, but I guess that's her husband's name, right? I don't know much about her, except as a boss."

"Right," said James, still trying to wipe the keys clean.

"Well, I guess she'll be glad to get her keys back," said Wilhelmina. "But is this what we're here for? To find her keys?"

"I don't know," he said. "You'd think they'd have the courtesy to glow or something." Then he narrowed his eyes at the gravestone with the howling dog. "Wilhelmina," he said, bending down, peering at it more closely. He held his hand out, so obviously meaning for Wilhelmina to come to him and take it that she waited, quietly, for him to realize what he was doing.

He glanced at her, then looked down at his extended arm. He sighed. "Right," he said, then moved back so she could move forward. When she did, she saw that the animal atop the gravestone was not, in fact, a dog; it was a wolf. No dog had teeth that big. And the name on the grave was Lupa.

"Wait, what?" said Wilhelmina, turning to look at James. "Lupa, like your building? What does that mean? Was Mrs. Mardrosian visiting the grave of the people who own your building?"

"Maybe?" said James.

"I thought you talked about a management company. Not, like, a family."

"A management company is just a company that manages properties," said James. "On behalf of someone else who owns them."

"And who owns the Lupa Building?"

"I don't know," said James, pulling out his phone. "I'll ask my parents."

But while James was texting his parents, Wilhelmina found herself staring at a nearby grave, a plain one with no angels or wolves. The family name was Mardrosian. Under the name, on the left, it said, LEVON 1952–2020. On the right, it said, GRAZIANA LUPA 1955–

"Graziana Lupa Mardrosian," said Wilhelmina, pointing at the grave. "That's Grace Mardrosian."

"What?" said James, looking up from his phone.

It was hard for Wilhelmina to imagine a neighbor of hers owning an office building. How could any one person own an entire office building? But the clues fit. James's family owed money to the Lupa Building, Wilhelmina was supposed to help them, and now they'd found Mrs. Mardrosian's keys and her future grave. Graziana Lupa Mardrosian.

"I think Graziana Mardrosian owns the Lupa Building," she said.

"YOU'RE RIGHT," James said grimly a few minutes later, his face bent to his phone. "My mom says the owner is named Mardrosian. She says they used to be able to communicate with a Levon Mardrosian, who was, like, a human, with a conscience. But then he died, and since then, everything has to go through the management company."

Because when Levon Mardrosian died, thought Wilhelmina, his wife needed help managing the office building she now owned all by herself. "She owns other things too," said Wilhelmina. "She let Frankie stay in an apartment once that she owned, in Boston. But now she's demanding your back rent?"

"Right," said James. "So I guess we were supposed to find these keys? Like, in the cosmic course of events. But for what? To hold them hostage, until she agrees to forgive tens of thousands of dollars in back rent? Cuz I don't think that's going to happen."

Okay, that was a massive amount of money. Far more than Wilhelmina had realized, or could even comprehend. She stopped herself from exclaiming, because James already looked depressed enough.

"What do you think?" he said, staring at the ring of keys in his palm. "I mean, I think we're supposed to return her keys, right? And what? Talk to her?"

Wilhelmina tried to imagine that conversation. *Hello, Mrs. Mardrosian, remember how I changed your tire in the snow? Don't you think you owe me tens of thousands of dollars?* "She's not . . . the nicest person," said Wilhelmina reluctantly. "She was a pretty terrible boss."

James's shoulders sank. He was rubbing the back of his head, and she wished now, as she'd wished many times before, that she could see his face, even if it was only to confirm what she already knew: that he looked worried, discouraged, and sad.

"She's my neighbor," said Wilhelmina. "Why don't you let me talk to her?"

"Alone?" said James, clearly horrified. "Of course not!"

"She's not going to hurt me," said Wilhelmina. "She's my neighbor."

"Everyone who hurts people has neighbors! Anyway, it's my family's thing!"

"Okay," said Wilhelmina. "We'll go together."

"Okay," said James, shoving the keys into one pocket and his phone into another, then sighing. "I need to get back to the shop soon. Want to go tomorrow?"

"Okay," said Wilhelmina, but her heart was snagging on his obvious unhappiness. "I wish I could give you a hug."

"I need a hug from you," he said forlornly. Then he pulled his mask down over his chin, and gave her a sad little smile. "The vaccine's coming, right?"

Sure, but when? thought Wilhelmina. "You told Delia you were always covered in sugar."

The tips of his ears turned pink. "Yuh-huh. I can prove it." Then he sighed again. "Want to walk a little more? Not for clues, just to walk?"

"Yes, please," said Wilhelmina.

AFTER THEIR WALK, Wilhelmina climbed into her car, then sat quietly, watching James drive away. A bumper sticker on his car said, BIRDS AREN'T REAL. IF IT FLIES, IT SPIES. It made her snort a laugh, which felt good.

She was thinking about rule breaking. About sneaking around and lying to her family, to be with James. To touch his skin, test him for sugar. Kiss his face, kiss his mouth, do whatever they wanted. She could imagine it. No one would have to know. She liked what she was imagining.

And then she imagined James passing her the virus, which she passed to her aunts and her asthmatic dad. She imagined passing James the virus, which he brought home to his sick father.

Nothing was worth those consequences.

She remembered then those early weeks last spring, as she, Bee, and Julie had begun to comprehend what was happening, and what being in the same room together could mean. She remembered the three of them piled together on Julie's bed playing *Starcom: Nexus*. Julie was the hands and fingers and the source of occasional advice, while Wilhelmina made the decisions. Bee provided running commentary; then, at some point, Wilhelmina noticed that he had a runny nose. When she went down to her own apartment later, she snapped at Theo.

"Bee was sniffling," she said, holding a hand up to ward him off. He stopped. Comprehension touched his face.

"Doesn't Bee get some allergies in the spring?" he said gently.

"Just stay away from me," she said, then spent the next few days anxiously monitoring her own breathing, agonizing every time she coughed or needed to blow her nose. Wilhelmina had been terrified of killing her father. She still was. It wasn't a feeling you got used to.

She picked up her phone and touched Bee's text thread. *How r we?* he'd written. *Could we talk today?* Tears were running down her face again. What was with all this stupid crying?

I'm in Mount Auburn Cemetery right now, she wrote. *Want to go for a walk?*

As she hit send, she realized that of course Friday morning was not a good time for Bee to take a walk. Bee had school.

There in 10, he wrote back.

———————

BEE WASN'T A MORNING PERSON, nor was he a virtual school person. When he climbed out of his car, he was in pink sweatpants and a plain gray T-shirt Wilhelmina was pretty confident he'd slept in, and his hair was all piled up on one side of his head. But he was wearing his elephant necklace.

"I forgot about school when I texted," she said, stepping out of her own car awkwardly, not sure what to say to him. "Sorry."

"Fuck school," said Bee. "This is more important."

"Okay," said Wilhelmina uncertainly. "Well. How are you?"

"Um, I've been better?" he said. "You're sad? Julie's sad? I'm sad? The world's on fire and this is the most stressful week I've had in, like, years, and I'm scared I'm losing my best friend?"

"You're not losing me, Bee."

"Well, it doesn't exactly feel like things are going *well*, does it?" he cried, throwing his hands in the air. Bee was crying. And there were people parking nearby, climbing out of their cars and staring at them, which probably should've embarrassed Wilhelmina. Instead, she found herself comforted by how emotional Bee was being, by the feeling of him being demonstrative in person. He felt exactly like her Bee.

"I'm really sorry, Bee," she said. "I know I'm the one who created this situation. Let's walk, okay?"

"I contributed to it," he said. "But okay."

"We're supposed to wear masks."

"Oh, fuck masks!"

"I need you to wear a mask, Bee," she said. "My dad and my aunts."

"Yeah," he said, digging a mask out of his pocket, then inhaling once slowly to pull himself together. "I'm a mess here. Sorry." He put his mask on. It had a picture of an anthropomorphized avocado eating avocado toast.

Wilhelmina directed Bee up the same stone steps she'd taken

with James, then nudged him in a different direction, because this was a different conversation. Bee was still dabbing his sleeve to his face and sniffling behind his mask. Bee had always given her his feelings like a gift. She was never left guessing who he was, or what he needed. Wilhelmina wondered if she'd been taking this for granted for too long.

"I've realized there's something I need to tell you," said Bee.

"Okay," she said, stepping off the road onto a grassy path that led to golden trees. "What is it?"

"I'm not sure I can make it clear," he said. "It's going to sound like a criticism of you, but it's really about something *I* struggle with."

"Okay," said Wilhelmina, wary now. Wasn't this one of the classic frameworks for breaking up with someone? *It's not you, it's me.* Which the person never truly meant?

"It's hard for me when someone puts up a barrier," said Bee. "Like, a wall, to protect themselves. Like, when someone decides to stop thinking about something or talking about something, because it's too painful. And then it starts to feel like they're pretending that thing doesn't even exist."

"Okay," said Wilhelmina, who was a little lost. "Are you saying I do that?"

"It gives me this feeling like I get from my mom," said Bee. "Like I used to get from my dad. Like there's something in front of our faces that's so screamingly obvious, but they're going to pretend it's not there, because that hurts them less than admitting the truth. But the problem is that their denial hurts *me*. They're choosing to let it hurt *me*, so it won't hurt them. You know?"

"Yes," said Wilhelmina, because she did know. She'd watched this dynamic play out in Bee's life always, starting way back, when he—and she—had both been too little to understand it, but not too little to feel the force of it. His dad was dead now, but his mom was still closed up behind that barrier. She never acknowledged to Bee what the truth of his life had been. The silence still hurt him.

"Bee," said Wilhelmina. "Are you saying I do that? That I'm hurting you the way your mom does?"

"No!" said Bee. "I'm trying to explain why I struggle sometimes to be the friend you need." He veered them off the path onto a carpet of yellow leaves, ginkgos. "You've put up a barrier, and I know it's not about me," he said. "It's different from my mom. I get why you put it up. When Frankie died, your heart, like, *exploded*. I know. But you did put me on the other side of the barrier, or at least, that's how it feels sometimes. I think it hurts a little extra for me, because of how barriers like that have operated for me in the past. I get panicky. It's not your fault. I'm just trying to admit to you that sometimes I struggle with it. I was struggling with it before the pandemic ever even happened, and maybe that's part of the reason I didn't stop to realize how hard the last few months have been for you. Which I'm sorry about. I think we should change our routines. We all need to, like, go on a long walk together every day, and everyone else can just deal with it."

Wilhelmina had wandered with Bee into the ginkgo leaves, but she hardly knew where she was. "I put you behind a barrier?" she said, her voice cracking, because she was picturing Bee, young and small and sad, trapped behind a wall she'd built.

"Wil, sweetie," he said, in a very gentle voice. "I mean, it's a meta-phor. But yeah, you kind of put *everyone* behind the barrier. Everyone and everything. Hey," he said, when Wilhelmina sank to her knees. He came closer, then stopped himself with a frustrated noise. "Wil. Your heart broke. You needed to, like, build reinforcements. This metaphor is starting to get really annoying, but it was a normal thing to do. I mean, look at the world."

"You don't build barriers."

"I don't know *how* to build barriers," he said. "I'm always just out in the wind, crying, and giving my friends the job of taking care of me. I'm not sure that's any better."

"You don't put your friends behind barriers."

"Wil," he said, "you need to give yourself a break here. Your heart broke. I know. I saw it happen. And the world was already on fire when it happened, and everything's only gotten worse. You think I can't stand behind your barrier for however long while you get your shit together? After all the times you've been there for me? Fuck!" he suddenly said. "It's killing me that I can't give you a hug!"

"It's killing me too," said Wilhelmina, who was crying.

"It's going to be group hugs all the time when this is over," said Bee.

"Is Julie going to want to hug me when this is over?" said Wilhelmina.

"I mean, on the one hand, that's obviously a question for Julie," said Bee. "On the other hand . . ."

"Yeah?" said Wilhelmina.

"Wil," he said. "When are you going to start having more faith in your elephants?"

"What?" she said. "I have so much faith in you guys!"

He took a step closer, then stopped, clearly frustrated again. So he knelt in the ginkgo leaves, six feet away from her but at her level. He spoke earnestly.

"When my dad died," he said, "he left a lot of shit behind, you know? But he also took a lot of the bad shit with him. A few of my problems just went away, Wil, you know?"

"You suffered a lot," she said.

"Yeah, I suffered," he said. "But my dad wasn't my light. He wasn't my magic. When Frankie died, you didn't gain anything. It was all loss. And it hurt too much. I remember; I was there. You turned out the lights, Wil—you just turned it all off. You had to. But you need to come back sometime. I know the world isn't exactly"—he waved a hand—"hospitable right now. But you know you have Frankie's magic in you, right? You have it, whether she's here or not. I miss you, Wil. When are you going to come back?"

AT HOME, Wilhelmina smelled bread baking, then found Esther in the kitchen, grating ginger. Esther smiled at her brightly. "Hola, Wilhelmineleh."

"Hola," said Wilhelmina. "You seem cheerful. Did something happen?"

"Oh, just Biden and Harris's lead growing in Pennsylvania," she said. "Once they win Pennsylvania, that's the election. How are you feeling?"

"Fine," said Wilhelmina. "Are you making challah?"

"Your eyes do not deceive you. Now, tell me, noodles or matzoh balls in the soup?"

"Matzoh balls," said Wilhelmina. "Are you taking a vote?"

"No, you get to choose," said Esther. "I'm letting everyone under the age of nineteen choose one part of dinner."

"Phew," said Wilhelmina. "I made it in under the wire."

"You did," said Esther, who was studying Wilhelmina curiously, as if she didn't quite believe in her great-niece's airy banter. *Because she knows about my barrier,* thought Wilhelmina.

"Oh, honey," said Theo, hurrying into the kitchen from one of the bedrooms, looking harassed. "You're home. Hi. By any chance, are you free to supervise math with Delia? She has a test, so it should be quiet, and your mother has clients, and something's come up at work—"

"I can do it, Theo," said Esther.

"Esther! I know you and Aunt Margaret have been wanting to walk," said Theo. "It's seventy-five degrees out!"

"I don't mind."

"I can do it," said Wilhelmina.

"Oh, thank you, hon," said Theo. "I'll send her out. Your options are . . ." He paused. "Your own bedroom. Sorry, I thought for a second you had more options."

"It's okay," said Wilhelmina, moving toward her bedroom.

"Are you all right, Wilhelmina?" Esther called after her.

Wilhelmina was trying to reflect people's moods back at them. Competence and gravity for her father; cheerfulness for Esther. She was trying to be what people needed, but she knew it wasn't working, because of the big, hurtful barrier she was dragging around that probably everyone besides her could see and feel.

"I'm fine," she said.

"Are you still upset about that card you found?" said Theo, following her, stopping in her doorway. Clearly still a little perplexed about that. Delia pushed in behind Theo, wearing her backpack and carrying her school laptop. She stopped to glare at Wilhelmina, then trudged to the desk and began to set up.

"No," said Wilhelmina. "Don't worry about that, Dad."

"Well," said Theo. "Okay. I'll let you get to it. Good luck on your test, honey."

"Thanks," said Delia in tragic tones, then, when Theo closed the door, sighed dramatically.

"Are you anxious about your test?" said Wilhelmina. Delia was good at math—she was good at all her subjects—but Wilhelmina wasn't sure which test this was.

"Nah," she said, "I just hate moving around the apartment for school. It makes me feel so disorganized. Like, the only place I'm ever organized is inside my own head."

It surprised Wilhelmina that Delia was organized anywhere, but she kept this to herself. "That makes sense."

Delia shot her a skeptical glance. "Why are you being so friendly?"

"Because I don't think I've been very nice to you lately," said Wilhelmina.

"You mean like yesterday?" said Delia. "When you tried to kill me with your driving?"

Wilhelmina remembered shouting at Delia, and Delia's crumpled face. "Yes."

"Humph," said Delia. "What's up with you and Bee and Julie anyway? You're not fighting, are you?" The eyes she turned to Wilhelmina were big and unhappy, and her voice sounded very young. It pulled at Wilhelmina, brought her forward to the edge of her bed.

"Delia," she said. "Are you so worried about me and Bee and Julie?"

"Why wouldn't I be?" said Delia. "Geez! Be quiet! I have a test!"

Wilhelmina wondered if a barrier might make her selfish, if when she barricaded other people off, her own focus had nowhere else to go, so it turned toward itself, endlessly spiraling inward. How many things was she missing? She didn't want to be missing other people's feelings, their needs. That had never been part of her plan. But what could she do? She couldn't just snap her fingers and make it disappear. She remembered the summer the builders had renovated the aunts' carriage house. They'd had to take the old walls and the ceiling down carefully, piece by piece, so that the whole thing wouldn't collapse all at once and hurt someone.

"Would you like to learn how to build a shield, Wilhelmina dear?" Aunt Margaret had said to her one morning, the summer Bee's father had died. Wilhelmina and the aunts had been in the living room together, waiting for Theo, who was on his way to pick Wilhelmina up and bring her home.

"A shield?" said Wilhelmina. "What do you mean?"

"To protect yourself from energy that might destabilize you," said Aunt Margaret.

"I don't—feel like energy is destabilizing me, Aunt Margaret," said Wilhelmina.

"But it might be useful to you someday," said Aunt Margaret. "For instance, if any of Bee's family members have destructive energy and you're stuck interacting with them."

"*Bee* needs to learn how to build a shield," said Esther grimly.

"You could learn so that you could teach Bee," said Aunt Margaret.

"All right," said Wilhelmina, capitulating, because it wasn't like she had anything better to do while they waited for Theo.

Aunt Margaret had taught her to locate the steadiest part of her own body, then reach down into the earth from that steady place. To thank the earth for the strength she gave. Then to draw the earth's sweet, powerful, protective energy up into her body and use it to begin to build a shield around herself.

"Let the image come to you of whatever your shield is made of, Wilhelmina," said Aunt Margaret, sitting on the couch with her eyes closed and a serene expression on her face. "Mine is a kind of flexible, knitted cord."

"Mine is candles," said Esther. "All aflame."

"Mine is vines and flowers," said Frankie. "I wear a helm of lilies."

Wilhelmina's shield material hadn't been anything, because she'd thought this was rather silly. But she'd kept her opinions to herself and pretended to build herself a shield. "When your shield covers you completely," said Aunt Margaret, "the world's harmful energy won't be able to get through."

"But what about the world's good energy?" Wilhelmina had asked.

"You must think about that as you're building," said Aunt Margaret. "You must think about how to make some parts of your shield permeable, so that the things you want to get through—*only* the things you want—will be able to enter. To be sure, that can include pain. We're not trying to block out anything important or true. But false things often bear blocking. It's like a selective kind of armor. It's not meant to close you off from the realities of the world; it's only meant to keep you steady when harmful things clamor around you."

How convenient, Wilhelmina had thought dryly, *that armor should have the ability to be so selective. Now teach me how to build a sword that will stab only assholes.*

On her bed, Wilhelmina was crying again, trying to do so quietly. She was thinking of Frankie in one of her gardens, surrounded by flowers and vines. Frankie's shield. She was remembering Esther, speaking at Frankie's memorial service. "The day after the 2016 election," Esther had said, "Frankie got into the car and went to the nursery. Then she came home and planted spring flowering bulbs. Poet narcissus and fringed tulips. That was how Frankie always confronted darkness: with light."

"Wilhelmina?" said Delia. "Wilhelmina?"

Wilhelmina came to herself with a start. Delia was patting her arm, her face scrunched up with worry. "Wilhelmina!" she said. "What's wrong?"

"Oh," said Wilhelmina, dabbing at her cheeks with a sleeve. "I'm sorry. I was just—I was thinking about Frankie. I miss her."

"I do too," said Delia.

It was another thing Wilhelmina should've known, but didn't. "I've been really self-absorbed," she said.

"Teenagers are supposed to be self-absorbed," said Delia. "Your frontal lobe isn't fully formed yet."

Wilhelmina snorted through her tears. "Who told you that?"

"I read it online."

She noticed Delia's earbuds, lying on the desk beside her laptop. "Aren't you in the middle of a test? Won't you get in trouble for going offscreen?"

"You were crying!"

"You're really generous, Delia," said Wilhelmina. "I'm sorry. Let me know if you need me to talk to your teacher. Are you, like, too big for a hug?"

Delia threw herself into Wilhelmina's arms. *I am hugging the heart of a lion,* Wilhelmina thought nonsensically, squeezing Delia with her heavy, aching arms. When Delia went back to her test, Wilhelmina found the foam roller and lay on it, closing her eyes, stretching her shoulders. Trying to breathe her tears away.

On the floor of her room, she experimented with letting the world soak into her consciousness. Outside, a bird sang a soft, chirpy tune. One of the crows cut through the sound with a screech, and a group of faraway crows answered. Now and then, Delia tapped on her keyboard or scratched her pencil on paper. Theo was in his bedroom on the phone, Cleo in the aunts' room on a video call. Wilhelmina could sense these things somehow, from the nature of the sound or the weight of the air, just as she knew that Philip was napping in his tiny bed beside Theo and the aunts had left the apartment entirely. And Julie—Julie was upstairs, in her bedroom, with her apartment to herself, one floor above and two rooms over.

With the awareness of Julie, heartache consumed Wilhelmina. She didn't want to start crying again.

But she thought about her barrier, which she needed. She wasn't ready to knock the barrier down. But—what about a very small door? Owl-sized. Sparrow-sized. Tarot card-sized.

Wilhelmina pushed herself up. She crossed to her dresser and pulled the shirt off the mirror. The angel in the Temperance card poured water from cup to cup, his wings unfurled behind him, like James in the cemetery that morning. *Temperance,* the card said. The balance between what was real and what you wished for. "Remembering the mundane makes us smart," Frankie had told her once. "Remembering the magic makes us brave."

Wilhelmina had never really understood what that meant. She didn't understand it now. This mundane reality made her frightened and sick, and magic wasn't real.

But she returned to the bed and grabbed her phone. *I'm starting to see the ways I've cut myself off,* she wrote to Julie. *You called it my disappearing act*

A minute later, Julie wrote back. *I've missed you, Wil*

Wilhelmina thought about that. *I think I've been pretty lonely,* she said.

That makes me really sad for you, wrote Julie.

Wilhelmina thought about that too. *Will you wait for me,* she said, *while I try to come back?*

When Wilhelmina was sixteen, her family took a trip to Pennsylvania together on a weekend in May.

It was an unusual thing for them to do, especially a few weeks before school was ending. Usually the family drove to Pennsylvania in June, to bring Wilhelmina.

"Can I go?" Delia had started asking that year, as spring began to turn toward summer. Delia was eight. "I want to go to the aunts for the summer too! Wilhelmina, how old were you when you started to go?"

"Oh, sweetie," Cleo would say. "You're right, when Wilhelmina was your age, she was spending her summers with the aunts. But they're older now, and Frankie is very sick."

One day, while Wilhelmina was putting her boots on in the living room, she heard Cleo and Delia in the kitchen, having this familiar conversation.

"If Frankie is sick, I can help!" said Delia.

"It's true you're very helpful," said Cleo. "But Frankie is so sick right now that I'm afraid even Wilhelmina is unlikely to have her summer."

"What?" said Wilhelmina sharply. She was on her way out to a driving lesson with Julie and Julie's mom. She could hear their voices outside, and the car doors closing.

"Oh, hon," Cleo said, coming to stand in the short hallway that connected the living room with the rest of the apartment. "I thought you'd left. We'll talk about this later, okay?"

"Whatever," said Wilhelmina, stepping into the vestibule and shutting the door hard behind her. Cleo had had that compassionate, understanding expression on her face again, even though she had absolutely no understanding of what it was like to be Wilhelmina right now, constantly overhearing Cleo and Theo speak about how extremely sick Frankie was, in a manner designed for overhearing. Seriously, how many times did they need to loudly agree that she was very, very sick? They were doing it deliberately, because Wilhelmina kept rebuffing their attempts to talk to her about it. This conversation Cleo wanted to have later was for the purpose of imprinting information upon Wilhelmina's soul that she didn't want. Anyway, she knew. She knew, okay? She knew, and she was keeping the knowledge spread out thin, like a lotion that only barely sank in.

When Theo knocked gently on her bedroom door later that day and stuck his head in, she said, "Dad, I know, okay? I'm begging you, don't make me sit here listening to you telling me something awful that I already know."

Theo had tucked his chin to his chest, then studied her for a moment. "Okay, hon," he said. "Would you like to talk to a therapist?"

Wilhelmina had zero interest in talking to a stranger who would stare at her with her mother's compassionate expression, acting like she understood what Wilhelmina was going through. So she said, "Maybe that's a good idea. Let me think about it," because that was the answer most likely to cause Theo to leave her alone about it for the longest stretch of time.

Then came the unexpected weekend trip to Pennsylvania. In the car, sitting in the back seat, pressed against Delia, Wilhelmina considered how much her pain had increased lately. She pretended to sleep, trying to find a position for her head that stretched her neck and stopped the sharp shooting heat in her palms. Delia, who was fidgety and bored in the middle seat, kept exhorting Philip to improve his pronunciation of all the words he knew. Philip was nearing two, and his pronunciations were adorable. He called Wilhelmina "Weenwuh." He wasn't a car puker, and she wished she wasn't blocked from his car seat by Delia.

"Now, when we get there," Theo said, "we'll have to reduce our volume. Frankie will be resting, and we must take care not to disturb her. Do you understand that, Delia?"

"Of course I do!" said Delia. "That's why I'm teaching Philip now!"

By the time they reached the aunts' house, Wilhelmina's pain was worse, pounding into her head and down her arms.

"You go lie down, bubeleh," Esther told her. "We have plenty of helping hands. We'll bring you a cold compress."

"I don't want anyone to have to climb all the steps to my room," said Wilhelmina.

"I'll bring it!" said Delia.

"Delia, you are a treasure," said Aunt Margaret. "You go and rest, Wilhelmina."

Wilhelmina took the stairs to the second floor and walked down the corridor. The house was quiet here, and cool; all the noise and activity were below, Esther and Aunt Margaret and her parents chatting, unpacking the casseroles Theo had made, deciding which should go in the fridge and which in the freezer. Philip was bursting explosively back and forth from kitchen to living room, Delia chasing after him making shushing noises. Everyone was downstairs except for Frankie. Frankie was in her bedroom. Through her own thumping pain, Wilhelmina could feel her, burning bright behind her half-closed door.

"Wilhelmina?" came Frankie's voice.

"Frankie?"

"Come in, dear," said Frankie.

In Frankie's room, Wilhelmina found a bird version of Frankie lying in bed. Tiny, with dark, luminous eyes and a bony, beaky nose, and wispy white hair like feathers. Her body hardly made an impression under the blankets. But she smiled at Wilhelmina, and her smile was the same.

"I'm so happy to see you, dear," she said. "Are you in pain?"

"Yes," said Wilhelmina. "My exercises haven't been working so much lately. Esther told me to go lie down. Are you in pain?"

"Yes," said Frankie simply. "But it's not too bad right now. Go upstairs if that's more comfortable, but you're also welcome to lie down here. I don't take up much of the bed."

Wilhelmina climbed onto the bed and lay down next to Frankie, on top of the covers. It was amazing to stretch out flat and let all the muscles of her neck and scalp release. "Ahhh," she said.

"Tell me, love," said Frankie. "How are you coping with all your pressures?"

As it had in the cemetery the summer before, this question brought tears springing to Wilhelmina's eyes. "My pressures aren't much compared to what you're dealing with, Frankie."

"Nonsense," said Frankie. "What I'm dealing with has become fairly straightforward. I mean," she said, nodding, "I acknowledge it's one of the hard ones to accept. It's hard to accept that we don't win every fight. But it is reality. My reality has become fairly uncomplicated. *Your* reality, sweetheart, is much more complex. You're coming of age in a time of great political difficulty. You're learning to drive. You're figuring out what to do about your attractions. People are probably prodding you about college. And I know this is very hard for you," she said, with a glance down at the tiny lump under the covers that was her own body. "I want to hear all about you, Wilhelmina."

"Probably someone is going to come up soon and tell me to let you rest," said Wilhelmina.

"They most certainly will not," said Frankie, "or if they do, I'll banish them. I can decide for myself when I need rest. You stay right there until you want to leave or I kick you out."

During that visit, Wilhelmina stayed with Frankie as much as she was permitted. Avoiding all thoughts about it; just being with her when she could. If she could be in the room with Frankie, then she was fine. Often they weren't even talking. Frankie would doze, or maybe they'd listen to a podcast. Sometimes they listened to LeVar Burton telling a story, and Delia would join them on the bed, listening too. Wilhelmina would text with Julie and Bee. *Hey elephants.*

Hey elephants, they would respond, one after the other. On Saturday, they reported that they each won their soccer games. On Sunday, they reported getting doughnuts at Alfie Fang's together. It was weird to be with Frankie on a May weekend. *This is weird,* she kept texting to Julie and Bee. *But fine.*

Frankie slept a lot, or maybe she wasn't sleeping. She came awake with a start once, saw Wilhelmina beside her, and said, "Oh, Wilhelmina, it's you. Was my father just here?"

"No," said Wilhelmina, confused enough by the question that she added, "At least, I didn't see him."

"I talked to my father before he died," said Frankie, who still seemed half-asleep. "I think he understood, in the end, that I did what I had to do. I never talked to my mother. She hurt me too much. But I loved her. I hope she knew." Then Frankie stirred. She looked over at Wilhelmina with eyes that burned. "It is a skill to love people well, Wilhelmina. No one's born knowing. We learn, over and over."

Wilhelmina thought of the Wheel of Fortune. Of Frankie as the Fool, moving through the world, gaining wisdom and experience. Claiming her tools the way the Magician did. Meeting helpers, such as the Empress. Confronting the Devil. Her heart breaking, like the Tower. Then moving through the confusion cast by the Moon, until she reached the clarity of the Sun. Finally, containing the entire World, then starting over again. Starting over again. The wheel wasn't supposed to stop.

When it was time to go, Wilhelmina's pain returned. It happened all at once, dramatically, as if the pain gods had thrown a switch. As her family drove out of Pennsylvania, she felt like she was being dragged away from some inner part of her body, a long red tether of muscle or viscera pulling tighter and tighter until it snapped and she cried out, "Pull over!" and emptied her stomach on the grass at the side of a New York interstate.

At home, over the course of the following days, her pain became unmanageable. Her appetite also plummeted. Her appetite, Wilhelmina began to realize, had been poor for some time. Her clothes weren't fitting right, which she hated. When a girl at school praised her for it, Wilhelmina didn't know whether to cry or scream.

In the middle of finals week, her worried mother brought her to her doctor—or rather, to the doctor who'd been assigned to Wilhelmina ever since her lifelong doctor had retired.

"Do you want me to come in with you, honey?" Cleo asked.

"No," said Wilhelmina, glad to be certain about something.

The new doctor looked Wilhelmina up and down. She barely asked her any questions or glanced at her chart, then told her that her pain was probably getting worse because she needed to lose weight. "Doing so will release some of the pressure in your thoracic outlet," the doctor said.

Wilhelmina recognized what was happening. Theo had warned her about doctors like this. "You come to us if anyone dismisses you like that," he'd told her. But now a doctor was dismissing her, and Wilhelmina was so shaken that she wasn't sure what to do.

She went out to her skinny mother, who was in the waiting room, bent over some papers in her hands and mouthing words to herself. Cleo was writing a speech about the unique work of the conspiracy theory therapist, whose job was not, as most people thought, to walk conspiracy theorists back from their false convictions, usually an impossible task. It was possible, though, to help with the shattered relationships. Cleo helped people to coexist, people who loved each other but had developed opposite and unbridgeable beliefs. Often she worked with the loved ones of the conspiracy theorist, to help them accept their new reality and grieve the person they'd lost.

"Mom?" said Wilhelmina, confused by her own nervousness.

"Honey!" said Cleo, looking up, startled, then narrowing her eyes. "Is everything okay?"

"She told me the problem is that I need to lose weight."

Cleo's mouth went hard and thin, and instantly Wilhelmina felt steadier.

"Did she, now?" said Cleo, her voice going deep. "Despite the fact that your increase in pain has coincided with a loss of weight?"

"Yeah," said Wilhelmina. "But she would've had to learn things about me in order to realize that. She knew what was wrong just by looking at me. She didn't even need to examine me. She's like a miracle doctor!"

Cleo shoved her papers into her bag and stood, hefting the bag onto her shoulder. "All right," she said. "I will be calling this office with my thoughts, and we will be finding you a doctor whose head isn't up her ass."

Wilhelmina's new doctor, Dr. Taft, talked with her for a long time.

"Tell me about your appetite loss, Wilhelmina," she said. "Do you remember when it started?"

"April, maybe?" said Wilhelmina. "May?"

"Are you under a lot of pressure at home or at school?"

"No," said Wilhelmina, then hesitated. Dr. Taft was kind, but also efficient, matter-of-fact. She reminded Wilhelmina a little of her mother. "Not at home or at school."

"Somewhere else?" said Dr. Taft. "Maybe among your friends?"

"No," said Wilhelmina. Then she touched the area around her collarbone with the flat of her hand. "Here," she said, then her voice cracked. "My—my aunt is really sick," she said. "I feel so much pressure here."

"I see," said Dr. Taft. "May I?"

Dr. Taft spent a while pressing different parts of Wilhelmina's neck, collarbone area, and shoulders with firm but gentle hands, while asking her more questions. "Well, no wonder you're in pain," she said. "These muscles are a wall of rock. Tell me, do you clench your teeth?"

"I—don't know," said Wilhelmina.

"Do you ever wake with an aching jaw," she said, "or notice that your teeth hurt when you're eating? Especially in the morning?"

"Yes!"

Dr. Taft nodded, then touched her fingers gently to the sides of Wilhelmina's face. "I think the muscle tension in your jaw and your entire thoracic area may be exacerbating your syndrome," she said. "And I suspect anxiety and stress are contributing to your muscle tension. Possibly also to your appetite loss. Anxiety, stress, and maybe grief. Does that ring true to you, Wilhelmina?"

Wilhelmina's parents were always talking about anxiety and stress: hers, their own, Cleo's clients', Theo's boss's. But this was the first time anyone had suggested to Wilhelmina that she might be experiencing *grief.* The word found a crack and stole into her, squeezing her throat so that she couldn't speak. But she could nod. So she did.

Dr. Taft advised her to make an appointment with her dentist, who could fit her for a nightguard for teeth clenching. She also prescribed her some new physical therapy, during which the therapist was supposed to teach her stretches and exercises, but also give her neck and shoulder massages. Wilhelmina had never been so motivated to go to physical therapy.

Dr. Taft also wanted her to see a therapist.

"All right," Wilhelmina finally said, after repeated nudges from Cleo. "But no one you know personally."

Cleo found Wilhelmina a therapist named Eileen whom Cleo didn't know personally. But even though Cleo didn't know Eileen, Wilhelmina rode the bus to the first appointment feeling like *she*, Wilhelmina, knew her, she knew what Eileen's goals were, she knew how she was supposed to answer every stupid leading question. She also knew that Bee was helped enormously by his own therapist, but still, some part of her couldn't believe that anyone was ever really okay with this. That anxious, grieving people would come to Eileen, or go to her mother, and tell them, total strangers, things they wouldn't even admit to themselves. Wilhelmina knew what she was supposed to say. She knew it, okay? How would it help to say it to this human? And who was Eileen anyway, to deserve such precious words? She went three times, to prove that she'd tried. Then she stopped going.

On a morning late in June, the call came. When Theo and Cleo appeared at Wilhelmina's door together very early, she knew.

"Honey," said Theo. "Frankie died in her sleep last night."

Wilhelmina pulled her covers up and turned away from them. "Okay," she said.

"Aunt Margaret said she went peacefully," said Theo.

"Okay."

"Honey," said Cleo, "would you like me to tell the Dunstables why you can't come today?"

A protest was planned in Boston that day, and in cities all across the nation, in response to the president's immigration policy that was separating children from their parents at the Mexican border. Wilhelmina had seen photos of children in cages. "I want to be the one to tell them, and I want to go," she said.

"I'm not sure that's a good idea, Wilhelmina," said Cleo, after a short pause. "Frankie's death is a lot to process."

"Frankie would want me to go," said Wilhelmina. "I want to do it for Frankie." It was a lie. If Frankie had known what was happening inside Wilhelmina at that moment, she would never have sent her into a crowd of emotional people on a hot summer day. Nor was Wilhelmina doing it for Frankie. She was doing it for herself. But it was the statement most likely to shut down her parents' objections. They went away and talked about it. Then they let her go.

On the bus to the train, Julie and Bee kept shooting concerned glances at each other, and asking Wilhelmina what was wrong. She wanted to tell them. She couldn't. She kept opening her mouth to say it but her throat would close up. At least she was with them; she wanted so badly to be here with her friends. It was the only bearable thing; it halted her disintegration. While Bee and Julie were in earshot, talking and joking in their dear, familiar voices with their dear, familiar energy, Wilhelmina could pull herself together and build herself up, barricade herself in with rock that was impenetrable, and be normal. Go to the protest and feel powerful, like they could win this fight with their passion and resolve. Stop feeling like nothing good was possible. "I'm fine," she croaked. "Just tired."

But when they got to City Hall and the march began, there were too many people. Too many signs with too many words; too much noise. People were shouting, "No kids in cages!" People were shouting, "Love, not hate!" It was too hot. Wilhelmina was crowded and jostled on every side, and her barricade wasn't working. Her heart began to flap in her chest, too fast to be alive. She couldn't catch her breath. She was dying like Frankie; Wilhelmina was dying. She dropped to her knees in the middle of the flow of protesters, and Julie and Bee cried her name, dropped down with her and took hold of her while people around them started calling for EMTs. A woman, a fellow protester, appeared who knelt with her and took her pulse, told her how to breathe. "I'm an ER doctor," the woman said. "You're having a panic attack. I know it feels terrible, but you're going to be okay." The crowd was still moving around them, parting respectfully like a stream around a boulder. As the terrible dying feeling receded, Wilhelmina began to cry. She tried to speak and began to sob; the words forced themselves out.

"Frankie died," she said. "Frankie died."

"What?" Julie cried. Julie's face was wet with tears. Julie was hugging her.

"Oh, Wil!" said Bee, in a voice younger than his deep, fifteen-year-old voice. Bee was crying too, and hugging her too. "You idiot! Why didn't you tell us? Why are we even *here*?"

"I thought it would make me feel better," said Wilhelmina. "I wanted to be with you guys."

"We could've hung out at home," said Bee. "Let's go home."

"But you wanted to hear Elizabeth Warren!"

"She would understand!" said Bee. "Fuck the speeches! Come on. Let's go."

As Julie and Bee helped her up, the crowd was still moving around them, slowly parting. "Will you both come with me?" Wilhelmina said. "When I have to . . ." She couldn't say the word "funeral." ". . . go there?"

"Of course we will," said Julie. "Right, Bee?"

"Of course," said Bee.

"Don't leave me, okay?" said Wilhelmina.

"Elephant," said Bee. "What are you afraid of? Do you think we're going to abandon you in this mob of liberals?"

It felt strange to smile, but she did, because she knew it would help Julie and Bee look a little less worried about her. She didn't want to tell them that even with one of them on each side of her, their hands clamped to her arms, their bodies close, and Bee's giant height cutting a path to the edge of the crowd for them, she felt like she wasn't really there. She was nowhere, in a cold, dark place, and it was too late. She was already alone.

Wilhelmina was having her recurring dream, the one where she was waiting for Frankie.

This time, she sat on the low wall outside the library. Her head was too heavy; her neck hurt. The giant maple stood tall and strong behind her, wearing its knitted tube dress, branches full of birds, and Wilhelmina was waiting for Frankie.

Wait, she told her sleeping brain, knowing how this always went. *Let me stay asleep. Let Frankie arrive, please, please, before you wake me up, please let Frankie arrive. No! Stop!* She was waking up, as usual. Frankie was close, but it was too late.

"Wilhelmina, dear?" said Frankie.

Wilhelmina's eyes shot to the voice, to the blurry creature standing before her. Was it Frankie? Or was it a giant bird? The creature came into focus. Oh! It was Frankie! Frankie with a body that had heft and health, and long white hair in a crown of braids, and a radiance that came from her smile, and she had wings. They were soft and gray and voluminous. She wore a gown that seemed to be made of flowers and vines. She had lilies wound into her hair.

"Frankie," said Wilhelmina, dazzled. "You came!"

"Of course I came," said Frankie.

"What do you mean, 'of course'?" said Wilhelmina. "I've been waiting for you in my dreams for years!"

"I've been here every time," said Frankie. "This is the first time you've let me in."

"What?" said Wilhelmina. "But I could never find you!"

"You weren't ready," said Frankie. "You know why."

"No!" said Wilhelmina. "I don't know why!"

With a small humphing noise, Frankie came to sit beside Wilhelmina, tucking her enormous wings awkwardly behind her. "Bit unwieldy," she said, struggling with the one on the left.

"Don't they fold in?" said Wilhelmina. "Albatross wings have hinges."

"That would be a nice feature," said Frankie. "Could you arrange it, dear? It's your dream."

"What?" said Wilhelmina in alarm. "But what do you mean? Aren't you real?"

"I'm real in the same way that magic is real," said Frankie.

"Huh?"

"People think it's easy," said Frankie. "Wave a wand and your problems are solved, the pain goes away, voilà. That's not what magic is. You have to pay attention. You have to do the hard, mucky work. But it is *real*, Wilhelmina." A ruminative expression crossed her face. "Maybe that's why you can't touch the magic unless you let reality in."

"Wow, Frankie," said Wilhelmina. "That really clears things up." Then she began to laugh. As her laughter grew deeper, her head suddenly began to feel less weighty, her neck freed from its burden.

"Look, Wilhelmina," said Frankie, who was leaning back, gazing in wonderment at the top of Wilhelmina's head. "Your helm is made of stars!"

"What?" cried Wilhelmina, reaching up to touch her head. It felt strange on her fingers up there, like sunshine. A great splitting sound resonated from somewhere deep inside her. Looking down, she saw cracks forming all across her body, and light shining through.

"Frankie!" she cried, grabbing for Frankie's hand. "Frankie! I'm scared!"

"Oh, Wilhelmina," said Frankie, holding her hand tight. "I know you are, but really, there's no need to be scared. It's wonderful! You're finally starting to crack open."

"What?" cried Wilhelmina. "That sounds dangerous!"

"Yes, there are risks, of course, dear," said Frankie. "But aren't you a little bit curious about all that light?"

ON THE DAY WILHELMINA STEPPED INTO HER OWN, she woke to the feeling that it was summer. She was a child in her bedroom in the Pennsylvania house and sunlight was streaming through her window. The aunts, all three of them, were downstairs. She could smell French toast. That meant it was probably Saturday, because sometimes on the Saturday after Esther made challah, Aunt Margaret made challah French toast. She was warm, too warm. She kicked her blankets away and Delia's voice said, "You are such a weird sleeper. If you ever get married, you're going to break your spouse's leg."

Wilhelmina sat up in her Massachusetts bedroom and groaned.

"It's so stupid that the election was on Tuesday and we still don't know who won," said Delia.

Wilhelmina groped for her glasses. Delia came into view across the room, sitting in bed with her legs crossed, Theo's laptop in her lap. Wilhelmina pulled out her nightguard.

"Hacking the Minuteman library system?" she said.

"Here are the states where that centipede is suing because he can't accept he lost," said Delia. "Okay? Are you ready?"

"That's offensive to centipedes," said Wilhelmina, "but go ahead."

"Pennsylvania. Michigan. Georgia, Arizona, Nevada, and Wisconsin," said Delia, reading the laptop screen. "He has no evidence. He just doesn't like being a loser. And all these protests are happening, with all these people who are, like, waving guns. And they believe him! And all these other people who should be like, *Hello, he's making it all up*, aren't saying anything at all! I don't get it, Wilhelmina! What is *wrong* with everyone?"

She lifted Theo's laptop and plopped it back down in her lap for emphasis. She seemed quite upset.

"I know," said Wilhelmina. "It's mind-boggling."

"But what's *wrong* with them?" Delia cried again.

"I don't know, Delia."

"I've decided I'm *Cor*delia."

"What?"

"*Cor*delia. I mean, it's my name. So I want people to call me it."

"Oh," said Wilhelmina. "Okay." She tried it out. "Cordelia."

"It's okay if you forget," said Cordelia, "but it's not okay if you say it wrong on purpose."

"Thank you for those clear parameters."

"You should take a chill pill about your own name, and those dashes," said Cordelia. "I mean, who wouldn't want 'helm' in their name? It's, like, badass."

"I don't feel very badass this morning."

"Maybe that's because you haven't embraced your name," said Cordelia. "Take a chill pill, Wil." She squealed in delight at her own humor. "Take a chill pill, Wil!"

"I'm disowning you," said Wilhelmina.

"Hey, it's Doughnut Saturday. When are you going?"

"Don't I smell French toast?"

"Yes? So? Is French toast doughnuts?"

"No, but they are both delicious breakfast items."

"Whatever," said Cordelia. "It's still Doughnut Saturday. Can't you text James and ask him to bring us some?"

"No," said Wilhelmina, "because he's not our personal delivery service."

"Then you have to go," said Cordelia. "Also, Aunt Margaret has an eye appointment."

Closing her eyes, Wilhelmina sighed. She'd forgotten about Aunt Margaret's Saturday eye appointments. This one was her one-week checkup. "Anything else you require of me?"

"I just want to know when you're getting the doughnuts so I know how much French toast to eat."

"That is an important calculation," said Wilhelmina, checking her phone. A text from James said, *Hows 11:30 for Mrs M?* "I have a lot to do this morning. Doughnuts'll be on the late side. Eat as much French toast as you want."

Pushing Theo's laptop away, Cordelia jumped out of bed and pattered across to the door with bare feet. "Yay!"

Left alone with her own fluttering heart, Wilhelmina reread last night's text thread with Julie.

I'm here, Wil, Julie had written.

Then she'd added, *Maybe we should hang out in the yard every day. Didn't you used to have some old rusty lawn chairs?*

Finally, she'd said, *I'm sorry, Wil. I mean, for pretending I hadn't guessed what a hard time you were having. That was shitty of me*

Everything is forgiven, Wilhelmina had said. *I'm sorry too*

Morning, Wilhelmina wrote now. While she was hitting send, Bee texted.

Morning elephant

Morning, elephant, she wrote back to Bee. It felt different somehow, not their same old exchange, even though the words hadn't changed. Wilhelmina wasn't taking a single syllable for granted.

AUNT MARGARET'S EYE APPOINTMENT was at ten. As Wilhelmina emerged from the shower with a towel on her head, she considered the day that lay before her. The appointment, then she and James would bring the keys to Mrs. Mardrosian. And what? Confront her?

"When are they going to call Pennsylvania?" she heard her father moaning somewhere nearby. "When are they going to call Pennsylvania?"

In her room, Wilhelmina went to her closet. There she chose a sundress composed of bright panels of leaf green, fuchsia, and scarlet roses, because it complemented her red glasses and set off her pale skin and dark hair, and also because it fit her perfectly. It gave her a hint of cleavage that pleased her whenever she caught a glimpse of herself in the mirror, and it had a pocket for her phone. She slipped Frankie's owl onto her ear, mussed her hair up artfully, and did her eye makeup. The she put on lipstick, a deep, glimmery red, trying not to think too much about why she was bothering. Lastly, she put on her elephant necklace. *Later,* she thought to herself, *I'll find a new one for Julie. Right? That's the right thing to do?*

She found Aunt Margaret sitting quietly in the armchair in the living room, touching her fingers to Frankie's birds on the windowsill. Someone had dismantled Wilhelmina's fort, and placed Frankie's blanket in a neat, folded pile on the sofa.

"Wilhelmina, dear," Aunt Margaret said, tapping Saint Francis's head, "I believe that we should entrust these treasures to you when we go. I can tell they're drawn to you."

"Are you going?" said Wilhelmina.

"Oh, no, not now," said Aunt Margaret. "But of course, we won't be here forever."

Wilhelmina had a moment to be surprised by her own ambivalence at this statement before Aunt Margaret turned and said, "Oh, Wilhelmina! How stunning you are. You look like . . . someone. I can't quite place it."

In that moment, Wilhelmina remembered the dream she'd had

last night. Frankie had arrived in time. With wings! Frankie had held her hand, while she'd cracked open. Wilhelmina felt the warm light all around her, seeping out of her own body.

"Do I?" she said to Aunt Margaret. "Is it you? Don't you think we look alike?"

Her aunt smiled sweetly. "I will accept that compliment, but no, that's not it. May I borrow your glasses?"

Slightly bewildered, Wilhelmina relinquished her glasses, then stood there taking in the fuzzy scene of Aunt Margaret slipping them on over her one good eye and her eye patch, then swinging her head back and forth like the snow goose, studying the room. In fact, Aunt Margaret reached out and nudged the head of the snow goose so it swung back and forth too.

"Lovely," she said, handing the glasses back. "Shall we go?"

Outside, the weather was almost too beautiful to be believed. "High of eighty today," said Aunt Margaret.

"Aunt Margaret," said Wilhelmina as they got into the car. "Why do you keep putting on my glasses?"

"Oh!" said Aunt Margaret. "I thought you understood, dear. I like to see the world the way you see it."

"Ah—" said Wilhelmina. "But—" She was flummoxed. "I don't think you see what I see when you put on my glasses, Aunt Margaret. I mean, I see clearly through them. Because of my prescription. Don't you"—this seemed inconceivable—"don't you understand how glasses work?"

"Well, of course I do, in the mundane sense," said Aunt Margaret. "But I meant via my affinity for objects. If I wear your glasses, I can get a sense of—well, you know. What you *see*."

"What I see," Wilhelmina repeated, pulling the car onto the road. She didn't want to ask, but the compulsion was too great. "And what do I see?"

Aunt Margaret opened her mouth, then closed it again. "It's very hard to express in words," she said. "But the apartment is very small, isn't it? Too small for so much family and an invasion of aunts. And Frankie's blanket shines like chain mail, and the snow goose—well. You keep a lot of memories in the snow goose, don't you?"

Wilhelmina was stunned and confused; then she was angry. "That's private!"

"Oh my!" said Aunt Margaret. "Wilhelmina, I humbly beg your pardon! I thought you understood!"

It was unfathomable to Wilhelmina that Aunt Margaret could think that anyone who lent her their glasses would understand—like, as if it was a normal, knowable thing—that she would be able to see their private thoughts. That wasn't normal. It wasn't normal! Who would think that? As they drove past the man with his STOP THE STEAL sign, Wilhelmina gritted her teeth and made a strangled sound.

"Yes," said Aunt Margaret. "It's very hard to take, isn't it? This win we're all waiting for today—I fear it'll be a brief reprieve only. That man isn't going to concede. He's going to break everything he can on his way out, Wilhelmina. I'm scared to see what the damage will be."

"Yeah," said Wilhelmina tiredly. "I am too."

"I'm really sorry about your glasses, Wilhelmina. I won't ask again."

"It's okay," said Wilhelmina. "I understand that you—thought I knew."

"How are you coping with all of your pressures, dear?"

Yesterday, that question would've made her cry. Now she just felt a small, inevitable sadness. "Frankie used to ask me that."

"I'm not surprised."

"I haven't been coping very well lately, if I'm being honest."

"I hope you won't mind me saying, Wilhelmina," said Aunt Margaret, "that I've wondered if you'd recently reached a breaking point. Not the bad kind, mind you. The good kind—or maybe that's an unfeeling way to put it. The *necessary* kind."

Wilhelmina was quiet for a while, driving. Thinking about breaking points. About cracking open, and what happened then. The people on the sidewalks wearing shorts and sandals disoriented her. She'd done this same drive last week in a snowstorm.

In Harvard Square, she pulled into an empty spot down the street from the building that housed Aunt Margaret's eye doctor. "The necessary kind of breaking point?" she finally said.

"Exactly," said Aunt Margaret. "I've wondered if you've been letting some of the hardest truths in. I mean about the world, of course, but also—well," she said. "I've wondered if you've begun to accept that Frankie is dead."

Wilhelmina turned to stare at her aunt. Aunt Margaret looked back at her serenely, short and round, her hair long and white, one eye behind an eye patch.

"I dreamed about her last night," Wilhelmina said.

"Oh, what a gift!" said Aunt Margaret. "Did she have any messages for you?"

Wilhelmina took a breath, then sighed quietly. "She told me that you can't touch the magic unless you let reality in."

"Very true," said Aunt Margaret. "It's *hard* to let the reality in that according to the count so far, over seventy million people have voted for that horrible man. But unless you do let it in, you can't appreciate what it means that over seventy-*four* million people have voted against him. Those people are our neighbors in this world too, Wilhelmina."

"But aren't both of those things reality?" said Wilhelmina.

"Yes, of course, dear. But magic *is* real, after all, you know. Tell me, how did Frankie seem?"

Wilhelmina was becoming annoyed with this conversation. "She was having some trouble with her wings."

Aunt Margaret nodded. "Yes, I can see that wings might be troublesome in ways we wouldn't appreciate, being wingless. I'm sorry to leave abruptly; I've just noticed I'm going to be late. Oh! But Wilhelmina, I've been meaning to mention. You know that our house is your house, don't you? You can go there anytime. With whomever you like." While Wilhelmina was trying to figure out what Aunt Margaret meant by that, exactly, Aunt Margaret added, "Oh! Wilhelmina! I've just realized who you remind me of in that dress. It's the Empress! You know, in the tarot? She's all greens and pinks and roses."

"What?" said Wilhelmina. "No! She's pomegranates, Aunt Margaret!"

Aunt Margaret reached for the door handle with one hand and made a dismissive gesture with the other. "You're her," she said. "I can practically see your crown of stars. Or maybe in your case, it's a helm of stars?" Then she smiled once, incandescently—a true Frankie smile—pushed out of the car, and tottered away.

Wilhelmina watched her go. Aunt Margaret pulled a mask over her face and raised her phone to her ear as she walked, calling the office for permission to enter. Then she turned, gave Wilhelmina a little wave, and disappeared inside.

Something new was falling apart inside Wilhelmina. She could feel it, and as she probed it, she wondered if it might be her understanding of the aunts.

It didn't make her cry. The tears of the last few days had washed Wilhelmina clean, and now she didn't need to cry so much anymore. But it did make her wonder. What was happening today? She had a lifetime of experience dismissing the odd things Aunt Margaret said. Why, today, was it burrowing inside her, that her aunt had put on her glasses, then known something true about her? That she'd called her the Empress, then known about her helm of stars?

"I do wish people would stop talking about my helm," she said out loud, reaching a hand up to the space around her head, feeling for the sunlight she'd felt in the dream. But of course it was warm up there. It was eighty degrees outside.

Wilhelmina sat quietly for a while, thinking. She wondered if, during this year between high school and college that she was unexpectedly spending with her aunts—this year that she'd always intended to spend with them, learning from them, and here they were, and it wasn't like they would be around forever—she was wasting precious time.

HEY, texted James, while she was still waiting in the car for Aunt Margaret. *U somewhere w a device?*

Yes, she wrote, immediately on high alert, because of the election, the monster. Any number of things that could be going wrong. *What's up?*

Albatross, he wrote. *Laying her egg.*

"ALL IS WELL," said Aunt Margaret cheerfully, climbing back into the car. "Later today, I get to take my eye patch off if I want."

"That's great news," said Wilhelmina.

"You look a bit different, dear," said Aunt Margaret, surveying her one-eyed.

"Not the Empress?"

"Oh no, still the Empress," said Aunt Margaret. "Maybe even more the Empress. You look . . . in readiness."

"In readiness?" said Wilhelmina. "For what?"

"Well, for anything," said Aunt Margaret, as if it were obvious.

At home, Wilhelmina found Cleo lying on the floor again, taking slow, deep breaths.

"Still haven't called it?" she said.

"That's right, hon," said Cleo. "Rick Santorum." Deep breath. "Pat Toomey." Exhale. "Mitt Romney."

"Republicans telling the truth about his lies?" Wilhelmina guessed.

"Yes, that's right," said Cleo. "There aren't very many of them, but they calm me."

"Will everything be okay here if I meet up with a friend for a bit?"

"Yes, go ahead," said Cleo. "Esther and Delia—Cordelia, I mean—are having a walk, and I'm going to make lunch with Philip soon."

The plan was to meet James outside Mrs. Mardrosian's house. But when Wilhelmina got there and remembered what a big place it was, with at least a dozen windows facing the spot where she stood, she felt exposed. Continuing to the stone wall that separated Mrs. Mardrosian's property from that of her equally giant-housed neighbor, she pretended to be admiring the flowers. Except that Mrs. Mardrosian's flower garden was startling, choked with tall weeds and with some kind of ivy that seemed, now that Wilhelmina was looking more closely, to have a stranglehold on much of the yard. Mrs. Mardrosian's yard needed mowing, and someone needed to get a handle on that ivy. Wilhelmina was pretty sure she remembered this yard being neat, well-kept, and quiet. Orderly—almost a little too orderly. She remembered being amazed by rows of tulips standing precisely to attention, like an army waiting for inspection.

She saw James walking up the long hill while he was still some distance away. She watched him climb, his shoulders straight and his legs bending at his knees in their usual extraordinary fashion, and he watched her watch. He smiled as he reached her.

"You have a gorgeous smile," she said.

"Thanks," he said, his smile growing softer. "I love your dress, Wilhelmina."

He was wearing a T-shirt that said HICKORY RUN STATE PARK and carrying a small pink box from Alfie Fang's, which tugged at her heart, because she knew it was for Mrs. Mardrosian. He was ready to argue his cause. She couldn't bear for him to lose. "Okay," she said, pulling up her mask. "Let's do this."

It was a while before Mrs. Mardrosian answered the doorbell. First they heard furniture scraping inside, like wood screeching across a floor, then an exclamation of some kind, in a shrill voice, then a crash. Their eyes met in alarm.

The door burst open. Mrs. Mardrosian stood there in a lavender silk bathrobe and slippers, flinching at the sunlight, clasping a struggling white bichon frise to her chest.

"What is it?" she said. The dog was plainly trying to launch itself out of her arms and into the sunny world. "Wilhelmina Hart? Is that you again? Come in, before the dog gets loose."

"We won't come in, Mrs. Mardrosian," said Wilhelmina.

"You've rung my doorbell, haven't you?" said Mrs. Mardrosian. "Come in!"

"We can't come in," Wilhelmina repeated more emphatically, "because of the pandemic. But thank you." She paused, knowing that a considerate neighbor would hand the keys over and go away, so that Mrs. Mardrosian could get back inside and stop struggling with her dog. "Have you met James Fang?" she said.

"What?" Mrs. Mardrosian almost shouted, and then she did fully shout, at the dog. "Bartholomew!" She gripped him around his chest, away from her body, so that his frantic little legs couldn't use her as a launchpad anymore. "Behave, this instant!" Then she spun around and disappeared into the house, the dog held out before her.

Still standing on the front porch, Wilhelmina and James considered each other doubtfully. "Does she think we're going to follow her in?" said Wilhelmina.

"Maybe?"

"I guess we should just stand here and wait for her to figure it out?"

"I guess?"

Wilhelmina moved closer to the open door, peeking into Mrs. Mardrosian's large entranceway. It was a room entire, with long, low windows to left and right and French doors straight ahead, opening to the rest of the house. Old black-and-white photos covered the walls, ornately framed. Most seemed to be family portraits, but one was a photo of men in trousers and rolled-up sleeves, carrying a statue of a saint along a street lined with onlookers. Part of a parade? The saint looked heavy.

Beside Wilhelmina, James let out a sharp breath, then made a small noise of pain.

"James?" she said, spinning to him. "Are you okay?"

On a table beside the French doors stood a giant taxidermied bird, black and white, with a red crest and a long, pale beak. "That's an ivory-billed woodpecker," said James.

"Okay," said Wilhelmina, who could tell this was a very bad thing, though she didn't know why. The bird looked a lot like the pileated woodpecker they'd seen in the forest, except much bigger. "Is that . . . a favorite bird of yours?"

"It's extinct," he said, "or anyway, there haven't been any verified sightings in forever. They were all murdered, and their habitats destroyed." Then his manner changed. Wilhelmina remembered how James got when he was angry: stiff and quiet. Deliberate in his movements, measured in his speech. "She is flaunting it like a trophy."

"I see," said Wilhelmina. "That's really upsetting, James. But don't forget, we can't assume she knows what it means. I think her son is into taxidermy. So maybe it was a gift, right? She didn't murder the woodpecker herself."

"Someone somewhere paid someone to murder it," he said. "And now, she's proud of it. It's the most beautiful bird, Wilhelmina. It mates for life. The parents build a home together in a cavity in a tree and take turns sitting on the eggs and feeding the babies, just like the albatrosses. This one's a male. You can tell by the red crest, see? Females have a black crest. He was probably murdered a hundred years ago, around the same time all his companions were being murdered all around him, and now she's showing him off to everyone who visits."

"Yeah," said Wilhelmina limply. "I hear you, James. But don't forget that we want something from this woman."

Suddenly, Mrs. Mardrosian came marching toward them from the depths of the house, without her dog. She was still in her bathrobe and slippers. When she stopped in the entranceway, James and Wilhelmina backed up, because she wasn't wearing a mask.

"I put him in his kennel," she said. "He never behaved that way with Levon."

"We're so sorry for disturbing you, Mrs. Mardrosian," said Wilhelmina. "We wouldn't have, if it weren't important. Have you met James Fang?"

"No," she said, and only then seemed to notice the pink box in James's hands. Her eyes flicked to his face. "Fang?" she said, stepping back just a fraction, reaching for the doorframe.

"Yes," said James. "My parents own the doughnut shop."

Mrs. Mardrosian seemed confused then, and a little angry, and very thin and bony in her overlarge bathrobe. "Well, it's nice to meet you," she said sharply. "I should check on my dog."

"Wait just a moment, Mrs. Mardrosian," said Wilhelmina. "We found your keys."

"What?" she said. "What keys?"

"The ones you dropped in the cemetery," said Wilhelmina, as James pulled the keys from his pocket and held them out. "You remember? It was snowing?"

"Of course I remember," said Mrs. Mardrosian, snatching the keys from James and plunking them onto the table, next to the ivory-billed woodpecker. "How kind of you. Thank you. I'm afraid I have to go now."

"James also brought you doughnuts," said Wilhelmina hastily.

"I'm on a diet," she said, moving away. "Excuse me."

"I get the feeling you've guessed why we're visiting, Mrs. Mardrosian," said James.

"Oh, here we go," said Mrs. Mardrosian, with an obvious flash of annoyance. "Yes, I've guessed why you're visiting, and it's unacceptable. Like all of my tenants, you were told to communicate with the management company. Not come to my door! I very specifically instructed them not to supply my address or phone number!"

"But you're our neighbor, Mrs. Mardrosian," said Wilhelmina. "And James and I found your keys."

"That does not give you an invitation to come to my door, interrupting my day, and begging. Talk to the management company!" she said, backing up a step.

"But the management company represents *you*," said Wilhelmina. "And maybe they haven't explained to you that James's family could go out of business. They could lose the shop they've had for twenty years."

"Wilhelmina Hart!" said Mrs. Mardrosian, in a voice of great offense. "Do you think I don't understand the situation? Maybe you should try walking in my shoes. Imagine what it's like having people like you knocking on my door, expecting *me* to take the hit for *your* business losses. Telling me your desperate stories, and trying to make me feel guilty! Do you know that I gave the dentist's office another month's extension—another month!—and still, they want more? Would anyone have treated Levon like this? No one would've walked all over Levon the way you're trying to walk over me! It's not my responsibility to bankroll other people's problems!"

Every time Mrs. Mardrosian said the name "Levon," water flew out of her eyes. She kept glancing over her shoulder too, as if she were hoping for him to emerge from the back of the house and step in. Wilhelmina didn't care. "If it's not your responsibility, then why do you feel guilty about it?" she said, noticing that her cello voice was back.

"How dare you, Wilhelmina," said Mrs. Mardrosian haughtily.

"If the people who have money aren't going to help the people who need money, then who is?"

"Don't tell me how to run my business, young lady!"

"Okay," said James, in a quiet voice. "Wilhelmina, let's go."

"No, James!"

"It's her money," said James. "She gets to decide. She doesn't want to help, and she wants the money she's owed."

"Your dad has cancer!"

"Yeah," said James. "She doesn't want to help with that."

Mrs. Mardrosian emitted a small, protesting breath. "You are trying to *guilt* me," she said, "into canceling an absolutely enormous debt. It is not my fault that your father has cancer. It does not give you the right to try to manipulate me."

For one sudden moment, James turned glacial again. He directed steady, cold eyes at Mrs. Mardrosian, and he seemed very tall.

Then his shoulders slumped. "Yeah," he said. "I guess I can see how it would look that way to you." He glanced at the woodpecker, then turned to go. "But we're just trying to survive."

Wilhelmina watched him walk down the porch steps, his head hanging. She wasn't ready yet; she had more fight in her. Frustrated, she aimed one last contemptuous glare at Mrs. Mardrosian. Standing beside her extinct woodpecker, the woman looked confused, and stricken, and old. She had a long, brown stain on the lapel of her silk bathrobe, and white roots at the top of her dark hair. She looked like a rich old lady who couldn't get her shit together.

Turning her back, Wilhelmina went to James, who stood in the yard, still holding his doughnut box. He was staring down at it dejectedly.

"Do you have hand sanitizer?" she said.

Nodding mutely, he reached into a pocket, stretched out, and handed her a small tube. Wilhelmina squeezed a generous amount into her palms and rubbed them together.

"You too," she said, passing it back to him. He didn't react or ask why, he just wedged the doughnut box under one arm and used the hand sanitizer, his face like stone.

When he'd returned it to his pocket, Wilhelmina stretched out again. This time, she took his hand.

That woke him up. He blinked at her in surprise, then started blinking a lot more, like he was trying not to cry.

"Thanks," he said, moving as far from her as he could go while still gripping her hand tightly. His hand was warm, and alive, and it fit hers perfectly.

"Yeah," she said. "I'm sorry. Maybe it's my fault, for getting all mad."

"I like you mad," he said. "Your mad voice sounds like you're about to throw lightning. Let's go, okay?"

"Yeah."

"Seven months," Mrs. Mardrosian called after them.

Wilhelmina and James turned slowly on their wide radius, still holding hands. "Huh?" said Wilhelmina.

Mrs. Mardrosian had come out onto her porch and was watching them. Her face was wet with tears and her eyes seemed wild with fury.

"Levon died of the virus," she said. "Seven months ago. I wasn't allowed to go near him. They took him to the hospital, and I never touched him again. No one who loved him was allowed to go near him."

"Oh," said Wilhelmina, who was winded suddenly, remembering her last visit to Frankie. She'd puked on the long drive home, because she'd known what was coming. At least Esther and Aunt Margaret had been with Frankie. She hadn't been alone. "I'm really sorry, Mrs. Mardrosian. That's terrible."

"Yeah, that's really awful," said James.

Mrs. Mardrosian swallowed. Then she nodded, as if she'd decided to accept their sympathy. "Seven months," she said.

James and Wilhelmina glanced at each other. "Yes?" said Wilhelmina.

"I'll give you seven months," said Mrs. Mardrosian.

James's grip on Wilhelmina's hand tightened. "Seven months'—extension?" he said.

"Seven months' rent forgiveness. In memory of Levon."

"Oh," said James, on a great outrush of air. "Thank you, Mrs. Mardrosian. Thank you!"

She seemed distressed by his gratitude, almost frightened of it. "It's probably a terrible idea," she said aggressively. "I'll call the management company when I go inside. The matter is now closed. Have a nice day."

"You too," said James, stepping toward her. But before he could approach, she retreated into the house, firmly shutting the door.

James was in a daze. "Do I—put the doughnuts on her stoop?"

"No," said Wilhelmina. "We leave quickly, before she comes out and changes her mind."

"Okay," he said, letting Wilhelmina pull him down the path to the sidewalk. "Do you want them?"

"What?"

"The doughnuts?"

"Oh. Yes, I'll take them."

"But I didn't bring a bag," he said in confusion. "Isn't it hard for you to carry things without a bag?"

"I live right around the corner, James. I can manage."

"Okay," he said. "I'm sorry I can't walk you home. I have to get back to the shop." James seemed flustered, and kind of out of it. He was holding on to her hand like it was keeping him from dropping into a well. "I guess I should go tell my parents?"

"Yes," said Wilhelmina. "You should go tell your parents."

"But will I see you?" he said. "Want to go for a walk with me later?"

"Yes."

Slowly, almost finger by finger, they let each other's hands go, and stepped back from each other. James pulled his mask away from his face, then smiled a flushed smile at her. "I think I'm free at four," he said, fishing his phone out of his pocket. Something else came out with it: a stone that dropped onto the sidewalk. It was a blue stone, glowing palely where it landed. He reached to pick it up.

"James?" said Wilhelmina. "Where did you get that stone?"

"Oh!" he said. "In Pennsylvania, actually. I've had it forever. My grandmas told me it has protective magic." He flashed her an abashed grin. "You know how my grandmas are."

"Did someone give it to you?" said Wilhelmina.

"Yes," he said. "A girl on a beach."

"A good swimmer?" said Wilhelmina, remembering Aunt Margaret's swimming bag bumping against her body as she swam. Sunlight warming her cold body, and a thermos of Frankie's ham and bean soup, and a snaggle-toothed boy who'd given her a doughnut. The sweetness of that moment. The feeling that everything was right.

"Yes," said James, who was watching her now with a funny expression, his face scrunched up in confusion. "Why?"

"James," she said. "That was me."

AFTER JAMES HAD GONE, Wilhelmina walked up the road a little bit. Not far, because she had the doughnut box, but she wanted to think before heading home. She needed her feet to clomp along the sidewalks of Mrs. Mardrosian's neighbors, while she tried to bring back memories of a boy a long time ago, in a different place. When you stumbled upon memories that way, they were like pebbles glowing on a beach.

Why had she forgotten that boy? Why had it taken her so long to connect him with *this* boy, with her James? He looked completely different; he was a grown-up now, and, well, he was dishy. His voice was deep, his teeth were even, he was made of light. But if she focused hard on the feeling of him, she had an instinct that he felt the same. James felt just exactly like that long-ago boy. Just like James's grandfather had been familiar, because he felt exactly like that long-ago boy's grandfather. Wilhelmina remembered the beach now, and she also remembered the boulder field. Frankie had talked to Rudy there, while James and his cousins were clambering around on the rocks.

She understood then, the glowing pebble Aunt Margaret had handed her this morning, when she'd made that random remark about the house. Aunt Margaret had meant, *You can go to the house with James. Take a break, and disappear from the world for a bit. Give yourself a gift.*

Wilhelmina wondered, did James have the sort of life he could get away from for any stretch of time? Did she? What would that be like, to be there together? What would they discover?

"Wait a minute," she said out loud, stopping in her tracks. A new memory was tickling her brain. She shot James a text. *Hey! Did you take that fucking teapot?!!?!*

He replied with a string of question marks.

Eggshell blue, she responded, *with brown spots and a bird on the handle!*

How do you know about my grandma's teapot?!! he wrote.

OMG, she responded. *I'll tell you later. Teapot thief!*

I didn't steal it!

I know, she responded, *you're right. It was an unjust slander upon your character. I apologize. But wait till you hear this story*

UR cute, he wrote.

In a house nearby, a person opened a window, stuck a trumpet out, and blew a few cheerful notes at the sky.

That was weird, thought Wilhelmina vaguely, still thinking about Pennsylvania. Trying to tug the past closer.

Then, across the street, someone else opened a window and started banging on a pot with a wooden spoon. A person a few doors up the street did the same thing. Wilhelmina stopped, coming to attention.

Down the road, a door slammed. "Vice President Kamala Harris!" someone shouted. "Vice President Kamala Harris!" It was Bee's little sister, Kimmy, running up the sidewalk with Julie's sister, Tina, at her heels, the two of them jumping, shouting, giggling, screeching. "Hi, Wil!" they yelled when they saw her. "Did you hear?"

"I hear!" Wilhelmina called to them, raising a hand and smiling. They turned and ran back the way they'd come, and Wilhelmina decided it was time to direct her own feet home. She wanted to enjoy her family's joy.

Her route brought her past Mrs. Mardrosian's house again. For some reason, at the wall that separated Mrs. Mardrosian's yard from her neighbor's, Wilhelmina stopped. She turned to face the overgrown flower garden. Why? Was it the squawk of a crow? She ran her eyes absently over the weeds and the vines, but no crows appeared. No owls swooped and nothing glowed. She looked down at her own body, then raised a hand to the space above her head. Nothing glowed there either.

Locate the steadiest part of your body, Aunt Margaret had said to her once.

Wilhelmina did: it was her thighs, broad and strong.

Reach down into the earth from that steady place, Aunt Margaret said.

Wilhelmina did, sort of. You couldn't "reach down" with your thighs; it was stupid, but she imagined it as best she could.

Thank the earth for the strength she gives, said Aunt Margaret, *then draw her sweet power up into your body. Use it to begin to build a shield. As you build your shield, let the image come to you of what it's made of.*

Wilhelmina felt very silly standing on the sidewalk outside Mrs. Mardrosian's property, pretending to draw energy from Mother Earth to build herself a shield. But she had an imagination. She could see the shield in her mind's eye, growing in the air before her. It was only a step away. It was shaped like her body. In fact, it was a suit of armor, and as it grew, it became steadily more dazzling. It was made of the light of suns.

With a sense of inevitability, Wilhelmina stepped into her own armor. It was soft and warm, like swimming in a perfect summer pool. As she stood there marveling at the sensation, she felt a helm of starlight descending upon her head, as if placed there by the hands of everyone who loved her.

Okay then, she said to herself. *I'm suited up. Now what? What's the point?* She turned in circles, but nothing happened. Inside her armor, she was steady, but it wasn't because anything in the world had changed. She could feel malicious things throwing themselves against the glow of her armor. They were like little metal moths that bounced off and then hurled themselves back again, so that she was surrounded by a whirling nimbus of harm. Seventy million votes for the monster. Baseless lawsuits. Liars. Cowards. People who were too scared to cope. People in denial.

But they weren't touching her. She was shielded from their poison. She asked herself, *What do I let in?*

The answer came quickly: Julie and Bee. And with Julie and Bee came their joy, and also their sadness, their own anxieties, their love for Wilhelmina, and every drop of hurt or anger or awkwardness they felt toward her. Inside her armor, it was very still. She could focus. And so she could find the feeling of her friends.

Wilhelmina turned to Mrs. Mardrosian's flower garden and stepped into the ivy. She pushed her way through a tangle of mostly dead lilies that left watery orange streaks from their stamens on her legs. In a dying patch of purple aster, to the sounds of pot-banging and that trumpet starting up again, she bent down and dug her hands through the leaves and dirt, until she unearthed Julie's necklace.

AT HOME, Esther and Delia—Cordelia—sat on the front stoop together, stretching their bare feet out into the sun and smiling. Esther had glittery purple toenails.

"Wilhelmina!" shouted Cordelia. "Did you hear?"

"Hear what?" said Wilhelmina, because she knew Cordelia wanted to be the one to tell her.

"They called Pennsylvania!" she said. "It's over!"

"Finally!" said Wilhelmina. "That's great news."

"You got doughnuts?" said Cordelia. "Isn't that kind of a small box?"

"More doughnuts can be acquired later," said Wilhelmina, handing her the box.

"Why is it dirty? And why are your legs striped orange? And what are you holding? Oh my god, your hands are filthy. Where have you *been*, Wilhelmina?"

"Listen, the doughnuts are clean, okay?"

"But where have you *been*?"

"In a flower garden," said Wilhelmina.

"Whose flower garden?"

"Cordelia," said Esther, who was smiling with her eyes closed, her lined face raised to the sun. "I want to know the answers to these questions too. But right now, I'm sensing that Wilhelmina needs to pay attention."

Wilhelmina was, indeed, trying to pay attention, in a way she remembered paying attention before. A long time ago, it had been uncomplicated. She hadn't wondered about it, or pushed the feeling of it away, or dismissed it when it happened. She'd just woken up in the aunts' house and known where everyone was, and how their feelings were sitting inside them. Or gone to sleep in her apartment and known that Julie was sleeping upstairs, nearby. Or felt the aunts' love in the stones they'd touched, or sensed a kindred spirit in a boy on a beach, or found a hidden piece of Julie, Bee, and herself in a flower garden.

"Bye, guys," she said, then turned and walked around the house to the backyard.

"Why is she so weird?" she heard Cordelia ask. "Pay attention to what?"

"I admire your bottomless curiosity, Cordelia," she heard Esther say.

"Thank you!"

The yard was steep and full of holes, but Wilhelmina made her way to the trees that stood outside Julie's high window. Then she turned around. Julie, who was curled up in her window seat, put her book down. Her window was open. She propped her chin in her hand and her elbow on the sill and leaned out, looking at Wilhelmina hard.

"Wil," she said, "why do you look both super hot and like you've been . . . wrestling in a flower bed?"

Wilhelmina had wiped the dirt off of the little winged elephant as best she could, and untangled the flower detritus from the chain. She perched the necklace in her palm and held her hand up to Julie, so that Julie could see.

"Because of my heroic quest to find this," she said.

Julie's eyebrows rose. She looked tired, and sad, and a little bit frightened.

"I'm really happy to see that," she said. "But are you a hundred percent sure you want me to have it?"

"A thousand percent sure," Wilhelmina said. "More than anything."

Julie took a long breath, then let it out. Then she did it again. It felt like it lasted forever.

Finally, she spoke. "I was just reading an article about a safe way to hug your pandemic friend," she said. "Interested?"

A tear ran down Wilhelmina's face. "Yes, please."

"Okay. I mean, it basically involves turning my head away and hugging your ass, but hey, I'm into it if you are."

Now Wilhelmina was smiling. "Come down from your perch, elephant?"

Julie was dabbing her face with her sleeve. When she emerged, her smile was beautiful. "I'll be right down, elephant," she said.

A NOTE ON THE WORLD OF THIS BOOK

Wilhelmina lives in Watertown, Massachusetts, which is a real place and my own home as I write this note. In fact, Wilhelmina's apartment is modeled on my apartment during Election Week 2020, right down to the noisy furnace in her basement, the long hill, and the steep backyard. Mount Auburn Cemetery is a real place, a cemetery but also a botanical garden and an arboretum, and I did happen to visit it during a snowstorm on the Friday before the election. There is a giant maple tree outside the Watertown Free Public Library, and it was indeed wearing a knitted tube dress that week. Several restaurants in Watertown Square closed during the pandemic, including my favorite Italian restaurant and a Tunisian sandwich shop I loved. There is a little forest path connecting Oliver Street with Marion Road near the stadium, just like the path Wilhelmina and James walk together, spotting a pileated woodpecker on their way. The man Wilhelmina regularly sees standing in the middle of an impossible Boston-area intersection with a MAGA sign is based on a real person. There was an outdoor mask mandate in Cambridge. When you went to the glasses store to pick up your glasses, they did come to the door to unlock it for you, and you weren't allowed to touch anything in the store besides your glasses. My dental hygienist was dressed like an astronaut; maybe yours was too.

All of this is to say that a lot of the details in this book are drawn from real life. Many others, however, are made up. There is no Lupa Building in Watertown, nor is there an Alfie Fang's, unfortunately. Readers familiar with Watertown might be able to follow Wilhelmina on her walks around town, but her driving route to the grocery store might leave you scratching your heads a little bit. There is no Museum of Armenia in Watertown, but the

Armenian Museum of America is on Main Street, and I recommend a visit. Watertown is the home of many descendants of the survivors of the Armenian Genocide of 1915–1917.

James's bird cams are real, and wonderful beyond description. Go to the Cornell Lab Bird Cams channel on YouTube and scroll down; you'll find the Panama cam and the Royal Albatross cam easily. In a moment of serendipity, albatross female LGL did in fact lay her egg on November 7, 2020, the same day the election was called. If you decide to spend some time with these gigantic, funny, beautiful albatrosses, I hope you will find, as I did, that watching the careful ministrations of the rangers from the New Zealand Department of Conservation who devote their time to caring for these gentle giants makes you feel a little bit better about humanity.

The aunts' home in northeastern Pennsylvania is in a town I left unnamed, but is loosely based on my own childhood home in rural NEPA. The Bunker Hill Monument in Boston was closed to tourists during the early months of the pandemic, and I don't know whether park rangers were providing private tours in reality, or only in my imagination. Brian Sims and Steve McCarter, both Democratic members of the Pennsylvania House of Representatives at the time, made national news on October 3, 2013 when they introduced legislation to legalize same-sex marriage in Pennsylvania. The election results and news headlines Wilhelmina's family is coping with during election week 2020 are all real.

James's "Birds Aren't Real" bumper sticker is a reference to the Birds Aren't Real movement, a satirical conspiracy theory developed by Peter McIndoe in 2017, for the purpose of making fun of other conspiracy theories. The idea is that birds are actually drones, developed by the US government to spy on American citizens. If you decide to look into it, you're in for a treat.

The outer space exploration game Julie and Wilhelmina play together, *Starcom: Nexus*, is a real game, created by an independent game developer who happens to be my husband. I hope you'll forgive the indulgence of this coded love note. I put at least one in every book, but this one is more noticeable than the others.

Finally, an important note about Wilhelmina's health. When I wrote and rewrote this book in 2021 and 2022, I modeled Wilhelmina's thoracic outlet syndrome after my own long-term experience of hand, arm, shoulder, and neck pain, diagnosed as thoracic outlet syndrome two decades ago. However, in the summer of 2023, around the time this book was about to enter copyediting, I began to experience an extended period of unexplained dizziness. Eventually, an MRI informed us that I had a brain condition causing my cerebellum, the lower, back part of the brain, to be pulled into my spinal column. The cerebellum orients us in space. Mine was under pressure; hence, my dizziness.

The condition, called Arnold-Chiari Malformation Type I, is correctable by surgery. When I met with my new neurosurgeon, he shared some of the other symptoms of Chiari: hand, arm, shoulder, and neck pain. Tingling in the hands. I told the neurosurgeon that I had those symptoms as part of my thoracic outlet syndrome. He told me that in fact, my symptoms were classic Chiari, and that thoracic outlet syndrome is difficult to diagnose. He told me that it was likely I'd been *mis*diagnosed.

It's scary to sit in a neurosurgeon's office and understand that he may soon be drilling into the back of your head. It's confusing to learn that something you've known about your health for decades might in fact be wrong. Nonetheless, one of my first thoughts in that moment was, *Oh no! But if I don't have thoracic outlet syndrome, Wilhelmina probably doesn't have it either!*

My characters are real to me. I expect many readers can understand this, because your favorite characters are real to you too. It was distressing to discover that I might have misdiagnosed my girl, leaving her vulnerable to unexplained and unresolved suffering. But it was also too late to revise the book. There are some changes you can make in copyediting, but casually inserting a brain condition for which your protagonist needs brain surgery is not one of them. Even if there had been time for a change like that, it wouldn't have been right for the book.

And so I asked my editor, Andrew Karre, if he thought it might make sense for me to talk about this in my author's note. Because just as I modeled

Wilhelmina's disability off of my own experiences, I'm now in a unique position to predict some things that might be in her future. As I write this note in late November 2023, it's been five weeks since my own surgery to create more space for my crowded cerebellum. It's been a strange time, but I've gotten through it, and now I'm healing. Here's what I solemnly believe: if Wilhelmina, like me, has a symptomatic Chiari Malformation, I believe she'll find out about it at some point in her life when she's equipped to handle the information. If she has surgery, I believe that the surgery will resolve her symptoms. Many, many people will support her. The resilience she's worked so hard to develop will serve her well. It'll be a challenging time, but she'll be surrounded by love. Wilhelmina is going to have a good life.

ACKNOWLEDGMENTS

I could not have written this book without the help of many people. Thank you to my editor, Andrew Karre, whose enthusiasm buoyed me and whose excellent instincts guided me toward the book I wanted to write. Every problem has multiple (fascinating) solutions when you work with Andrew. Thank you also to my agent, Faye Bender, my biggest cheerleader and advocate, to whom this book is dedicated. We've been working together for a long time. My gratitude grew too big to fit inside my chest long ago.

For their careful readings and generous feedback on early drafts, I extend thanks to Catherine Cashore, Dorothy Cashore, Deb Heiligman, E. K. Johnston, Malinda Lo, Jamie Pittel, Cindy Pon, Marie Rutkoski, Amber Salik, and Tui Sutherland.

A number of medical experts generously answered my questions. I'm extremely grateful to Lisa Arcikowski, NP, for her help with Frankie's ovarian cancer; to Dr. David Kroll for his help with Bee's father; and to Dr. Rachel Haft for fielding general questions about Covid. In fact, Wilhelmina's Dr. Taft is named after my Dr. Haft, out of gratitude for her invaluable help across the years. Any medical errors or inconsistencies that persist in the book are my fault entirely.

For help on a number of topics (including but not limited to Cuban endearments and slang, parenting, perennials, grounding and shielding, and Rudy Giuliani's stint as mayor), I extend thanks to Judy Blundell, Anthony DePalma, Eve Goldfarb, Deb Heiligman, Marthe Jocelyn, Kevin Lin, Jamie Pittel, Jess Quilty, Margo Rabb, Natalie Standiford, and Rebecca Stead. Thank you to Imogen Flowers for the story of playing chess with a genius five-year-old who couldn't write his notations because he hadn't learned to write yet. Thank you to Isabel Flowers for helping me with age-appropriate phrasings for Cordelia ("Take a chill pill, Wil!").

For their skill, care, and devotion, I extend thanks to the team at Dutton Books and Penguin Young Readers Group who turned this book into a beautiful object and are now connecting it to the world. Thank you to Melissa Faulner, Natalie Vielkind, Janet Rosenberg, Kat Keating, and Rob Farren. Thank you to Jen Loja, Elyse Marshall, Emily Romero, Amanda Close, and Debra Polansky. Thank you to my publisher at Dutton, Julie Strauss-Gabel. Thank you to Anna Booth for her elegant design work and Jessica Jenkins and Theresa Evangelista for a cover that beautifully captures the feeling of Wilhelmina's strange but hopeful week. Please see the Credits page for the names of more people who deserve my thanks for their support.

The encyclopedia passages that Wilhelmina transcribes in her letters to Bee during the summer of 2012 are lifted word for word from the 1924 edition of *Compton's Pictured Encyclopedia*. The Temperance card posters that hang on Frankie's bedroom wall are based on the Temperance cards from two of my favorite tarot decks: *The Light Seer's Tarot* by Chris-Anne and *The Wild Unknown Tarot* by Kim Krans. The tarot deck that Frankie uses is the Rider-Waite-Smith deck, originally published in 1909. You may have heard it referred to as the Rider-Waite deck, created by academic and mystic A. E. Waite. In fact, the deck was a joint project with Pamela Colman Smith, who did all the illustrations, but has only recently begun to receive credit for her work.

I had a lot of conversations and read a lot of books about magic and witchcraft in order to establish a theory of magic for this book. I wanted to create magical practices that were unique to my characters and to this book's fantastical world, but also respectful to real-world practitioners and cultures. Some of my favorite reads were *Witchery* by Juliet Diaz; *Making Magic* by Briana Saussy; *Becoming Dangerous*, essays edited by Katie West and Jasmine Elliott; and *The Tao of Craft* by Benebell Wen (which is where I found the phrase "practitioner of craft," used by James's maternal grandmother to describe her own practice).

I also worked hard to establish a theory of hope for this book. Some of the books that helped me most were *Hope in the Dark* by Rebecca Solnit; *The Impossible Will Take a Little While*, essays edited by Paul Rogat Loeb; and *World As Lover, World As Self* by Joanna Macy, especially Chapter 8, "Despair Work."

Special thanks to my sisters Catherine and Dorothy, for introducing me to those hope books, for knowing everything there is to know about birds, and for keeping me company on the bird cams during the long pandemic.

Thank you (again) to Dr. Rachel Haft and her team, and to Dr. Philipp Taussky and his neurosurgery team at the Beth Israel Deaconess Medical Center in Boston, for your care of my body and my brain as this book moved through production. Thank you (again) to Andrew Karre for stepping in to make copyediting and proofreading so easy for me as I worked through an unexpected health crisis.

And a final thanks to Kevin Lin, who helped, loved, carried, and supported me every day through every part of this project, never once complaining about the screeching of albatrosses from the laptop I left in the living room.

CREDITS

DUTTON BOOKS AND PENGUIN YOUNG READERS GROUP

ART AND DESIGN
Anna Booth
Theresa Evangelista
Jessica Jenkins

CONTRACTS
Anton Abrahamsen

**COPYEDITORS AND
PROOFREADERS**
Rob Farren
Kat Keating
Janet Rosenberg

EDITOR
Andrew Karre

MANAGING EDITORS
Madison Penico
Natalie Vielkind
Jayne Ziemba

MARKETING
James Akinaka
Christina Colangelo
Alex Garber
Brianna Lockhart

Danielle Presley
Emily Romero
Shannon Spann
Felicity Vallence

**PRODUCTION
MANAGER**
Vanessa Robles

PUBLICITY
Elyse Marshall

PUBLISHER
Julie Strauss-Gabel

**PUBLISHING
MANAGER**
Melissa Faulner

SUBSIDIARY RIGHTS
Micah Hecht

SALES
Raven Andrus
Jill Bailey
Andrea Baird
Maggie Brennan

Dandy Conway
Nichole Cousins
Stephanie Davey
Nicole Davies
Sara Grochowski
Lauren Mackey
Mary McGrath
Carol Monteiro
Colleen Conway Ramos
Jennifer Ridgway
Amy Rockwell
Devin Rutland
Michele Sadler
Judy Samuels
Kate Sullivan
Nicole White
Dawn Zahorik

**SCHOOL AND
LIBRARY MARKETING
AND PROMOTION**
Venessa Carson
Judith Huerta
Carmela Iaria
Trevor Ingerson
Summer Ogata
Gaby Paez

LISTENING LIBRARY

Linda Korn
Rebecca Waugh

THE BOOK GROUP

Faye Bender